THE APOCALYPSE BEAD

BY RIO VARGAS

To Habiba, every page is a testament to our friendship, thank you from the bottom of my mongrel heart.

Special Thanks to
Blake Allen and Stuffeddogdigital for Cover Art
Alicia Cata for editing this mess
Dawn Black for the beautiful formatting
Helena, Margar and Rose for reading my unedited ramblings
And my husband for putting up with me through the whole thing

CONTENTS

CHAPTER

1

• ● •

Article XXVIII

The existence of alternate magical realms will be recognized by all
branches of the government. Further, The term "Human" is now
a classification that is exclusive to persons born without magical
abilities or connections to any realm besides the mundane realm.

-Preternatural Licensing and Enforcement Bureau Archives

The heat was horrendous. It was, maybe, 105 degrees
out and the lingering promise of rain was still weeks
away. Theia stood staring at the thick brush of the Sonoran
Desert in a mood. She was in a mood because, thanks to
some upstart Invoker trying to kill the president, the business
of making a living as a post-human person was much harder.
Prior to the 28th Amendment, while post-human abilities

were not recognized as a skill set, there was no regulation by a government body to use magical gifts. Now, instead of telling a grieving woman that her husband had passed, and his body could be found in a strip of desert east of town, she had to find the body herself if she wanted to make a profit on it.

So here she stood, in capris and an airy white blouse, wearing a state issued license clipped to her sleeve, auburn hair pulled into a braid and squinting even with sunglasses on, into the light. Her business partner Mason was 6' with a stocky frame and cropped hair. In khakis and a bright yellow dress shirt, he seemed as annoyed as she was.

"We had an appointment..." he said reaching down to pet the large, wolfish mutt at his side. Nosam, as the hound was known, was pure white with piercing violet eyes that betrayed his otherworldly nature. Nosam met Theia's gaze and a feeling of ancient knowledge creeped into her mind. While she had become used to the creature it never got easy to make eye contact with him.

Theia sighed and checked her watch for the 207th time.

"Well, the Bureau doesn't pay it's pencil pushers well enough to be prompt." Theia commented. Almost as if summoned, a woman pulled up in a gray, government issued sedan. As she got out of the car, Theia noticed that she was wearing a pencil skirt, sensible heals and a tan blouse, that were all going to get ruined in this heat,

"Runic." Nosam thought/said. Indicating to Theia that the woman was a fully human practitioner. Only humans could work in a government position.

"She's gonna want to know how you found it." Mason added in a grumpy tone.

Theia had known Mason for many years now. When they started the firm, their caseload was mostly made up of the few true believers they could find, and jobs from the greater supe community. This was always fraught with very real danger, especially because of her reasonably buxom personage. Now that everyone south of normal was outed, and magic was legal and regulated, Mason was vocal about how much he hated the red tape. Shamans like himself faced a lot of strange claims and accusations as their magic was mostly inscrutable to practical practitioners like "Miss Government 9 to 5".

"Good morning!" the overwhelmed woman called as she stepped out of her car balancing a coffee and clipboard. She checked a paper on the top of the clip board. "Body identification?"

"Body retrieval" Theia corrected. "You're supposed to have the coroner with you." She tried her hardest to be professional, but this woman's whole job was to know these things.

"My notes say that you are an Oracle, and, as prophecy and fortune telling is still only 30% accurate, we only call-in support services after identification." She said taking a sip from her, most likely, caramel latte.

Nosam let out a growl and Mason quickly reached down a hand to calm him. Theia sighed and turned toward the empty desert behind her. Before regulations, it was common to be questioned, as there were a lot of people falsely claiming to be psychic or able to see the future. However, now, all of those charlatans were given equal weight in the government's eyes, leading "so called" Oracles to be more critically viewed then others within the greater magical community. Mason had it even worse, as he was still classified as a religion or faith, and unable to gain a license for himself. Hence, the reason why he was on the books as security at the firm.

"Well, my associate here can pinpoint the exact location, I was able to narrow it down to a mile radius." Theia braced herself for what came next.

"With what method?" The woman said putting her cup on a rock formation and producing a pen.

"Tarot and pendulum." Theia stated as plainly as she could manage. She had been working with her therapist on answering pointless questions.

"Are you incapable of scrying or do you just prefer nonvisual methods?" She asked not even pretending to remove the condescension from her tone.

"Scrying wouldn't have helped much as most of the desert valley floor looks exactly the same." Theia said the heat rising to meet her mood.. Dr. Fohg had told her there would be days like this. "Just think of her as a child, it's much harder to be angry at children for asking stupid questions." She imagined him saying.

"Yes, but in these situations, a fine could be issued if an agent was called without visual confirmation and no body identified." The talentless woman shot back as if reciting lines from a play.

"Look, do you want us to produce a dead guy or argue about possible fines." Mason grumbled reaching into his bag.

"Very well, please attempt whatever it is you are going to do." The 'you' was very pointed. Clearly, little " Miss Government Regulation" didn't care for Shamans.

Without comment, Mason produced a length of chain weighing about 15 pounds, with symbols etched into each link. He made contact with the valley with the chain. Both Theia and Pencil Pusher, who had yet to identify herself (but Theia knew her name was Meredith) could feel the surge of the valley rising to his call. Very few Shamans had the intimate connection that Mason had with his territory. An elemental the size of the desert called "Sonora" was momentous. There was a feeling of connection, heat, life, and longing. When Mason called to her he could feel the immense love, she had for him.

"Very Impressive Mr. Wallace, but I must have a physical manifestation, or I will have to report potential obstruction of evidence." The earth itself let loose a flash of annoyance at her Shaman being questioned by someone so insignificant, but suddenly, a woman stepped through the haze of heat rising from the ground. She seemed average to the untrained eye, a deeply tanned woman with impossibly, long dark hair, not quite black, festooned with gravel and plant debris. Save for the cloak she wore which was made from gently falling sand which joined with the earth beneath her seamlessly. Her movements were ethereal and did not disturb the world around her. Plants seemed to join the cloak as it passed over them and then return to normal once it had passed. It was impossible not to feel completely in awe of her, him, it. The elemental chose to appear as a woman because that's how

Mason thought of her, not because she truly was the creature before them.

"Satisfied, bone caster?" The Sonora spoke, the heat intensifying around her. Meredith balked at the slur but quickly composed herself. Mason turned away from her and smirked as Nosam let out a canine wheeze that sounded suspiciously like a laugh. Mason stepped forward and bowed his head, Sonora planted a gentle kiss on his forehead, and even fell to her haunches to ruffle Nosam's mane, before promptly rising and turning, moving deeper into the desert. Mason stepped after her, instinctively avoiding placing his boots on any plants or fragile tunnels. Theia managed to keep pace and annoy only a few plants. Meredith trudged and cursed as the plants seemed to almost unavoidably catch on her clothing. The walk was easy, unless you had insulted the literal manifestation of the desert itself. After a few moments, Mason politely asked Sonora to make a path for Meredith, ever the diplomat. A gentle giant, Theia thought. After that, they made much better time.

Ten minutes later the smell came upon them, sweet carrion. Theia and Mason were used to it , but Meredith must not have been very seasoned, because she gagged. Mason muttered something to Nosam that Theia couldn't quite catch. Nosam seemed to scan the horizon.

The body was half unburied, probably coyotes. Most of the face and chest were devoid of flesh and several insects had burrowed deeper into it . Mason made a wordless gesture to Sonora and the body rose to the surface as if the ground that still encased it was water. As it settled on the surface, Theia removed a rag from her back pocket and bent over the body. She turned the wrist that was still fleshed to show the tattoo on it. A small crescent moon hung with two stars. For his wife and daughters, Theia suddenly thought. Meredith gasping for air, nodded and walked a good 10 yards away. Removing a cell phone and calling for someone to come and retrieve the body.

"Any idea who did it?" Mason asked quietly.

Theia closed her eyes and felt for past traces on the body. A chill came over her, and the expanse of a great cold tapestry splayed out before her endless and unknowable. She felt along the cloth for some thread that tied him intensely to someone else at the end of his life line.

"Frayed, meaning at least a moderate talent. I'd need my tools to get anything, assuming they aren't strong enough to scrub any evidence." Theia was angry. This man had two girls at home. She had known he wasn't alive, but had held out hope that he had died an accidental death. The fact that someone else had severed their connections to him made the act even more heinous. Whoever had done this not only had magic, but was also smart enough to remove any trace of magical evidence.

"There are pack rats in the area, I could try and ask them if they could describe someone, but we all look the same to them." Mason offered. Theia always loved watching him talk to rodents, but with Meredith here it might not be the best idea. He shouldn't appear to do too much of the heavy lifting beyond what his security duties allowed. So far all he had done was summon an entity, which is technically possible for even vanilla humans, but, anything more might complicate the paycheck on this one.

"No, the fray was sloppily done. I'm confident I can get more back at the office, maybe loop in Ne…" She had almost said her name. Nessa had made it clear they wouldn't be working together anymore, but old habits die hard. Mason understood.

"She made the call; it wasn't your fault." Mason proffered while Nosam licked her hand, breathing his warm doggy breaths.

"Still, it would make this easier if we could talk to him." indicating the dead man. She ignored the regret and anger that flared up. It had been almost a year, and she was doing very well in therapy. Dr. Fohg told her you couldn't win at therapy, but Theia was sure he said that to all the competitive sorts. Meredith returned and produced a slip of paper, kind of like a coat check ticket.

"Identification and location rights go to…" She checked her notes. "Your firm…Unseen Forces." She smiled at the name.

Theia grabbed the slip of paper and added it to the satchel at her hip. Meredith seemed to want to say something, but a quick read of the threads around her clearly indicated it was going to piss Theia off.

"It must be frustrating, making a living this way. With a talent like yours you could clearly make a fortune from a broom closet." She said instead. It was a trap; it was always a trap. Get you to admit to some misuse of power. It was doubly offensive from a runic, who knew full well the consequences of such a brazen abuse of her powers.

"It was easier before no-talents were given the reins." Theia remarked and turned on her heels to head down the hill towards Mason's jeep. Undoubtedly Meredith would report the insult, but they could add it to the pile of such complaints. Theia even smiled a bit when she heard Nosam's howl of laughter, and Mason's insincere apology on her behalf.

Someone was killing normies, Theia thought. Maybe it was isolated, but she had seen the thread entwining with her threads. It was strong, unavoidable and not at all a color she liked.

CHAPTER

2

• ● •

Post Human

Postie, Posty, Indigo Child ; Denotes a person/human who develops
inherent magical abilities, usually around early - late adolescence.
Post Humans are considered human as far as the law is concerned
and have equal rights, however they must be licensed by the
Preternatural Licensing and Enforcement Bureau to use any
magical abilities professionally.
-Preternatural Licensing and Enforcement Bureau Archives

M ason was tense. Insulting the woman from the bureau
wasn't a smart move, but he trusted that Theia knew
what she was doing. He checked the rear-view mirror; Theia
was watching the desert roll by as they bounced along the
rough back road.

'All things will be as they will be, Mason' Nosam said directly into Mason's mind.

'I worry.' Mason replied similarly. He took stock of the situation. A man had been murdered, either by magic or more mundane means. The killer had obscured their involvement using magic. As suspects went, Mason could think of several post-Humans that would be capable of it, fewer true supernaturals, but there were still quite a few.

'The Fey had visited the grave; you too saw the signs.' Nosam thought.

'I can't help her with that, especially if they refuse to meet in neutral territory.' Mason was tense, almost afraid to broach the subject with Theia. He checked the rearview again. Theia was watching him; she had learned how to tell when Nosam and Mason were talking.

"What is it?" she said, smiling with little mirth.

"We noticed signs of Fey visiting the grave. Could the dead guy have been of the blood?" Mason intoned. He wasn't going to lie to her, no matter how worried he was that she would pursue such a perilous lead.

"Well so far, we are only being paid to find her husband. We haven't been retained to locate or identify who killed him." She said, knowing full well that was coming. They drove in silence until they reached the outskirts of the city. Tucson was a weird town, almost seamless in its transition from wilderness to civilization. That balance had been what had drawn Mason to the valley. He had always heard from his mentor that when a shaman finds his territory, it would fill them with a sense of purpose that couldn't be found anywhere else in creation. He hadn't understood then, but from the moment he first felt Sonora, he had known he would never leave her for long.

"Drop me off at the office, it might be useful for you to do the legwork on the Madison case." Which, Mason knew, was Theia for 'I need to brood.'

"I'm sure she would appreciate confirmation on what her husband has been up to." he said. Mason hated the adultery cases. The clients were always petty, and none were ever happy with the results of the investigation. Either they couldn't find evidence, which the client never believed and would just move on to the next P.I., or they did find something, and the client made it their problem just the same. In any case they were in for tears and anger.

The Unseen Forces offices were in the One South Church building downtown, on the 9th floor at Mason's insistence. It wasn't a large space, just a waiting room, an office and a copy/records room, but it had been heavily modified. As parking downtown was always more trouble than it was worth, Mason dropped Theia off at the entrance and headed for his house to pick up his camera equipment.

Mason lived in a small neighborhood just north of downtown. After the firm's first big windfall, Mason had bought two things: a very nice houseboat and a plot of land in a downtown historic neighborhood. Back when the railroad had been rolling through the valley, Dunbar was where several Black and Chinese families had settled, both while the railroad was being built and after. He loved the feel of the area, and the Loci was amenable, if not a tad distant.

Which was preferable to a noisy Loci, that pestered him all night and day about flower placement and the number of pollinators visiting. As Mason pulled up to his bought and paid for lot, he was, again, incredibly grateful they had not yet decided to start an HOA, because amidst a sea of flowering plants and low mesquite trees, squat in the middle of the lot, sat his half-buried houseboat.

He had paid a pretty penny getting it hooked up to electric and water, and had suffered no end of passive aggressive notes taped to his wrought iron fence, but it was everything he'd dreamed of. Mason was a bit of a black sheep in his family, the few good memories he had of them had been of traveling over water. He'd grown up on boats and loved them, but as a solid, true blue earth shaman, he had always felt uncomfortable with his feet off the ground. This was a perfect marriage of the two.

Nosam bounded to the gate as soon as Mason had gotten the Jeep parked and had already lowered the wards enough to safely pass through. While the wards weren't hazardous to the average person, someone with any kind of magical energy rattling about in their pattern would find themselves in quite a bit of pain. Even though Mason himself was somewhere between post human and true blue supe it was still best to be cautious, even with his own wards.

As soon as his boot touched the sidewalk, he could feel Dunbar reach out a questioning tendril of energy. Dunbar wasn't nearly as old or powerful as Sonora, and rightly lived within her essence. Loci, like Dunbar, were often difficult to hear, but he still seemed determined to communicate.

'Worry.' came the thought. Dunbar was asking after his mental state. Mason sighed, smiling to himself. A shaman's duty was to the elementals, flora and fauna of whatever territory claimed them, but the Loci, being greater elementals, tended to act like concerned parents.

"I'm fine big guy, just a lot on my mind." Mason said back aloud, his nosy neighbor Phyllis watching him with judgmental eyes, from her living room window.

'Consume. Breed. Rest.' It proffered. Loci, like most elementals, had limited understanding of biological creatures. They knew they liked to eat sleep and... be merry, so they thought these things made us happy, which was honestly pretty true. It had been quite a while since Mason had satisfyingly done any of those activities. He sent back a happy thought and climbed onto the deck of his boat.

After some scrounging and cajoling with subpar storage solutions, he located his camera and a frozen peanut butter and jelly sandwich, set them both near the exit, because he would surely forget them, and plopped down on his couch/bed. Nosam came down the stairs after a pleasurable roll in the flower beds and leveled a gaze at him.

"Pensive. Tense. You are little good to anyone so unfocused." Nosam said aloud, surprisingly.

"For the last time, you are not my husband, I can take care of myself." Mason rose and moved to the entirely too small bathroom.

"No, but you should take a mate soon, you do not grow younger." Nosam managed to eke in before the door closed. The door meant nothing to the two of them. While they had separate minds, they shared a soul. What Mason wanted, Nosam yearned for, and there was no way to keep secrets from him for long. Mason looked at himself in the mirror. He was only 27, green eyes, and not nearly as pale as the rest of his clan thanks to his mother's mixed heritage. His bright, red hair was eternally unruly so he kept his haircuts short. He wasn't tall, compared to his brothers, only just barely clearing 6' feet on his tippy toes, and while he kept fit, he was far from ripped.

Mason was deep into self-evaluation mode and was considering getting his septum pierced when Nosam's voice traveled to him.

'Horace approaches.' Mason was taken aback. Horace was the only other practicing human in the neighborhood. An Invoker, they often gave each other a wide berth, unconsciously dividing the neighborhood a bit so they didn't have to run into each other often.

"Any idea what he wants?" Mason splashed some water on his face and hustled to the bedroom to put on a less dirt covered shirt. He quickly found a gray one with an obnoxious pattern, threw it on, and joined Nosam in the 'living room'.

"Can't be anything particularly pertinent to this day's tasks." Nosam reminded him. Nosam was a big old stick in the mud, duty first, everything else later; a real, clear your mind and get to business type. Ignoring the gentle prodding to his assignment, Mason stepped up the stairs to the front deck of his house.

Horace, a balding, middle aged man, who looked like he could be living in his mother's basement, was wearing a suit jacket and slacks. The sleeves were adorned with stylized black flames and demonic symbols. Mason was actually taken aback, as he had never seen him out of a polo shirt and cargo shorts before today.

"Ahoy! , he said. "If you're after flour I'm afraid I used all of mine celebrating Baphomet's bris." Demon humor was in terrible taste, but Mason still had a painful hellfire burn on his thigh from the first time they had realized they were neighbors. Horace sighed deeply and stood quite purposefully on the edge of Mason's wards.

"I've come today in an official capacity." Horace said crisply in the fading remnants of some eastern European accent. Official could only mean one thing, the demon prince he served forced him to seek Mason out specifically. Nothing else would force Horace to darken Mason's doorstep.

"We're listening." Mason said as he felt Nosam join him on the deck. Horace hated Nosam. Can't blame the guy, he still limped because of their first meeting.

"Neutral territory, Catalina Park, Midnight." He said dragging it out like a demand.

"I'm afraid that's well after my office hours." Mason knew he would be entirely too curious to not attend, but you don't agree to meet with demon sock puppets too hastily. Horace sighed, which was a promising sign.

"My lord is willing to offer one petty service in exchange for the meeting, to be performed by myself personally." There was the rub. Horace looked annoyed, because he was being offered as an errand boy to some up jumped tree hugger. He could already feel Nosam's annoyance as the thought rose to the surface of Mason's mind.

"Any petty service, meaning just about anything that wouldn't put you in obvious physical harm?" Mason needed to be sure of exactly what was on offer. Demon deals were fickle, if you ask for too much you may end up in debt, which was not advantageous.

"As my lord knows you are a purveyor of male flesh and strange appetites, mild physical harm is permitted if it pleases you." Horace was disgusted with the mere mention of this caveat. In fairness Mason was also repulsed by the thought that Horace was offering himself up for kinky sex in exchange for a conversation with him.

"Uh, I don't feel either of us would be happy with that arrangement, and kibble is not a strange appetite when you share soul space with a majestic member of Canis Familiaris, thank you very much." Didn't want Phyllis, another local Loci, who was clearly listening intently, thinking he was a post-human, sex hound, pervert, which was only two-thirds correct.

"Then name the task, and I am duty bound to complete it by the time of the gathering." Horace said, somewhat relieved. Mason didn't like the sound of this "gathering." One Invoker was bad, several were more than capable of killing one thirty year old Shaman and his faithful hound.

"There is a man named Kent Maddison, his wife believes he is unfaithful to their marital bed." Mason said in his supe approved, serious voice, "Bring me proof of his dalliance, and myself and my Circle shall attend your gathering and hear your demon daddy out." Horace blanched at the term daddy but swallowed hard and met Mason's gaze.

"It will be done; I assume you need mundane proof?" Horace said overconfident, but still quite annoyed.

"Legally obtained, and visually confirmable." Horace could very easily just ask a demon to confirm the man's sins, but that wouldn't satisfy a Normie client. Horace huffed out what could have been a curse or angry retort but composed himself and said a very chilling set of words.

"We accept your task and will fulfill it soon." With that he turned on a heel and walked back up the street. Mason watched him go and then looked down at Nosam.

"Why didn't you stop me?" Mason asked, semi-incredulous.

"I too am curious as to what a Demon prince could want from us." Nosam said thoughtfully. He sat in a pointed canine way and looked out to the street. "We have not been duly tested in this lifetime... and I'm afraid you are not ready for what may lie ahead. I have done you a disservice as a guide."

"You taught me everything I know, forged me into the man I am, watched over me every day of my life. Even if I die tomorrow, you have already done more than I could repay." Mason said, feeling the hound's emotion.

"Then we had better not die." Nosam said, his tail wagging despite himself.

CHAPTER

3

•●•

The elevator was slow, arduous and very inconsiderate. Theia was barely aware, eyes closed and trying not to focus too hard on anything in particular. Her gift was an active and passive power; it gave her insight into the world around her, but it also answered to conscious thought. If she was worried about something, it could try to find an answer to her concerns. But, if the information was too broad or actively changing, it could lead to a killer of a headache.

The elevator finally announced, in its fashion, that she had arrived at her floor. She stepped off. She looked across the hall at the lawyer's office that shared the 9th floor with them. He was nice man, who dealt mostly in post-Human Rights law, so they got on famously and even sent each other clients on occasion. In her tapped-in state, she saw a sadness leading to his office, maybe a death in the family? She would invite him to lunch, maybe he'd talk about it.

The door to the Unseen Investigations office was solid reclaimed steel, at Mason's insistence. The older a man made object was the more spirit it had. And, the more spirit it had, the more he could interact with it. If someone entered the door that wasn't supposed to, Mason would know. Upon approaching, Theia greeted the door, offering a small tidbit of energy to it. While not necessary, it always helped to be on good terms with your staff.

She stepped into the reception area and must have startled Zoe, as she let out an "eep" of shock. Zoe was around Mason's age, a few years Theia's senior. She had wild, raven black hair that she wore in a variety of crazy ways. Today it was in two ponytails on either side of her face, poofy and charming. Her skin was tanned betraying her Mexican heritage, and she was wearing a floor length, floral sundress.

"Theia you scared the crap out of me! Were you supposed to be in today? I had the whole morning blocked for the Randall case." Zoe said, bringing a schedule up on her computer screen.

"Went faster than we thought. I wanted to get some work done." Theia was fishing the charm attached to her keys that would disable the wards on her office. Zoe and Mason could do it using their power, but Oracles had to do it analog style.

"Ho ho, she came back without Mason!" a voice from above her called out.

"Probably, buried him up to his neck and covered him in honey!" a second voice called back.

The reception area of the office was unique. While one half was a small seating area and coffee station with mismatched antique chairs and a plush loveseat, the back half, behind Zoe's solid desk, was floor to ceiling bookshelves. Flanking her office door were two thick stone columns topped with a pair of particularly pig-like gargoyles. Theia and Mason had acquired them when a construction company remodeling a church into a real estate office grew to think the building was haunted, as disembodied voices kept insulting the workers. They had quickly discovered the Gargoyles and recruited them. They made great research partners, when they weren't busy theorizing about how all the staff might murder each other one day.

"He is working the Madison case today. I would never leave that much evidence behind, Waldorf." Waldorf erupted into a hearty guffaw, as if murdering her business partner were the epitome of comedy. They had named the two after Statler and Waldorf of Henson fame, as Gargoyles rarely named themselves anything polite.

"We will probably have clients today, so I expect you to get the tasteless jokes out of your system now." Zoe said in her mom voice. Theia ducked into her office, the charm tingling as she passed through the wards, as the gargoyles began a litany of terrible 'humor'.

Theia's office had a small work area with an inlaid silver circle in the center of the room, a plush chair pushed into it. Against the large windows stood her more traditional desk, neat case files stacked into categories and a decent computer. The rest of the room contained books, books, an unreasonable number of books. The entire room smelled of lingering incense, herbs and old tomes.

She crossed the room and leaned her body into one of the shelves. A small click sounded, as it swung out on well-oiled hinges, revealing a locked cabinet painted with symbols and runes. Most of the rune work she had done herself, and she was quite proud of it.

Ritual magic like that practiced by that horrible woman from the bureau is technically possible for anyone with the discipline to learn it. Neither Zoe nor Mason had ever bothered to master more than the basics, but Zoe had more of an understanding of the practical applications. Theia had wanted some independence and had studied the art as well. Being used to the pomp and circumstance of Oracular showmanship, she found the rituals and tool use familiar. She'd even made the ward charm herself, surprising a smug Mason when she had cracked his patterns.

Growing impatient with her own wandering thoughts Theia removed the heavy wooden box where she stored her tarot deck. She had been working with it for almost 10 years now and it was her preferred divination method. Having a flash of intuition, she also grabbed a vial of rose oil. She placed the rose oil near the door on a small table, and then moved to her worktable settling into the comfortable plushness of the familiar chair. Mason said the chair had a bit of an obsession with her, and an ego that annoyed the rest of her office, but she did love the chair and did her most important work there.

As soon as she had placed the box containing her cards on the worktable it slipped and fell open cards fanning out of the box. Three faced her: The Tower, The Hierophant, and the Judgment cards. All high arcana and not in a configuration she liked. She immediately got a flash in her mind, and a new thread in the tapestry of her awareness. Sure, if she had been paying attention in the elevator as opposed to trying to avoid a headache, she would have seen it. With a heavy sigh she pushed herself out of the chair and returned to the office door.

"… a pair-a-moors!" Statler finished. Zoe reached out a hand and snapped and the gargoyle fell silent as if slapped.

"Yes, Theia?" she said sensing the dread enter the room.

"Has the mail come yet?" Theia said in a surprisingly calm voice. Zoe pointed to a mesh basket full of envelopes.

"Haven't had time to sort it yet." she cocked an eyebrow, "Bad news?" Theia reached into the stack and found the envelope floating in her mind. As she had known it would, it bore the emblem for the Bureau. Ripping it open there was a small hiss, and a bit of smoke erupted from the page. Startled she dropped the envelope.

"Anthrax!" Waldorf called.

"Finally!" Statler echoed.

"No, it's a receipt mark. Runic's use them. Look on the first page. It should kind of look like a wavy circle." Theia trusted Zoe. She kept her around for two primary reasons, extraordinary organizational skills, that both Theia and Mason lacked, and an avid knowledge of the inner workings of most of the supe communities.

Theia retrieved the envelope and sure enough on the first page was a slightly charred wavy circle just under the address information for the bureau. Zoe nodded sagely.

"They use them to track if the letters have been opened. They can also usually tell if the letter made it to the right place. But only the Runic who drew it." Zoe looked at the papers. "What does it say?"

Theia already knew full well what it said, but she skimmed it anyway. Oracular sight was very accurate but had a tendency to have a wide lens, so confirmation is always smart.

"We are being Audited..." Theia said a thin veneer of rage escaping. "Claims of job tampering in an effort to prove false claims of foresight."

"Dunlap..." Zoe said all too knowingly.

Mr. Todd Dunlap had been a client of theirs the summer prior. He was certain his father's will had been tampered with. He insisted that his post-Human sister had done the deed, though he hadn't used proper state approved terms. Theia had checked the threads around the situation, and had Mason talk with the lawyer's desk. They had even coughed up the fee to have it studied by a third-party practitioner. Nothing had panned out, and there was no tampering. Theia had known, though, that while his sister had moved their dying father into her home, and cared for him while he died, Todd had tried every underhanded trick he could, to get control of his company before he died, and the will got involved. He had sworn revenge in no uncertain terms and here it was.

"He must have paid a fortune to get us audited." Theia said. Zoe squinted at the papers in Theia's hands.

"Technically, telling someone you don't know, or can find no evidence isn't even fineable." Zoe sighed. She rose and started up the espresso machine.

"I mean even if he gets my license revoked, or me thrown in prison, it still won't change what a piece of paper says!" Theia was about to throw the papers into the trash when she saw the name of the auditor assigned to the case. It wasn't a real shock, she had known that they were becoming entwined destiny wise, but she still stared at it: Meredith Carson.

"Either something about that letter has a deeper meaning I'm not aware of or you are trying to set it on fire, either way I'd love to help." Zoe added in a cheerful tone.

"The Auditor Meredith, she never gave us her name, but she was at the retrieval this morning. She was kind of the literal worst." Theia set the papers back on Zoe's desk, while setting them on fire might make her feel better, it wouldn't stop the threads radiating from it to stop existing.

"Kinda tricksy for the Bureau. She must have something against Oracles." Zoe said looking over the letter.

"It wouldn't surprise me if she has issues with post-Humans in general. She wasn't overly kind to..." A knock cut Theia off mid-sentence. Theia looked to Zoe for some kind of explanation as to who it could be.

"No one on the books this early." she said shrugging. Theia crossed the reception area and opened the door. It was odd she knocked. While the door is warded it knows not to harm clients.

Standing on the other side was a youngish woman with mousy brown hair, capris and a t-shirt, and a startled expression.

Theia recognized her as Mrs. Randall. Why she was here was unclear, even with a cursory glance at her threads.

"Hello, Ms. Morgan." while slightly nervous, she still managed to put an odd amount of emphasis on the lack of an R in the title.

"Mrs. Randall." Theia added, in as unamused a tone as she could bring to bear. Zoe instantly moved from behind her desk, tucking the offensive letter into a drawer.

"Tina! We weren't expecting you to stop by today. Come in and have a seat." Zoe motioned to a nicely plump white chair, before moving to the coffee station. "Coffee?" she called over her shoulder.

Theia, feeling awkward at the door, crossed the room and leaned against Zoe's desk and gave a side glance to Statler who just grinned.

"No thank you, I was just hoping you had an update on my... husband." the tone seemed to indicate she was unsure if she should still call him that. Tina was under the impression her husband had run off with a somehow younger woman.

"Theia just got in, so I don't know if she has compiled her notes for a consultation. If you want to come back tom..." Theia cut Zoe off abruptly.

"He's dead." Theia announced, and watched as Tina went through the motions of shock. Something wasn't right about this. Tina was giving off only strong threads, meaning there was little delineation in her choices and actions. That usually meant a planned or at least practiced set of events.

Zoe shot Theia a glance that may have been a hex, and sat next to the woman comforting her. One thread stuck out more than any of the others. When it would come up was still unclear, but it was easy enough to follow it to a vague notion that she was working towards.

"I don't know what happened to his wedding ring." Theia supplied, briefly shocking the woman genuinely.

"It was taken?" she said through what could be real tears, Theia was never particularly good at feminine wiles.

"Neither I nor Mason saw any ring, jewelry of any kind really." Theia replied, memory wasn't included in the whole foresight package, but she did have a good one regardless. The body had been a horrendous mess, but they had checked it.

"Do you know what happened to him?" Mrs. Randall asked. Theia got tense, it's not technically on the up and up to provide information that couldn't be backed by evidence, and she was staring down the gun of an audit.

"Not at this time." Theia said looking at a spot on the carpet.

"The coroner will be able to tell you more sweety." Zoe cooed.

"So, I guess that means case closed for you, right?" Tina said a backbone forming in the words. She was going to do it.

"Yes, your account will be settled and after I finish writing a case report Zoe will send you an invoice." Theia tried to make it sound as final as possible, lest Tina get the impression she wanted anything more to do with this case.

"Would it be possible." She began.

"I can only provide certain services under the law, mam, so anything else regarding this case would be up to the police department." She was being rude, but if she was kind, Tina would beg, appeal to Theia's better nature, and probably convince her to help anyway.

"Finding a missing object... would that be illegal?" Tina said the briefest of smiles playing at her lips.

"It would not... no." Theia said defeated.

"I'll get a blank contract." Zoe said rising from Tina's side.

CHAPTER

4

• ● •

Mason, finding himself suddenly having the day off, had taken a nap. He wasn't used to sleeping during the day, or really much at all with all of his duties to the agency, so he woke up groggy and dehydrated.

"I've been storing up excess liquids in case your nap went as expected." Nosam said from the love seat. Almost instantly Mason began to feel better as hydration flowed through their connection and his symptoms began to abate.

"It had better not have been from the toilet." Mason said moving towards the bathroom himself. Nosam let the implications hang between them and didn't respond. The bathroom was the one area that Mason had made some changes when converting the houseboat. While still quite small by home standards, he'd made it more comfortable to move around in. Ignoring the potentially damning splash marks near the toilet, he began to relieve himself.

Everything was going great until the faucet on the sink made a horrendous groaning sound. Mason hurried to finish his current task as a black sludge began pouring and splashing into the sink, bringing with it a smell of mildew and general unpleasantness. Nosam pushed the bathroom door open and locked eyes with Mason.

"Deep Court…" They said simultaneously. The sludge began to coalesce into a roughly shaped sphere.

"Mason of the second world," It hissed through a bubbling surface. "You have been summoned to the court of the Deep Queen."

There were three fey monarchs in Tucson. The Queen on High, who presided over the mountains and changed with the seasons, The King in the Valley, who held power as long as snow did not touch the mountains, and the Queen of the Deeps, who oversaw the massive caverns beneath the valley and all the deeply upsetting fey. Of the three, Mason could think of not a single one he'd want anything to do with.

"I am under no obligation to meet with the fey monarchs. I am only bound and obligated to creatures of the second world." Mason grabbed a hand towel and held it to his face, growing increasingly nauseated by the scent of the messenger.

" No obligation. Payment is offered for any services rendered." The black sphere gasped. Well, that was a different matter. As creatures of the Fey lands, they weren't bound to human laws, and as such, there would be no regulatory barrier to accepting payment for his abilities. On the other hand, it was the fey, and even fair payment could be dangerous to accept.

"Do you not have a Druid you can call on? This sounds like a job for them." Mason added, still looking for an out.

"Dead, and no replacement within the courts reach. As one bound to the second world, the task would then fall to you." Mason was not enthused to hear the Druid of the valley had died. There should be a Facebook group or something, so the different two-natured could keep tabs on each other.

"I am honor bound to another, a mortal woman, I cannot accept any such offer without her expressed consent." Mason had hoped that the concept of their being a mortal obligation would dissuade them. Binding him when he already had a geas would be problematic for them. If the claim of a task offered in good faith was true that wouldn't bar the proceedings, if it was an elaborate trap, they would resist her involvement.

"Gather your fellowship and call to me at any drain, I will appear and show you the way." It hissed and began to dissolve.

"What is your name, who do I call for." Mason said a bit desperately.

"Coincleach." it burbled as the last of the sludge seeped into the drain. The name almost sounded like clicking with some vowels thrown in. Aside from the strange blue stain in his sink, Mason had made it out of this encounter with nary a scratch on him, and when dealing with the fey that was impressive.

Mason pulled out his work phone, and sighing at having to admit he didn't have anything on the Madison case yet, he dialed Theia. She answered almost immediately which was a parlor trick of hers, knowing when you were about to call and usually about what.

"Honestly, Mason, you have terrible timing." she said in the tone she used when she was trying not to sound angry in front of clients. She was much better at being an Oracle, than she was at controlling the tone of her voice though.

"I know, but it's all too convenient. We find a body, traces of the fey left behind. The boogey lady of the near fey suddenly summons." Mason left the rest of his thoughts unsaid knowing she would connect the dots.

"I don't have time to really be traversing the planes of existence right now, but I agree you shouldn't go alone." Theia seemed to ponder. "We got a new case and the tapestry around it is suspicious." She added, "There might be some wisdom in seeking out some outside intel. I can be at your place after I finish up here." With that, she promptly ended the call. Mason put the phone away. He was a Shaman, hopping through different planes of existence was inconvenient at best.

The reason most PLEB agents had a hard time with Shamans was they didn't fit neatly into the classification system they had established. The whole system hinged on the level of humanity inherent in the individual. The Constitution only claimed that all men were created equal. Men in this context meant humans. Ironically, the 'discovery' and subsequent adjustment to the concept, that magic was real had actually done a lot to unify people along lines that used to divide them. Now it didn't matter as much if the new guy in the neighborhood was Gay or Black, but did they turn furry at night and bring down property values.

So now there were four classifications of Americans: Humans who were either completely without magical talent, or practiced safe forms of magic like Runics, and some Invokers. No matter how human you were, dealing with Demons was still frowned upon. Post-Humans, people who had been normal in childhood, but developed their inherent magical gifts later in life, like Theia or Zoe. Demi-Humans who were hybrids and only spent some of their time in human form, like shifters or vampires, and finally Supernaturals or Paranormal Creatures, things that were never or could never be considered humans like Coincleach or Nosam.

Post-Humans were allowed to attain licenses in order to use their abilities in ways PLEB found fair and not exploitative. Demi-humans could hold down normal jobs, but there were no laws protecting them from discrimination. So, if you're boss finds out you're not human enough, there is nothing stopping them from canning you. Supes usually don't care about money as they had never fit into human society to begin with. A unicorn rarely thinks about retirement.

Shamans, and other dual-natured humans, however, were hard to classify. Officially they were a restricted class of post-Humans, and , technically, they fell under a religion as far as discrimination was concerned. However, as all DNH's have two aspects, one human and one tied to a different plane of existence , an argument could be made for Demi-

Human. And, to further confuse the issue, if the DNH and their supernatural partner are intrinsically bound, did that make them Supes?

Mason was lucky that he had been born bound to the second world, the closest of the other planes. So close in fact that it was easily reached from either side. Nosam could manifest here with only a whisper of energy spent. Other dual-natured beings tied to more distant realms, like the infernal or the fey, were much more suspect to the general public and the gulf between their two selves could be hard to surmount.

"You won't be able to come with me." Mason said to Nosam, even though both he and Nosam already knew what traveling to the Fey would entail.

"And you will be unable to call upon any pledges or oaths you've made. You will have to rely solely on Theia's runic magic for protection." Nosam added in a dire tone.

"Well, I can think of worse company to have at the end of your life." Mason made an attempt at humor, but it fell into the silence of the small bathroom and died.

• ● •

Theia arrived at Mason's 'house' within the hour. She had taken the time to switch into a more appropriate outfit for traversing the fey realm. She had undone the braid and pinned it into a bun, mostly to use the iron chopsticks she had had commissioned. She also now sported a heavy leather jacket that fell perfectly to the waist. It had been payment for a job a few years ago. It was made with salamander skin so was all but fireproof, and even in the harsh Arizona sun she felt perfectly cool. More importantly, it was laced on the inside with fey chain mail and so was very sword and bullet proof, unless you had an iron sword, but it was highly unlikely anyone at the fey courts would be wielding one of those.

Mason was waiting for her on the curb; most likely Nosam had felt her coming. He looked much the same as earlier, save for the bastard sword strapped to his back.

"Expecting trouble?" Theia asked with a smile.

"It is my job, so yes, always." He said sliding into the seat next to her. Placing the sword gently in the backseat.

"Didn't this blob thing offer us a ride to the Deep Court?" Theia asked. Mason had said as much in his lengthy text message filled with info she already knew about the Fey. Theia used to call him out for man-splaining, but had learned over the years that he only did it out of worry for her, and a need to go over things himself. He often coped with the stress of their lives through gentle instruction.

"I can guarantee you any path Coincleach would open for us would not be pleasant to non-slime-based people." Mason intoned , slightly disgusted.

"So, what's the plan then?" Theia had already pulled away from the curb, checking her rearview mirror to make sure Nosam had somehow made it into the back seat. He was laying down next to the sword with a doggy grin.

"Head to the University. There is an oak grove there we can use to cross. It will be more of a walk, but more pleasant by a long stretch." Mason pointed east toward the campus, but she already knew where it was he was talking about. He spoke of oaks often. Oak trees were special to him and the fey. It was a place he often visited just because he liked the ambiance.

"How long of a walk are we talking about? I can't afford to lose a week traipsing around in the Fey realms." Theia was scared to bring up the audit. Not because she feared his reaction, but more out of a displaced guilt that she hadn't seen it coming. It's hard not to blame yourself for not seeing problems ahead of time when you can see the future.

"Got that covered." He reached into his pocket and pulled a Dora the Explorer watch out and quickly attached it to her wrist. Even Theia could feel the spirit crawling around inside and was a bit taken aback by how strong it must be. "I made these last summer when all of those red caps were terrorizing the train station. I had assumed we would have to travel to the Deep Wild to deal with it. Anyway, these will keep us in time with the our world."

"A lot of people would pay a lot of money to be able to attend a fey rager and make it back by Monday." Theia whistled.

"Well, it took me a lot of time to convince a strong enough spirit to imbue them, and an even longer time to find vessels it would like." Mason said producing a My Little Pony watch of his own.

"So, an ancient and powerful time spirit." Theia began.

"Elemental." Mason corrected.

"A time elemental spirit, chose these watches specifically?" Theia turned the watch on her wrist and could feel the jubilation from the spirit inside.

"Apparently it is a fan." Mason said with a shrug. Theia understood some of the basics of how Mason's abilities worked. He would scoff if she called it magic, but it was deserving of the title. He used to call these items fetishes, but referred to them as charms now. Too many clients giggled at the term "fetishes". They contained a portion of the elementals set to a specific task in exchange for a small amount of the user's essence.

"How long til it taps me out?" Theia was mostly concerned, because her pool of essence was quite smaller than Mason's. He waved a hand dismissively.

"I've had a year to charge these babies when I had excess. They should be good for about two relative weeks." He said off handedly.

"Okay, so time isn't an issue. What about getting lost.?" Theia knew that while Nosam had a near perfect sense of direction, Mason did not, and Nosam would not be able to join them.

"I called in a favor and got us a guide." Mason said with a smile.

"It had better not be Jackson…" Theia said with a warning tone.

"Think he ironically goes by Jack now." Mason said, purposefully not meeting her gaze. Jackson, or Jack now, was a member of the local Drove of Were-Hares. While he was a great pal, he could be unreliable in a crisis.

"We are going to die." Theia put enough fake gloom into her voice for the both of them. Mason pointed her to a parking meter he knew, and she backed into the space it ruled over.

"He's familiar with the back roads of the fey, if we follow him, we don't need to get into any fights. Then it won't matter if he hides or runs away." Mason said as he collected his sword and stepped out of the car. He walked over to the meter and had a short nonverbal conversation with it. As she watched, it added several hours to itself, as if he had paid in coins.

"Aren't these meters relatively new?" Theia asked, referencing the belief that most of the things Mason dealt with had to be antiques in order for him to talk to them directly. The older something was the more of a spirit it had.

"Usually I wouldn't be able to, but Shithead here, is a prodigy. When he was installed, he had an error that caused him to reset every 20 minutes, regardless of how long you paid for. Led to a lot of people personifying him. Hence the name." That made things a little clearer.

Objects, Mason had often explained, especially those with lots of moving or electronic parts, rarely have spirits. When they either receive a lot of energy, or are personified frequently by one individual or by a lot of different people, they tend to become what people think of them. The elevator that just loves one particular song, or the camera that just seems to have a life of his own, probably has one of these spirits. Shithead here was fond of screwing people over because so many people thought he had malicious intent.

"He should behave for me, though, it's in his best interest. Worst case scenario we get a ticket, and we call in a favor." They had done a lot of work with law enforcement, so, a favor like fixing a small parking fine was the least they could do.

"I'm still not sure what the plan is. Every time I've plane hopped, it's been through a local opening, or a door." Theia said, giving Shithead a warning glare.

"I happen to know the door man!" Mason called jovially over his shoulder, Nosam giving her a doggy grin. Theia sighed deeply and jogged after them. As they entered a small alcove between buildings, a space was ringed by eight tall oak trees, the ground covered in the red gravel common to Tucson. Jackson was already waiting for them. He was thin but wiry, wearing a mechanic's overshirt and a pair of work pants.

"Hey Mason, Theia." Jackson had an upbeat and optimistic sounding voice that always made you wanna be as hopeful as he was. Jackson was a prominent member in the Tucson Drove, a group of Hare Shifters. Given their numbers and the fact that herbivore shifters didn't disquiet humans nearly as much as the predatory kind, it was relatively easy for them to fly under the radar and avoid licensing and registration. As such they were better off than most Demi-Humans in being able to give others of their kind a leg up.

"You sure you know the way to the deeps, Jackrabbit?" Mason said handing him a Powderpuff girls watch. Mason had a million and one nicknames for just about everyone he met, but Theia felt that "Jackrabbit" was a pretty lazy one, even for him.

"Sure do, got a client that likes to ride the deep roads on a sweet little suped up..." Jackson had been about to expound on the specifics of a model of motorcycle, but remembered that Mason and Theia were particularly disinterested in motorcycle minutia. "Anyway, I often do house calls as it's hard to dredge a bike from the deep."

Mason was busy talking with the largest tree in the center of the small grove. After a time, he reached up and picked something from a low branch. He turned and handed each of them a smallish acorn. He put his in his mouth and gestured for them to do the same. Theia sighed and put hers in her mouth, knowing how bitter acorns taste and dreading step two.

Theia felt the circle close around them. Mason hadn't even gestured, but, then, he did specialize in these things. Most magic, especially the kind meant to affect the world around you, could just be unleashed. But magic dealing with moving around, or that might be tainted by outside forces was best done from within a protective circle. Theia would have had to draw a circle, or use a pre-existing one like the one on her worktable, but Mason had just willed his into existence.

Theia looked about just to be sure, and sure enough, small mushrooms were forming around them in a perfect circle. Soon the magic began to build energy, filling the space. Knowing the drill, Theia added her own energy to the workings, and soon also felt Jackson mingling his energy as well. With a loud crunch, Mason disappeared. Taking his lead, Jackson and Theia met each other's eyes and bit down hard on the acorns, and the world around them exploded with color.

CHAPTER

5

———— • ● • ————

Mason loved the Near Wild, or the Fey as many people think of it. In some ways, it was much like the real world, with the Oak grove standing silent and brooding above them. The buildings, however, had been replaced with towering mesas, their sides peppered with flowering desert plants and cacti. The Oak trees, too, were taller, greener, and you could almost hear them breathing in their nearness. Mason was so taken in by the scene unfolding, that he completely missed the inherent danger. Theia called out an alarm.

"Mason, get down!"

Mason was confused, until she plowed into him, an arrow impacting off of her enchanted jacket. Jackson, who had appeared around the same time as she did, was already shifting his face and body, sprouting the tawny hair of his hybrid form. After a moment, Mason noticed them, Goblins. Terrible little creatures who were more teeth than sense.

The three of them ran to a small alcove, where in the real world there was a covered walkway, and assessed the situation. Red feathered arrows planted themselves at their feet as they ran.

"This makes no sense! Goblins are Deep Fey, they should not be this close to the border." Mason said in a stern voice, unstrapping the sword from his back.

"Well, they clearly don't know that, Mason! What are our options?" Theia yelled out, removing a glass dowel from her satchel. Jackson was fully shifted, and now stood behind them a slightly shorter but muscled half hare, half man. The Motorcycle shirt he wore oddly tamped down the fluffy fur on his arms.

Mason thought, there was really no reason Deep Fey would travel this far. While the Near Fey almost exactly mirrored the real world in geography and even appearance, the Deep Fey was a realm of madness and violence that made Alice's Wonderland look like a children's book, which it really wasn't, if you had ever read it.

"Technically by fey law we have more right to be here than they do. If the Valley Court knew they were here, they'd kill them on sight." Mason provided, wishing he'd brought more weapons on this supposedly peaceful ambassador mission.

"Perfect." Theia stepped out of cover briefly and raised the glass dowel , gathering the small spark of power needed to direct the spell held within. She leveled it at a goblin, who had just knocked an arrow and shouted, "Fulminous!" a streak of lighting flung from her, snapped the bow with its heat , and carved a bloody ruin of charred flesh across the goblins mostly mouthy face.

This seemed to concern the remaining Goblins, who looked at each other. She must have tagged the leader, she thought, her ability to see the future giving her excellent timing. Theia ducked back into the stone alcove as arrows began peppering the ground again. The remaining goblins overcame their shock. Mason looked at the dark stained-glass dowel. Theia had maybe one more shot in it before it was completely burned out.

"Any bright ideas, Mr. Security?" Theia said, with just a tad too much scorn. Mason thought, they were much too close to a boundary for them to be this aggressive. The King in the Valley should be swarming the grove with a powerful vengeance by now. He looked about, his eyes falling on a crack in the floor , and sighed deeply.

"One, but none of us are going to enjoy it in the slightest." Mason stated matter of factly.

"Well, unless you got very good at throwing swords in the recent past, I don't think we have a choice." Theia said, in her "I'm-remaining-calm" voice. Mason produced a canteen he had brought from his bag. He had meant to have it in case they were dying of thirst , but as long as they were dying, it made sense to use it. He poured it liberally on the crack, hoping it was deep enough to qualify as a drain.

"Coincleach." He said clearly and with power behind it. Not a demand per se, but definitely a summons. Almost immediately, black, awful smelling sludge began to pour from the small crack. It spread out along the floor.

"I am never speaking to you again." Jackson said flatly, as he realized what was happening. Arrows were continuing to whiz into the alcove deeper than before. The goblins were getting bold.

"Mason, we have two options to get out of here without too many consequences." Theia said her eyes distant and faded. "One involves harming the trees, the other, harming you." It was clear she was hoping for the trees to be the target, but the pain that settled on her face meant she must have seen the real answer.

"Leave the grove." Mason said gravely. Theia nodded and moved to the mouth of the alcove as black slime began to crawl up their ankles, a wet slimy, cold suffusing them all.

Theia raised the glass dowel in both hands and, with a sharp intake of breath, snapped it in two. A crack of lightning and flash of a much too bright light, seared the air. Mason had looked away , but the Goblins, and sadly, Jackson, had not known what would happen. They would get their eyesight back in an hour or so.

Pain lashed through Mason's shoulder, a goblin arrow piercing it straight on. He called out in pain but was quickly drowned out as black sludge reached his mouth and began pouring down his throat. He blacked out in a very heroic fashion.

• ● •

Theia was never going to be clean again. As the slick wetness retreated, and she found herself in perfect blackness, she reconsidered whether getting them filled with arrows was not the better option.

"Mason?" Theia called in a hoarse whisper, her voice unwilling to return too quickly after its slimy ordeal. There was a presence close by, a cold , deep magic that thrummed through the seemingly infinite darkness. Theia reached for one of the small , chemical lights she had packed in her satchel.

"We would not." Came a voice, clearly feminine in tone but composed of a thousand voices.

"We wouldn't, or can't?" Theia answered back. She could hear Jackson's heavy staccato breathing.

"Our form would be unpleasant to you." The voice originated from the same general direction as the power that was awash within the space. Theia followed the sensation with her eyes and found a dozen glowing blue orbs, most likely eyes. But, they were not arranged in a way that screamed human.

"Mason!" Theia called with a tad more urgency than she intended.

"He is not conscious. The combination of the goblin barb and his transportation, overwhelmed him. He informed us that you are capable of speaking for him." It was clear, now that Theia had calmed a tiny bit, that this was the Deep Queen. So, they were safe, in the broad sense of the term.

"Well, I would ask why we are here then," Theia began, "Mason made it seem like you asked to speak with us." Theia was proud of herself for not swearing in front of extra-dimensional royalty. It was tempting though.

"We have summoned you because we wish to retain the services of your guild." The voice paused, "You are an investigation guild correct?"

"We do often serve that purpose, yes. I am an Oracle, Mason assists me with gathering information." Theia could feel Mason stirring.

"What do you know of our people." the voice asked, more pleasantly. Theia likened it to slowly sinking into cool waters, shocking at first , but soon refreshing.

"I know that the near Fey serve as guardians and wards between the Human world and the Deeper Realms. Almost every major city has its own courts. Typically, they are based around the seasons, but in Tucson they are determined by altitude." Theia hoped the few primers she had studied on the topic weren't offensively incorrect.

"Yes, and to serve that duty, we employ spies in the human world. Creatures of human birth with fey souls and magic." Mason was fully awake now and decided to add his own voice.

"Changelings." He said in a rough voice, the sound of it indicating he was standing.

"Ah, speaker, you are awake." The Queen said.

"The Drove has a few Changelings in it, it's considered a blessing." Jackson said, his breathing returning to normal, and by the tone of his voice he had shifted to human form.

"Yes, hence, why so many of your kind are welcome in our realms. We appreciate the chances to mingle our peoples." The Queen responded.

"The Queen of the Deeps does not broach topics frivolously. Has something happened to the Changelings?" Mason responded smartly. Theia hadn't even considered that the Queen might be building to a point. Most of Theia's interaction with the Fey had been with missing persons cases. Most of those ended with dragging a college kid home from a primordial Bacchanalia.

"Indeed, you are correct, we grow concerned. Several of our agents have been attacked, none have survived the ordeal." The Queens sadness was palpable and was almost overwhelming.

"I mean no disrespect, but would this not be a job for a Druid?" Mason retorted. Theia wasn't aware that "Druid" was a job you could have.

"Our Druid was slain during the last moon." The Queen intoned, "His surname was Randall."

Ryan Randall had been an agent of the Fey. That raised a lot more questions than it answered. Had Tina known what he was? Even dead, there should have been some energy on the body indicating a post-Human. Perhaps he didn't have much juice.

"Hence, why you approached me, a speaker for the closest nation to your own." Mason seemed to ponder. "I cannot make an oath until I have consulted with those I am obligated to." Theia wasn't sure if he just meant Nosam, or Sonora as well. Mason seemed to have differing levels of commitment to several different entities.

"I ask not for an oath, but present a quest with due reward." Almost on cue, there was a wet sliding sound and suddenly, a light sprung into existence. In its center was a wooden treasure chest, just like out of a video game. Inside were gemstones, a lot of gemstones.

"If you require no Oath, I feel comfortable accepting your terms." Mason said, a tinge of greed on his lips. Jackson's nervous energy was rising to a peak.

"Deep Queen." Jackson said in a timid voice, with a bit of rigid respect to it. A deep, unfathomable presence fell on the shifter. "When we first crossed, we were attacked at the border by goblins. Has something changed in the valley kingdom?" Theia hadn't even thought it would be worth broaching with the queen. Mason had said Jackson was a bit of a fey expert, perhaps he was a changeling himself.

"Regrettable." Came the queen's voice. "The Queens of the Deep Wild must be in conflict. Wild Fey have been displaced throughout the near kingdoms. I had to send Coincleach to you, as all of the crossings have become treacherous." she finished, the pressure of her words abating.

"ALL of the crossings have been guarded?" Jackson said a bit incredulous. Mason seemed to pick up on his thought.

"That is pretty, tidy and organized for creatures like goblins." Mason made a thinking noise.

"It has prevented us from sending our own to investigate the missing changelings. Few fey can slip in and out of the mortal realms as easily as Coincleach." , there was a pleasant, burbling sound from near the floor at the queen's words.

"So, it could be related, a Wild Fey trying to interfere?" Jackson said rubbing the stubble on his chin.

"The Wild Courts don't really work like that. They barely even acknowledge the human realms." Mason provided.

Theia was reminded of a long conversation she had had with a researcher of the Fey Realms. The Realms were separated into roughly three sections, making up the whole of the plane. The Near Fey was almost an exact mirror of the first world. Although, the exact things in it might look very different, like the buildings around the grove becoming mesas in the Fey realm. The Deep Wilds, however, were more conceptual, having only a vague resemblance to the Near. It was all primordial forest and ancient fantastical castles. The Wild Queens, each representing one of the four seasons, and constantly at odds with one another, ruled there. Beyond that, there was, presumably, a barrier with some deeper even more alien realm called the Far Wild. Goblins, and other unaligned fey lived in the lands between the realms.

Mason was right to assume that, the fact that goblins were there to ambush them, was exceedingly suspicious. If it hadn't been for Coincleach, they would not be in as unscathed a position as they were.

"I'm sure in time you will find the answers you seek." the Queen's focus seemed to wane and disperse, "Jackson you shall be of assistance to these Heroes, per your obligations." A whine from Jackson.

"Of course, my Queen." he quickly corrected.

"Then your business here is done, you have your quest." With this dismissive tone, Theia felt her body turn to fuzz and her consciousness waver. Soon, she was blinking her eyes open against a very bright sun in Mason's front yard. The smell of flowers was everywhere. She looked about and saw Mason and Jackson lying nearby.

"Maybe it was a dream," she said to the two men. She sat up and looked over at them. Mason was a bit further away, and Nosam was sitting near his head looking concerned. Mason had lost his shirt, and the tapestry of his skin was covered in tribal tattoos of various creatures and plants masking his otherwise pale flesh. Where the arrow had struck him was now caked in mud. The arrow was gone.

Jackson had a concerned look on his face, and stared up into the sky. His face was a tad furrowed, as if he was strongly considering fleeing at the earliest possible moment. As Theia watched, he composed himself, and took on a determined countenance. Hares weren't known for bravery, but they could be plenty stubborn.

Mason sat up, rubbing at the mud at his shoulder. He looked at Theia's face, their long friendship making it easy to read. A lot more had happened than either of them had been prepared for that morning.

"Well, we better get in as many office hours as we can." Theia said, rising to her feet and offering Jackson a hand. He took it, and the two waited patiently as Mason put on the tank top that Nosam had brought him.

CHAPTER

6

•●•

Theia was riding in the back of Mason's jeep. It wasn't a long drive from Dunbar Springs to downtown, but she had been out of the world for a spell. While the watches had worked perfectly, she was still worried that the space/time tapestry might have shifted since she last looked.

She closed her eyes and let the threads spread out in front of her, weaving themselves into the whole cloth of infinite possibilities . She then focused on her and Mason's immediate future. Parts were not filling in correctly, meaning there must have been powerful players involved , who were able to hide themselves from the casual use of her powers. One particular section glowed with inevitability, however.

"Mason." Theia said opening her eyes.

"By your tone, I'm assuming there's trouble a brewin?" Mason said with levity.

"Is there a particular reason you would be having a disagreement with Gideon?" Theia watched Mason's eyes in the rearview mirror and saw the momentary 'oh shit' twitch.

"Well, I may have made a deal with Horace... But it was only to meet, not perform any tasks." Mason was being slightly evasive, and while Theia was upset, she also had news for him that she was waiting for a good time to share.

"He's waiting for us; I don't know if we will be able to avoid him." Theia spread her metaphysical 'hands' over the ethereal tapestry. "Even if we play it perfect, he finds us eventually, and while the details are muddy, it's better for us to face him now."

"Where?" Mason pulled over so she could look, but she had already picked a place.

"Veinte de Agosto." She said without hesitation. Veinte de Agosto was a park right across from their office at One South Church, and the area around it was heavily populated, so the chances of violence breaking out were slim. The park had the additional benefit of being a close, personal friend of Mason's. It was really just an upstart median with an, admittedly, cool water feature and a statue of Pancho Villa, which could be a tad problematic. With two major roads on either side of the park, it was never really not being observed.

Mason nodded and gestured for Jackson to exit the vehicle.

"Meet us at our office. You know what floor?" Jackson nodded and hopped out of the jeep. Mason quickly found an open meter on Pennington and pulled his seat forward for Theia to get out.

"Don't say it." Theia anticipated, particularly tuned in, though, it was starting to give her a headache.

"Gideon can be dangerous, and I doubt you packed that bag with much that would phase him." Mason was right on that one. A casual traipse through friendly fey territory, and fighting a Nephilim were two very different tasks. Theia hadn't really had much time to make much in the way of quick use gear lately, either. Nothing worse than an under-prepared seer.

Nephilim were bad enough, being the supernatural equivalent of Demi-gods, think Hercules or Thor. The PLEB had classified them as Demi-Humans, but most agents were resistant to policing them, as most people thought of them as angels. Gideon was on the laxer side of claiming divinity , understanding that while he was powerful and his power was drawn from a celestial bloodline, he didn't see any difference between himself and a shifter or Changeling.

On a good day, Gideon was a casual acquaintance, maybe even an ally, but if what Mason thought was true, he could feel compelled to get involved. Gideon was also an accomplished Invoker of a potent celestial creature. He never said which one, but he would always jokingly inform you that you'd heard of him. So, they weren't looking down upon a strong Demi-Human, they were looking down the barrel of a celestial cannon pointed at their proverbial pontoon boat. Not to mention, he and Gideon had dated for a bit.

"Getting any details yet?" Mason asked hopefully. Sometimes, when dealing with less momentous odds, Theia would get a play by play of the fight, sometimes, even actual visions like she had with the goblins. Gideon, however, had enough pull on the ethereal tapestry that it warped around him and could pull her right in with it, if she wasn't careful.

"The park is our best bet, lots of people around, and it's a home-field advantage." Theia said, going over the contents of her satchel. She had a couple snap circles, mainly meant to repel fey, but a protective circle offered resistance to most things, regardless of specific purpose. Also, a canteen of factory run off, super deadly to fey, not so much to angel babies. She did have a magic dampener, essentially a silver rod, that when activated, sapped the magic in a given area. That would work on an Invoker. Theia wasn't sure how it would affect Mason, though.

"Nosam." Mason said, and the Wolf-Hound's eyes began spilling light as his form dissolved into energy, floating to Mason in a slow cloud of white-hot motes. It began to settle on his shoulders and arms, forming thick leather sleeves. The sleeves were covered in corse, white, canine hair, ending in powerful, clawed glove weapons, called cestus, on the hands.

Now, the flow of energy between them would be instantaneous and some of the toughness of being a totemic spirit would transfer to Mason. Theia had only seen him do this a few times. Mason and Nosam didn't like to be fused in this way, because while inseparable, they liked to maintain a semblance of individuality.

"You should probably hang back, or go back to the office." It was sweet of Mason to be concerned, but she could tell by his tone he already knew the answer to that.

"You do better with me there." Theia supplied, which was half true. As they got closer to the encounter, the threads where she was involved became longer. But, hers were becoming much more secure at avoiding the situation, and there was a fair bit of free will at play. Seeing the future was complicated. In a guided consultation with specific questions and tools involved, it was easier to read the most likely outcome. Yet, when reading wild tangents of an ever-changing situation, it was much harder to get a concrete answer. Everyone involved could change their minds in a million different ways, resulting in a web of possibility that was near impossible to read, save for milliseconds into the future.

"We are here, looks like he hasn't arrived yet. I'm gonna get Agosto involved." Mason stepped into the grass, kicked off his boots, and closed his eyes. Theia had always been a tad jealous of Mason and his abilities. Most Post-Humans had very active and flashy abilities, while her gift was more passive and reactionary. It was hard to feel accomplished when your best friend can control the very earth beneath your feet, and all you can do is guess at what is going to be delivered in the mail that day.

The thrum of the park rose to the surface at Mason's call. Theia, never tiring of the sight , watched as Mason's legs seemed to merge with the grass. The grass slowly creeped up his legs, and appeared as if he wore boots made out of soil and grass. The water from the fountain behind them also seemed to pull toward him and splash in a haphazardly fashion.

The moment of admiration was short lived, however, as Gideon soon arrived, stepping into the park from the south.

Mason's eyes shot open as he felt the sudden presence. Theia looked Gideon over. He had the look of a much older man, with his all-white hair and pale skin, it didn't help that he insisted on wearing suits that made him look like Colonel Sanders. The suit did hide his impressive physique, and, it was only when you got closer, that he began to appear much younger.

Gideon stopped about 20 feet from them and put his hands in his pockets. In the bright afternoon light, you could barely see that Gideon glowed slightly, and that glow washed them in a gentle warmth. He didn't look dangerous, but felt safe, and comforting. Theia and Mason suddenly felt that to be facing him with hostility was wrong. He was here to help.

"Mason, Nosam, Theia I'm not here looking for a fight." he said, gently. Theia felt all tension leaking from her body, and wanted to lay down in the grass and look at clouds. His voice had that effect. She knew better though, and quickly shored up her mental shields forcing his aura from her mind.

"Theia?" Mason asked, in a half growl. He was looking for her guidance and making sure she was in the moment. Theia spun out the weave before her, and gripped Gideon's thread, much clearer, now that she was this much closer. She spread it out and looked at its branches.

"Forty-five percent." Theia supplied. This was the survivability assessment. It was probably closer to 56%, but Mason was cautious and preferred the most critical of scenarios. Some things Theia would consider survival. He wouldn't.

"That doesn't seem terribly peaceful." Mason said with finality.

"Well, there must be something I can't foresee with my pitiable grasp of future events." Gideon sighed, and brought his hands to his side in a clear sign of non-aggression. "I know Horace came to see you. You must understand, that the situation that is brewing right now will bring us into conflict. Promise me you will ignore his summons, and I will walk away right now."

This was the definite point of contention in the weave. If Mason agreed, they would all walk away from here and all be the best of friends, happy and healthy. The problem was, it would be a lie, and while there was a small chance Mason might pick that option, his bullheaded pride was going to get in the way. Nosam being so close to the core of them, also made Mason more aggressive.

"I don't take orders from Infernals OR Celestials, Gideon. I'm not involved in your war." Mason said with more force than he might have intended.

"Warning Shot." Theia said clearly as she saw the thread solidify. Gideon, barely noticing her words, let loose with a searing bolt of pure, white light. He had barely moved his arm. The Light scoured a divot maybe 6 inches deep and 6 feet long just to the right of Mason in between him and Theia. If she hadn't warned him, Mason would have dived to the left putting distance between them, and probably rapidly escalating the fight. As it were, Mason only flinched a little.

Recognizing Theia's involvement, Gideon smiled slightly. "You have me at a disadvantage, clearly." Gideon seemed to ponder.

"Fifty-four percent." Theia said more quietly this time. If Gideon was catching on, she'd have to rely on Nosam's exceptional hearing.

"Gideon, you know as well as I do, that once I made that deal I couldn't back out." Mason said. "That would be more dangerous than just going to the meeting." Mason was gaining clarity and was able to affect a more compassionate tone.

"I should have come to you first." Gideon scuffed the ground with his foot. "Things may have been different."

"You can't possibly be thinking of starting a fight in the middle of downtown?!" Theia called out incredulously.

"I don't see too many people." Gideon said with a smile on his face. A pair of luminous wings unfurling from his back, his eyes fiercely glowing, even in the sun. Theia took stock and realized that, in fact, the streets were empty. No cars drove by, no pedestrians wandered past, and no transients slept under the shady trees. Aside from a few annoyed birds and trees, they were alone.

"How in the..." Theia was impressed. Celestials were known for their ability to affect the minds of others, but this was something else.

Gideon didn't hesitate, Theia felt the power growing beneath her and with a quick glance saw his intentions. In the glowing white lines, a complicated magic circle was forming along the ground at her feet. He was trying to remove her from the conflict, trapping her in a circle, where she would be cut off and safe, but unable to see the weave. She sidestepped, planting a foot right in the path of the circle just in time for her foot to meet it. It began to fizzle.

Mason ran a hand over his chest, where Theia knew his tattoos lived. Without warning, birds streamed from the trees dive-bombing Gideon, who was already distracted by willing the protective circle into existence. Neither side seemed too interested in harming the other, but that wouldn't last long. All Gideon had to do to achieve his goals was put Mason in the hospital.

Gideon began a haunting chant in what was most likely Enochian. He stuttered though, as birds ricocheted off his head. While Theia was familiar with the language in its written form, it was a dead language, and she had never heard it spoken with clarity. Power built around Gideon in a steady thrum as he chanted. Mason didn't hesitate and tree roots exploded from the earth forcing Gideon to dodge backwards to escape their sharp points.

Theia almost smiled to herself as a metal hoof struck Gideon in the back. The statue of Pancho Villa having removed itself from its pedestal, had joined the fray, forcing Gideon to weave his way through a barrage of hoof beats that could have shattered bone.

Mason pushed the attack, gesturing wildly, as the ground underneath Gideon grew unstable and uneven, further complicating his defense. Theia watched the threads and saw an opportunity. She moved to flank Gideon, as he danced away from the Statue. Gideon, getting a solid foot on the ground, launched himself into the air, and with a strong burst, rose out from the statue's metallic assault. This also put him well out of range of the park's root structure. Theia found what she was after, a sprinkler that was in desperate need of some TLC. One swift kick, and the top of the sprinkler went flying, and while no dramatic jet of water flew into the air, Mason instantly caught on to her plan.

Mason reached out a furry arm to the gurgling sprinkler and clenched a fist. Water began gushing from the ground in a torrent right at Gideon. Now water would not be too much of an issue for Gideon, if he had been a bird or was on the ground. But, running water made it very hard to maintain magical constructs, like spectral wings. Gideon tried to move away from the torrent but even as he moved, another burst of water would erupt into being, as Mason expanded on Theia's plan. The wings flickered and eventually gave into the deluge and Gideon fell to the earth. He managed to turn the fall into an impressive forward roll, but the roots were waiting for him, and one managed to pierce his calf muscle painfully.

With that injury, Gideon couldn't move with the grace he had displayed thus far. Quickly, the topsoil got a hold of his feet, and before long he was buried up to his knees in earth, the front hooves of the mounted Pancho Villa statue hanging over his head. All movement seemed to stop, and Mason held his arms stock still.

"Concede Gideon." and after a beat added, "Please."

Gideon looked from Mason to Theia, concern on his face. They were at a crucial juncture. Theia looked at Mason and shrugged a bit, indicating she wasn't sure which course of action had the best results. It was really up to the men to decide for themselves.

"I'm uniquely placed in a conundrum." Gideon spoke. "I both trust and fear what you might do, once you come to realize the stakes involved in the conflict to come." Theia knew full well that Gideon was much more lethal than he had been playing at, during this whole encounter. The fact that they were all talking, and not seared to a crisp, was evidence of his hesitation and restraint.

"It's a meeting, Gideon. I don't take jobs from Demons, and I have no intention of making you my enemy. I need you to trust me, buddy. Please." Mason lowered his arms and the ground pinning Gideon's legs receded, leaving him kneeling in a small dent in the ground. Amazingly, the wound to Gideon's calf already seemed to be healing over. He was a celestial after all.

"I suppose faith is in order." He said, in the kind of pretentious, but good intentioned way people with a lot of faith say things.

"I'll keep him in check." Theia added.

"That does make me feel better, and truly I don't crave animosity between us." Gideon closed his eyes, thinking. Theia's weave frayed before him, coalescing as he made his decision. "Very well, do what you must. I shall stand down for now."

"What could be so contentious that you are coming after people who only MIGHT get involved." Mason asked, the tension gone from his voice, the earth covering his legs slowly receding.

"In the past, you and the others were more tied to the Material realm, and have been neutral to the greater conflict being fought. The time for that luxury may be passing. Soon you may have no choice but to pick sides." Gideon said dramatically, and then slid his eyes to lock with Theia's.

Pain and light filled her mind, visions too fast to follow flowed through her. Screams, pain, heat, despair, she felt them all, almost too quickly to register. She tried to hold on to power through it, men were watching, and she really didn't want to faint. In the end she took a very dignified power nap.

CHAPTER

7

• ● •

Mason reached out and caught Theia, before she crumpled to the ground, and turned murderous eyes on Gideon, who looked just as mortified.

"What did you do!" Mason screamed, his voice a cacophony of rage and anguish.

"Nothing! I just made eye contact and she collapsed." Gideon gestured to himself trying to prove his innocence. Mason looked at Theia, and she was already fluttering her eyes and waking. She winced at the sun light and gently pushed Mason away, as she steadied herself.

"You, okay?" Mason asked, hovering over her. The fuzzy armor on his shoulders was breaking apart and fading, and before long, Nosam appeared, licking at Theia's hand.

"Yeah, it was just an intense vision." Theia looked about, not seeing a bench. Mason sent a shock of energy down into the park, who responded by forming a mound of soft grass at bench height. Theia sat down gratefully.

"So, you saw it." Gideon finally said, with a strange finality.

"I saw something. It wasn't normal, it was like seeing someone else's dream." Theia shook her head. Mason wasn't sure what they were talking about, but he kept Agosto's awareness close to the surface , in case Gideon tried something aggressive. He knew that he was being paranoid, but when he wasn't sure of himself, he got protective as a default.

"Does it have to do with the plane-ist stick up Gideon's Ass?" Mason asked. Plane-ist was a word he had thought up during the years when all the different supe groups were still mistrustful of each other. Before they banded together, for the most part, versus the vanilla humans.

"The Infernal realms are far from just culturally different. They prey on all living things!" Gideon said defensively.

"And the Celestials don't?!" Mason said gaining some heat, "They are supported by the churches, churches that condemn the rest of us! All because you can just make them love you!" Gideon looked hurt and sad all at once.

"I know you don't have the best history with the Church, Mason, but we aren't all like that." Gideon said in a soft de-escalating tone. Mason bristled but didn't push the issue, looking down at Theia who was shaking her head.

"Is that vision what's got you so concerned?" Theia asked. She rubbed her face and looked up to Gideon, her eyes damp with residual emotional shock.

"Yes, almost everyone tied to the Celestial realm had similar visions. No one knows exactly what they mean, but

we are sure the Infernals have something to do with it."
Gideon avoided looking directly at Theia , perhaps in fear of
inflicting the vision again.

"So, you had a nightmare, and you just automatically
assume it's Demons." Theia asked skeptically. That seemed
to take Gideon aback.

"I mean classically..." Gideon began to explain himself.

"Classically, terrible visions are misinterpreted and lead
to people making lethal and stupid assumptions!" Theia
interrupted loudly. "Ever heard of Cassandra , or self-
fulfilling prophecy? These things cause wars, genocides, and
on a lesser scale, bone headed Nephilim attacking innocent
people in parks!" Theia thrust herself to her feet and pushed
past Gideon. "Mason shouldn't have agreed to meet with
Horace, but a couple of really scary images doesn't mean
he's involved.

"Theia." Gideon tried the calming tone again.

"Fuck off, Gideon!" Theia stopped him, her mental
shields flaring dramatically. "Honestly, I don't want to hear
from you unless you have a thoughtful apology for Mason,
and a better grasp on this supposed doomsday scenario."
With that she walked to the street, and waited for the now
suddenly heavy traffic to relent so she could cross.

Mason looked after her, feeling both foolish for agreeing
to the meeting, and happy she had stood up for him. Nosam
gave Gideon a wide berth as he chased after Theia. Mason
rose to his feet, fetched his boots, and walked past the
befuddled Celestial with a shrug.

"If I hear anything that might support your hypothesis, I'll get a hold of you." He said as nonchalantly as he could.

"Please do." Gideon was already heading the way he had come. Mason turned and jogged after Theia, not looking back, as he knew Gideon had already dramatically disappeared.

• ● •

Theia glared at the door to the Unseen Forces office, as if it had dared her to cross it. It unlatched and swung open without any protest. The scent of calming incense within, did little to improve her mood.

Zoe was at her desk, which was awash with several file boxes, files, and miscellaneous paperwork. She was likely doing a pre-audit, making sure **PLEB** didn't ding them for a missing invoice or some other such nonsense. Theia hadn't even thought to do any of that , and was reminded of how pivotal the Witch was to their operation. Zoe took one look at her stance and pushed a strand of hair out of her face.

"Fey shenanigans, or Mason shenanigans?" She said with a gentle humor to her words.

"I bet she sold him to the Deep Court!" Statler supplied.

"Drowned him in muck and his own regrets!" Replied Waldorf. Theia shot one look at them and they switched to a hushed tone.

"Mason has some explaining to do, but I'm mostly upset at Gideon." Theia said slumping into one of the plush chairs. Mason and Nosam entered soon after.

"What did Gideon do?" Zoe gestured to a small paperweight of a black cat on her desk and the enchantment within animated the small statue. The small cat opened a drawer in the statue's base, and in moments a new even more calming incense began burning.

"Determined not to learn from history." Theia said, throwing her head back in frustration. "Team meeting. Too much is going on for us not to all to be on the same page." Zoe moved to her desk and produced a pad and paper and sat in one of the waiting room chairs. Mason sat on the loveseat and Nosam crawled up and sat next to/on him.

"Sorry about not telling you about Horace. It seemed pretty innocuous at the time." Mason supplied.

"What does he want?" Theia said, wanting to remain on the high ground before admitting she too was hiding something.

"His patron wants to meet, tonight at a park nearby. No reason why was given, but Horace had to perform a service to even get me to agree to go. And, I couldn't help annoying the guy. It was arrogant and lazy, and I'm sorry it got us into this mischief." Theia had known Mason a long time, Lazy, was a pretty good descriptor. But, so were loyal and determined; his positive traits far outweighed his laissez-faire nature.

"Well, there is trouble on the home front as well." Theia bit the bullet. "PLEB is sending an Auditor. That hapless bureaucrat from this morning is coming to review our license."

"And I started a fight in a public park and dragged you to the Fey." Mason looked down, "Both of which wouldn't be positive arguments for us." Theia felt awful that instead of being upset she hadn't told him, he was upset he could have made things worse.

"Don't worry about it. The meeting with the Queen had some interesting implications, and you were the one who got shot by an arrow." Theia gestured to Zoe. "Plus, we have our super organized paperwork whiz on the case." Zoe looked up from her note taking to smile.

"All of the anti-scrying spells are still fully intact. Some looked tampered with, so it seems they have been remotely testing us already." Zoe pointed her pen at the boxes on her desk. "Not surprisingly, all the boxes that were tampered with have files pertaining to Todd Dunlap." So, Theia thought, it had been Dunlap who set the feds on them after all. Typical, humans really were the worst.

"Alright, so what do we know." Theia said, sitting forward in her chair.

"One dead Druid left in the desert. The probable killer had enough mojo to cover their tracks from easy magical or mundane forensics". Mason surmised. "Someone is either tampering with or killing changelings in the city. To make matters worse it seems the Infernal and Celestial powers within the city are also gearing up for a conflict.".

The door to the bathroom came open, and Jackson sauntered into the room. He was drying his hands on a paper towel and looking at all of them.

"I just got a text that two of the changelings in the Drove were attacked a couple days ago, but were able to get away." he supplied.

"Attacked by what?" Theia asked.

"Weirdest thing, apparently a giant spider..." Jackson said, as if, even he, didn't quite believe it.

"Alright, while that is definitely fuel for several nightmares, what does it tell us?" Theia put her head in her hands, willing her mind to make connections.

"Well, there is also the misplaced deep fey gathering at the border. That can't be just randomly happening." Mason supplied.

Zoe looked up with a surprised look.

"The Deep fey are involved?" She asked, pointedly.

"It was presented to us by the Deep Queen, as a coincidental development. Hard to say with that Druid dead." Theia said through her hands.

"Okay, and this might be my ignorance about how these things usually shake out, but aren't Druids kinda hard to kill?" Jackson asked, settling into the next plushiest chair.

"Yes and no," Mason began. "Like myself, Druids live in two worlds at once, having a fey body and a human one, tied together by a shared soul." Mason gestured to Nosam. "If the druid had been able to call his other half to the confrontation, or even to cross into the Fey itself, he could have made himself a significant threat. But, unlike me and Nosam, the Fey is further removed from the Material world. Meaning that it would take a lot more energy to call his other self forth, and perhaps he didn't have the resources at that moment."

"So, if the killer had planned it right, the Druid would have been pretty vulnerable." Jackson concluded.

"We should assume that the killer didn't fully understand what Randall was." Zoe added. "If the Queen has accurate information, the killer has been targeting Changelings. A Druid, while similar in some ways, is a very different beast and wouldn't offer the same sort of challenge or even benefit. "

"Benefit?" Jackson asked.

"Well, Unlike Mason, or Mr. Randall , Changelings are Demi-Human, meaning they have a lot more magic on their own." Zoe supplied.

"And even if you did manage to kill a druid, his other would just fade back to where it came from taking its magic with it." Mason crinkled his forehead. "If the killer is after Magic, could it be some kind of Fey obsessed vampire?"

"Unlikely, as there weren't any signs of blood draining , and doing an extraction any other way would take way too long." Theia said only mildly dismissive.

"If I may." Statler interjected. Theia raised a tired look to the gargoyle and put on a patient face. "The bunny mentioned a giant spider, which not only rules out most vampires, but does point to a human practitioner. They really like to summon things to do their dirty work." Statler looked to Waldorf.

"Ah... and most spider supes are pretty much vampires when it comes to draining their victims." He added hastily.

"Still no injuries to suggest blood loss." Theia reminded them.

"Well, you've only seen one body that, by your own admission , doesn't match the killers' profile. Could they have realized their mistake and just dumped the body?" Waldorf continued. The gathered humanoids all looked a bit stunned at the implication.

"So, we end up with not enough information." Mason said shrugging into a yawn.

"There is still the audit issue." Theia said tensing. "Unrelated to the case."

"We have a flawless case record! If Dunlap had taken that case straight to PLEB they would have determined the same result." Mason said incredulous.

"Regardless, that's why Pencil-Skirt was so superfluous at the body dump site." Theia unconsciously envisioned Meredith Carsen's involvement with their own corner of the tapestry. "And it doesn't look like she is going anywhere anytime soon."

"I've been shoring up the office records, but you never know what angle they are gonna come from." Zoe said flatly.

"Well, I can find out at least." Theia pushed herself off her chair and moved to her office, determined. She didn't wait for anyone to follow, and moved to her worktable. Her cards were still splayed where she had left them. She licked her finger and placed it on the metal circle inlaid on the tabletop. There was a snap of energy as the enchantment snapped into place. The cards twitched and formed into a neat and tidy stack awaiting her whims.

She thought about just doing a blind reading on this Meredith character, but was worried she would have sensors in place if she tried. It was difficult and very inaccurate to read your own future, as inherent bias skews everything. So instead, she decided to see what kind of interaction she would have with Mason in the near future. She could have done it without the cards of course, but she had been using her gift a lot this morning, and the beginnings of a mondo headache were forming.

She gestured to the cards, and they shuffled and arranged themselves into a familiar spread of her own design. She allowed them to channel her gift, and let it flow from her beleaguered mind and into them. They flipped over a pattern indicating a test of sorts. Theia plied the cards for clarification, and they revealed a pattern. She saw a phone call, death, and then strangely, the connection faded abruptly. Either Mason would stop associating with Meredith for a time, or something was tampering with the flow of events. One made sense and the other scenario was deeply concerning.

Theia ran a finger along the metal circle, releasing its energy, and replaced her cards into her hidden cabinet. Satisfied that she had the timeline locked in, she moved to her office door and waited a few beats, mostly for the drama of it, and threw it open as the phone began to ring. As Zoe moved to answer the phone, Theia smiled.

"Tell Meredith we can meet her at the crime scene in 30 minutes."

Zoe answered the phone , giggling in spite of herself.

"Why yes, Ms. Carsen, we can be there in 30 minutes."

CHAPTER

8

—————— • ● • ——————

Zoe had insisted on coming with them. Mason wasn't convinced that it wasn't a ploy to meet Pencil-Skirt, who was beginning to seem like a fixture in their lives. Though in fairness, a witch of her caliber really could go wherever she pleased.

The new body had turned up at a private country club on the eastern side of town. The building had a colorful history, and within the post-Human community it had been especially infamous as the home of a particularly notorious Infernal Invoker in the late 1930's. The tall, Italian cypress trees lining the property gave it a sense of privacy, and if you looked closely, you could see several telltale signs of its past.

"Is that fountain just a huge watery pentagram..." Zoe asked, a tad incredulous.

"Stone Ashley is full of that kind of stuff." Theia answered. "Mason, any word on the club itself?"

"Not really. No one is even quite sure who is and isn't a member." Mason looked to Nosam for confirmation, but he gave a doggy head shake. "I'm assuming Vampires."

Vampires were drawn to secret societies and privacy. Even more so than other Demi-Humans, they attempted to live deeply in the closet. While most of them abstained from drinking blood, their demonic half still needed to be fed. Most did this by slowly draining the life force from their families and friends, not enough to be noticed. But, then again, they rarely stayed with the same people long term unless they had a large social group.

Sipping at the life force would keep them alive, but, it was kind of like using an eyedropper to drink a glass of water when you're dying of thirst. Popping someone's vein and drinking them dry was vastly more satisfying for them. It made vampires a tad anathema to the rest of the supe community. Even Post-Humans had blood, so associating with vampires meant they sipped at you while around them, or worse, made you vulnerable if they fell off the wagon.

Pencil-Skirt was wearing dress slacks and a puffy sleeved white blouse, and ordering a bunch of uniformed officers around, when they arrived. Her plastic, librarian glasses turned to the newcomers and was quickly followed by a squint of suspicion.

"Ms. Morgan, Mr. Wallace," She paused at Zoe and referred to her ever present clip board. "Mrs. Halston." She put a strong emphasis on the "Mrs".

"Ms. Actually I'm divorced." She said, with a "try me bitch" smile.

"Honorifics are fascinating, but can we see the body?" Theia stepped in before Meredith got herself hexed.

"Shouldn't you be able to find the body? If not you, then definitely Mr. Wallace." she smiled knowingly. Mason, out of pure defiance, tried to contact the Loci of the estate and was almost thrown from his feet by the sheer perversion of the presence that answered. It was waiting , eager to sip at his magic in exchange for the information. Mason could feel its hard teeth seeking a chip in his soul's defenses. He pushed the elemental away, and raised his mental shields even higher.

"Definitely Vampires." Mason said quietly to Zoe. Theia, seemingly having read ahead a bit, started walking to the back of the property. Mason and Zoe wordlessly fell behind her, much to Pencil-Skirt's annoyance.

Theia came to stand beneath a balcony, where a man was suspended about 10 feet off the ground from the third story. He was in a very expensive suit, looked to be in his early 20s, and was currently too blood spattered and bruised to tell much else. In a horrifying display, the man was hanging from what seemed to be his own intestines fashioned into a harness about his torso.

"We are still searching the property for evidence, but it seems the Killer is done hiding." Meredith said with a quiet respect.

"You have it wrong." Theia said finally, her eyes closed and frantically flickering as she was lost in her power.

"I'm sorry?" Pencil-Skirt said skeptically.

"Fergus Vasser, here, was a casualty, a bit of collateral damage." Theia opened her eyes and met Meredith's gaze. "The other four are in the hidden basement beneath the bar of the lounge. I'm surprised you haven't found it yet, as the blood trail leads right to it."

Meredith stepped away and began talking into a walkie talkie, clearly disturbed by the news. Mason stepped forward and placed a hand on Theia's shoulder. Her pattern had become pretty exhausted,, and as Mason let some of his energy flow through the touch, she unconsciously drank deeply of it. Between the fight with Gideon, and the psychic wounds she sustained running through events like these, it was pushing her to the limit.

"You need food and a nap." Mason said with a bit of authority.

"She's going to keep us here for at least another couple of hours, until I've read the bodies. She hadn't even identified this one yet." Theia's gift always amazed Mason, though he knew she didn't think very highly of it.

One of the people here must have had significant dealings with the hanging body, Theia thought. It wasn't possible to glean much information from lifeless objects, including corpses, unless someone had a karmic connection to the object. A pen doesn't have much of a destiny unless someone either is or was going to handle it in the future. Strong emotion and repeated handling strengthen these Karmic Bonds. Stronger bonds meant more information and a clearer read. If these bonds were present, Theia could read what a corpse's life might have been like if it hadn't been killed, and who it was or would be close to.

"Any idea what did it?" Mason said hopefully.

"Threads are cut again, just like with Randall." She said. As they spoke, Zoe's eyes locked on something that had escaped the notice of the uniformed officers. She subtly gestured and whispered, and a strong wind picked up in the area sending sand and small tree debris whipping everywhere. Most of the official investigators moved their arms to their eyes at the sudden windstorm. Zoe locked eyes with Nosam and pointed while everyone else was distracted , and the hound ran in the direction indicated.

"What was that about?" Mason said, a bit annoyed at the sand in his eyes.

"I think I found a clue, and my intuition says Pencil-Skirt isn't interested in solving this case." Zoe rubbed at her eyes, as if she was terribly put out, as the wind swiftly died down again.

"It is odd that I can't deep read her tapestry. I Had assumed it was because she was Runic." Theia said, a deep line forming between her eyebrows. Meredith returned to them in time to hear the word 'Runic', but not the beginning of the sentence.

"'Runic' is a slur, we prefer the term 'Practitioner'." Meredith said. Mason tried not to roll his eyes at the woman. 'Practitioner' was a very underhanded phrase to other post-Humans, several of whom were just as capable of 'practitioning' as any human wizard was. Many human's took umbrage with the term 'Runic' as it referred to their inability to cast magic without certain rituals, which mostly involved Runes.

"Apology, old bad habits." Theia apologized.

"Well, they found the basement hatch, and I'd like you to go over the bodies." Pencil-Skirt was making notes on her clipboard, and didn't seem to care anymore about the slur in the slightest.

"Are you ever going to address the fact that you were sent to spy on us?" Zoe said crossing her arms. Meredith gave a deep sigh and met Zoe's eyes. It showed a bit of courage, as most humans were scared to look a witch in the eye.

"I sent the appropriate notification, and I know that Ms. Morgan received it." Meredith turned to Theia, seemingly hoping she would cow her employee.

"Yes, but you haven't taken any of the appropriate steps. You are just attempting to spy on our records haphazardly." Zoe said. Now, Theia raised an eyebrow and crossed her arms.

"Auditors are permitted to test magical precautions on those who are being reviewed. As far as what is appropriate, each auditor is permitted to conduct their investigation as they see fit. Bringing Theia in on this investigation will be more than sufficient opportunity to see if she is what she claims." Pencil-Skirt clicked her pen, and moved away from Zoe. She stood with her back to the witch and turned her face to Theia. "You should consider using less emotional employees. Witches can be very temperamental, and their powers are very unstable."

Mason, and Theia were both aghast at the statement, and moved to say something, but Zoe raised a hand indicating for them not to get involved. Meredith, seeing them cowed, waited for Theia to fall in line behind her,and dismiss Mason and Zoe from the conversation. Theia threw an apologetic shrug their way and moved to follow the woman. PLEB was unavoidable in the current political climate, and if you wanted to operate as a business, you just had to deal with a certain level of prejudice.

"If I was even slightly inclined to emotional instability, I would make that woman's hair fall out." Zoe said, her fingers twitching slightly in anger.

"I'm sure she is expecting you to." Mason said thoughtfully. "You taking aggressive action would reflect on Theia and the business, and Meredith doesn't seem to need any additional motivation to deny our license."

"Theia has proven her gift at least a dozen times since we got here. Any auditor with any level of sense would see that." Zoe grumbled.

They had moved down the tree lined driveway and out on to the major street. The police blockade didn't impede them, and Mason gestured down the street to a chain taco restaurant just a bit away from the estate. As they sat down in a booth, having ordered just enough food to not be considered loitering , a woman cried out in alarm as Nosam strolled into the restaurant. He put down something he was carrying in his mouth and turned to the woman.

"Calm down, I'm an emotional support animal for a very critically, mentally disabled person." He said, giving her a doggy grin. He retrieved his parcel and moved to Mason and Zoe's booth.

"For the record I will not bail you out of the pound." Mason said, not too offended.

"Man has not constructed a jail that can contain me." Nosam said dropping the object on the table. He had found a plastic bag, and was nosing it open as he looked to Zoe.

"Perfect." Zoe slid the bag over to her and removed a very old dagger. "I know it's not exactly playing fair, but if PLEB had found this, they would have probably destroyed it instead of using it to gather information." She held the steel dagger . It was thin and very old, and kind of got wider toward the end of the blade before tapering to a fine point.

"And what is it that we have salvaged from the horrors of PLEB containment?" Mason asked.

"No clue, but it is magical for sure, and not in any way infernal." Zoe turned it , using the plastic bag to handle it. She rewrapped it and handed it to Mason. "I assume you would want an excuse to visit the professor." Mason immediately went scarlet, and Nosam's tail wagged happily.

"We will go right away." Nosam said excitedly.

"Now hang on." Mason attempted to protest.

"Great! I'll wait here, and me and Theia will catch an Uber back to the office." Zoe said, ignoring Mason.

"This is evidence tampering." Mason protested.

"It's decided!" Nosam said, jumping down from the booth seat. His tail threatening to cause a hurricane. Mason sighed and retrieved his keys from his pocket and took the proffered artifact.

"Primals , save me from well-intentioned friends." Mason said mostly to himself. Nosam had already ran ahead, and was holding the door for him.

• ● •

When the Government finally admitted that magic was real, and a significant portion of the population wasn't nearly as human as everyone had thought, there was a rush to commodify as much of magic as possible. One such tactic, led to doctoral programs specializing in magic, its theories and its implications throughout history. America was hard pressed to let an earning opportunity pass it by.

One of the fastest universities to jump on the, magic should be studied, bandwagon, was the University of Arizona. Within a month of the governmental announcement of proceedings to suss out the post-Human population, it had restructured several programs to make room for a wide range of magical studies. Its crowning achievement, however , was the Museum of Alternate Human History. This sprawling building was filled with mostly innocuous displays of Post and Demi human history, with a smattering of simulated creatures, and art inspired by other realms of reality.

Mason stood awkwardly in the entrance hall of the museum underneath a, mostly accurate , simulated dragon sculpture. Mason knew a few Dragons, and they weren't nearly as large as the display. It stood to reason that one this large could exist, but Mason hadn't met one. Mason was torn from his musings by an excited bark from Nosam.

Benjamin Rey Aguilar, had probably started the day in a reasonably put together suit, but had since removed his jacket and loosened his tie. His olive toned skin and blue-black hair were dappled with sweat, and the telltale signs of long bouts of concentration. He was clearly of Hispanic descent with a strange of mix of Asian features. Ben had told him once that his great grandfather had been of Chinese descent leading to the intriguing mix.

"Who's the best boy!" He said, falling into a squat to ruffle Nosam lovingly. Mason could feel the warm affection Nosam had for the man, trickling in through their bond, and it made him blush all over again.

"'Best' might be a stretch, but surely you mean me." Nosam said in a playful tone.

"To what do I owe the pleasure." He said mostly to Nosam. Mason reached into his waistband and presented the dagger to him.

"Sadly, Mason isn't ready to admit he has a crush on you, so it's just business." Nosam said as Mason choked in embarrassment.

"Nosam Ecallaw! You can't tease poor Mason that way! We are colleagues, not dolls in a playroom." Ben's perfect pronunciation of Nosam's name was endearing.

Everyone in Ben and Mason's life seemed to be trying to force a relationship between them, seeing them both as too stubborn to give in to what was obvious chemistry. In truth, they had dated for a few months, but found their views on monogamy had become an issue. Mason had never been raised in a monogamous culture, and adopted a more polyamorous view to relationships. But, Ben was much more traditional in that regard. So, while there was definite chemistry, they both attempted to keep things at a professional level.

Regardless, Mason's eyes still lingered on the flexing of Ben's thighs as he moved to stand and moved toward him. He even had the audacity to smell amazing, Mason thought.

"So, business then?" Ben held out a hand for whatever artifact Mason had brought this time. Peeling the plastic bag like a banana peel, Mason showed him the dagger. Ben looked at it closely. "Well, I can tell you immediately this isn't a weapon. It's a Kopis, A Grecian kitchen knife." He said, turning it over. "Have you determined what the metal is?"

"Steel." Mason had an affinity for metals, and could smell most alloys and materials.

"Meaning it was forged later in the period." Benjamin stood abruptly and began to walk toward an employee door. "Better bring it down to the lab, I can at least give any enchantments a once over."

Mason was nervous. If Benjamin were to find something truly dangerous, he would be required to quarantine or destroy the Dagger and they needed it to find the killer. Nosam rolled his eyes at him and moved to follow Ben. Mason did as well, reluctantly.

The lab was in the bowels of the museum , and was mostly a warehouse with a small corner dedicated to the identification and study of the artifacts that came in. Most of what came in had long since lost any active magical effects , but a few retained a kind of fingerprint of some past enchantment. A large Runic magic circle wrought in Silver, Copper, and Iron, as well as a few other metals, dominated the space.

Benjamin took the Dagger from Mason and stepped within the circle, and paused , inviting them to join him. Mason politely declined. While the Circle wouldn't adversely affect either Mason or Nosam, it would disrupt the flow between them, which was something they avoided when they could. Ben bowed his head in acknowledgment of the sentiment, and slipped off his shoes. He wore socks that had a small hole in the bottom, and when his skin touched the metal, Mason could feel the circle snap closed.

"I know your job is dangerous, but this level of security must have been very expensive." Mason said with a whistle.

"Well , the possibility of releasing some ancient evil onto the campus is an ever-growing concern." Benjamin said with a smile. Benjamin turned to the table and began donning gloves and other protective gear. Mason recognizing that this was going to take a while, turned toward the assembled artifacts on the nearby shelves. He couldn't feel much. if any, magic on most of them, but after reading the tags on them, was very glad they were no longer a part of this world.

"What's an Avulsion?" Mason asked off-handedly.

"I'm busy, Mason, look it up on your phone." Benjamin said, only slightly annoyed.

Mason took out his phone and immediately regretted the curiosity. The innocent-seeming finger trap on display now nauseated him immensely. Nosam, less interested in the trappings of human flesh removal via children's toy , busied himself making contact with the various elementals of the warehouse.

While Mason was on good terms with the overall Loci of the University, it had its own Shaman and was less inclined to acknowledge Mason. It was one of the few areas in the valley that didn't recognize Mason as an authority. Still, Mason thought, It was always nice for him to be out of the area of responsibility that he was usually forced to exist in. Trees demanding care or attention from him, and stagnant water hissing at him as he walked past, did get tedious.

In his boredom, Mason eventually gravitated to a crate filled with miscellaneous objects. A Pez Dispenser shaped like Heathcliff the cat, a small amber bead, a hand mirror which sported a screaming face in place of glass, and many other charming and innocuous objects. Sensing that this was going to take longer than he had the patience for , Mason politely asked the concrete floor for a place to relax , and a chair formed near the circle. He lounged and pulled out his phone to mindlessly scroll for a bit.

CHAPTER

9

— • ● • —

Theia left the crime scene drained, annoyed , and more than a little stressed. Reading the future of a corpse was one thing, reaching backwards through the horrors of their death was another entirely. Add to that an intense woman hell bent on proving you a fraud at every turn, and it just added to the mystique of it all.

As she rounded the corner of the restaurant where Zoe was waiting, she shut her gift down entirely. It was like closing her eyes after a binge watch of the entirety of a teen drama. It was cathartic , and she was stricken with instant relief. So, her first sign of additional trouble was Zoe's raised voice ringing through the store window. Theia moved into a ladylike hustle and threw the door open.

Zoe was standing in a defensive position, while a large man gestured at her wildly, all the while yelling in Spanish.

Theia wasn't nearly as fluent as she would like to be, but even she could make out the word 'Bruja', the Spanish word for witch. Zoe saw Theia enter, and managed to ask her for help in controlling her temper and not vaporizing this man, without saying a word.

"Is there a problem?" Theia asked , acting like she was a new patron who was being ignored. The entire staff and most of the patrons seemed laser focused on the drama unfolding in the dining area.

"Owner is kicking out a non-human for threatening a cashier with a dangerous familiar." the youngish dishwasher or cook, judging by the numerous food stains on his shirt, answered.

"What did the familiar do?" Theia asked, moving to a distance so that she could act if she needed to.

"Claimed to be a service animal, as far as I can tell." the young man answered, with mirth in his voice. Theia closed the distance, and the large man took notice. He seemed to almost recoil , and began pointing and shouting at Theia as well. Theia tried not to dwell on the irony that this man was sensitive enough to pick a post-Human out of crowd, but not self-aware enough to realize what that meant. Noticing Theia being unmoved by his tirade, he moved to the phone and began emoting that he was calling some kind of authority on the issue.

"Shall we leave Mason's mess?" Theia asked.

"Gladly." Zoe said moving towards the door. The man almost popped a blood vessel in his effort to yell loudly enough to be heard through the glass. Theia sighed deeply.

It hadn't been that long ago that Hispanic men, like this one demanding that God smite them for their wicked ways, had been themselves the target of much the same treatment.

"We can head up the road a bit and call a car." Theia said. Zoe already had her phone out with a driver app open. "Tell me what you found."

Zoe, in a furious display of multi-tasking , described the weapon she had found in great detail.

"Did he blush when you brought up the professor?" Theia said with a smile. Zoe rolled her eyes conspiratorially.

"The man is hopeless." she tittered. Theia let herself laugh for a moment as well.

"I'm worried Zoe." Theia leaned against a tree set artistically around the empty lot. "There are too many pieces on the board, and too many unknown variables. Makes it hard to know what happens next." Zoe closed the distance between them and gripped Theia's elbow.

"Now, you know how the rest of us feel." They stood in companionable silence for several minutes, Theia trying to construct a series of events from the past few hours.

"The killer is powerful, and I'm starting to surmise that she's not native to Tucson. I think she might be from one of the far realms." Theia said suddenly.

"She?" Zoe asked.

"Yeah, the first victim was going to hit on a woman. He died instead, but that tells me we are definitely looking for a woman. No way of knowing more, as she is able to omit herself from even their potential futures somehow." Theia checked the horizon for insight, hoping for an omen.

"Okay, so she drains her victims and has a least enough magic to completely sever herself from her victims. A woman, probably reasonably young and attractive." Zoe checked her phone. "Vampire?" Theia shook her head, not finding any insight in the sky.

"No, the victims would have expected treachery from their own kind. Not a one of them suspected danger til it was upon them. So that rules out almost everything Infernal."

Vampires aren't quite the undead monstrosities they are in the stories. All Vampires descend from a singular Demonic Lord, who had a penchant for human life force. He passed on that hunger to his children. Being Demonic, they are extremely sensitive to Infernal energies. If a Demon none of them had recognized wandered into their country club, they would have known right away.

"Where does that leave us?" Zoe said, thoughtfully.

Theia thought about that. There were only a few realms that had paths to the material world. The Mirror realms were those close enough to mirror the material world, like the Near Fey. The Second World, or, The Nether, was all dead things that have little use for Changelings. In the Orphic World, no one really ever left the dream realms, or the Deep realms. Much less was known about the Deep Fey, or the realm of Primal. If it was the Primal, Mason would have more insight, as that was where Nosam was from. The Celestial was possible, as they hate Demons, but they had a non-aggression pact with the Fey. If it was them, it would have to have been an independent agent.

"We should look into Randall; do we have an address?" Theia asked finally. Zoe typed quickly on her phone.

"Odd." she said.

"How odd?" Theia asked , sensing a new tangle.

"I looked it up on our database , and Ryan Randall did not live at the address Tina gave us on her paperwork." Zoe showed her an address in the foothills.

"Now, why would she do that?" Theia expanded out her senses, and realized she couldn't quite pin down Tina's thread. "And why is she so hard to read, I wonder."

"I changed our destination." Zoe informed her.

"I owe you a bigger bouquet on Secretaries Day." Theia smiled.

• ● •

The Randall Estate was a grand one, and set back from the road. The driver seemed surprised they had tipped him in cash; rich people this far north must be awful stingy. The large gate at the entrance of the driveway was at least 500 feet from the front door of the house, and was very locked.

"We could jump it?" Theia said, shaking the 7-foot-tall ornate gate.

"Oh yes, I love jail this time of year." Zoe said, approaching the little keypad that controlled the door.

"If Mason were here, he could ask the gate to open..." Theia didn't want to come back later. Something momentous was here, but she couldn't quite make out its shape yet.

"We don't need him!" Zoe removed a spool of a very fragile looking thread from her bag. She placed it on top of the little keypad, and then rummaged around further in her bag , finding and placing a pad lock, and a six-inch piece of copper wire next to the thread. Then finally, a polished gnarled stick that looked like it might be a wand in a horror movie. The keypad was on a small pole next to the driveway, and she drew a circle with her foot around it fairly easily.

"Okay, but what do any of those things have to do with getting us inside the gate." Theia inquired. Zoe shushed her, and waved a dismissive hand. She wrapped one end of the copper wire around the curved top part of the padlock and then clicked it closed. She tucked the free end into a small seam in the keypads casing. She then un-spooled some of the fine thread and wrapped the lock in it.

"Spider Silk." She said, seeing Theia's confused expression. "To bind the lock." Holding the gnarled stick to the padlock , she began chanting in a rapid-fire Spanish. Even on the other side of the crude circle, Theia could feel the magic swirling inside. Witches magic was inherently wasteful, and tended to be much flashier than runic magic. So,, in order to cut down on the personal cost , most witches used magical tools and ritual to mitigate the burden. The copper wire started to glow with heat , and after a crescendo of chanting, Zoe dramatically turned the key on the padlock. Theia released a breath she didn't know that she was holding, as Zoe broke the circle and magic poured out.

The large Gate swung open of its own accord, as Zoe started packing up the bits and bobs she had used. Theia crossed her arms somewhere between impressed and annoyed.

"I could have done that if I had my Spellbook." Theia said, in a tone matching her crossed arms.

"Yes dear, but we didn't have all day." Zoe said, patting her arm. They walked together down the long driveway up to the front of the house. The property was clearly owned by a druid, as the front lawn was lush with healthy grass and plants of all different types, all of which would simply not grow well in the Tucson sun. Trees could even be seen poking up over the roof from the backyard. If the man wasn't tied to the fey wild, he had the highest water bill in the valley.

The front door was made of thick oak, and depicted a Satyr serenading a very, anatomically correct nymph lounging on a rock. He must not get a lot of visitors, or his HOA would have thrown a hissy fit. This door was also locked, and this time, Theia could feel threads of magic laced throughout.

"And now, door number two." Theia said, with a heavy sigh. Zoe whistled as she looked at it. Her irises were ringed with red, red being the color of her magic, and the rings indicating she was looking into the magical spectrum.

"I can crack it, but its gonna take me awhile to find the cracks in the wards. I'm honestly surprised how many of them survived his death." Zoe began tracing her finger in the air tracing the lines of the spells. Theia, determined to be useful in this impromptu B&E, closed her eyes and plunged her hands into the tapestry. She found Zoe's thread, and found the failed branches, and compiled a cliff notes version of the wards. Zoe wasn't able to solve this doors puzzle, not without setting off several magical countermeasures. However, a combined effort between she and Zoe, had the door could be handled quite simply.

Theia opened her eyes and took out a set of readers she had purchased at the drug store. Drawn on the lenses were several runes intended to let one see magical matrices. While Zoe could do this naturally, Theia required a bit of assistance. Once the pattern was clear to her, she put a hand on Zoe's shoulder.

"Let me try something." She said with a knowing smile. Adding a small thimble to her index finger, and an added small silver blade, she began to draw a large symbol upon the door, snapping magical threads as she went. Zoe gasped in horror as several of the spells flared, but were immediately silenced by the severing of the next line. Soon, and with little preamble, they stood facing a mundane unlocked door.

"I feel like you cheated." Zoe said flatly.

"I couldn't have done it without you." Theia said, as she turned the copper doorknob and entered the foyer.

The house was sparse on furniture and décor, but compensated with an abundance of houseplants. Each seemed to have its own space within the home, and it was clear Randall had cared for them meticulously. Moving into a comfortable and plush living area off the main door, it was clear the man lived alone. There was only one small couch, one chair at the breakfast nook, and a tendency to only have flat usable surfaces on only one end of the seating areas. It was clear he didn't entertain much, and only focused on his own comfort in the space.

"I don't see any of Tina in any of this." Zoe said, stroking the large leaf of a prominently displayed potted plant.

"Separated?" Theia asked, feeling that couldn't be quite right. Zoe shook her head conspiratorially and moved to a dusty bookcase.

"Tina didn't seem like a jaded ex-lover." Zoe said, running a finger across the books on display.

"Counter-point, she didn't seem to care, or be particularly surprised he was dead either." Theia's eyes alighted on a laptop sitting on the breakfast nook table. She pulled the computer open to find that it was in desperate need of a power cable, which she did not see anywhere near it. She focused on the object's potential futures, but the cable had always been brought to it, which did not reveal the cords current whereabouts.

"AHA!" Zoe proclaimed triumphantly. "Photo album!" She pulled a plain-looking album from the shelf and brought it over to the small couch, positioning a t.v. tray in front of her.

"Let me know what you find. I'm gonna check the bedrooms to see if I can't find his power cable." Theia said, moving to the exit.

"He probably left it plugged in near the bed or something." Zoe said, turning the pages. Theia moved through the back hallways of the house trying not to feel like a Victorian ghost in a tragic romance novel. For one, she did not have the constitution for corsets or the coordination for long dresses.

In her search of what were essentially climate-controlled plant bedrooms, she came to a very ominous looking bright, red door. Popular fiction and intuition told her this door was probably more ominous than it really was. She did a cursory check of the next moments, and found the door didn't explode, but the dread at what was behind it was palpable.

It's hard to read your own future, it's why most serious seers avoid it. It's impossible to remove the ego, and one's own wish fulfillment, from twisting your reading of the future events. If you see great happiness in a reading about future love, the tendency is always to interpret that emotion as finding true love. Whereas, if you are reading for someone else, you would look harder for the actual source of the happiness, being more skeptical of the baseline emotion. So, dread was easy to read as danger, however, this may not necessarily be the case. So, Theia pushed forward.

Behind the ominous red door was a sparse but functional bedroom. The bedspread was a beautiful scarlet, and was surrounded by a romantic canopy of sheer, deep, green fabric. The pillows were plump and clearly rarely used. It would have been an ideal guest bedroom, if it hadn't been for the stage lights, high quality cameras, and the wall of torturous sex implements.

"50 Shades of Yikes!" Theia said, to no one in particular. Well, either Tina was a lot less tight laced than she seemed, or their separation had come about before the sex room. A plainly obvious two-way mirror and suspicious closet stood to Theia's left, and she sighed and moved toward them. The closet contained the larger, and not as easily displayed sex toys. As she looked, she noticed there was a false wall in the back, behind which was a large editing room with rows and rows of DVD cases.

A masochist to the end, Theia sat at the bank of computer monitors and sound boards and pushed a power button. While the system powered on , Theia shut down her gift hard. What she was most likely about to see was going to be horrific enough ,without knowing what the participants were feeling at the time.

Once the computer had spent the eternity it needed to open fully, she began perusing some of the recent projects being edited. She found what she was looking for. An attractive, even beautiful Satyr man with light blonde fur filled the screen. The fur was trimmed to a less shaggy length to 'enhance' his anatomy. He was participating in wanton sex acts with every flavor of post, demi or non-human imaginable. Theia didn't spend much , if any, time on any particular video, as she was trying to distance herself from the content, but the Satyr was always center stage in all of them. It wasn't much of a leap to guess that this was Randall's other self, the creature that tied him to the fey realms and made him a druid.

Being tied to such a sexual creature must have played havoc on the man's mental state. Theia wasn't sure what a Druid's place within greater fey society was, but if it was anything like Mason, she didn't see how he settled many disputes while securing this much footage.

Supe-Porn wasn't technically illegal, but it was difficult and expensive to get the insurance to film some of the more dangerous demi-humans, and legally dubious whether sex with a Kirin was bestiality. Regardless, she highly doubted Randall's business was registered and working above board. She took out her camera and took some pictures of the room and equipment. She knew that they were breaking into a dead man's house, but who knows what might be important down the road. PLEB would eventually toss the place, but they would have layers and layers of magical defenses that would take, admittedly even Theia, a lot of time and resources to get through. From their perspective, many supe crimes didn't get cleared very often, as the supe community rarely cooperated with PLEB; so PLEB would hardly be motivated to risk its staff on breaking into a dangerous, post-human home.

Theia thought about taking some of the DVDs, but was worried about the legality of even owning or being in possession of bootlegs of this... magnitude. She settled on grabbing a little, black book that appeared to hold contact information, presumably of clients or actors, hopefully both. As she left the room and closed the door behind her, she heard Zoe exclaim in victory. Theia walked to the living room to find Zoe taking pictures on her phone of the photo album.

"What has you all riled up?" Theia asked, leaning on the door frame.

"Wedding photos." Zoe said, putting her phone aside, and holding up the album for Theia to see. A young woman stood next to a younger Ryan Randall wearing a simple, but elegant mermaid cut wedding dress. Her deep, ebony skin was radiant, she was extremely beautiful.

"First marriage?" Theia asked, not sure why Zoe was so excited. Zoe smiling, turned the page to them signing a marriage certificate. A decorative copy of the document was on the following page: Ryan and Tina Randall.

"Tina has either changed a lot in the years after her marriage, or someone is pulling a fast one on us." Zoe said,dramatically, thumping a finger on the page. The shock of the situation made Theia's concentration slip, and her gift clicked back into her conscious thought. The thread for Meredith was quickly entwining with Zoe's. So, Theia probed. She could see oppression and despair, a sacrifice of freedoms, and a sudden bout of judgment.

"Leave the album. We have to get to the backyard very quickly." Theia said, moving to where she hoped the kitchen and a back door were. Zoe, knowing better than to question, placed the album on the table and scooped up her cell phone.

"What's about to happen?" she asked.

"Well, my good friend, we are about to be arrested." Theia moved through what had been the kitchen to a second living room. Perhaps it was a den, she was never quite sure what the difference was. Thankfully, the den had a sliding glass door that emptied out onto a spacious, back patio. There was no sign of PLEB yet, so she moved to the door, unlatched it, and stepped outside. Zoe followed , and slid the glass door closed behind her.

"I can lock it from here, but it will cost me with no prep." Zoe said, tension in her voice.

"Can you lock all of them from here?" Theia was watching the threads entwine , solidifying their fates. They needed those doors locked.

"Will do." Zoe threw out her arms and her eyes rolled back. Raw, untethered power rushed from her and into the house. Theia watched as nearby plants started to waver and brown. With a resounding thunk, the door behind them locked itself, and Theia hoped she had managed to get them all.

"You, okay?" Theia reached out to support her. Zoe sagged into her arms, but managed to nod. Magic isn't cheap or easy, and for all her skill, Zoe didn't have a very deep well. She was a whiz at finding the perfect tools and crafting a spell that saved her a lot of effort, but spontaneous magic was never going to be her forte.

"Couldn't get to the gate, too far." She said, a bit out of breath.

"Its fine, that should be enough." Theia began a countdown in her mind and moved Zoe to a lounge chair nearby. Three minutes later, just has her countdown reached two, not perfect, but pretty good, Meredith Carsen and two suited PLEB agents moved up to them from around the corner.

"Hi!" Zoe called out from the lounge chair. Theia smiled at them and hooked a thumb at the house behind them.

"If you're looking for Tina Randall, she isn't home." Theia said.

The two agents held in their gloved hands two small leather bags, and began crushing the bags in their fingers. The sound of chalk snapping, and the sudden rush of magic emanating from the bags, was concerning. White runes began forming all over the two men's suits. Theia recognized their purpose, magic warding; the agents were scared that Theia and Zoe would start using magic on them.

"Theia Morgan, Zoe Halston you are under arrest for the murder of Ryan Randall." Meredith said, with a lot more smile in her voice than was necessary. Theia held out her hands, as the two nervous men took her satchel and camera bag. As handcuffs came out, Theia made a mental note to remove Meredith from her brunch list.

CHAPTER

10

• ● •

Mason was bored, his phone offering him very little entertainment in the quiet space beneath the museum. He watched Benjamin work for a while, impressed by the precision in which he scribed circle after circle on the dagger. Mason was always fascinated by Runic magic, but didn't have the patience for it. He knew a few runes enough to avoid walking into a trap or ward, but not nearly enough to even suspect what the man was looking for.

Nosam had rejoined him at some point and looked longingly at Ben slaving away over the dagger. Mason had thought that the Loci of the Museum was thoroughly uninterested in speaking with him, as he was considered a foreign Shaman. Still, an overzealous ceiling light seemed to acknowledge him, and spilled all the tea regarding the goings on of the warehouse. But, the info was limited to security guards goofing around on the job, which the light found appalling, but Mason didn't care.

"Okay, well I think I have enough to give you the basics." Ben suddenly said to the room in general. He looked up and spied Mason lounging in his stone throne, and rolled his eyes. "That had better not leave a crack in the floor." Feigning shock, Mason stood, and the stone chair slid back into the floor leaving no imperfections.

"Heaven forbid." Mason said. Ben sighed deeply and dropped the circle around his workstation and waved Mason over.

"Like I said earlier, in its time this was more of a cooking utensil than a weapon. However, this particular dagger has a truly sickening resonance: vengeful, angry, lack of a better word, its murdery. However, I do think that these are inherited traits from a long-time user, and not any kind of personality of the dagger itself. Its main granted function seems to be to sever karmic relations." Ben said quickly and concisely.

"So, it was designed and enchanted to remove someone from being detected by others?" Mason tried, paraphrasing.

"It has also been used to murder a lot of people. A lot." Benjamin seemed almost afraid of the blade. Mason looked down at it and quested a tendril of his magic down to it. It voraciously consumed the energy, and began pulling at it seeking the source. No voice, no thought , it was just mindless and hungry.

"That is one nasty butcher knife..." Mason was about to wrap it back in its plastic bag, when he felt the lasso close. "Shit." He turned but Nosam was already gone.

"What's happening!" Ben could sense that something had changed, but wasn't familiar with this kind of magic. A lasso, as it was referred to in the Supe community, was primarily used to trap and or catch creatures that were prone to slipping physical bonds. It involved encircling and area , and then shunting people ensnared to a plane of existence the subject had little to no connection with, usually an opposed mirror plane.

Mason watched as everything in the room changed subtly. Being in a human constructed building, the change wasn't as drastic as it would have been above ground where the topography could shift. The furniture and structures around them seemed to decay or corrode as if they were much older and neglected.

"Nether." Mason said, to no one in particular.

"We have crossed into the land of the dead?" Benjamin asked accusatorialy.

"At great cost, I'd imagine. Do you know what the Museum's Mirror in the Nether is?" Mason asked, moving to the stairs. He looked over his shoulder for the knife, but it ,of course , had remained in the Material.

"No, unfortunately plane-walking is… frowned upon." Benjamin said reluctantly.

"Well, the PLEB have no such compunctions." Mason reached out with his magic trying to establish a connection with Nosam. Nosam was a Primordial spirit of the second world, and as such, wouldn't usually be able to cross into a different mirror realm. When he received no whisper of a response, he sighed. "And unless you keep several Runic doodads on your person at all times, I don't think we are gonna be much of a match for whatever they send after us."

"Why would they send something after us?!" Benjamin reached into his jacket and produced a charcoal dowel.

"Well, usually when they attempt to capture people like myself, they lasso them," Mason indicated their current situation. "And then, send in some golem, or other creature they have managed to gain control of, to finish the job. PLEB doesn't really understand how we work or how to imprison our other selves, so they try to manufacture pretty lethal methods of dealing with us."

"You're Post-Human. You have rights." Ben said incredulously.

"True, but not if they get enough probable cause, then, we get shunted right down to full monster status. I mean to be fair, Nosam isn't human in the slightest." Mason was about to launch into a diatribe about these inconsistencies with the current classification system, when they felt the first shake. Something was slamming into the floor above them.

"That cannot be good for us." Ben said.

"No, it can't." Mason calculated the distance. Whatever it was, would have to survive a two story fall before engaging with them. Which included a lot of possibilities, in theory.

Mason had to do something, but the Nether was pretty foreign to him. He had visited a few times with Nessa, when they had been working on combining their gifts, so that she could be a medium of the Nether. Mason closed his eyes and felt for the flow of this world. It was there he felt beneath the floor, a cold sluggish thing. It felt his mind and bubbled up to him.

"Amica periculum, Videte frater." Mason said to the flow. He could feel her shudder with understanding, but was unsure if she would get to him in time, or would even be able to break through the lasso.

There was a resounding crash from the ceiling as something broke into the warehouse. It fell with a loud crack, and an absurd amount of dust and sand shot into the air, making Mason and Ben cough and cover their eyes. When Mason could finally see, he saw it. It was a creature that was pure muscle and bone, shaped into the vague likeness of a person. It shuffled about eyeless, and emitting a terrifying keening. It must have been capable of sensing them in some way, as the thing zeroed in on them immediately.

The creature lunged forward, its arms flailing. It was surprisingly fast, and Mason had to roll away to draw its attack from where they had been hiding. The Golem reeked of rotting meat , and spun at the hip to land a glancing blow on Mason's back. It knocked the wind out of him and sent him flying. When the ringing in his ears stopped, Mason opened his eyes to see the creature hesitating before an elderly gentleman.

Despite the man's apparent age, he stood straight and upright,. And instead of leaning on the solid wooden cane he carried, he held it like a rapier, stopping the creature in its tracks. The man wore what seemed to be a ship captains' uniform, and Mason recognized him immediately.

"Thanks for the assist, Captain." Mason said through winces.

"As a creature of flesh in the Nether , it fears me for now,." The Captain said quietly, " But, quickly it will realize I cannot act against it while Nessa is absent. I'm afraid I amount to only a timely distraction, my boy." The captain never looked away from the dripping abomination as he spoke. The dust settled enough where Mason could now see Benjamin take his feet and a take a confident step forward.

Ben held the charcoal dowel aloft and in the direction of the creature. Mason had never seen Ben use offensive magic before, but doubted that whatever he was about to do would matter much to a golem this size. Ben snapped the dowel and a burst of flame the size of a minivan erupted from him engulfing the creature. The keening grew to a painful register as the Golem's flesh bubbled and blackened. It fell to the ground in agony, but did not stop moving.

"Mason! How do we get out of here!" he called, removing something green from his jacket pocket.

"Captain?" Mason asked.

Without taking his eyes off of the creature, the captain shook his head, he could not help them escape.

"We are on our own, and I don't know the Nether or the College well enough to know what would resonate well." Mason called back. The Golem was trying to get back on its feet. Benjamin thrust the green dowel at the ground and drug it across the floor . The smell of plant matter filled the air , as vines as thick as Mason's wrist erupted from the floor and wrapped around the Golem. The vines tightened and pinned the creature to the ground, and much to Mason's surprise, started growing pumpkins. Mason looked at Ben in shock.

"Something I've been working on for Halloween, " Ben said, "Still haven't gotten the vines to not attack people." He said with a shrug. The Golem strained against the vines, and it was clear it would not be held for too long. A long-mangled hand thrashed out, pulping one of the growing pumpkins.

"Okay, well." Mason was finding it hard to focus, being as broken as he was in that moment. He managed to get to his feet and look around. All of the hideously ancient objects were gone from the shelves, not having an equivalent here in the Nether, so, there was no chance of exploding the thing with some ancient super weapon. Nosam was out of reach, and the Captain, while a welcome sight for sore eyes, was only able to do so much without his Medium. And Benjamin, sweet, handsome, very much in danger Benjamin, who was trying so hard and having a measure of success; Mason realized that he had to do something. It just wasn't fair that Ben could be a casualty in something that Mason had dragged him into, and that he had nothing to do with.

Mason focused and settled his breathing. He took all of his pain and exhaustion and pushed it from his mind. Being on his feet helped him feel more in control , but, he knew that he would need one extensive recovery time after all of this was over. He moved to put himself between Benjamin and the creature, and opened his magical senses as wide as they could go. He saw what he had expected to see. They were in the Nether Realm, and that meant he could see little to nothing. An aura of familiar magic poured from the captain, and he could see the magic thrumming from

Benjamin's Vines. Everything else looked very mundane, as well as, creepy.

Oddly, there was something about Benjamin himself, and Mason began to focus in on him. There was a steady stream of energy connecting him to the Vines, which Mason knew should not be happening. Runic magic borrows nascent energy from the world around it, a reason why most post-humans refuse to use it. After Ben had cast the spell, it should have been absorbing magic from the environment and then fizzling out. This one was pulling magic from Ben. Runics aren't able to do that.

"Benjamin, are you human?" Mason could have worded it better, but, he was trying to ignore several aching bones at the moment. Benjamin, to his credit , tried very hard not to be confused by the question.

"Yes, Mason I am." He said, in a tone that indicated that now was not the time.

"Are you sure? Your magic is behaving very oddly. If you have secretly made a covenant, I promise not to judge, and we could really use the assistance." If Ben had entered into a contract with some powerful being from beyond the mortal realm, it would explain why his magic was behaving like it was. And, there was nothing inherently wrong with being an Invoker.

"No, never, my mother would kill me." Benjamin scoffed, but Mason noticed he was concentrating on the vines, shoring them up and making them stronger.

"You are actively manipulating a spell with your mind, Ben." Mason said bluntly. This was shocking enough to Ben, that his concentration slipped, and the Golem pushed a good six inches off the floor before Ben refocused. In refocusing, however, he saw the truth in Mason's words.

"Okay, so I'm obviously breaking several laws of magic currently. I can acknowledge that, but how does that help us?" He said, now doubling down on the spell, a veritable stream of magic flowing from him into the spell.

"Well, for one thing, you are pouring more magic into that thing than I think is safe." Mason looked back at the Golem. The vines were so tight the flesh was bulging around the vines.

"I am getting a bit light-headed." Ben said offhandedly.

"I bet. Now, we have no idea what flavor of post-human you are, and right now it's not overly important. What IS important, however, is whether you are the kind of post-human who can rip a hole between the realms. The Nether is pretty close to both the Orphic and the Second World, I personally would be happiest with the Second World."

"How do I do that?!" Ben said, incredulous at Mason's calm tone.

"Well, Zoe, if she had enough juice, could just force a hole, and barring that, would come up with some spell that would lessen the magic draw and open a door of some kind. " Mason rambled, "But, I assume you have been focusing on the Golem, so that might not work." Benjamin gave an enthusiastic nod. "If Nessa were here," Mason continued, "we could join energy and form a bridge. The Captain could reach out to Nosam through me and then overlap the worlds, as it were. It was what we were working on before she left the agency."

"Wouldn't I know if I was a medium?!" Ben asked, sweat forming at his brow.

"More than likely, but not always." Mason reached out a hand to Ben, "May I check something?" Ben nodded, and Mason placed a hand on the back of his neck. He let energy flow between them. It was incredibly intimate , and very taboo in most non-human groups, and a bit thrilling. Mason could feel the core of Benjamin, who he was, who he strove to be, how he felt about Mason. Better ignore that whole can of worms, Mason thought, and he followed the flow of his magic back to Ben's core. Some would call it the soul, but Mason had complicated thoughts about souls.

Mason found himself in a large, metaphysical space teeming with magic. Energy was pouring in from the Nether at alarming rates. Even Nessa, with her strong connection to the captain, would be hard pressed to pull this much energy this quickly. Benjamin was strong, and it was exceedingly odd that he had never discovered this part of himself before. There was an oppression to the space, confining it, like bars Mason couldn't see. Something had sealed something inside this man, like putting a mesh grate on his magical plumbing.

"Captain!" Mason called out, while still immersed in Benjamin. Mason immediately felt the presence of the Captain, a cool, numbing presence. "Can you feel this lock on his connection to the Nether?"

"I do." was all the shade offered.

"Can it be removed?" Mason asked.

"Not by me, but you could." The captain said, in that aggravatingly cryptic way spirits had of talking.

"I have no power in this realm, without my other." Mason corrected the shade.

"I speak not of magic, but of community. Draw him into your circle." The captain droned , annoyed.

That took Mason a second to comprehend. A Circle was a very generic term for a lot of different kinds of supernatural groups. Jackson and his Drove were the easiest kind to understand. Whenever non humans formed into a group that transcended mere communion, they formed what was in essence a magical network between their members. Mason and Theia had formed such a connection, but it was something they kept to themselves. Post-Humans were usually very opposed to mixing magical types as it were, and here was a spirit casually telling him to make a type of connection that far surpassed family or romantic bonds. And with a man he had had an awkward romantic history with.

"That shouldn't be done under duress." Mason said flatly.

"If you care for this man's well being, it must be done." The Captain said plainly. "You and Nessa were on the precipice of such a connection. It would have solidified your bond if you had not been so opposed." There was the rub, he was here again, being asked to bind himself to an unknowable fate. Mason raised his awareness back to a surface level, saw that the Golem was almost to its feet, and saw Ben panting and wheezing with the effort of holding the thing.

"I might have a solution, but it's not something I can ask casually." Mason said to Ben, in as grave a tone as he could muster.

"I don't see a lot of options, Mason." Ben said straining.

"The Captain seems to think that if we bind ourselves to one another, I might be able to break this seal someone put on your magic." Mason considered his next words carefully. "But, it's not a one-time thing. It would be for the long haul. Your problems would become my problems, your success becomes mine, we would walk the world together."

"It beats dying , Mason. What do I do?" Ben met his gaze, a determination there behind his fear.

"Just accept me, yourself, Nosam, and Theia. Understand that our steps are your steps 'til there are no more roads to wander." Mason held his hand aloft. Ben raised his hand and placed it in his.

"Sounds like a plan." and their paths converged.

CHAPTER

11

•●•

Theia hung up the phone. She had left a strongly worded voicemail on Mason's phone about his lack of commitment to her wellbeing, and at least three disparaging comments about his lack of focus in times of strife. She looked over at the burly man who was watching her quite fearfully. Ever since 'The Matrix' came out, people thought that Oracles could hack the world. Sure, she could probably dodge a few bullets if she could see them coming, but Neo she was not.

"Well, he didn't answer, so I guess it's back to Detainee Room 4?" Theia asked pleasantly. She was trying to be upbeat, but she was scared shitless. PLEB was not known for its attention to due process, If Mason was even suspected of foul play, they might just kill him , as opposed to trying to bring him in. The Dual-Natured were very misunderstood by humans, and notoriously hard to keep in a jail cell to boot. No one was telling her if Mason was also under suspicion. The charm they had placed on her neck cut her off completely from her sight. Which, if Theia was being honest, was kind of nice for a change. Seeing the future isn't always the peachy walk in the park that wizards in books made it seem.

She was also worried about Zoe. They had separated them early in the interrogation process, and she was most likely bound and gagged for their protection. Making a magic blocking charm for witches was kind of like trying to plug a bursting pipe with your thumb, not very effective. But, then, again, it goes to show how ignorant the PLEB were in thinking that gagging witches did much of anything, either.

Theia had called Matthew Davis, the lawyer across the hall from their office, and briefly asked if he could come down to PLEB and bail her out., His secretary had told her that she would inform him once his meeting was over, which could mean anything. Theia had made the mistake once of being honest with the woman in regard to a reading about her son. Most people really hate it when you tell them the truth about their future.

Regardless, as far as interrogations go, she found this one pretty lacking. No one had come to speak to her, and when she insisted that she was owed a lawyer, they reluctantly let her make some phone calls. She had tried to ply some information from the goon who had escorted her, but had gotten nowhere. So, she sat in the small room they had assigned her. They hadn't even had the courtesy to cuff her to anything.

The room she was in did have a window, however, so she busied herself with people watching and, to be honest, people judging. Theia had never understood the appeal of PLEB to humans. Maybe it was a prejudice thing, maybe the pay was a lot better than she thought it was. She may never know, as she was barred from any participation.

Meredith suddenly blew into the room flanked by two brutish looking men with protruding tusks, their foreheads marred by long singular horns. They had a reddish tone to their skin, and Theia guessed they were Oni. That was interesting. Oni were primarily feared in the community as magic resistant bogey men, and most definitely not human.

"I see PLEB isn't above employing infernal helpers." Oni weren't exactly demonic, but, the expression immediately drew angry expressions from the Oni, which had been her goal in using it.

"Antagonizing them won't make this go any easier." Meredith spread some papers out in front of her and produced a pen. "Now let's forgo the usual and get to the point. Why were you at the Randall estate."

"We were doing a welfare check on our client Tina Randall." Theia lied easily.

"Tina Randall has been dead for 6 years, try again." Meredith jotted down a note. Theia imagined she was keeping a tally in some twisted trivia game.

"I met with her in my office this morning, my secretary can corroborate." Theia was fully aware that whoever that woman was, she wasn't Tina Randall, but to know that, she would have had to gone inside the house.

"Alright, assuming you believe that to be true, what evidence did you have that a welfare check needed to be done." Meredith pushed forward.

"We had an encounter with Gideon Smith that led me to believe she may have been in danger." Theia tried not to smile at the attention she was drawing to the Nephilim.

"Mr. Mason Wallace is dual-natured, correct? His non-human half being a Primordial shape of a large dog?" The question threw her a bit with its sudden topic change.

"Nosam, yes."

"Could you tell me what 'Nosam' removed from my crime scene earlier today?" Meredith smiled as if to say check mate.

"I'm afraid I don't know." It was a plausible lie; she hadn't been present at the time, so, couldn't know for sure.

"Ms. Morgan, lying to me won't help your case. You are an 'Oracle' under investigation by the Preternatural Licensing and Enforcement Bureau, involved in a murder investigation with a dubious, fake client. Things do not look well for you." She emphasized the point with a click of her pen.

That was an understatement. PLEB needed to solve cases in order to prove to those above them that they deserved the budget afforded to them. Even if they didn't think she did this, they might still try to make something stick just to keep the public happy.

"I was not aware that my client was 'dubious' until you told me, and, as far as I am aware, I've been an asset to your investigation using my abilities." Theia said, without breaking a sweat.

"Although, it would be easy to pretend magical clarity if you were involved in the crimes themselves, wouldn't it?" Meredith countered.

"That may be true, but no one on my staff would have been capable of the crimes committed at the country club. Also, if you had a decent coroner, it could be determined that whatever killed Mr. Randall obviously has skills we don't possess." Theia was swallowing her nerves; can't let bureaucrats see you sweat.

"I'm afraid we have no idea what you are capable of Ms. Morgan. Especially if we find that your oracular abilities are exaggerated." Meredith said with a smile.

"Well, I guess it's all in your capable and fair hands, then." Theia shifted in her chair in a dismissive manner.

"I wouldn't make any long-term plans." With that, Meredith stood and collected her papers. The Oni held the door for her while she strolled confidently from the room.

After she was sure Meredith wouldn't be within sight, Theia turned back to the window. A woman, wearing a floral blouse and a tangle of bright red hair sat at her desk, but was only pretending to work. Then, her full attention became glued to a particularly handsome beat cop giving a statement to a suited PLEB agent. Theia missed her gift in that moment, as she would have loved to see if she would be able to work up the courage to talk to him. She was musing about the red- haired woman's potential future when she heard it.

Music from a wooden flute trickled into the office. It was all at once everywhere, and also just outside of her perception, music not meant for her. It did, however, seem to affect the PLEB officers she could see from her tiny room. They all stopped what they were doing and stood at attention. Gently swaying to the ethereal music. Theia became very concerned about this development, and wondered what it could mean for her personage in its fragile state. As she watched, a man dressed in a medieval style garment, strolled into the office, all the while playing a flute. He looked about, but, never ceasing his flute playing.

As his gaze fell on her, she could feel a power pouring from him. It was tinged with the smell of lilacs and roses, and fell over her in a heavy but comforting way. He strolled, maybe frolicked, to her, keeping a rhythm with his playing. As she watched, a rat fell from his shirt and wriggled under the door. Faced with the rodent, Theia was suddenly at a loss for words.

"You are Theia of Cassandra?" It squeaked, in accented English. Theia recognized the naming convention, and was suddenly glad she was on the up with the local fey. At least she assumed she was.

"Yes I am." She finally managed to say.

"Your imprisonment is inconvenient to the Deep Queens wishes of you. However, she has bade us to defer to you as to which course our actions should take." The Rat managed a tiny bow, which admittedly, was rather cute.

"I do not wish for any humans to be harmed, but I'm otherwise unclear what you can do for me." Theia was trying to play all of the angles in her mind.

"We can erase you from their minds, make them sleep as long as the music holds sway. They shall obey." The Rat responded.

Theia took a quick stock of her priorities. The brand that blocked her abilities was Runic, so she doubted the fey would be able to do much about it. She could walk out of here, find Mason, and make sure he got to the meeting with Horace. There was a killer on the loose, and pinning the murders on Theia would be a big score for Meredith, however, erasing their memory of her wouldn't erase any records they had.

"Can you make them believe I'm still here? That I haven't left, and make them ignore me?" She asked.

"Yes," the Rat answered, "but only for a time. Come sunrise the magic will be broken." That made sense. Most spells, unless very powerful, don't stand up to the big three: Sunrise, the stroke of midnight, or something like a sacrifice born of true love, or some other nonsense like that. The Fey were especially bound by the fairy tale norms.

"So, as long as I return before sunrise, they won't realize I'm gone?" she clarified.

"Such is within the Piper's power." The Rat squeaked.

"There is another, Zoe of..." She struggled with the proper title. "Oak Blood?" The Rat seemed either unmoved or not understanding.

"You are the only one Imprisoned the Queen owes favor." The Rat said finally. "An arrangement can be made though..." There was the rub; he had been paid to collect her, but anything extra would come at a price.

"What is your price for removing Zoe Halston from the minds of the Humans of PLEB." Theia asked sighing.

"Safe Haven, for one cold season for our brood." the Rat said immediately. Theia thought about her house being overrun by rats for an entire winter. Safe Haven also meant she would have to provide for them.

"Done. Free her and erase the human's minds of her." Theia had a thought, "Two cold seasons if you can manage to destroy any evidence of her as well." Theia could feel the magic of the pledge flow between them, and then snap closed as the deal was accepted. There was a stinging at her neckline. She looked and a pair of tiny rat tattoos had appeared there.

"The pact is concluded; the humans will unlock your cell." With that, the Rat wriggled under the door again, and crawled up the leg of the Piper. The music shifted. Humans began moving again. One came and unlocked her door, and several more began collecting paperwork and shredding it. The woman in the floral blouse was furiously typing, most likely removing digital records. The Piper did what can only be described as a jig in the middle of the room.

Theia moved to the door, pulled it open, and surveyed the room. Zoe stood in the hall rubbing her wrists and looking about bewildered. She saw Theia and mouthed, 'this you?' before gesturing at the frantic activity. Theia pointed at the Piper and gestured for Zoe to follow her. They moved together through the office finding any door that would have impeded them being held open by a member of the PLEB.

"Was that THE Pied Piper?" Zoe finally asked as they stepped into the night air.

"Apparently the Fey are very motivated to find who is killing changelings." Theia supplied. "Can you do anything about the brands?" She gestured to the sealing mark on her neck. Zoe closed her eyes and held a hand over her own, slightly different, brand. In moments it began sparking and smoking and then evaporated from her skin.

"Easy enough to short circuit mine, the Runics have no clue how Witch magic works." She looked at Theia's mark. "Unfortunately, they have a much better grasp at blocking Oracle magic. I'd need Mason's help in frying yours. I just don't have the juice."

"Well, let's go save him from whatever is keeping him from answering his phone." Theia took one last look back at the concrete building, and moved into the night walking to the beat of an ethereal flute.

• ● •

Mason could feel the binding slide into place; it was heavy and momentous. He wasn't sure which of them was pulling the other, but , this was not how it had felt when he had joined with Theia. That had felt like a gentle mixing, like finding a long-lost friend you had never known existed. This binding felt like an obligation, a dread destiny pulling him into Benjamin's orbit.

"Now what?!" Benjamin screamed drawing Mason back into the moment. The Golem let out a keening scream, and finally freed itself from the vines. It lunged forward with an awkward gait; the vines having sapped it of some of its gumption. Mason pushed Ben out of the way and dove into the creature's lunge, falling into a forward roll under its massive arms. As soon as he recovered his feet, he dodged to the right, only taking glancing blows from the creature's legs and clawed feet. Who puts claws on feet?

"You need to figure out how to open a door out of here!" Mason cried, reaching out to the vines and questing with his magic. Time slowed as the vines roused at his presence. 'I need a weapon.' he thought furiously at them.

'What is weapon, what are us?' the Vines were a brand-new existence a literal newborn, but enough of a natural plant to respond to Mason's gifts.

'I wish I could take the time to help you during this transition, but I don't have the time.' He began to think furiously formed thoughts about the form and properties of weapons at the vines. They began to writhe and wrap around themselves in a twisting shaft, hardening and stiffening. In seconds, a long pike of almost stone hardness dislodged itself from the mass of vines. Mason flooded the vines with gratitude and magic and brandished the spear at the Golem.

It had turned awkwardly, but seemed conflicted. It was looking between him and Ben as if it was confused as to whom to go after. Mason was suddenly concerned; had the binding mixed he and Ben's energies enough where it couldn't tell them apart? The main advantage Mason had had was that the thing had been trying to kill him specifically, but, if it suddenly thought otherwise…

Regardless, it was hesitating, which meant Mason had time to try something. He moved in close and got a bare hand on the sticky flesh of the creature. Golems were dangerous to send after Shamans, and, yes, if the thing had never hesitated it would easily kill him. But, if it was this unsure, he might be able to further confuse the issue. Without Nosam, he couldn't force anything, but he was still a shaman, and perhaps he could reason with the thing's parts.

Golems are made out of stuff. This one was made out of dead stuff, and Mason excelled at befriending stuff. His magic found the corpse of one of the many corpses used to make the greater creature. It resisted, not wanting to be separated as an individual, But, the magic that Mason was creating, was helping it to feel safe. Wanting to be a part of a greater whole, it eventually 'turned' to Mason.

'I am.' it said, in a strange, wheezing voice.

'You are.' Mason poured magic into that one thought , and quite suddenly, meat and bone poured out of the Golem. Not a lot, but, enough to enrage the creature, who solidified its attention on Mason. Mason used the butt of the pike to brace himself against the flesh of the Golem, so, as it turned to maul him, it pushed him out of its reach. He then spun the pike so that the business end and cross bar were between them. Being the mindless thing that it was, it charged, impaling itself and pushing Mason backwards. The pike groaned and almost gave up on its new form, but Mason assured it that it could handle this and more.

Benjamin retreated behind a shelf, feeling particularly helpless as Mason struggled with the creature. He wasn't sure where he had gotten a spear from, but his understanding of post-Human magic was limited. He had to stop thinking that way, as he apparently wasn't nearly as human as he thought he was. If Mason was right, he could get them out of here, he just had to do something. He closed his eyes and reached for that part of himself that Mason had touched. It had been so intimate, that if he had not been in mortal danger, he might have been embarrassed.

The space felt almost raw, and had the feeling of a fresh bruise. He tried to move it to do something, anything. He thought over and over, DOOR. He practically yelled at this new sore part of himself for it to make a door. It laid silent and throbbing, but he could feel a barrier around it muffling his will. He pushed against the barrier, it felt flimsy now, not the rigid mesh it had been before he had tied himself to Mason. He hooked metaphorical fingers into the spaces in the obstructing force, and pulled at it.

He was assaulted by strange images of a tower, the rushing of wind, his parents speaking softly, pain in his shoulders, a burning that threatened to overwhelm him, a ring, and loss, such a vast and unending loss. He pushed past all of it and tore the mesh down from its core. It was his birthright, no one could keep him from it anymore. He was free.

The pain swelled to a crescendo, and then he felt heavy, a weight across his shoulders that threatened to push him to the ground. Then, in that moment before he lost consciousness, he felt it, a trickle of cold that spread over him. It brought clarity and calm, and a deep, profound understanding that all things will pass, and all things have an end.

'I have waited.' a feminine voice touched his mind.

"Who...?" Ben managed to say, tears running down his cheeks.

'We have all waited.' the voice returned.

"Nosam, door." Benjamin managed.

'You must know...' It said calmly. Benjamin was so tired, more tired than he could ever imagine being. What did this thing want? They needed to escape.

"I don't..." Benjamin started, but the presence flared angrily.

'You MUST!' It screamed painfully. Benjamin took a breath and let his intuition bubble to the forefront of his mind. He put aside decades of putting his life into tidy lines. He took the rules he had always known and ripped them from his mind.

"The Consumed." He said in a whisper.

'Hello again, dear heart.' the presence almost cooed, as the room began to spin. The floor rushed up at him, and the world went dark. He slept and hoped Mason would survive.

CHAPTER

12

• ● •

Theia and Zoe arrived at the U-Store that was close to the PLEB headquarters. They had purchased the storage space in the off chance they needed to either escape the PLEB, or maybe have a walk of shame in the area.

"Storage lots always give me the creeps." Zoe provided. She was clearly tired from shorting out her brand.

"Well, this creepy dark lot you know." Theia said, tearing open an inner pocket of her jacket and retrieving the skeleton key that would open the storage unit.

The unit was lit by a single bare bulb, and had a rolling rack of clothes and several shelves of odds and ends. Theia walked to a shelf containing a plastic bin of cell phones, and removed one and checked it for any damage. On the back of the phone there was a small cartoon dog sticker. She removed it and the phone chirped to life. Zoe plopped down onto a metal folding chair in front of a small vanity.

"Is that one of the clone phones the Wiz made you?" Zoe asked, rubbing her neck.

"Yeah, useful as hell. Pull one adorable sticker and your phone transfers to it seamlessly." The Wiz had made several of them, after they had helped him with a particularly hard to pin down stalker some years back. The ability it had to both wipe a lost phone and get everything from contacts and battery life from it was priceless in their business.

"Anything from Mason?" Zoe asked, sleep dripping from her voice.

"Still booting up. There is a cot in the corner. Pull it out and try to power nap. Protein bars and water in the bin next to it." Zoe would be useless if she didn't get her reserves back. The witch dragged herself out of the chair, pulled the cot down from the wall, and placed it and herself to good use.

There were several messages on her phone, but not from Mason. Nessa had called her 8 times and left 15 text messages. She scrolled through them expecting to be blamed for some new development in her life, only to find she was texting about Mason. He had been lassoed near the U of A. The Captain was with him, but she was too far away to be of more help. Theia turned the phone off and dumped a second bin on the floor, grabbing a pair of truck keys, and turned to leave. Zoe stirred and half sat up.

"Gonna go grab Mason. You nap. That's an order." Theia said in a calm but stern voice. Zoe gave a small salute and fell back onto the cot. Theia reached the parking lot, and hoped the old man she paid to keep the truck in a drivable condition hadn't been slacking off. The small white pickup chirped to the key fob, and she slid into the driver seat. She took a hopeful breath and turned the key. When the engine rumbled happily, she let out a sigh of relief , and threw it into drive heading toward the campus.

• ● •

The Explosion of energy caused both the Golem and Mason to stop their fighting and look about. Mason could still feel the lasso, but the contents of the little pocket dimension had shifted. They weren't in the Nether anymore, they were in the Second World. The Loci of the warehouse instantly touched his mind, and, being a place whose purpose was to keep things safe, it took a distasteful view of the mindless Golem in its demesne. Mason felt it reaching out to him and seeking his help in repelling the creature. Mason gladly acquiesced, and felt the cold roughhewn stone of the floor crawl up his legs seeking skin contact.

As soon as he and the Loci had gotten on the same page, his awareness of the warehouse became truly omniscient. He could tell how many cracks were in the floor, how many spiders were in the rafters, and how important the things entombed here were to the Loci. With a gesture and a gentle prod of magic the floor warped and spun away from the Golem, throwing it off balance. With another flick of his wrist, the unused crates near Benjamin's work area splintered into jagged pieces, the resulting inertia carrying them to the creatures exposed flank.

It howled and leaped at Mason. A white blur slammed into the Golem, and when Mason realized what was happening, he saw Nosam's jaws locked on the throat of the monster. They slammed to the floor to the right of Mason, and the creature's screaming intensified.

Convincing a Loci to do much of anything is usually a slow and arduous process. It can take months to convince it to do something for you sometime in the future, and even then, it rarely wanted to break too many of the laws that physics and the physical sciences set for it. But, the Loci of the warehouse was not only pissed off, and, as they were in the Second World, those rules were given respect, but were not binding in the least. Mason gathered the essence of the warehouse, and with a dramatic gesture, dozens of shafts of concrete as thick as his wrists shot up from the floor and pierced the Golem from all angles. It wheezed one last ragged breath and ceased moving, the magic animating it no longer able to repair the amount of damage it had sustained.

Mason went limp, but, the concrete of the warehouse floor kept him standing. As it receded, the danger passed, he was able to catch himself on one knee, panting heavily. He looked about for Benjamin, and spied an expensive, but practical, shoe sticking out from behind a shelf.

"I shall tend to him." Nosam said. The large canine padded over to the passed-out man and let out an unconscious yip.

"What is it?! Is he okay?" Mason forced himself to his feet and began to shuffle over to them.

"He is fine, but you should see this." Nosam backed away so Mason would have room to lean on the shelf.

Mason put his weight against it and looked down. He understood what had Nosam so shocked. Lying on the floor, half propped up, was Benjamin. Surrounding him was a charred circle embedded into the floor of the warehouse. Mason recognized it, of course, as it was a pledge written in symbolism and dead languages. Mason himself had produced a similar effect when he and Nosam had promised themselves to each other. It had caused quite a stir, because the average two natured person manages to lay a three to five layer circle, indicating the strength of the bond. **B**ut, Mason and Nosam had produced nine layers.

Benjamin had produced eighteen. What had he bound himself to, and where was it now?

• ● •

As Theia pulled up to Shithead, the parking meter, she saw him. Mason was carrying an unconscious Benjamin in between buildings towards his jeep. She instantly hit the hazard lights and jumped out of the truck.

"Is he okay?!" She yelled over the music of the restaurants across the street.

"I think so, but we should probably get him to a hospital regardless. He is very tapped." Mason said, laying him in the passenger seat of his vehicle.

"What happened?" Theia said, pulling one of the clone phones and handing it to Mason.

"Thanks, the damn lasso fried mine." He said taking the phone and pulling the sticker.

"How did you get out?" Theia hadn't even thought to ask the Piper to do anything for Mason. "Was there a PLEB team?"

"You would think, but when we crossed back over , there was not a suit to be seen." Mason rubbed at his neck. "Whoever it was, I think they were after the Kopis."

"The knife we found at the crime scene?" Theia was taken aback.

"The very same. The warehouse can't remember who grabbed it, but it was the only thing missing when we got back." Mason let out a sigh. "Whoever it was had access to a particularly large Flesh Golem that almost cooked my ass."

"How did you get away?" Theia removed a small, enchanted patch that she had snagged from the glove compartment and slapped it on Mason's bare arm. Mason winced as the stored magic poured from it, and into him, but didn't complain.

"Apparently, Mr. Benjamin Aguilar is not quite as Human as he has always insisted. Look Theia I have to tell you something." Mason looked worried, and Theia couldn't use her gift to soften the blow.

"It's okay, unconditional." It was her way of telling him she was there no matter what.

"I added Benjamin to our Circle. It was the only way to get us out of there." Mason looked at him, a worried expression on his face. Theia sighed and handed him a second patch.

"Get him to a hospital. We have time to figure out what that means. No need to rush it." Theia pushed a stray strand of hair behind her ear and checked her phone. Midnight wasn't that far off.

"I'll get him squared away and then meet you at the park. I'm running on fumes, and if this meeting goes bad, I'll need your support." Mason placed a meaty hand on her shoulder and walked to the driver's side and pulled the door open. Theia didn't know exactly how to tell him she had nothing to offer at the moment, but, seeing Benjamin's pale face was enough to convince her to cross that bridge later.

Theia wracked her brain trying to think of who she could get to back them up. Several names came to mind, but none of them seemed practical in any way. She sighed and dialed a number into her phone. After a few rings Jackson answered.

"Theia?" Of course, he had saved her number on his phone. She never remembered to do it herself, being a virtual human caller ID. Well usually.

"Yeah, in order to do what the queen wants, we need to get through the next few hours, and even though you are conflict... averse I could use the muscle." Theia said, not trying to hide her desperate tone.

"Oh..." Jackson said after a pause. "Yeah, text me the address and I will meet you. I hope it won't take long, I have a shift in the morning."

"Demons tend to be pretty flowery, so I would expect you will need to call out in the morning." Theia said, a smile in her voice.

"Demons!" Jackson sighed heavily.

"Just the one, really." Theia replied.

"You're right, that's much more reasonable of a request." Jackson hung up the phone in a tiny bit of a huff. Well, even if he was annoyed, she hoped he would show up. She texted the name of the park with instructions to show up a bit early.

She got back in the truck and backed it into the space ruled over by the surly parking meter. She stuck her head out and gave him a hopeful thumbs up. The Parking Meter whirred for a moment then displayed 20 minutes.

Theia rolled down the windows and leaned into the back of the driver's seat. It had been a long day, no matter how you looked at it. She fully intended to take the 20 minutes the uppity meter had given her for some much-needed self-reflection. Suddenly, there was the sound of wing beats and, out of nowhere, Gideon was in her passenger seat.

"Shit!" Theia yelled, as she reached for her door handle, but Gideon laid his strong calming hand on her shoulder, and she stopped.

"I didn't mean to startle a seer." He said with a small chuckle. Theia pulled her hair to the side showing him her brand before speaking.

"PLEB blinded me, just vanilla right now." She said putting her hands on the steering wheel.

"I assume this is the same run in where you mentioned my name?" Gideon removed a small satchel of what seemed to be lavender and held it to his nose.

"Yeah, I figured you could handle the heat." she answered.

"Well, they wasted no time trying to reach me for questioning. We are having a merry chase." Gideon smiled offering the small satchel to her. She politely declined, but relaxed her grip despite herself.

"Well, to what do I owe the visit then. Trying to get me lassoed?"

"No, I'll be gone before their diviners find me. I came to see you and to entreat you, that when you find it you will bring it to me..." He said mysteriously.

"It?" She asked genuinely confused.

"You'll know. I'm almost certain it will be you now. You aren't the only one with a bit of precognition." Gideon considered, "When it returns of course."

"No chance I can get you to zap this off of me then?" She said losing hope.

"I feel it best serves my goals if you remain in the dark a bit longer." Gideon reached out and laid a hand on hers.

"Gideon." Theia warned.

"If you didn't have your gift perhaps you would be calling my name in a different context." The sultry tone spoke of many scenarios.

"It doesn't work out Gideon." She said removing her hand from under his.

"It most likely doesn't work out. You let your gift decide your fate; bar you from the mystery of 'maybe'." Gideon opened his door and stood holding it open. "Someday you will have to give 'maybe' a chance."

Just as suddenly as he arrived, Gideon was gone, leaving a white feather resting on her side view mirror. Theia wanted to call after him, but she had seen where that ended up. She had seen where every 'maybe' ended up. It made her lonely, but it beat the alternative.

She looked in her mirror to see that the meter still showed 15 minutes, but she was far from relaxed. She pulled the small crystal pendant from the rear-view mirror and gave it a tiny spin on its chain. To her surprise, it began quite visibly tugging toward the museum. She was branded ; her magic shouldn't be working at all. Maybe PLEB didn't understand Oracles as well as they thought.

She exited the car and let the hunk of crystal tug her toward the museum. While she got her steps in, she pondered what it was that Gideon could be after. Was it the Kopis? Someone out there with a lot of power had made that disappear. The dagger didn't initiate anything particularly world ending as the vision had implied. She was so deep in thought that she almost tripped over the first step leading up to the museum entrance. It was very closed, and while she was branded and without a sturdy brick, it seemed a pretty big nope as far as gaining entrance. She sighed and put the crystal in a jacket pocket. She would have to come back here and try to figure out what was so important.

She returned to the truck, giving the meter an appreciative pat, and got inside. The sky was clear, and the moon was full enough to cast a surprising amount of light down. As she started the truck up, she took a moment to appreciate her thoughts. Being this close to the campus always made her feel old, and the weariness that plagued her didn't help in the slightest.

CHAPTER

13

• ● •

Mason left the hospital with very little travel time left. Apparently, bringing a passed-out man to the emergency room raised a lot of questions that weren't easy to answer. Luckily, Benjamin had gotten enough juice from the patch to tell the very concerned staff that Mason was a hero actually, and not some creep who had kidnapped him. Nosam was already sitting at attention in the jeep when he reached it.

"Clearly, you see now that Ben is meant for us." the hound said thumping his tail against the seat.

"Well, being in a circle complicates things. We aren't shifters. Being this tied up isn't natural for us." Mason said, ignoring the bigger conversation.

"Excuses." Nosam said plainly.

"Regardless, we don't have time to debate it. We only have time to meet Horace." Mason said, putting the jeep into reverse. As he drove, Nosam never took his gaze off of his Human.

"You could make it work; you don't need to be hidden from me." Nosam said finally.

"I shouldn't HAVE to make it work. It should just work." Mason retorted.

"Fine. Do we know who Horace has made a pact with?" The dog said, changing the subject. Relieved, Mason pondered this.

"I've never put much stock into it. Horace definitely wields fire, but, I had always thought of him as a solo worshiper. This talk of 'we' changes the situation." Mason rubbed his eyes and needlessly adjusted his mirrors.

"There are many princes in hell, but few command the loyalty he displayed earlier today." Nosam said thoughtfully.

"Well, we are two short blocks from finding out, I guess." Mason took the turn into the neighborhood and was surprised to see the parking lane packed with cars. It wasn't uncommon to see so many cars while school was in session, but not usually this far from campus. A quick inquiry to Sonora showed him a parking spot on a side street near the park. It was blocking someone's mailbox, but he didn't plan to be here that long.

The short walk to the park was tense, and when it finally came into sight, he was shocked. There was a full-blown block party going on, at midnight, on a school night no less. The attendees all seemed like common suburban fare. Karen haircuts and Hawaiian shirts were as common as tasteful capris and cargo shorts. Mason checked his phone to see if maybe Horace had changed the meeting place, but there was no such text. He did, however, see Theia and Jackson sipping from plastic cups near the fringes of the gathering.

"Just couldn't wait to drink the Kool-Aid?" Mason called out to them, as Nosam sniffed Jackson thoroughly.

"It's 'Country Time", actually." Theia said, correcting his flagrant lack of knowledge in the area of powdered drinks.

"Don't worry, I can smell most poisons." Jackson provided. Mason wasn't 100% sure why the Shifter was present, but he trusted Theia and her reasons.

"Are these all..."

"Demon worshippers? Oh yeah." Theia finished for him. She gave an amused look around. Mason followed her gaze and started to notice the odd things, the lack of children running about, infernal jewelry, a group of soccer moms drinking from a decanter of much-too-thick-to-be-wine.

"Takes all kinds, I guess." Mason shook his head. "Nosam, care to see if any of the natives are amicable to our side?" Nosam gave a nod and fuzzed into the Second World to talk to the trees.

"So, when does the summoning from hell start?" Jackson said in as light a tone as he could muster.

"Probably already happened. Someone in this park is not like the others." Mason said with a whistle. The stench of Infernal magic was thick in the area. It made sense that Jackson couldn't pick it out, but Theia was usually better at this than most. He shot her a questioning glance.

"I should probably explain what happened while you were busy with Benjamin. Theia gave Mason the diet version of the events at the PLEB Headquarters. When she was done, Mason shook his head.

"You should have told me; I would have had you wait at the office." Mason scolded.

"Hence, why I didn't tell you. Plus, Jackson here is honor bound to assist us. No way of knowing that these folks AREN'T killing changelings." Theia said with a shrug.

"Well, now that you're here, I don't really have time to give you a lecture you won't listen to." Mason said to Jackson.

"Mansplain me harder, daddy." Jackson piped in.

"Shush, Mr. Bunny." Mason said dismissively. Theia snorted, but remained composed and aloof.

Suddenly, they could see that Horace had torn away from the group of homogeneous, middle-aged party goers and approached them. He was wearing very earnest robes with a deep cowl. It looked so out of place in this crowd that it was almost comical, and it was clear from the snickering the rest of the group felt similarly.

"Mason, you have most fortuitous timing, my Lord is ready to receive you." Horace said with a comically, deep bow.

"We had a deal, Minion." Mason used the less than PC term for an invoker to see if he could get a rise from him, but Horace didn't stoop to his level.

"It would be easier for my Lord to explain why we were only partially successful." Horace said holding out an arm for Theia, who scoffed at it and moved in the indicated direction.

The crowd didn't part in a dramatic fashion, but it was clear they knew the newcomers were guests, because they shifted subtly, and without much cajoling. Horace brought them to a stunningly, handsome middle-aged man with long auburn hair, and a rugged, if not angelic, countenance. He wore nothing but a pair of cut off jean shorts and an apron that read DILF in a bold no nonsense font. The D had tiny red horns. Oh, and his skin was covered in half impaled rusty nails each securing a slip of paper with Aramaic symbols. It made for a wholly disappointing, arousing, and horrifying first impression.

"Mason Wallace, you stand before Samael, Venom of God, Ha-Satan, Masshit, Fallen Angel of the Deathly Host." Horace said with enough gusto to quiet the gathering, either in cringe or respect.

"Thank you, Acolyte Finn, that will be all." The Demon gestured for the small man to leave.

Mason was a tad gob smacked. This was no second-rate prince of Hell. Samael was a major player in the war between the Infernal and Celestial realms. Something young Nephilim were terrified of, something he was terrified of, and here he was in a novelty apron flipping burgers.

"I'm not sure what the proper title is here... Sir?" Mason said for lack of anything better to say.

"Smil will be fine, this is meant to be a very informal gathering as you can see." He gestured to the suburban crowd who all cheered in unison before returning to whatever it was, they had been doing.

"Alright, Smil, what did you want to talk about." Mason said trying not to shrug.

"Well, someone is trying very hard to wipe out Existence." He said very matter of factly, before taking a swig from his Light beer.

"I'm sorry?" Jackson said for all of them.

"Yes, the Fey have been guarding, hmm, not quite. Holding an artifact for us." He said flipping some of the burgers on to a paper plate.

"And it is THAT dangerous?" Theia asked a bit incredulous.

"Probably a lot worse than you are thinking, honestly." Smil pulled up a plastic chair and managed to sit in it without destroying it utterly. "Got the entire heavenly host all riled up with visions and portents."

"Alright well the end of the world is bad, but what does it have to do with us?" Mason asked.

"Well, whoever this is has been working their way through the fey population, for whatever reason, and I think they may have stumbled onto the damn thing." Smil seemed very put out by the whole sordid affair.

"So, our murderer might have the end of the world in their pocket. No pressure." Theia added.

"Exactly, the higher echelon of Demons wants a war with the angels, and if this thing isn't accounted for, they are going to get it. That's where you come in. Catch this murderer, bring us the artifact, and all the little sheep get to live." Smil began picking at his teeth absentmindedly.

"What is it?" Mason asked, annoyed by the utter lack of gravitas Smil had countenanced.

"A bead."

"Like from a tacky sweater?" Theia interrupted.

"Yes, grab it for me, and I'll put some credit toward a reward of your choosing." He stood and held out a punctured hand. "Deal?"

"I'm not entering into a casual, verbal agreement with someone called the Venom of God." Mason said flatly.

"Alright, then, go be a hero, for all I care, just make sure the Bead stays in neutral hands." The demon plopped back down into his camping chair.

"No scheme? No attempt at getting the Bead for yourself?" Mason was dubious.

"Nope, the damn thing is like an atom bomb. If either side gets it, the other will escalate the whole thing, and it will be ceaseless war all over again." Smil said rolling his eyes.

"I gotta say, for a being as old as the universe, you seem not to care all that much about all of this." Mason didn't know if he wanted him to be more conniving, or mistrusted the facade.

"I would like to see the end of the Universe too. I fell because I wanted freedom, not so I could serve in hell. A bunch of dead humans just means less praise, adulation, and sacrifice for me." Smil stretched his legs out, "Killing all of you in one go isn't good for business. Think of the long-term profits."

"Any idea what this thing is?" Mason changed tactics.

"The murderer? It's not Mortal, whatever it is. Not Infernal either. It wouldn't be so off the rails if it was. Probably not Fey." He put a clawed hand to his chin. "Could be Celestial, but I doubt they'd be so worried if it was."

"So, to be clear, we are under no Obligation or Oath. You just want to make sure we find this bead?" Mason clarified.

"If you can find whoever is killing the Changelings, that would be a big help as well. If you find the time." Smil said with a nod.

Mason and Theia shared several knowing looks. Finally, they shrugged almost in unison and looked back to Smil.

"Well, no promises, but, if we find a bead of infinite, destructive power, we will put it someplace safe." Mason said.

"Under no circumstances can the light and love angels get a hand on it." Smil rushed to say, "If they do, things won't go well for the mortals, maybe even worse than if it stays missing."

"Why, on earth, would the Fey hold on to such a thing for you in the first place? They hate being involved in inter-realm conflict." Jackson intoned, mostly to himself.

"It's why they were created, to stand in the middle of all our shit. Sure, they've gotten a bit big for their britches and formed their own sovereign corner of existence. Great pretenders to the pedigree of the on high and the fallen." He paused. "But that's not really important to what you need to be doing right now."

"You... created the fey?" Jackson said with wonder in his voice.

"Personally? No, though if I'm honest I wasn't really paying super close attention to the physical realms back then. That is the company line though." Smil was clearly getting bored with the conversation.

"Well..." Mason said to break the tension. "I just need the agreed upon payment." He said with a slight yawn.

"Oh, yes. Unfortunately, Mr. Randall Madison was one of mine. As such, he will be punished for bringing attention to himself. He will provide proof to his wife of his dalliance, and the Cult will pay what your firm is owed." Smil said in a rush.

"That wasn't the agreement." Mason said cautiously.

"It's in the spirit. You wanted proof in order to close your case with the wife. I have circumvented the need for that. Tidy." Smil said, his smile faltering a tad.

"Fair.." Mason said considering.

"It's been lovely." Theia added.

"Enlightening." Jackson almost whispered.

"I hope after all of this is over, I can convince you that Demons aren't nearly as heinous as you thought. Maybe, even do you a favor." Smil grinned and a magical weight settled over the trio. Mason was immediately on edge, but they hadn't made any concrete promise or deal. He was entirely too tired to deal with all of that mess though, and let it go. Confronting him further might almost be worse than living with it.

"I will see you to the street." Horace said with a submissive tone. He seemed nervous about the conversation in some way. Guilt maybe? It was hard to read someone as conniving as Horace.

As quickly as they had come to face Samael, they were just as summarily standing on the sidewalk looking back wistfully. Mason was kind of amazed that being enslaved to something as ancient and powerful as Samael could look so mundane, even boring, from the outside.

"We should have asked him to remove your brand!" Jackson exclaimed.

"No." Theia and Mason said at the same time.

"Favors from a demon are fraught with risk and backstabbing. Even if it seems straightforward, it never is." Theia said plainly.

"You guys forget that I deal with the Fey on a regular basis." Jackson rolled his eyes, "He's asking us to save the world. A brand is a small asking price."

"That's where you are wrong, He was asking us to do something we would have done regardless. Sure, he was pretending he was doing us a favor, but come reward time, there would be an imbalance. Next thing you know, you are strangling a man to death under demonic compulsion." Mason had heard that could happen. He avoided demons like he did credit card debt. Not worth the hassle. Jackson gulped at the prospect and dropped the subject.

"Well, back to PLEB for me." Theia said unceremoniously.

"I'm sorry, what?" Mason was taken aback.

"Temporary reprieve. Fey Perk, but its only til sunrise, and taking a nap there means I don't get pumpkin'd." She explained.

"Pumpkin'd?" Jackson asked.

"It's a Posty phrase. Forget a loophole, cost of a spell, or something else and get caught up in consequences. Like your carriage turning back into a pumpkin while you're inside it." Mason added.

"And, escaping from federal custody, is just not the look I'm going for." Theia concluded.

"Get some sleep Jack, we will tackle our delinquent in the morning." Mason stretched and kneeled down to pet Nosam.

"You can sleep after that?!" Jack squealed.

"Honestly, that went very smoothly." Theia said with just a tinge of suspicion in her voice.

"Mason didn't get stabbed or anything." Nosam said, trying not to enjoy the scratches he was receiving.

"Honestly, its in the top five 'didn't get stabbed' moments for me." Mason said sluggishly.

"Well, I for one couldn't sleep if I wanted to after all that. To just casually broach the topic of the creation of an entire nation of people?!" Jack went right on ranting to himself as he straddled his bike and put on his helmet. Soon he was waving and peddling off.

"I, for one, am off to bed," Theia supplied. "First thing tomorrow, we need to get this off my neck." Theia motioned toward the brand.

"I can help Zoe with a jump start. She should be able to fry it." Mason paused. "About Benjamin."

"No worries, if he truly is one of us, and you are okay with it, its fine by me." Theia said dismissively.

"I mean, he's gonna need a lot of guidance, coming into his power so late in life." Mason hedged.

"You being in likes with him complicates things." Theia smiled as Mason blushed.

"Good Night, Ms. Morgan!" Mason said in a Meredith impersonation.

"Tell Benjamin I said hi." Theia couldn't resist dialing the blush up to an eleven.

• ● •

Convincing the emergency door to open for him had been easy, and Nosam had sweet talked the security cameras to ignore them the first time they were here. Security cameras were pretty vain and self-important, and there were so many tv shows and movies about them and their heroic deeds, that it was relatively easy to talk them into just about anything.

Regardless, he didn't want to overstay his welcome, so he just wanted to look in on Ben and make sure he was doing okay. Unluckily, Ben was awake and waved Mason and Nosam over to his bedside. Mason sighed as if he was put out, and crossed the small, sterile room to Ben's bed.

"How did your meeting go?" He said with the practiced ease of someone who small talked often.

"Honestly, you had to be there to really grasp the scope of how weird it was." Mason ran a hand through his hair. "But no one died, so I'm happy."

"Are you?" Benjamin put a hand on his. "I get a feeling that you're a bit overwhelmed. You push yourself too hard all the time. Trying to be everyone's hero." He squeezed Mason's hand.

"If I didn't try to save the frail damsels, I'd never get a date." Mason said, wiggling his eyebrows.

"Ha! I saved you!" Benjamin pulled his hand away in mock anger.

"Well, after several attempts at swooning at my manliness, you did manage to be pretty helpful."

"I did not swoon."

"I did say 'attempts'."

Benjamin laughed, and then quickly ran out of breath and coughed a little. His color was back, and he seemed fine. Mason was struck by how handsome the man was, how strong. He had been through a truly horrifying ordeal, and yet, came out on the other end able to laugh easily. That encounter in the warehouse would have killed most humans, and yet, he seemed to come out much stronger for having been through it. Then again, Benjamin was clearly not human anymore, if he ever had been.

"What happened to me in that warehouse? I don't feel any different." Benjamin asked, when his breathing normalized again.

"It's hard to say for sure this early, but it looks like you might be two-natured like me. A Medium of the Nether Realms." Mason said dramatically.

"Two-Natured, so a Shaman like you?" Ben said, with an eye roll at Mason's drama.

"Yes and no. The two-natured are… complex." Mason continued. "For whatever reason, whether you believe we all came into existence at the same time, linked by some divine will, or were just randomly assigned, all two-natured beings share a soul with something or someone from one of the other realms of existence. Two unique entities, one shared soul."

"So, the entity I met in the Nether... we share a soul?"

"If you are in fact like me and Nosam, then yes, that is the case." Mason shrugged. "We are kinda rare, even among post-Humans, and many of us believe we have a duty to both of our realms, some duty that makes our existence meaningful."

"Hence, why you're an overprotective stick in the mud who does favors for trees?" Benjamin teased. His throat was getting scratchy again, so he reached for his ice chips.

"Those of us tied to the Second World or the primordial, do tend to be a bit reverent, but that is mostly because, unlike the rest of our kind, our other selves and the other world we live in is so very close to this one. Nosam is always right there, the trees are always right there, waiting for someone to listen. The very ground we tread upon complains to us." He reached over and rustled Benjamin's already ruined coif. "Unlike some who would go to the literal land of the dead in order to call theirs."

"Okay," Ben looked at himself in the black tv screen and began to fix his hair. "But why all the pomp and circumstance around forging the initial bond? If we share a soul, why do you need to agree to be together?"

"It's curious, but me and Nosam think it's similar to other rules in the supe community, like the Fey being unable to lie, or Witches being bound by a statement made three times. Until you decide to walk side by side, you share a soul, sure, and that can be a powerful advantage in some of the other realms. But, that doesn't bring either of you to power. Once the bond is formed, you can do things that other post-Humans just can't, and to be fair, its different for all of us." Mason explained.

"So, should I expect to be haunted forever?"

"Nessa used to say that the dead both covet and despise the material world of the living. Always seeking to bask in its energy, but powerfully opposed to its essence." Mason tried to think of conversations he had had with The Captain. "As far as I know, spirits in the Nether, at least those that would bind in this way, are more archetypes or concepts, creatures who may have been individuals but are also something more."

"The Consumed..." Benjamin said, with an appropriate amount of awe.

"See? Less Karen from accounting, and more of a vague concept of death or remembrance." Mason said with a smile.

"This is going to be an odd question, but should I, like, call or summon them?" He looked down at his hands, the little heart monitor clip still attached.

"After the warehouse, it is very clear you have a lot of juice to bring to the table, but even if they wanted to visit the human world, most of the beings you could be bonded to live deep in the Nether realms. It might be a bit of a tug on their reserves to manifest physically."

"I just don't know what's polite in this instance." Ben said sheepishly. Mason laughed.

"That's like asking your arm if it is comfortable! Sure, some respect is surely necessary, but you are more than bound. You ARE. One being, two bodies, two minds. No need to stand on ceremony." Mason reached a hand to Nosam. "If the being wishes to speak with you, or bond as it were, they will let you know."

"Might have been a little nicer to have a fuzzy, and handsome companion like you, Nosam." Ben said in a high-pitched voice.

"Unfortunately, all the other totems aren't as cute as myself, so you would be out of luck, sir." Nosam said his tail wagging.

"So, when should I meet with Theia?" Ben seemed nervous.

"Whenever you are ready. She trusts my judgment, and she likes you. Calls you "The Professor'." Mason said, ruffling Nosam absentmindedly.

"In that case, I'd love to speak with her tomorrow and get it out of the way, while I feel like I'm on solid ground."

"We are in the middle of some… cases at the moment, so she is a bit tied up. But, I will be going down to see her tomorrow." Mason hedged.

"So, I should wait til tomorrow afternoon?" Benjamin pushed, able to subconsciously feel Mason's apprehension now.

"I'll ask her about it, get some sleep. Let's see when they release you from here." Mason smiled. He waited til the other man fell asleep and then rose to leave.

He felt the cold first. A sudden shift to frigid temperatures. Mason spun around to see what could have been a woman floating over the sleeping Ben. Large chunks of her flesh had been eaten away and she/it floated there almost lovingly. She raised her eye-sockets, the flesh of her face ravaged and the eyes missing.

"He returned our wings." She said, flexing a pair of ravaged and torn wings that rose from her back.

"Awful kind of him." Mason said. It was never good to panic when dealing with new supes.

"You will serve him well. He has made good choices." This was an odd choice of words on her part. Circles were not structured in a way that would constitute service, not in a very long time.

"Thank you for saving us." Mason edged into gratitude.

"It was his will, and he gave me my wings." The creature, The Consumed, stroked Ben's face lovingly with, Mason now knew, an avulsed hand, then faded to where she had come from. Mason sighed to himself and turned to Nosam.

"If this day gets any weirder, I'm gonna quit. Move to Montana."

"Good land up there, but you'd be bored." Nosam said with a doggy grin.

"Boring is looking better and better." he said as he walked past a very flustered nurse.

CHAPTER

14

• ● •

Matthew Davis was a forthright and warm individual. His very expensive suit, briefcase, and easy smile, were just outward signs of his attention to detail and professionalism. He was a good lawyer as far as Theia knew, and he was here to see her.

"Your secretary already took care of the nitty gritty, so, regardless, I'm gonna get you out of this, but let's go over the particulars." He fanned out the case file and leveled his serious, brown eyes at her. "Did you kill Mr. Randall?"

"No, I did find his body, which is my job." Theia answered, but she felt something pull at her. A gentle presence that even in her cut off state she could perceive.

"I apologize, but I had to be sure." He said putting his hand to his mouth.

"What was that?" Theia asked, annoyed.

"Tasted your thoughts. It tells me if they are honest or not. Baku thing." He seemed contrite, but also giddy. Matthew was a Baku, which was an Orphic Supernatural tied to eating dreams. This meant he could nibble at her brain waves, get a taste for her state of mind. She had been thinking about how his deep brown skin complimented the plum of his button up... with maybe a tad too much appreciation. Theia refused to blush.

"Alright, now that you believe me what is our next step?" She said, ignoring what he may have tasted.

"Well, I'll be honest with you Ms. Morgan..."

"Theia."

"Theia, they don't have much. If I had to venture a guess, they are holding you just to get you off the street." Matthew put on a grumpy face. "These justifications are paper thin. Did you anger Mrs. Carsen?"

"She's auditing me. An angry client sicced PLEB on me." She made sure not to think about his impressive shoulders or physique.

"Well, being arrested could go a long way in justifying a license revocation. I know a few good eggs at PLEB, I'll see if I can't get her reassigned. She is way too far into conflict-of-interest territory." He placed his paperwork into his briefcase.

"Condolences, by the way." Theia said before she could stop herself. Matthew was shocked for a moment, then remembered what she was and put on a grim face.

"My father was a good man. I'm not sure why anyone would do that to him."

"Wait, what happened to your father?" Theia was intrigued by the wording.

"I assumed you knew. He was killed about a week ago. Looks like possibly a vampire, but its inconclusive." Matthew seemed uncomfortable, but curious.

"Once I get this brand off, I would love to do a reading. It might help a case I'm stuck on." Theia tried to be calm, but this might be the break she was looking for.

"Let me get you out of here, then. If it can help catch the monster that did that to him." Matthew clicked his briefcase shut and knocked to be let out of the room.

"Thank you, Mr. Davis." Theia said, with as much emotion as she dared.

"Matt."

•●•

Mason sent a lizard some hours later. He was a sleepy little Gecko ,with an x marked in sharpie on his tail. To Theia, It signified that they wouldn't be able to come see her. Theia gave the little guy a boost up into the corner of the room, where she had spied a spider web. At least one of them should eat something decent. Meredith had brought her a very stale donut and shitty coffee as a smug screw you gesture this morning. She would have offered some to the Gecko, but she didn't want Meredith to think she had touched it.

Speaking of horrible people, Todd Dunlap strolled into the room. She could see Matthew on his phone, but, before Matthew could protest, the door was pulled closed by a stocky PLEB Agent. Theia could hear Matt raising his voice, but the door didn't open.

"Ready to change your tune, bitch?" Todd Dunlap was maybe 5'7 and 250 lbs. of rage and misogyny, wearing a tacky, off the rack suit. His pink cheeks made him look like a spoiled child, which he probably was.

"Mr. Dunlap, unfortunately I'm not in office at the moment, but if you'd like to make an appointment." Theia said in her best, business voice.

"This," Dunlap said, gesturing to the room, "Won't stop til I say it does, you'll never work in this town again."

"For a man of your means, inheriting more money hardly seems like it would solve any of your problems." Theia said, bored.

"You're spayed, little girl. That brand makes you just another helpless cocksucker." the disgusting man gave his crotch a grab for emphasis. The urge to bash his skull in with her chair notwithstanding, Theia knew if she attacked him, even in self-defense, it would ruin her.

"I assure you, if you care to push the issue, I will gladly go to prison." She said, a cold murder in her voice. Todd was visibly shocked by the tone and removed his hand from his 'manhood'.

"Keep it up. You'll see how hard I can make your life." He said backing toward the door.

"It's okay, while I was reading your cards, I saw the blood clot. I won't have to worry long." She said smiling. She, of course, had seen no such thing, but the pale clamor that came over the man was worth any consequence that came from the lie.

"Open the door!" Dunlap yelled pounding on it. As the door came open, Matthew was there.

"I will be adding this to my complaint! This man could have caused grievous harm to my client!" Matthew was screaming, as the door closed again. Theia considered figuring out a way to pin these murders on Todd Dunlap, but knew her conscience would get the better of her.

After about 20 minutes of planning a horrible accident for Todd Dunlap, the very top of her 'angry-harm-fantasy' list strolled in. Meredith Carsen was wearing her signature pencil skirt and peasant blouse looking entirely like someone's divorced aunt, more than she did a prominent member of the government.

"You have a very good lawyer, Ms. Morgan." Meredith almost hissed.

"I take it, that means I can go?" Theia tried not to gloat.

"Yes, but the brand stays on, and it's removal is considered grounds to rearrest you. I will know if its removed." She said with venom.

"So, why are you so hell bent on ruining my life for a man like Todd Dunlap?" Theia asked.

"Who? Oh, yes, the 'Complaint Maker'. I'm just the Auditor unfortunate enough to be assigned to your case." She said, fiddling with her necklace. Theia actually recognized the figure depicted on the necklace from a long lecture Benjamin had given at a party.

"Is that the Goddess, Ceto?" Theia asked almost haphazardly. Meredith quickly tucked it into her blouse and reached for her glasses.

"Are you a fan of ancient Greek history, Ms. Morgan?" Meredith was smiling in a predatory way that made Theia very nervous. But, Theia had rarely paid attention to Benjamin's lectures, and she was not very knowledgeable on the subject.

"Not really, I've just seen that depiction before." She lied. Whether Meredith was buying it or not, was hard to tell. The woman stood and turned to the door.

"It might serve you to brush up on your history." With that, she knocked on the door and exited the room. Soon after, Matthew, complaining as to her treatment, and a very annoyed looking PLEB agent, came to release her.

"You're free to go, Theia. I will call you later with our next steps IN SUING THE LIVING DAYLIGHTS out of this dog and pony show!" Matthew continued to rail, as Theia walked toward the exit smiling.

• ● •

Theia was at a bit of a loss. She could head back to the office to see if anything new had shaken out on the case, or could head to the Museum to investigate what that odd feeling had been. She fiddled with the crystal pendant in her pocket. The responsible choice would, of course, be to head back to the office, but the lure of the unknown was strong.

In the end, she found herself parking at the campus and removing the pendant. It immediately pulled away from the museum, which was curious. She followed the call from the little hunk of stone, and found herself standing in front of one of the shabbier dorms on campus. Almost as if making the decision for her, a young woman in sweatpants and a weary expression was holding the door open for her, half asleep.

"Forget your keycard?" she asked blearily. Theia, much too old to be living in the dorms, rolled her eyes at the woman.

"Thank you." was all Theia said, as she followed the tug of the crystal.

Soon she found herself standing outside a dorm room. There was a sock on the door, and the room, indeed the whole floor, was strangely silent. Theia knocked and received no response. In for a penny in for a pound, she tried the door handle and found the room unlocked. As the door came open, there was a ripple of energy, like steam escaping an oven. She stepped in and the smell hit her.

A young man, wearing a janitorial jumpsuit, lay dead in a large pool of blood. Written on the floor near his hand was an ominous message, 'Nothing Remains'. Theia had a moment of clarity and took a step back. What was she doing? Why was she here? Then came the pull from the crystal. She stepped in the room, careful to not tread through the man's blood. The crystal and its presence filled her mind, and she kneeled down and put her fingers into a pile of clothes that was laid near the small sink in the room.

Her hand came away holding an amber bead. Not terribly large, it was the size of a pea, a smallish pea. She was mesmerized by it; she could feel it reaching out to her but the brand stopped it. She didn't have any magic to respond with, currently. Though impossibly tiny, her vision was drawn to the bead, and she could almost make out something frozen within it. She looked away. She knew that if she stared long enough, she would discover what was inside it, and she knew, inherently, that she should not, in fact, know what it was.

Theia reached for her satchel where she kept small drawstring bags for containing pieces of hazardous magic. Whatever force had called her here, whatever made her yearn to peer into the bead, screamed with rage. It filled her mind with searing pain. She fought through the sensation, and grabbed a runed leather pouch from her satchel. Unable to see or stop her hands from shaking, she got the bag open and dropped the bead inside. Her hands not wanting to release it, she pulled the draw strings closed.

Clarity came to her like a bucket of water to the face. She sat in the empty dorm room, no corpse, no blood, just the trappings of daily dorm life. Theia stood for the first time, noticing the strong scent of college boy assaulting her senses. She looked at the containment bag and the sealing runes were glowing under the strain of the object. Unaware of the protocols for coming out of a fugue state, she looked casually at the desk of whoever lived here. From the pictures on the desk, she determined that the dead man from her... vision? Dream? did in fact live in this unit. She remembered

Smil had been looking for a bead, and she couldn't shake the feeling that she had indeed found it.

"What the hell was that?" Theia whispered mostly to herself. Knowing that she needed to, not only find a more permanent home for the thing, but, to check in with a probably, very worried Mason, she exited the dorm room. She almost crashed into Levi Frost who was approaching the room at a run.

"Sorry... Theia?" Levi was short, and in full panic mode. Levi was the shaman for the U of A campus, and an acquaintance of Mason's. Levi's other half was a 5'10" Flamingo by the name of Bertrand, and as Theia thought of him, he manifested a few paces behind Levi.

"What's the rush?" Theia asked, trying, and most likely failing, to look nonchalant. Levi looked her up and down. While Theia wasn't at her freshest, having spent the night in federal detention, Levi looked as if he had just woken up. He wore a half open hoodie and a pair of flannel pajama pants, no shoes, and looked from Theia to the room behind her.

"The Loci was in a blind panic about something." Levi ran a hand through his aqua green hair that was mussed with sleep. "Why are you here?" Theia froze for a moment, why was she here? What was that energy that had called to her?

"Following up on a lead. Guy in question isn't home." Theia lied a tad too quickly. Bertrand squawked meaningfully and scratched at the floor.

"Well, whatever it was, seems to be gone, and in its place I find you." Levi had never really liked Theia. He and Mason had had a fling earlier in the year and Theia had been staunchly opposed, knowing, in her way, that the relationship was doomed from the start.

"What are you accusing me of, Levi?" Theia said gaining some composure.

"Nothing yet, but its not often the elemental drags me out of bed to contain something." Levi put a quieting hand on the antsy bird behind him.

"Well, it was great catching up, but I really must be on my way now." Theia said, moving to walk past the pair. Bertrand let out a birdlike, angry noise and stepped into her path.

"I can't just let you walk away until I've figured out what's going on." Levi was no slouch in the Posty community, and Theia was not playing with a full deck at the moment, so a confrontation was low on her priority list.

"Look, you know where my office is, and I'm assuming you still have Mason's number. If something comes up, and you feel sour about it, you can get a hold of me." Theia was being very reasonable, but the large bird gave no hint of relenting.

"What's in your jacket pocket?" Levi raised a hand to grab at her before a man called out from down the hall. A well-dressed man, in his late fifties, stood at the end of the hall thumping a cane on the ground for emphasis.

"Mr. Frost, why are you accosting my guest?" the older man said authoritatively. Whoever he was, Levi cowed and lowered his arm.

"Professor Taylor, I wasn't aware she was here at the behest of the faculty." Levi said, suspicious still.

"Yes, it is a private matter. We felt you would be too close to it to be impartial, so, we hired outside help. Might I remind you, while you are honor bound to the stones of the university, you are not a recognized authority on all of its dealings." The man was unrelenting in his admonishment. A few of the dorm room doors began to open, and students were peeking out bleary eyed and hung over.

"Yes, Professor Taylor, the Loci isn't panicking anymore, so, whatever was going on seems to have resolved." Levi said as Bertrand stepped out of Theia's path.

"If there is nothing further, I would like to escort the young lady to her vehicle." Professor Taylor held an elbow out for Theia, and, while in most circumstances she wouldn't have taken it on principle, she now felt accommodating to this gesture. She slid a hand into the crook of his elbow and moved to the stairs with the man.

Once they were safely in the stairwell, and well out of earshot, the older man chuckled and put his free hand on hers, abandoning the pretense of needing the cane.

"Samael sends his regards and good will, young lady." He said it so casually, Theia almost missed it.

"How did he know I would be here, and why do I feel a trap closing in?" Theia said, removing her arm from his.

"All things proceed as they should; I assure you there is no need for concern." The old man said fire dancing in his eyes.

CHAPTER

15

— • ● • —

Mason sat in the waiting room at the Hospital, not sure what else to do. He had been barred from seeing Theia at the PLEB office, and was livid about it. He figured he might as well see if Ben needed a ride, but the hospital was being shifty about releasing any details. To make matters worse, they wouldn't even let Nosam inside to wait with him. So, Mason was on edge when Benjamin walked out in an undershirt and his slacks from the day before.

"They told me there was a big man asking about me. Real intimidating. They offered to let me out the back." Benjamin said, a laugh in his voice.

"Apparently, I'm a suspicious character." Mason said, his mood instantly shifting.

"Very dubious, what will the villagers say?" Benjamin sat in a proffered wheelchair, as an orderly wheeled him to the door.

"I don't know, but if they have pitchforks, my general advice is to tell them what they want to hear."

As they stepped outside, Benjamin stood and waved good bye to the orderly. Suddenly, Nosam appeared and almost knocked him over while greeting him.

"Well, hello Stinky! Did you miss me?" Benjamin said, hugging the canine.

"Desperately." Was his only response. Mason tried not to blush, as he was doing that entirely too much this week and was determined to cut back.

"Have you heard back from Theia, at all?" Benjamin changed the subject as to not embarrass Mason any further.

"Zilch, and it's starting to piss me off. Matthew, her lawyer, promised she'd be a free woman by noon, though." Mason adjusted the brim of the baseball cap he wore, trying to keep the morning sun at bay.

"Well, these things take time. Should we get breakfast? I might never stop being hungry at this point." he said, putting a hand to his stomach.

"You're eating for two, now." Mason said with a smile. The energy demands of being two-natured can be hard to adjust to, at first. Especially for Nether bound mediums, as their other selves rarely sought out their own food.

"Oh man, I'm still getting used to the concept. I need to find some time to talk to my parents to see if they know about any spell that was on me." Benjamin squinted at the sun, and Mason offered him his hat. Benjamin politely declined.

"Chances are, they were the ones who placed it on you." Mason whistled. "The allure of a human child was pretty tempting, even before the amendment." Mason said offhandedly.

"I can't imagine them doing that, and, this is going to sound odd, but, I feel like I've always had it." Benjamin struggled with a thought. "Do you believe in reincarnation?"

"I uh..." Reincarnation was a touchy subject in the magical community. The very existence of the Nether realms made it seem implausible. Furthermore, very few people were capable of accurate past life regression. "I do." Mason said, unlocking the jeep and holding the door for Ben.

"I did a past life regression with a colleague, and, for whatever reason, the spell failed every time. It was like something was stopping it dead in its tracks." Mason circled to the far side and piled in, fiddling with his keys, before starting the car.

"Me and Theia did one." he continued, "Found out we'd been around awhile, Nosam too. We don't talk about it much, because, well..." This had been a turning point. "There was a rift... Memory before, memory after, but just a void of experience somewhere in the middle."

"Okay, but, what does that mean?" Benjamin asked without judgment.

"We think that it might be the 'Gap'." Mason said flatly.

The "Gap" was a conspiracy theory within the magical community. It was the equivalent of the 'Flat Earth Society' among humans, not a popular opinion to hold. Essentially, the belief entailed the idea that a large swath of time couldn't be accounted for in history, and, that during that lost time, the world changed radically. Humans called it the 'Mandela Effect'. Supes called it the 'Gap'.

"Well, if the two most knowledgeable post-humans I know think the Gap exists, then consider me a believer." Ben said with a smile. Mason let out a sigh of relief and started the car. Even if Ben was merely humoring him, it meant that they wouldn't quarrel on the topic. They rode on in companionable silence, and as Mason signaled to turn into a burger joint for breakfast sandwiches, his phone chirped.

"It's Theia, she wants to meet ASAP." Mason said, turning his signal off.

"But fooood…" Benjamin said sadly.

"Zoe will have something for you." Mason said, a bit of scolding in his voice.

• ● •

Theia read Mason's text stating that he was 'on the way'. The whispering bead still hissed at her mind from the bag on the passenger seat. The sooner she could be rid of it the better. As she pulled into the parking structure for her building, she noticed that there was no gate guard. Puzzled, she turned on her hazards and removed a handgun from the glove compartment. The gate was never left unmanned, and she became very uneasy. Tucking the handgun into her waistband, she got out of the truck and moved slowly towards the booth that the security guard always sat in. Almost as a reward for her paranoia, the booth appeared very strange. Gravel filled the bottom of the small room, and there was stone dust coating everything. She opened the little door on the far side, and leaned down to inspect the stone pile.

She recoiled as she turned over one of the larger pieces of stone and saw Burt's familiar face frozen into a horrified expression. He was dead. She drew her weapon, and scanned the immediate surroundings. When nothing jumped out at her, she reached over and pushed the button to open the garage. With whatever or whoever had done that to Burt out there, she felt safer in a 2-ton death machine than on foot. She parked within sight of the booth, turned the car off, and pulled her phone out. Zoe answered on the second ring.

"Unseen Forces!" Zoe said cheerily.

"Zoe, it's me. Something happened to Burt, don't let anyone in." Theia said in a hushed voice.

"Should I come down there? You shouldn't be alone." Zoe should still be recovering from yesterday, but Theia knew better than to scold her.

"No, you're just as useful as I am, after yesterday. I'm gonna wait for Mason before looking around." Zoe wished her luck and ended the call.

Theia took a breath and put her phone away, before removing the gun and checking that it was in working order. She cursed the damnable brand on her neck, and checked her mirrors for anyone standing around suspiciously. After a few minutes, she got antsy. The whispering was driving her crazy, and this shit was the last thing she needed after a long night.

The woman pretending to be Tina Randall stepped into the view of her mirrors. She stood looking at Theia's truck, a strange blank expression on her face. It seemed like she was listening for something. Slumped in the large seat as she was, it seemed that she hadn't noticed Theia yet. As Theia watched, the woman reached up to her head and removed an earring, and then, she began to change. Her hair began to undulate of its own volition and the woman grew larger. Her legs fused into a large, thick, snake's tail. Her arms became long and bony with wicked claws at the end of the fingers. Her eyes reflected oddly in the side mirror, but all of that paled in comparison to what was happening to her hair. The writhing had coalesced into constant movement, as the once blonde tresses were replaced with thin, green snakes.

"Oh, fuck." Theia whispered. Tina Randall was a Gorgon. Poor Burt's demise made a lot more sense now, and Theia suddenly felt like her handgun might as well shoot rubber bands as bullets, against such a creature. As Theia watched in horror, the snakes seemed to whisper to the 'woman' and she slid her gaze to the truck's mirror.

"Theia Morgan, bring me the bead. Do it now and do it calmly. I have no grievance with you." The creature sounded like Tina, but the voice was deeper and sounded damaged in some way.

Theia looked at her bag. While she had no clue what that bead was, she knew giving it to a Gorgon wouldn't be a smart move. And, yet, how long before Mason got there? Would Mason be able to do anything about it if he were turned to stone. Theia also wasn't sure if Mason's connection with Sonora would be enough to protect him from something this ancient.

"I'm afraid I can't do that, Tina." Theia called from her seat. She cursed her decision to leave the window rolled down, but in Arizona, the temperatures made it impossible to keep them rolled up with the AC off. You would roast.

"You do not know who you deny." Tina slithered closer to the truck, maintaining a stance of negotiation, but closing in on a sight line that Theia wasn't happy about.

"Why don't you tell me about it. I feel like, whatever this thing is, it's not your everyday kind of magical object." Theia called out, wondering if sunglasses would protect her from turning to stone.

"My sisters and I need this object to complete our work. You will be compensated if that is what you wish." The creature was getting closer. Theia reached over and rustled through her satchel, found the pouch with the bead in it, and shoved it into her jacket pocket. As the creature bumped into the back of the truck, Theia moved.

She threw the driver door open and rolled onto the hot pavement, checking her sight line from behind her gas station sunglasses, and seeing the vague shape of the huge creature indirectly. She immediately felt her muscles harden, but was careful to look at the ground as she squeezed off two shots. She heard the creature hiss, but not much else, as she crab-walked deeper into the garage, away from the creature. She couldn't be sure if she had hit the thing or not, and didn't dare look to confirm. Hopefully, the gun shots would alert someone to call reinforcements, although she doubted this would all end in a tea party.

Her breath was ragged, and she was still tired from her long day yesterday. Where was Mason, and how could she warn him about the danger in the garage? She reached for her phone, but it wasn't in her pocket. It must have fallen out when she rolled. She reached for the pouch, and found it humming and warm in her pocket.

"Foolish Mortal, you need not make an enemy of me and mine!" The creature hissed and screamed. Theia could almost feel the bead recoil at the thought of going with the monster, as if it knew what was happening.

"I, Theia Morgan, invoke safe space to negotiate terms." Theia called out, unsure where Tina was in relation to herself.

"I, Medusa of Sarpedon, grant you parley in exchange for the Bead, offering you your mortal life." The hissing of her hair was growing louder and excited.

"Medusa, who was killed by Perseus?" Theia had met creatures that claimed lofty lineages before.

"As it was in the old world." The creature said with a deep satisfaction. Well shit, if this was indeed THE Medusa she was in deep shit. Theia, now very desperate to survive this encounter, looked about for anything she could use. Up near the ceiling, in one of the corners, was one of those mirrors garage attendants used to look around corners. In it, she saw the creature slithering up the wall to her left, almost within striking distance of her. Theia almost looked up out of pure reflex, but stopped herself and instead threw herself away from the Gorgon and dashed for the far side of the garage.

There were two distinct thumps, and the crunching of a car. Medusa/Tina called out in rage and pain. There was some kind of struggle going on. She could hear that large snake tail thrashing about, stone scraping on pavement. Something was tossed into the view of that corner mirror, and Theia realized that Medusa was fighting someone. Theia didn't waste any time moving toward the stairs in the corner of the garage. She was pretty desperate to put a good solid door between her and any stony eye contact.

Theia felt more than heard something large flying through the air in her direction, and threw herself to the ground. The seven-foot, stone body of Waldorf slammed into the door she was heading towards. The door warped around his body and dust fell from the ceiling. Waldorf was not in his much smaller stature form. Currently, he resembled a fat pig-man with large bat wings. His Stone face was twisted in pain, as he pushed his massive arm against the wall, tearing the cheap door from its hinges. He smiled a horrifyingly, toothy smile at Theia before launching himself back into the fray with a war-cry.

"Did you squash her!?" Statler called out in a strained voice.

"Just, oof, missed her!" Waldorf called out, clearly in a melee with the Gorgon.

"Next time maybe...!" Statler called, an sudden impact cutting his breath short.

Theia was too afraid to find much humor in the banter, though she had never been happier to see the two blockheads than she was in that moment. Being creatures of stone, they were particularly immune to the Gorgon. She did seem to be putting up a fight, though; it was tempting to look, but she didn't dare. Theia had to do something, though. The elevators were too far away to risk accidentally glancing at the creature, and she doubt she knew the garage well enough to walk there with her eyes closed.

The bead called to her incessantly, the force of it making it hard to think. Then it struck her. If she could use her gift, this whole situation would be simple to get around; and Zoe had said earlier, that enough energy could fry the brand. The bead appeared to have plenty of stored up energy. It was a stupid plan, not knowing enough about the bead to put it to use. But, so was sitting and waiting to die. She fished the pouch out of her pocket and pulled open the top. The bead sat at the bottom of the pouch glowing in a welcoming way. It didn't seem dangerous, it wanted to help. After a moment, she pulled the strings closed again, realizing that this was what the bead wanted. It was coloring all of her thoughts with its own agenda.

"Theia, you really must get out of here!" Statler called out in a weary voice.

"She shows no signs of slowing, and we are very out of shape!" Waldorf called.

"One look is all it takes, sweet oblivion!" Medusa called maniacally.

Theia knew she had to make the stupid choice. If she didn't, Mason, Ben, the gargoyles... the cost of all of that life was too high for her to do nothing. She plucked the bead from the bag and held it up to the brand on her neck. It burned her, ALL of her. She became nothing but heat and pain, a million emotions at once, a thousand lifetimes in a second. Then nothing. She was floating in an infinite dark void.

There was a man standing in front of her. It took her a moment before she realized it was Ryan Randall. He was dressed in a suit, but, long after the party had ended, his shirt untucked, his tie loosened.

"You're probably confused." Randall said, in a surprisingly calming voice.

"A bit. You're dead." Theia stated it as a fact, but honestly after the day she had had, who could know.

"Most assuredly."

"So, I died?" Theia had expected more of the Nether, but honestly, she had never visited.

"No, this is the last little bit of me tied up in the Bead." Randall said, lighting a cigarette.

"Why, did I do something that stupid?" Theia sat back against nothing and found a kind of nothingness chair there.

"The bead will do anything to protect itself. If that meant seducing you, coloring your judgment, making you hurt others…" Randall seemed to stare off into the middle distance. "Anything to keep what it contains safe."

"What does it contain?"

"The alive me knew. All the druids took a run at guarding the thing, moving it between us randomly." He gestured, and a seemingly infinite line of men and women stretched out from his right, out of sight. "The angels and the demons didn't trust either side to hold on to it, so they left it for us to handle."

"So, what does this ominous void chat mean, exactly?" Theia leaned back in her nothing chair.

"It's your problem now." With a strong exhale and a swirl of smoke, he and all the other Druids faded from view, and Theia opened her eyes.

CHAPTER

16

• ● •

Mason pulled into the garage on full alert. Zoe had called saying there was some kind of attack going on, and it had him on edge. Benjamin seemed to be holding his breath, as they looked out on a battlefield. Huge scrapes and holes in the structure were everywhere, Statler and Waldorf were in their natural forms, large and rotund, leaning back-to-back in a crater. Mason through his hazards on and jumped out of the jeep.

"What's going on!?" He called to them. Statler rolled his head up to Mason and answered in a weary tone.

"Gorgon attack, Theia drove her off." he yawned.

"Crazy fire magic, she's passed out over there." Waldorf pointed to a vehicle.

"Can you two make it back to the office?" It wasn't safe for them to be around this much sunlight.

"Yes sir!" they said in unison, and they kind of faded and disappeared. Mason ran to the vehicle they had indicated, and found Theia splayed behind the truck, a swath of ruin and a few small fires still burning around her. Her neck was a ruin of swiftly scabbing burns, an odd pattern that almost seemed intentional. Mason could see that she was still alive.

"Wakey wakey." Mason said, gently prodding her. Theia's eyes shot open. They were bright red. Not blood shot, the iris of her eye was now a crimson red that seemed to shift back and forth as he watched.

"Did we win?" Theia asked wincing.

"Gorgon is gone. I sent the boys back to their pedestals, no body though." Mason helped her sit up.

"If she really was Medusa, she will be hurt, but still alive." Theia began to rub her neck before crying out in pain.

"Yeah, something burned you pretty good. When did you start making fire magic?" Mason touched a link on the large chain he wore, and a small orb of cool water formed above his palm. He held it to the burns, and it glowed slightly.

"It was the bead." Theia visibly relaxed into the healing waters.

"Bead?" Mason asked concentrating. Water was very far from his wheelhouse. "Smil's bead?"

"It's a very long story, filled with very stupid choices, but it got the job done."

"You? Stupid choices? We can't both make a habit of doing that, Theia." Mason said calmingly. Benjamin joined them, but stayed a bit away from them. Mason could swear there was a shimmer at Ben's shoulder, but decided not to worry about it.

"It fused with the brand, it... defended itself." Theia tried to stand, but Mason held her down with a strong hand.

"Where did you find this bead?"

"Dorm Room. The University had summoned Levi and Bertrand and everything."

"Okay, well, I'm out of Lethe water, so let's get you upstairs." Mason helped her to her feet.

"Gideon is gonna be pissed, Mason." Theia said out of nowhere.

"Well, that's pretty normal for Gideon, so who cares." Mason said with a chuckle. Theia seemed to finally notice Benjamin.

"Hey! The Professor is here!" She said pointing at him. Benjamin gave a little wave, and continued to gawk at the ruined garage.

"Yeah, I picked him up from the hospital this morning after PLEB barred me from seeing you." Mason pushed the call button for the elevator.

"You guys are gonna kiss soon." Theia was clearly a little loopy.

"Theia."

"It is my job to tell you the future you will have, not what you want to hear Mason." Theia said in a mock dire tone.

"Nosam, can you run up to Zoe and tell her to get a cot ready?" Mason said to the hound, who yipped and faded from view.

"Do you need a nap?" Theia asked.

"No, but in a few minutes you probably will." Mason guided her onto the elevator and pushed the 9th floor button.

"Magic life is a lot more confusing than it seems, from an outside perspective." Benjamin chimed in.

"To be fair, it's been a weird week so far." Mason said, holding Theia up.

"Do you think when we kill Medusa, we'll get a flying horse?" Theia asked blearily.

• ● •

Zoe closed the door to Theia's office quietly, and turned to the men in the waiting room. Mason, Benjamin, and Jackson all waited pensively.

"She'll be fine, there was some rose oil out on a side table, so it was a breeze to get her to sleep." Zoe crossed the room to her desk and slumped down into it. "What is going on?"

"I'll admit, I'm a bit confused myself. Any clarification boys?" Mason said looking to the two gargoyles.

"Well, she was fighting a Gorgon so we moseyed down there and engaged with the beast. Waldorf almost managed to crush her, but missed." Statler said cheerfully.

"Then, out of nowhere, Theia stood up, her hair was on fire, and she started throwing fireballs at the Gorgon. With her eyes closed!" Waldorf finished.

"With a wand or?" Zoe asked.

"No, her bare hands! It was like she was summoning them from somewhere!" Statler said in awe.

"Might have been hellfire! Maybe she made a dark pact with that demon you met with!" Waldorf added.

"She didn't smell infernal." Jackson said, around a mouthful of Danish.

"It might be that. She did say something about a terrible choice, and Samael does grant hellfire." Mason said pondering.

"You met with Samael?!" Benjamin said, a bit breathless.

"He was a real Chad, honestly." Jackson added.

"Regardless, why did a Gorgon attack her in the first place?" Mason waved a hand to end all of the Smil talk.

"She called it Tina once, I think." Statler supplied.

"Yeah, she smelled like that femme fatale soccer mom, too!" Waldorf chirped.

"That makes sense. We did find some pretty damning evidence at the Randall estate. Tina wasn't who she claimed to be." Zoe said, scribbling notes.

"And, she was much more interested in Ryan's ring, than in knowing whether he was alive." Mason said rubbing his chin.

"Could this be related to the missing changelings?" Benjamin asked.

"Well, the Kopis, being of Greek origin, and the Gorgon, being a Grecian monster, does seem awful coincidental." Mason consented.

"But, that doesn't explain the giant spider, or the magical evidence." Jackson added.

"Gorgons aren't known for being particularly good with general magic, but, Theia had called her Medusa. Maybe that explained the spell work." Mason said.

"I'm inclined to think that there is an accomplice, that the Kopis had been used in some powerful spell work. I didn't see any signs of magic in the garage... save Theia's." Benjamin added hesitantly.

"Okay, but what do we do now? We aren't any closer to solving any of the problems we are currently dealing with." Zoe said. She had a point. The next steps to take, were just as important as tying off any loose ends. Mason sighed and checked his watch.

"I could go see the Admin." he said dejectedly.

"I don't know if we could afford him. One of our paying clients just tried to kill us." Zoe said.

"I'm sure we could work something out." Mason knew exactly what he would want in trade, but he was dreading giving himself over to that.

"The Drove is keeping an eye out for anything weird and checking up on the changelings we know. Nothing has shaken out yet." Jackson said, hopefully then dejectedly.

"I can ask around campus. Several of the professors have contacts in the greater magical community. Someone must have noticed a Gorgon moving around." Ben said, already texting someone.

"That's a good point. How DID we not realize that soccer mom was an ancient demi-god?" Mason looked to the gargoyles.

"That confirms it for me. She must be working with a powerful witch. Hiding auras and removing destiny from things is thoroughly in the miracles department." Zoe said slapping her desk for emphasis.

"Alright, until further notice, team good guy is officially using the buddy system." Mason said, standing up. "Every vulnerable member travels with a heavy hitter. Theia is safest in the office while she recovers with the dorks." Statler giggled. "Jackson, you're with me to see the wizard, and Zoe you watch Ben's back while he makes inquiries." Everyone nodded, and Jackson even managed a small whoop of excitement. Nosam turned to Benjamin with a doggy head tilt.

"It would be safest to use the Nether to travel." he said without preamble.

"In what way!?" Zoe interjected. "Gorgon or no, its still safer to take an uber."

"Not for Benjamin now, the Consumed will keep him safe." The dog was staring at Ben intently.

"I wouldn't know how..." Benjamin said, hesitating.

"Search your feelings, you know it to be true." The hound was quoting Star Wars now.

"Alright, Yoda, don't push the boy." Mason chided. Jackson headed for the door grabbing a Danish on his way out. Zoe turned off her computer and grabbed her purse. She was already on the phone with a car service. Soon, it was just Mason, Nosam, and Ben in the room alone.

"I just want you to know..." Ben started. "Even though most of this is your fault, I'm glad it happened." He seemed determined, but clearly scared.

"I don't see how I'm to..." Mason began, but Ben closed the distance and placed a hesitant but firm kiss on Mason's lips. Initially shocked, Mason quickly melted into the kiss, softening his lips and placing a hand on Ben's waist. As soon as it started, it ended too soon. "Clearly, an Act of God." Mason said, flustered.

"I just needed to do that in case I never get the chance later." Benjamin considered. "Now that we are connected, I can be more sure how you feel about me. It's like a warmth in the back of my mind. I can sense the fear too." He moved to the door and placed a hand on the handle. "I would never reject you, Mason." With that, he was through the door and gone.

Mason stood dumbfounded for a moment, looking after the man. Nosam put his head under his hand, and Mason ruffled his fur out of habit. Well, as always, Theia had been right. It was annoying, but, like Ben had said, he could feel the man in the back of his mind, the tender emotion resting there. It felt familiar and exciting.

"Well, as far as signs go, that one was pretty clear." Nosam said finally.

"Jackson is waiting for us." Mason said, adjusting his clothes and walking to the door determined.

CHAPTER

17

—— — • ● • — ——

Theia was definitely asleep; she was sure of that. Why she was standing under a tree, she wasn't 100% clear on. It could be a dream. She'd never dreamed about this particular tree before, but there was always a first. She looked about and there were a lot of other trees, but for some reason this one seemed very important. Her eyes fell on three crones, very large 9-foot crones standing around a stone well. They didn't seem to acknowledge her, and as she watched, one turned a crank to bring a bucket to the lip of the well. Another pulled it to her with a crook, before holding it to the third crone, who moved to the important tree, with large confident strides, and sprinkled the contents of the bucket with her massive hands, like rain down upon it. She then turned, strode back to the well, and each of them rotated so as to share the burden of the tasks equally.

It was clear to Theia that she was supposed to interact with these women. It was a dream after all, and you rarely got anywhere in dreams by just watching. She thought back to a book on dream symbolism Gideon had given her. It had been a sweet gift, but, Oracles rarely dream, and often the symbolism is pretty literal. The book had said that crones signified wisdom and foresight, both of which she could use a bit of. It hadn't said anything about how large they could be, however.

"Hello, my name is Theia of Cassandra. May I ask where I am?" Theia called out trying to sound momentous, and maybe a tad important.

"We know of you mortal." Each word emanated from a different giantess, but, so seamlessly it sounded like one voice.

"You have me at a disadvantage then..." Theia replied.

"You are at the center of the cosmos. We are Urðr, Verðandi, and Skuld. We tend The Tree." They continued with their work, their voices reaching her easily, despite their height.

"The Norns?" Theia knew of the Norns. They were Norse deities, and were said to shape human destiny.

"That is a name given to us, yes." they said in unison.

"Why am I here?" Theia said, moving closer, but avoiding the well-worn path to the tree.

"You've been pulled from your path." They seemed to consider for a moment. "Perhaps, onto the correct path... unclear the waters are."

"Is this about the Bead?" She touched the raw scars on her neck left by the trinket.

"Herald, it is what you are now. A herald of an end."

"End of what?" Theia hadn't considered how obscure her subconscious was going to be.

"There are many ends. Too many for any one Cosmos to contain, so, the Architects fashioned many worlds. For each to have an end." They stopped their work and turned their attention to her.

"End, as in end of the cosmos?" Theia didn't like the sound of that.

"You know of the ends, many are foretold. You have even seen one."

Theia was reminded of the horrible vision Gideon had unintentionally shared with her.

"What does that have to do with the Bead? How can I be in possession of it, if it's not of my world?" Theia pressed.

"So many questions mortals have. You should be happy. You continue to serve a purpose. Do not question it." Skald tutted. At least, she thought it was Skald, as it was hard to tell which was which when they spoke.

"If I'm to be a Herald, I have to understand." Theia demanded. This made the Norns laugh.

"The Architects grew fond of what they had created, and many of them did not want their cosmos to end. The ends had already been determined, however. So, many of them sought the boon of their siblings, and had them spirit away the ends and place them somewhere safe."

"The bead is the Apocalypse?" Theia asked incredulous.

"An, not the." They corrected. "From another Cosmos, some other architect's end."

"The Architects are... Gods?"

"Nothing so petty as that. Gods are born from the imaginations of men. Used to shape what they recall from when all the worlds were one. Gods cannot cross the borders."

"If Gods can't cross into another cosmos, how did I get someone else's bead?"

"We are not yet sure how it is you were able to find the bead. But, all Architects will care for another's bead. They are too dangerous to keep in the cosmos they were meant for."

"So, if I understand, some alternative universe put their apocalypse into this bead, and then chucked into our universe?" Theia said, gesturing the actions as she described them.

"It is possible that is how it happened." The Norns conferred silently. "We are but Gods, we cannot be sure what transpired before we came into being. "

"So, you don't know how it happened, why it happened, or if it should have happened, but it's my problem now?" Theia was trying not to be annoyed, but there were limits.

"It seems things have shifted for you. Something has drawn you from the threads that were laid out. The bead is not of our making, nor under our control, and, as such, you are on your own outside of this gathering." They were at least being clear about what wasn't their problem.

"Okay, so, do I wake up now or...?" Theia shifted her feet. The Norns grew silent and returned to their well.

• ● •

Ben was elated to be back in familiar territory. The car had dropped him and Zoe off on University Blvd., and the walk felt wonderfully normal. Only one of the professors he had texted had responded, and he was meeting them at his office. Ben didn't know how to start a casual conversation with Zoe, whom he didn't really know that well, without swerving into the dramatic events of the day before. She, by rights, seemed pretty determined to stink eye every person or thing that looked at them suspiciously.

"So, did you attend the university?" He tried, as she seemed very familiar with the route.

"Before I got married, yeah, Theater major." She said smiling warmly.

"I studied Art History before I got involved in Magical Studies." Ben had always loved how diverse art studies had been. If you grew tired of styles and techniques, you could shift focus and study history or cultural relevance. Then, when the university started teaching actual magic, he had been first in line to change majors.

"You're going for a Doctorate, right?" Zoe asked.

"I was. I'm not sure if that's an option now." The upper echelons of magical studies were very political, and staunchly human.

"After my oldest was born, I let myself prioritize parenthood, gave up on school. While I don't have any regrets, I'm not sure I would make the same decision now." Zoe said in a knowing tone.

"If I can make it work I will, but I might not get a choice." Ben could feel his companion spirit on the edge of his awareness, a cold and constant presence.

"You know, I don't think Mason noticed, but you might have more problems than you think." Zoe said is a serious tone.

"Great, please enlighten me." Ben said with a sigh.

"Too early to tell. If I'm wrong, it will only serve to confuse you. Let me sit on it for now, as annoying as that is. Indulge me." She winked which was charming enough that he didn't scream.

"Well, I'll try not to obsess about that. I didn't know you had a kid." He shifted the conversation as best he could.

"Two, actually, Lyra and Lynnete. They are living with their father in Oregon. Teenage rebellion, I'm assuming" she said, with a bittersweet twinge to it.

"Must be hard." Was all he said.

"It is, but I have the agency and that keeps me plenty busy." Zoe said. "I mean, Mason is basically a child himself, so you get to use those motherly instincts." Zoe laughed at that and slapped him on the arm, a bit too hard. "He's a good friend, and an even better man. His childlike wonder is part of that." Zoe said reverently.

They walked in silence for a time. The ice had broken, and both were thinking a tad too deep. Ben turned his thoughts to the quest at hand, and tried not to think about his future.

Professor Wooly was one of the only non-humans at the university. He had been hired because humans had completely failed to figure out Oneiromancy. With that in mind, they had little choice but to employ someone else familiar with the realm of dreams. So, Wooly, who was wholly non-human, had been hired with much controversy. His classes were popular, however, and he was well liked by the students at the college, even though he could have a frightening countenance. Ben had grown to know him quite well, as he crafted charms for him on occasion. Being a Mara, Wooly was mostly invisible to vanilla humans, so Ben often crafted illusions for him so that he could be perceived by others. They often had many a laughter filled luncheon, as they fine tuned his 'human disguises', as well as other more fantastical visages.

"Something's up." Zoe said sharply. Sure, enough as they walked along the path, mist had begun swirling at their feet. Fog wasn't completely unheard of in the valley, but on a bright sunlit day, in over 90 degree weather, it was very unlikely. As they watched, the mist grew thicker along the ground. Soon, when they couldn't see the path ahead any longer, tension began to run through them.

"What is it?" Ben was hoping some Practitioner had just left a spell running, and this was a side effect of that, but Zoe seemed much more concerned.

"If I didn't know better, I'd say someone was forming an Avalon." She said grimly. Avalons were mostly a theory within the academic magic community, named for the eponymous mists from the Canterbury Tales. Legend and theory both agreed that most supernatural creatures operating in the material world were tied to one of the mirror realms. There were, in fact, several creatures native to the first world. These creatures, at least the strong ones, were capable of forming hidden lairs and homes by severing parts of the material realms into a pocket dimension under their control. These lairs were "Avalons", and if what Zoe was saying was true, he was witnessing something very few people ever get to see. Mostly, because outsiders rarely survived these visits.

"Isn't that very bad, Zoe?" Benjamin said, becoming nervous.

"Oh yes, extremely. If the intent is to suck us into it." Zoe was removing things from her purse and moving them into her jacket pockets.

"How likely is that?" Ben felt very naked having no dedicated tools on hand.

"As far as I understand, if you can see the mist its already much too late to do anything about it." As if on cue, the mist turned into a proper thick fog, a sheer white wall of roiling vapor. Zoe grabbed Ben's hands protectively, and, after a few moments, the fog began to recede again.

They now stood in a stone hallway, about 10 feet long on all sides, torches on the walls flickered, creating extreme shadows. The stones were even, and comprised the floor, walls, and ceiling. They became very disorientated. The smell of stale air and stagnant waters filled the air, along with another, more subtle smell that Benjamin couldn't place at first.

Benjamin started to panic, feeling that the only anchor he had to the world was Zoe's warm hand, but then, he felt a steady touch on his shoulder. It was cold but solid, and as he looked over his shoulder he saw her, the Consumed. She hovered about a foot off the ground, dripping a black ichor from her gaping bite wounds, her empty eye sockets staring forward to some unseen horizon. He could feel the thread of power between them; through it, his warmth flowed into the ravaged woman and her cold, calm strength flowed into him.

"Oh well, that's a look." Zoe said, obviously able to see, and become unsettled by the Consumed.

"Death is rarely glamorous." The Consumed said aloud without moving her 'mouth'.

"There is glamour, and then there is pure horror." Zoe seemed to realize how rude she was being, "No offense."

"None taken, danger here." The Consumed 'said'. Ben reached for his magic, and found his senses being pulled to the Consumed. A cold well of energy laid there. "Yes, my love, I can help you, but my influence is not vast here." She must be reading his thoughts.

"So, we have to rely on Zoe?" Ben tried not to sound panicked as he said it.

"She sits upon the veins of the earth, but you are capable of more than you know." The Consumed ran her fingers along his shoulders. "When you begin to fly, you will not feel afraid any longer."

"No one tell Nosam, but I really wish you had bound yourself to the Second World." Zoe was wrapping her hands in some kind of yarn.

"Zoe, I don't think we have the liberty to look this particular gift horse in the mouth." Ben said trying not to chastise.

"True, true, so this is either some kind of dungeon, or maybe catacombs?" Zoe whispered a short incantation and copper filaments in the yarn began to brightly glow.

"Labyrinth..." the Consumed provided cryptically.

"Now, why would someone put a maze in our way?" Ben ran a hand along the wall. It felt very solid, and that added to his anxiety.

"Death blooms here." the Consumed provided.

"Okay, well, no one has every escaped a death trap by talking at it." Zoe stepped forward with a confidence Ben had not seen before. He removed a sharpie from his jacket pocket, and moved to draw a seeking spell on the stone wall.

"A moment, Zoe." He began drawing the circle and runes, mostly from memory. As he did so, he felt the cool magic of the Consumed flow into him, and his recollections gained clarity. He could see everything with almost photographic clarity, remembering many more complex theories and combinations. He met the eyes of the Consumed.

"Memory is the curse of the forgotten." she hissed.

"Well, that is quite handy." Ben finished the circle with a flourish, and it began to glow. Ben prepared himself for the feeling of being drained, the cost of even this simple of a spell, and found that while he could feel a pull, it was barely noticeable.

"Human no longer." the Consumed said with what could be considered a laugh. Ben tried not to dwell on the thought as he waited for the spell to finish.

As the light grew and then changed, a crude chalk outline looking very much like a photo-negative or cartoonish version of himself manifested on the wall. It stood regarding him blankly.

"I need to find the exit of the Avalon we currently inhabit." As soon as he had finished the sentence the image dispersed for an agonizing minute before reforming and pointing to the right.

"Well, Captain we have our heading." Zoe said continuing in the way she had started.

"Lead us." Ben said, in an authoritative voice, and the image began to walk briskly along the wall, doing its best to stay in sight. Ben was beginning to calm down a bit, when a loud bellow began to shake the walls of the hall. Then, an eerie silence settled back in.

"Shit..." Zoe added.

CHAPTER

18

• ● •

Mason was pensive as he drove down Aviation Highway. Jackson was fidgeting, and trying to think of a way to broach the subject of the strange middle stare Mason was giving the stretch of road ahead of them. Nosam made a throat clearing sound, impressive for a dog, and Mason looked at the rear view mirror to meet his gaze.

"Sorry, a lot on my mind." Mason said to Jackson a tad off-handedly.

"I mean, it has been an eventful few days. I mean, we just found out that the fey are basically babysitters for the celestial realms." Jackson trailed off, still struggling with the concept.

"If I'm honest, it's not that surprising and might even be a tad misleading." Mason squared his shoulders and refocused on the road. "It might be that the fey appropriated an existing realm, and in Demonic fashion, changed the narrative to make themselves seem more powerful. It's much more likely they only ,created the systems and balances within the fey courts than the entire realm and the people who live inside of it." Mason had met a few "Gods" in his day and, while powerful, none had ever really impressed on him that they could create an entire world. They claimed to sure, but he'd always wondered why they didn't do more, if they were as powerful as they claimed.

Jackson nervously opened the glove compartment and closed it again. "It's just hard to think of the Fey monarchy paying lip service to anyone."

"Of the Gods I've met personally, most of them were on a power level akin to the more powerful monarchs in the Deep Fey. The more local kingdoms, however could probably be bullied by other supes." Mason gestured for Jackson to leave the glove box alone. He then turned off into a mostly residential neighborhood and started looking at street signs. Mostly out of habit, as his general sense of the city meant he was rarely lost.

"Smil just seemed so confident; it's hard to rectify that with my old world view."

"The only thing I know for certain, Demons are the creators of Narcissism. Don't let it get to you, it's what he wanted to do." Mason said, turning onto a very unassuming street and stopping at a very rundown house.

"This is the Admin's house?" Jackson said, taking in the duct taped windows and the lawn in need of attention.

"Books and covers, my friend." Mason held the door open for Nosam, who glided through it like a wisp of smoke.

"It would be bad for business if people could tell something strange was going on next door." Mason paused, "You know this isn't something you should talk about, right?"

"I understand discretion, Mason, I am Leporine." It was a good point; his people had been the most successful of the shifters to sail under PLEB's radar. Most people in Tucson had met a were-hare, but few knew they had.

"Just doing my due diligence." Mason rang the doorbell, which made no sound, but then again, the Wizard already knew they were there. The door buzzed and Mason pushed his way into the house. While it might have looked shabby on the outside, inside the house looked like it had been in a magazine. Pristine, clean, and well decorated, and containing the trappings of a man with many hobbies and a fair bit of success. The entire home thrummed with magic, but not in a way that was immediately recognizable. Almost like the hum of an idle TV, or the ambient buzz of computer servers.

"In the kitchen!" came a familiar voice, and Mason walked in the direction of the kitchen, Jackson following close behind. A deceptively young looking man stood there, in a Dungeons and Dragons shirt and a pair of comfy shorts. He ran a hand through his dirty blonde hair, while clinking a spherical ice cube into a whiskey glass and shaking a tumbler.

"Hello Cole, we were hoping to talk with you," Mason gestured to Jackson, "This is my associate..."

"Jackson Thumper, mate and second in command to the current Lepus of the Tucson Drove, Artemisia Thumper. Who isn't even a shifter. There is a good story there for sure." Cole said leveling his piercing blue eyes on Jackson. Cole made it his business to know who everyone was. Jackson was clearly taken aback by the casual mention of his wife.

"Yes, and you remember, Nosam."

Having downed his cocktail, Coles eyes lit up and he beckoned the hound to him. Nosam, if not used to this behavior in humans, was very amicable to the attention in supes, and padded over to him directly.

"So, Mason, I know you don't drink, but would you like anything Jackson, I've been working on a few cocktails that might appeal to shifters." He said, in between nonsense baby talk and rhetorical questions of 'who's a good boy' directed at Nosam. Jackson perked at the offer and looked to Mason.

"Better make it a virgin, we are working, and while shifters have notorious constitutions, I'm sure Cole is capable of getting you sloshed."

Cole's kitchen was amazing. Gadgets and knickknacks filled the space without it being cluttered or busy, and he had quite the impressive bottle nook in one corner.

"Yes, what he said." Jackson replied to Cole. Cole wordlessly set about the task of resetting and then crafting a very pretty and fragrant cocktail for Jackson, with the practiced finesse of a bar tender in a detective movie. As he added a perfectly spiraled lemon peel into it, he finally seemed to grow curious as to their visit.

"So, I take it this isn't a social call." He walked from the kitchen to the back half of the property, expecting them to follow. Even Mason, who had seen the Admin's office on several occasions, was still taken aback by the size and scope of it. The size of a large banquet room, the space was organized into hobbyist sections. One here for music, there for whatever craft had taken his fancy, and one filled with maps from different decades, all with bright red marker on them. Of particular dread, was a large table in the center of the room, seemingly unassuming, but Mason was well aware of its true purpose and why it was so well lit. But, all of these items paled in comparison to his immense computer desk. Taking up most of the far wall with several monitors and buzzing server towers, and a very comfortable looking chair that Cole had already slipped into.

"No, not today." Mason said, trying to hide how impressed he was at the space.

"Is this an ESP, Eclipse Guitar, Exhibition Limited Original Series, Buckeye Burl?!" Jackson exclaimed, holding his hand out towards the instrument, as if the ugly guitar was radiating life sustaining energy.

"Yes, I needed something to practice with." Cole said sipping his cocktail while staring at a screen that was streaming code. Jackson,overwhelmed, sipped his own colorful drink and did another double take.

"This is wonderful!" he exclaimed. Mason turned toward him and gestured to him to at least attempt some decorum. Jackson blushed a bit and straightened up.

"Mr. Oxford, we were hoping you would have information for a case we are working on." Mason started.

"Really, Mason, you can call me Cole. We aren't in any way strangers." Cole admonished.

"Cole, do you know of any reason for, or the whereabouts of a Gorgon in the city?" Mason adopted a casual tone.

"Nothing overt. Someone has been moving very quietly throughout the city, causing all kinds of trouble. I haven't been able to pin down who or what, as they either avoid computers and cameras, or aren't comfortable with them. That being said, whoever it was, is not alone." Cole said, with only a tiny bit of dramatic flair.

"What makes you say that?" Mason hadn't even considered it could be a larger group. Maybe, a witch helping with magic shenanigans, but he assumed they would be local.

"You know my price." Cole turned in his swivel chair, looking at the prominent table in the center of the room.

"Cole." Mason began to protest.

"It's not a death sentence Mason just a few hours of your time. You used to love it." Cole said melancholy in his voice.

"I just don't want to get sucked in again, the agency keeps me so busy." Mason continued.

"One session and I can get you CCTV footage of my theories." Cole steepled his fingers under his chin, knowing he had won.

"Fine, one session." Mason relented.

"Be clear, Mason." Cole prodded.

"Oh, Mighty Dungeon Master, mayhap, I, a humble man, join you in the thrills of adventure to be held within your perilous tome?" Mason recited with reluctant enthusiasm.

"Perfect! We have a DnD stream on Sunday. I'll post you as a guest star." Cole began typing furiously.

"Wait a minute, I don't know about being on camera." Mason began to blush, his face approaching the red of his eyebrows.

"It's done, Mason." Cole said with a final dramatic key push.

"Dungeons and Dragons?" Jackson looked at both men, bewildered by the exchange.

Cole typed several commands into a second keyboard, and the whirring of a large printer, that couldn't be seen, began working. Shortly thereafter, Cole stood, presenting a stack of glossy 5 by 7 photographs to Mason who began to peruse them.

"These are the most likely individuals. Between not being recognized by Franklin, or having a strange effect of the cameras themselves, I suspect they are the most likely candidates."

"Franklin?" Jackson asked.

"My system," Cole gestured to the room around them. "I thought about doing the whole reversed name thing like Mason did, when Franklin and I were bonded, but Franklin sounded better to me than Eloc Drofxo." As if on cue, the monitors all blinked and crowds of people appeared, waving hello enthusiastically.

"Your computer is alive?" Jackson asked flabbergasted. The Drove and the Were-Hares in general didn't mingle much with the greater supe community, preferring to maintain their autonomy and ability to blend with humans.

"Much like our Shaman friend here, I am also dual-natured. I share my soul with Franklin, who is kind of an... Exspiravit en Machina." Cole provided.

"So, you are a... computer shaman?" Jackson shook his head.

"I think I prefer the term 'Digital Wizard', or my unofficial title 'The Admin'. I don't wanna get bogged down with any particular nomenclature as we are relatively new." Cole said typing away.

"There are others?" Jackson said his voice wavering.

"Our numbers are growing; the internet is new, sure, but it is by far the fastest growing mirror realm." Cole was printing out a character sheet, and Mason felt dread and worry at facing, yet again, his tabletop addiction.

"Wait, you can GO INTO the internet?!" Jackson exclaimed, eliciting a sigh from Mason.

"Not exactly, but I can interface with it in a… primal sense." Cole smiled smugly and flicked out his arms. Data and media of various stripes began streaming over the monitors, and they could see the data playing out in Cole's eyes. Jackson was gob smacked and looked on with rapture and awe.

"Cole." Both Jackson and Cole looked to Mason. "This picture is blurry." He held up one of the glossy photos and the person in it looked like they had been diffused with water. Cole looked almost offended for a moment, as he took the photo and slumped back into his chair.

"Yes, whoever THAT is can somehow obscure themselves from even the best cameras." Cole turned to his computers and typed what seemed to be fast gibberish. Several images from various angles appeared all with a similar obscuring effect.

"If you can't recognize her face, how can you…"

"Find her?" Cole interrupted Jackson's thought. "That's just it, the software IS recognizing her. It just can't properly record her image. Franklin knows who she is but can't convey it." Cole pointed to one of the screens that was an ATM video of the person's face.

"Definitely our witch." Mason said tersely.

"She'd have to be an Admin like me. Magic can't fool machines." Cole admonished.

"If she can rewrite her fate, Cole, messing with a picture of herself hardly seems difficult in comparison." Mason held the photo up to the light.

"Can't you just ask the photo to describe her?" Jackson asked. Cole and Mason looked at him dumbfounded. Mason made an odd face and looked at the photo again.

"That's... not a bad idea." Mason grinned like a mad man. "But it would have to be a photo with a spiritual significance, or barring that, taken with an old well-loved camera."

"Significance doesn't have to mean happy, lovey dovey feelings, right?" Cole asked typing away.

"No, negative emotion can also rouse the anima, but for more modern items it has to be protracted or frequent." Mason shrugged. Cole struck the enter key with gusto and a similarly blurry photo of a person driving filled the displays.

"Like a red-light camera?" Cole said triumphantly.

"Like a red-light camera." Mason smiled.

CHAPTER

19

• ● •

Theia shot awake in a cold sweat, her heart pounding, and a searing pain in her head. She hated magical dreams, they were dramatic and disrupted your whole day. Then, without so much as a 'mother may I', real life comes rushing back to you. Theia touched her neck. The brand was still hot and painful. She reached for her gift; it was there waiting for her, but it was painful to use. She could flex it sure, but it was the kind of sore that made you think that maybe you shouldn't. With a deep sigh she sat up. She was in her office, the scent of roses and sleep sweat everywhere. She patted the cot thanking it for a job well done.

She looked over, and Zoe had set her files on her desk, with several colored tabs sticking out the sides. She knew it was a subtle reminder that she should stay in bed and get caught up on paperwork. Theia sighed and rolled the little tray table into a position, so that she could stay in bed, propped up by pillows, and still read over the papers. The whole process was kind of nostalgic. Before Zoe had joined the team, Theia and Mason had almost lost the business to less than stellar record keeping. One particular morning, Mason began screaming at a file box of receipts and demanded they hire a secretary.

It had seemed like such a risk, an expense, almost an invasion, to the steady rhythm they had formed. Thank the Gods they had though. Now, Theia couldn't even imagine the office without Zoe's incense or cooling teacups strewn about. From a strictly business standpoint, she had also legitimized them to the Witch community, who were inherently distrustful of other Posties. Even as she initialed her 30th tiny little line, she still managed to smile thinking about it.

"Usually, the papers piss you off." Waldorf's voice startled her, and just about made her pass out all over again. She shot a look at the ceiling and found him wedged in a corner where he could watch the doors and windows.

"Why are you in my office?" Theia asked, once she had regained her composure.

"I was politely invited to do so, so that I could make sure you didn't expire whilst sleeping." The gargoyle said in a pleasant tone.

"Perish the thought." Theia said smiling despite herself.

"Eh, while novel, dying in your sleep would be a letdown." Waldorf went silent. Gargoyles were strange creatures. Talking with them made you feel a bit crazy. They never moved their lips, or breathed, or gave any indication that they were anything other than a statue, unless they were trying to kill you of course.

Theia touched the brand again, and memories flooding back to her, vague, sudden, violent. Yet, why couldn't she remember the exact details? How was the bead powerful enough to drive off something like Medusa? What was living inside her? The Norns had only confused her more. They were fading from her memory quickly, too, which, is why it's a terrible practice to be conveyed information in a dream.

Theia got halfway through the stack of files, before she was fed up and pushed the table to the side. She was not an invalid. She planted her socked feet on the plush carpet of her office and found them solid under her.

"Alright Theia, let's figure out how we can help the others." She stood and crossed the room to her silenced phone, no messages, no calls. She wasn't sure what she had expected to find, as her team had wanted her to rest. Well, if they weren't going to include her, she had her own ways of forcing the issue. Theia crossed the small room to her cabinet. She removed a Tucson road map, before remembering that her pendulum was still in the truck. She sighed deeply, and checked her pockets for the keys, not finding them either. They had either borrowed the truck, or hid the keys to thwart her.

Regardless, she spread the map out on her desk and stared at it. She could, of course, just check the tapestry. The use of her tools wasn't strictly necessary, however, it hurt to use her gift, so she didn't want to make it worse. She cast her eyes about her office. She had a million little baubles from past cases, small mementos, books, some emergency accessories, and her overnight bag. She unzipped the bag and felt around in the side pocket. Sure enough, there was a pendulum there, that she had purchased at a convention she and Zoe had attended in Dallas. She had bought it intending to replace her old one, but had forgotten all about it.

Smiling triumphantly, she plopped down in her work chair, and wrapped the pendulums chain around her fingers. She licked her fingers and ran them across the metal circle sealing it closed. She focused on Mason, and let a trickle of her gift flow into the crystal at the end of the chain. It pulled with a sudden force and plopped thoroughly on the Admin's house. That made a lot of sense, they probably should have brought him in to all of this from the beginning. He definitely would have seen PLEB coming. Well, as she didn't want to get pulled into a lengthy board game, she decided to leave the Admin to Mason. She let her thoughts shift to Zoe, and the pendulum went limp. Theia blinked at the stone. While this could mean a few different things, none of them were ideal. Either she wasn't in Tucson, or, Theia was being blocked by something else, or else she was...

Theia slammed her hands on the desk and began pacing the room, the release of the magic circle on her desk making the room smell of ozone. Worried, she turned to Waldorf, and even though his countenance didn't slip in the slightest, she could feel him get nervous.

"What does that look mean?!" Waldorf said with a panic.

"If you kill him, at least do it where I can watch!" Statler called out in a whine.

"Where did Zoe go?" Theia asked casually, trying to cut the tension that was pouring from her.

"Which one is that?" Waldorf attempted.

"Waldorf…"

"Zoe said you're not supposed to leave…" Waldorf protested. Theia waited patiently.

"Try to describe how she's torturing you!" Statler cried from the outer office. Theia felt a violent urge shoot through her. It surprised her; she'd never been a pacifist, but her anger was usually more subtle.

"And no offense, but Zoe is a lot scarier than you." Waldorf said, almost as a challenge. Heat flared in the brand, and shot down her arm which erupted in bright orange flame that reeked of burning chemicals. Theia, who had only a basic recollection of the Medusa fight, did the only thing a sane person could do at the moment. She began losing her shit.

"MELT ME!" Waldorf called out in ecstasy.

"Wait for me!" Statler responded.

Theia, unable to even really register the idiots, was desperately trying to get her jacket off. Her panic and adrenaline seemed to feed the flame, and it just grew bigger and the smell grew stronger. She had a moment of clarity and took a breath, letting memory flood into her.

• ● •

She was sitting on grass, it was cool, but the air was dry and oppressive. The sound of artificial waterfalls could be heard burbling, as well as, the laughter of some unseen toddler. There was the smell of stagnant water, duck shit, grass, trees. Mason's voice reached her.

"Energy doesn't understand emotion, intention or even control." Mason said pacing behind her. "Energy just flows down whatever channel is in front of it." He sat cross legged in front of her, a magic circle drawn in the earth between them. His eyes were the vibrant purple of Nosam and they overlapped into her memory.

"Okay, but what does that have to do with my runes exploding." Theia asked annoyed.

"Magic is energy. Emotion is a conduit for magic." Mason/Nosam said. "So, when we get frustrated that a poorly drawn rune isn't working correctly, the rune, which is meant to be the channel for the energy, finds an easier channel in emotion. Thus, the energy is released without the structure or control of the rune."

"Okay, but you don't even do Runic magic!" Theia said, the runes of the circle beginning to glow again.

"No, but the principle is close enough to what me and Nosam do." He said, in only a slightly condescending tone. "Plus, with our sparkly new bond, I can kinda get a sense for what you're doing." He took his stick and drew the one rune he knew really well. It represented unraveling and was primarily used to undue Runic magic. Annoyingly, he drew it perfectly. He then held out his hand/paw and energy flowed into the rune. The other runes in the circle, those drawn correctly, began to fade or unravel.

"Okay, but being shown and understanding are..." Mason held up a finger to stop her. She could feel the angry memory come forth, the emotion build, and, even as she watched, the rune began to spark and sputter as if dripping water on to a fire.

"See, the emotion is more conductive, so the magic just pours out." He said lowering his hand and opening his eyes. "You should really talk to my friend Ben; he is kind of a whiz at this stuff."

• ● •

Theia took hold of the situation and began breathing slower. Without quick access to a circle, she just kind of imagined one in her mind, a perfect circle made out of paper. Fire magic loved paper, and even though there was no actual paper present, the flame went out, now channeled in her mind's eye. When she finally felt calm enough to open her eyes again, she realized that both Statler and Waldorf were on the floor in front of her, arguing about who should get reduced to oblivion first.

"Enough boys." Theia said. The Gargoyles grew quiet.

Alright, so she had magic now, that part hadn't been a fever dream. Could the bead do other things? When she got annoyed with Waldorf, had that felt like danger to it? Was it intelligent? The number of things that she really didn't know about the bead, which was now living inside her, could hurt a lot of people. She, despite the pain, let the tapestry spread out before her, the threads un-spooling into the vastness of the void of her third eye.

Immediately she saw it, the odd pattern. The bead tugged at the tapestry around her, warping and mangling it. Sure, she could still see the threads outside the warping, but the connections to where she currently was, were almost impossible to read. She felt adrift in a way she hadn't in a long while. This meant she would only be able to see the strongest most obvious threads, the more subtle threads were too mangled to make sense of. It was kind of like someone had spilled water on a sheet of notes, the bold bits in sharpie weren't affected, but all the scribbling in the margins was unreadable. She opened her eyes again to see the gargoyles curled up looking like ugly statues placed randomly in the room.

"You guys, okay?" She asked.

"We just wanted to say... mind you, it's very hard for a gargoyle to admit, that we are glad you're the one who took us in." Waldorf said sincerely.

"And we're only kidding about hoping you die." Statler finished in his odd falsetto.

"What brought all of this on?" Theia asked not wanting to seem ungracious.

"Things are changing." Statler remarked.

"Fleshies take longer to see it, but we've been around long enough, seen enough to know." Waldorf said pensively.

"Change tends not to include us."

"We appreciate you making sure we got a perch."

"And plenty of opportunities to get killed."

"Oh man, so many."

Theia looked at the hideous creatures, cute with the right mindset. Gargoyles were one of the true immortals. The only way they could die is if something destroyed them very thoroughly. And like most immortals, they craved new experiences. In Statler and Waldorf, this craving seem to manifest as a weird death fascination. Theia sighed despite herself.

"You're welcome, wish I could do more." Theia placed a hand on Statler's oddly warm stone head.

"I mean, you could start dating again." Waldorf chirped.

"Yeah, a real Hannibal Lecter type." Statler supplied.

"Some guy who we'd have to protect you from!"

"With magical stone disintegration powers."

They devolved into their wild fantasies, all but ignoring Theia. She looked down at her coat, which was not even singed, and wondered at how much things were changing. She didn't trust a lot of people in the world, and even fewer fully trusted her in return. Being able to summon apocalypse fire wasn't going to help her overall image. She needed advice, and fast, and from someone she could more than trust. Perhaps someone she believed in. She took out her phone and did a quick time conversion, it was about 9 pm in Japan. She opened up a Wi-Fi chat app in order to save them both money.

'Hey, really need a consult' She typed. 'You available tonight?' Theia watched the phone for a moment, and sure enough the tiny '…' appeared.

'You in Tokyo?!' She responded.

'No, but if you're available, I think I can make it happen.'

'I'll start lighting candles.'

Theia closed the app and moved to her contact list. It took her a minute to find the text chain that was Matthew, as she was terrible at saving phone numbers, but she eventually figured it out. She didn't really want to waste time, so she called him.

"Theia, wasn't expecting to hear from you so quickly." Matthew's rich baritone reached her.

"So, if I'm understanding, it's your job to keep me out of jail, right?" She tried not to smile, as her plan was at the forefront of her mind.

"Not exactly." He was already suspicious.

"Well, being seen fleeing the country wouldn't be a good look, right?" Theia let his heavy sigh play out over the phone.

"No, it would not."

"Then, I need a very discreet ride." she said grinning maniacally.

CHAPTER

20

—— • ● • ——

Zoe had been the seasoned adventurer in the group, even counting one really bad company picnic with a few too many zombies. That was her old life, though. Since joining Unseen Forces, she had really embraced her craft and organized many filing cabinets,and brewed countless cups of coffee. However, without warning, here she was, facing down certain doom in a damp Avalon.

"Okay, don't panic." Zoe said, mostly to herself.

"Avalons can only be crafted by strong creatures, yes?" Ben was falling back on facts to remain calm, and that's why he wasn't panicking.

"Exactly..." Zoe said, only a bit of panic in her voice.

"And, I can count the number of creatures that would choose a maze to hang out in on one hand." Ben continued.

"It's definitely a minotaur." Zoe recognized bull noises.

"That's just it. The Minotaur, if it existed at all, was a one-off creature. Capital M unique, there are no hordes of bull people running about." Ben began, jogging after his tracer spell.

"Alright, now we know exactly how fucked we are." Zoe said, and began gathering ambient energy from the Avalon. It was thick as molasses, and that just made it harder to draw into herself. She had never been the best at it, in the first place. Her sister was a master, and was able to create a lance of ice in a sandstorm. Zoe, however, struggled to keep her lights on.

"My point is, what are the odds that the Minotaur and the Medusa are both in Tucson, both trying to kill us all, and no one has noticed?" Ben said, becoming breathless.

"Oh no, definitely related." Zoe squeaked a bit of victory as a tiny orb of flame popped into existence. She began forming a second.

"What would it take?" Ben said looking at her. Zoe was taken aback.

"What would what take?" She lost her concentration and the second tiny orb fizzled. She started over, wishing she had taken Mason up on those runs.

"To hide from an entire city, magically speaking. I don't know of a way to do it runically." Benjamin made a sudden turn, and Zoe lost the first orb.

"Technically, anything is possible with pure magic. With enough ritual or raw power, you could make the moon disappear if you wanted to, despite everyone expecting to see the moon." Zoe said, giving up on the fireballs, and removing a pair of knitting needles from her bag, she tucked them haphazardly into her hair.

"What do you mean?" Ben asked starting to sound a bit out of breath.

"Well, now hardly seems the time, but, the more real or expected something is, the harder it is to hide. It's harder to hide yourself from someone who is looking for you, but, it's easier to trick someone into continuing not to see you, if they don't see you in the first place." Zoe rolled her eyes. What was the University teaching these great stewards of magic? Ben suddenly stopped moving and studied the ground at his feet for a moment.

"They're dead!" Benjamin cried out.

"I mean, they might disagree with you, seeing as they are trying to kill us." Zoe gestured that they should keep moving.

"No, I mean both the Minotaur and the Medusa were killed. We've learned that bit of information all of our lives. It would be simple to hide something that literally everyone thought didn't exist!" Benjamin was in the thrall of this epiphany, when the Consumed hissed and pulled him back away from Zoe.

The wall to the right of where he had been standing suddenly exploded, and a very large, very naked man with the head of a white bull flailed about looking for something to throttle. Zoe fell back onto her butt in shock, and scrambled to get to her feet as the beast turned on her. Breaking through a solid wall must be disorienting, because she was able to get out of its reach. Once she had her feet though, she had no idea what to do. The thing was so massive and tightly muscled she wasn't even sure if stabbing the thing would work.

There was a bellow, and the creature reacted as the Consumed appeared at its neck biting deep into its flesh. Zoe could see the skin blackening around the bite, and could see the animalistic panic in the Minotaur's eyes. Zoe was emboldened. She knew she had a brief window while the thing was distracted to make something happen. She tugged the knitting needles out from her hair forcing it to cascade around her face. In the same motion, she brought the needles down into the, dishearteningly at eye level, thigh of the creature.

"Hielo!" she set the magic in motion, and the ambient and stagnant air began to crackle and cool around the creature. The creature slowed as ice flowed over it, causing its muscles to spasm and harden. Once the Minotaur fell to one knee, Zoe looked up and could see Benjamin getting to his feet, a gash on his forehead.

"Zoe!" He called out as he threw out his hand. The Minotaur had managed to raise its arm and was inches away from touching her. She was panicked, as she didn't want to be drawn into her own spell, which was very quickly draining her of everything she had.

Her stomach lurched and her vision blurred, and she was looking into Ben's eyes, his face a mass of exhaustion and blood from his head wound.

"Did you..." She tried to make sense of things, but Benjamin was already dragging her away from the creature, following the simulacra, as it quickly tried to calculate a route along the new path, they suddenly found themselves on.

"Yes," He said panting, "I conjured you. I wasn't sure I could do it without a circle."

"You could have conjured me into a brick wall!" Zoe cried, finding that being angry made it easier for her to flee in terror.

"Well, if we live through this, and you find something missing, I will be more than happy to pen you a formal apology." Ben said, with a bit too much confidence.

"Ok, sure, if we get out of here, I will lodge a formal complaint." Zoe said. There was a moment of relief, followed by one of abject terror as she realized her spell had stopped draining her. Which, sadly, meant that it was no longer affecting bull boy.

"Your energy shifted." Ben stated matter of factly.

"Bull boy is free." Zoe's lungs burned and her muscles screamed to stop running. She powered up the adrenaline, pushing her far past her limits. "We need a plan Benji!"

"I know, even the tracker is having trouble finding a new exit!" Ben was following the spell, but it was jerky and clearly thought the best path was behind them.

"Okay, how do we kill the Minotaur!?" Zoe had turned up her absorption of ambient magic as high as it would go, just to keep up with the physical exertion.

"I mean, Theseus killed him the normal way. There was no prop or magic tool he needed to do the job, he just kinda stabbed or punched him a lot." Ben slowed giving the spell time to orient.

"I am not particularly good at stabbing things." Zoe panted.

"Me neither, I'm not even good at it in video games." Benjamin was pouring energy into the tracker spell, which seemed to be mostly just following them at this point. Zoe thought on what Mason would do, and it probably involved facing the creature heroically, even if he died trying. Zoe didn't want to die, heroically or otherwise. The lights Zoe had conjured when they first arrived were flickering and wouldn't last much longer.

"Well, Mason would do that weird overlap thing, get buff and punch it a bunch." Zoe stumbled and leaned against a wall, unable to continue the pace.

"Weird overlap thing?" Ben said stopping for his own benefit.

"Yeah, he and Nosam, kinda like, wear each other. He says it makes him stronger, better able to anticipate danger and whatnot." Zoe tried not to gulp her breaths, she knew that wouldn't help. Benjamin turned to the plainly creepy being floating just out of sight.

"Can we do that?" He asked her.

"It would require practice; it would be unwise at this juncture." The Consumed stated.

"But we could, become strong enough to defeat him?" Benjamin pressed the chewed up angel.

"You could likely survive the encounter, for a time." The Consumed said cryptically.

"How do we do it?" Benjamin asked, and without thinking removed a sharpie from his jacket pocket seemingly to scribe runes. Once he realized he didn't need it, He, perhaps out of pride, more likely embarrassment, didn't return it to his pocket.

"Ben, she doesn't seem very confident in the idea." Zoe tried to reason with him.

"Yes, I do not wish to lose you so soon." The Consumed whispered.

"Well, all evidence we currently have, points to us dying a horrible trample-filled death, regardless of what we do." Benjamin pleaded.

"If you must insist, then I must also wish to try?" The Consumed seemed almost confused, the words being half statement, half question in tone. Benjamin spread his arms out, and the Consumed embraced him, holding him close and intimate like a grotesque lover. As tired as she was, Zoe could barely make out the exchange of energies. Something was happening, but she couldn't really follow it, like trying to watch an intricate action scene while half asleep. The physical changes evolving were drastic. Benjamin's skin grew gray and corpse like, his mouth expanded, growing and bulging with fangs, large, skeletal wings erupted from his back, and the passage grew cold enough to see your breath play out.

"Ben?" Zoe's breath was ragged.

"Rest..." Benjamin said it with the authority the Consumed exuded, but also with some of the care Benjamin usually had in his voice. Accompanying the words was a cold wind that was heavy with magic. Zoe drank it in and breathed easier.

"Thank you." She whispered, trying not to show how afraid she was for Ben, but also grateful for the much-needed energy. Her body's natural recovery assets kicked in, and she sat on the ground pulling her knees to her chest. She was trying to stay out of the way, but it was also getting uncomfortably cold. The lights at her hands began glowing strong again, making everything look bleak in the passage.

Benjamin raised his head as if smelling the air, and his now horrifying jaw hung open slightly. He moved further back the way they had come. Zoe was concerned she was going to be left behind, before she too felt it. Before, it had felt just like the ambient magic of the labyrinth, but it was clear, now, that something was seeking them. Brushing up against them in a tingly, invasive way, Zoe had chalked the strange feeling up to creepy vibes when they had first entered the Avalon. **B**ut, when she had frozen the Minotaur, the feeling had dissipated. Now, it was intense and a bit smothering.

Stone, again, erupted from the wall across from Zoe, several small bits leaving stinging gashes on her arms and legs, but luckily nothing worse. She was sure the Minotaur would kill her, right there right then, but nothing was happening. After what seemed like an eternity, she opened her eyes to see Ben and the beast struggling, neither able to truly overpower the other. Benjamin was losing ground though, and he looked so small next to the hulking Minotaur.

Zoe was so tired, but seeing the struggle invigorated her, and she managed to reach into her bag and remove some yarn from it. This was not special, magic yarn; in fact, it was still mostly attached to a hat she was knitting. Yet, it felt to her like reaching for Excalibur, something momentous and heroic. Once she had the squishy ball fully extracted, she began humming low and resonant. She tapped a rhythm with her toes, and her fingers drew invisible symbols all over the ball as it slowly began to float before her. The Minotaur had gotten some leverage, and was slamming a knee into Benjamin's side. The blows were merciless, and the sound they were making was troubling in a very primal way. Letting her mind flow over the yarn, ascribing purpose to every gesture, painting meaning over the reverberation of her voice, she lashed out her fingers, and the yarn became heavy chains. They wrapped about the Minotaur and began to constrict. The chain had caught the creature mid motion and pinned one knee painfully to its torso. It bellowed in pain, and Benjamin lashed out with that grotesque mouth, leaving a bloody ruin where the Minotaur's neck had once sat proudly.

"Benjamin!" Zoe called out, but, Ben was lost in the throes of conquest. Something primal had overtaken him, forcing him farther down the path away from his humanity. He was tearing chunks of flesh from the creature, hissing and screaming. "Benjamin!" Zoe tried kicking at him weakly. He turned toward her his face covered in gore, his eyes wide and mad. Zoe, still fearful, almost lashed out at her friend, suddenly very aware of her vulnerability.

"Zoe." Ben, said slowly, as if remembering something while drunk. He backed away like an animal, and a ripple of magic played along his body. The Consumed pulled itself away from his body, ripping its way back into the world. Zoe watched breathless, as Ben fell to the ground, eyes wide, looking very corpse like, before turning and retching on the stone floor.

"Get it out, you're okay." Zoe said moving to him and rubbing his back. The Consumed hovered nearby, clearly concerned.

"It was too soon; he was ill prepared." It said, melancholy coloring the words.

"Well, regardless, it may have saved our lives, not to mention your existence." Zoe said, trying to comfort it while also scolding it.

"I'm okay, Zoe." Benjamin managed to say between heaves.

"Like hell you are." Zoe shot a glance at the Minotaur. It twitched a bit, and as spell had worn off, the colorful yarn seemed almost comical played over its monstrous countenance. As she watched, it seemed to deflate slightly as if it was collapsing in on itself. The walls around them started to lose their substance, and in minutes they laid on asphalt, the mists swiftly dissipating.

"Pretty small club..." Benjamin choked out. Zoe fished in her bag for a bottle of water and held it to his lips.

"What club is that?" She said, trying to humor him.

"Me and Theseus..." He was smiling, the blood staining his face and clothes quickly fading into dust.

"I don't follow."

"We both killed the Minotaur." He said beaming at her. The sun broke through the mists and Zoe smiled despite herself.

CHAPTER

21

• ● •

Red light cameras weren't used in Tucson anymore. They had instituted them for a time at a few intersections, got Mason a ticket or two, and then had been decommissioned. It didn't surprise Mason in the slightest to learn that they were still collecting information, however. One of them, on the east side, was particularly hated by Tucsonans and as Mason pulled into the parking lot of a nearby big box store, even he was getting a little hot under the collar about it.

"I used to go out of my way to avoid this intersection, even when I was pretty sure I wouldn't run a red light." Jackson said squinting his eyes.

"It got me twice, both times I was just making a legal left turn." Mason said shaking his head.

"So.." he started looking at the busy intersection as Mason walked towards it.

"Don't worry, I have no intention of walking into traffic."
Mason said with a smile. Nosam yipped and rushed a bit
ahead, his form shifting and twisting until a white furry
archway appeared before them.

"Uh... What?" Jackson whistled.

"Next stop, the primal!" Mason said smiling at him.
Jackson took a step backward.

"Uh... Isn't that just as dangerous?" You could almost
imagine him thumping his leg with the stress of the thought.

"You give day tours of the Fey, and the Second World
gives you pause?" Mason gestured toward the archway.

"I might just wait for you here." Jackson said straightening
his clothes.

"Buddy system. You're my buddy." Mason pretended to
check his watch.

"Okay." Jackson walked through the archway, putting
a bit of defiance into his stride. Mason followed after him
rolling his eyes.

The Second World is much like the first, but it lacks
structure in place of concepts. The earth, plants, buildings
and people are all represented, but with a more colorful
brush. People milled about lacking outlines, and were not
fully formed, almost blurry. Things and people with a
stronger core were more defined. Jackson, a were-hare, with
his focus on community and sense of being part of a whole,
looked more generic, albeit, with more rabbit like features,
than the other individuals. Mason on the other hand, was
over-stylized, looking like a military captain straight out of
a propaganda film. Nosam, after changing back into his

doglike form, was the size of a horse. An unfelt wind rustled his fur, and a palpable energy within him screamed predator.

"The spirit is restless." Nosam added in a growling base voice.

"It does seem a tad agitated." Mason, of course, sensed him strongly. His spirit was, in this instance, more the general vibe of the Primal than any individual entity.

"Uh, Mason..." Jackson interrupted, "Why do you look like a literal poster boy?"

"Oh right, you don't come to the Second World much." Mason fiddled with his new outfit self-consciously. "The Second World and the Orphic realms are unique when it comes to how they affect other creatures. While a world like the Fey kinda just copies your physical form, in the Second World things appear in a more stylized reality. Some scholars on the topic say the Second World emphasizes what the world has already decided you are. If you are vilified by enough people, you might seem demonic or evil. I'm seen as an authority figure here, hence the getup."

"And the Orphic realms?" Jackson pressed.

"The Orphic realms tend to display things as they could be. Such as, an ideal self." Mason surmised.

"So, in the Primal you appear as others perceive you, and in the Orphic, it's how you perceive yourself?" Jackson wiggled his ears.

"Exactly." Nosam supplied.

"Regardless, I would like to get this over with." Jackson sighed. Mason indicated the camera.

"This guy is both a camera AND universally despised. He's going to be the literal worst." Mason said with a deep sigh.

They walked the short distance to the intersection. People kind of floated by, as most cars didn't have enough juice to really manifest here. The ones that did, appeared as either hopeless junkers or pristine examples of automobile perfection. A few others were personified in an almost cartoonish visage.

The Camera hung over the intersection, looking very foreboding and demonic. Its gleaming red eye protruded like a telescope. His body was very clearly male and rippled with muscle, and was quite textbook demonic-looking. Any cars that did take notice, seemed terrified of him hanging there, hyper vigilant.

"Good, Morrow!" Mason called out. Nosam bristled ready for a fight, and Jackson gave a small wave.

"Who dares speak with me?" The camera's voice was robotic and cold. No trace of emotion could be detected.

"I am Mason, Warden of the Valley, Consort and friend to the Loci of Tucson, beloved of Sonora, and partner to Nosam." Mason said with an impressive amount of gravitas. "May I ask what you are called?"

"I am Judgment." the camera droned. Jackson whistled and kind of glanced at Nosam, who managed to chuff with amusement. Judgment did not seem to notice or care.

"Judgment, I come asking for a boon. The safety of the city requires that you describe to me one of the subjects that you have passed… judgment on in the past." Mason said, trying to scold his companions at the same time.

"Long my memory is, but I am not bound by your authority." The mechanized voice stated without ego. Mason had been afraid that this might happen. Some things, especially government owned and maintained things, had a tendency not to recognize a Shaman as having authority over them. Mason had often, and before the 28th amendment, considered getting a government job just to get them to fall in line. That wasn't an option now.

"I am on official PLEB business." Mason wasn't technically lying; he had been called to a PLEB crime scene related to the case.

"PLEB has no authority over traffic issues." Judgment droned. Mason was stumped. The traffic camera was going to stonewall him.

"If I might interject," Jackson stepped forward. Mason stepped to the side, a smile creeping into the corners of his mouth. "One of your photos came across our desk, and the quality was abysmal. We couldn't even tell if the person in it was a man or a woman." Judgment recoiled in abject horror.

"Impossible." it stated, once it had regained its composure.

"Mason, if you will." Jackson said, and held out his hand, with an authority that even convinced Mason. Nosam let out another chuff of amusement. Mason made a show of scrambling for the photo, like a scolded intern, and handed it to Jackson. Jackson held it up to the camera. "Is this what passes as acceptable to you?"

"This photo has been tampered with." Judgment almost sounded angry.

"How is that possible without your say so?" Jackson continued.

"This slight on my performance must be amended." Judgment crawled, in a very inhuman way, down from its perch and snatched the photo from Jackson. "Magic has been employed, is this the reason PLEB is involved?"

"Uh... yes." Mason lied.

"I cannot improve the photo quality; the enchantment is too complex." Judgment 'narrowed' his glowing eye at the photo.

"Can you describe the subject?" Mason asked hopefully.

"I can attempt. The enchantment seems to have affected my ability to actively speak of the subject. However, I can inform you if I see the subject again, I can provide you with a current license plate. The one in this series of photos is no longer in service." Judgment rattled off.

"That would be good, for a start." Mason sighed.

"We look forward to hearing from you." Jackson handed the traffic light a business card. It was odd watching this mechanical horror take the card gingerly, and hold it up to its lens.

"There are other surveillance cameras I converse with. I shall inform them as well." Judgment nodded to the three of them, and reached an impossibly long arm to the metallic pole it sat upon and hoisted itself back into position. Mason watched it return to its odd stillness and gestured for Jackson to follow him back to the parking lot.

"Good work back there." Mason said clapping him on the shoulder. Nosam gave him a loving shoulder bump as he jogged ahead. shifting again into an archway.

"Honestly, I just channeled an old manager of mine. It was almost traumatic." He said rubbing the back of his head.

"You might have a future in the hero business you keep up this way." Mason said with a chuckle passing back into the bright sunlight of the parking lot. He didn't see the circle of runes til he stepped inside of it.

He realized there was a trap a millisecond before it clamped down. He reached out to Nosam drawing him into himself, and eliminating the archway, which meant Jackson would be trapped. However, Mason wasn't going to fall for the same trap twice in one week. The circle of runes on the ground was a gate, and he had stepped right into it. Before he could get a good read for where it was sending him, he was falling.

If you have never fallen into another plane of existence, it's hard to explain. It doesn't have the inertia of falling in the material plane. Wherever Mason was, it didn't have a solid concept of gravity, and while he was moving through space, it was hard to tell which direction he was heading. Worse still, until he could get his feet on the ground, he was cut off from a majority of his options. Mason had always assumed that mastering the earth element would mean he always had something to work with, and yet, situations like this kept popping up.

'What are our options?' he thought at Nosam.

'We are in Gehenna.' Nosam thought back. Mason was elated to hear his voice, and to be whole in this time of trouble. 'There should be elementals here, but I cannot seek them. If I stray too far from you, I'll be shunted out.' Mason certainly didn't want that.

"Hey!" Mason called out, but was surprised to find he couldn't even hear himself over the intense wind of the place. Wind. Mason changed tactics. He opened up to the wind letting its energy touch his, and soon several small wind elementals had flocked to him. They were invisible to the eye, but plain as day to Mason, as they began nibbling on him. Growing annoyed with the constant spinning of the fall, the tiny elementals began to steady him, and he hung limply in the air while they nibbled on his pattern.

'Now would be a good time.' Nosam supplied dryly. Mason sent back an impatient thought and set about it. He moved his hands through the air, drawing several of the elementals close to him, and tugged magically. The energy the elementals had pulled out of him went taught like a fishing line and they began to wriggle chaotically. Mason was not good with air. It was too nebulous and frantic, never sitting still long enough to talk.

'Nothing is free, my friends.' Mason thought/spoke at them. 'I've given of myself and now I seek balance.' While air has a desperate need to be free, and never stood still very long, even it understood the need for balance. The Air elementals stopped wriggling and flitted about impatiently.

'Task.' was all that they thought back. In all honesty, it was more like 'task, task, task, task.' repeated a dozen times a second, like they were eager to be done with it.

'I need a route to the Material, preferably close to where I entered from.' Mason pictured the concepts as clearly as he could manage.

'More.' was all they thought back. They were willing, but required a greater payment to achieve equilibrium.

'I fear I'm walking into combat,' Mason thought. " I will need my energy now, but I am willing to enter into a covenant.' Mason didn't like having too many outstanding debts, but he didn't know what he was going to be subject to once he escaped.

'Acceptable.' the tiny wisps sent back in a cacophony. A thin, silver chain manifested in Mason's hand. He gripped it and shoved it into a pocket. Then, he was hurtling back in the direction he was pretty sure he had come. It was hard to tell up from down in Gehenna. While he was madly spinning, he tried to remember who the big players in this particular infernal realm were. It might have been chosen because it was one of the more nebulous realms, but Mason suspected he knew who had sprung this particular trap. Before he could even finish the thought, he was thrust from chilled winds into harsh daylight and chaos…

CHAPTER

22

———— • ● • ————

Theia rarely flew, the ability to see the odds of hurtling to a fiery death were too tempting in dealing with the stress. Plus, she liked the contemplative nature of a road trip or train trek. Flying on the back of a Baku, who was usually an attractive office space neighbor was, well, she wasn't sure how she felt about it. However, the Orphic realms were truly breathtaking from the air. Dreamers were soaring through the air, dragons, and ancient gods flitting about, and a never-ending dreamscape with colors rarely seen in the First World surrounded her. As a counterpoint, Baku have very little to hold on to, and she had to clamp her eyes shut to avoid passing out.

'You asked for this, remember.' Matthew's disembodied voice touched her mind. Theia knew he could nibble at her thoughts to hear her, but wasn't sure what that meant for her mental health, so she yelled back at him instead.

"You said nothing of FLYING!" She screamed as he did a barrel roll. His jovial laughter returned to her mind.

'You know you can fly here, right?' Matthew said.

"Knowing the nature of the dream realm makes it harder not easier!" Theia screamed back angrily.

'Well, there's not a lot of people dreaming similar dreams in Tucson, so we have to hustle a bit to find a Tokyo exit.' Matthew explained. He had explained it before, but it was still too inconvenient for her to process at the moment. The Orphic realm didn't have any real geography. It was more of a collection of movie sets, similar dreamscapes all near to each other. To further complicate things, you have to try and find a particularly deep sleeper in order to exit or enter, without scaring the piss out of someone.

Theia closed her eyes, and even though it still didn't feel right, she laid the tapestry out before her third eye. It was still ragged and torn near her present, but she was able to skip ahead just enough to find the correct dreamer. It was a young woman dreaming about being eaten by her own hair, which was, admittedly, an uncommon dream. But, it was the easiest possible exit, as she was a very deep sleeper and had her first-floor window open. Matthew had found a Tucson man asleep at a bus-stop, dreaming of being eaten by his own feet, which was close, but it was still a bit of a journey. Matthew had insisted that they fly, as this part of Dreamland is particularly disturbing up close.

Matthew gave another midair twirl and began to descend. Theia's curiosity got the better of her, and she peeped an eye open just in time to see little scenes unfolding all around her, mostly of hair eating people. She closed her eyes again, and squeezed the lawyer's fuzzy body tighter. He landed and kind of shrugged, and a relieved Theia slid to the ground, which was cool and wet. She looked up and a naked woman was screaming soundlessly, as several strands of hair held her to the wall of her shower.

"Why can't we hear her?" Theia said.

'Well, its taking place in her mind...' Matthew began, and in an almost cartoonish puff of smoke, appeared in his human form. He finished verbally, "...and the mind is very good at compartmentalizing. The Orphic realms are old, but the sheer volume of new humans has really swelled its borders. If every scream, yell or scary howl was audible, nothing would ever get accomplished." Matthew spread his hands out, and the scene shifted to the woman thrashing a bit on her bed. If Theia squinted, she could still make out the scene in the bathroom, but she had no continuing urge to do that.

"So how close are we to the address I gave you?" Theia said shifting a bit nervously. In the Orphic realms the embedded bead radiated large, orange flames, making her look like a crazy fire spirit of vengeance or something. She caught Matthew looking at this furious conflagration nervously before answering.

"A block or two, but I cannot stress enough, please keep a low profile." He scolded.

"I have no urge to suddenly star in a new viral video." She dismissed him, but she was equally concerned.

"Do you even speak Japanese?" Matthew said as he moved to the woman's closet.

"Brought one of Zoe's potions, so, it shouldn't be an issue." She strode to the closet, and as he gestured for her to go first, she stepped forward and sound returned to the world. Even at 3 am, the city noise was a gentle almost soothing thrum. The woman whimpered from her prone position near the floor. Theia felt for her and looked to Matthew, who smiled and moved to the woman. He kneeled down and, in another ridiculous poof, reappeared in his strange tapir like Baku form. It was always odd to see true supes transform, and realize that your loved one or neighbor isn't really human at all, just really good at pretending. His trunk touched the woman's forehead, and a dark purple light pulled away from her and into Matthew's open mouth. The woman immediately sighed and calmed, her nightmare over. Matthew touched his front paw to a small Baku charm and whispered something in Japanese.

They exited through the open window; Theia as gracefully as she could, and Matthew flowing through the air as effortlessly as mist. Quickly, he coalesced back into his human form. He smiled at her and gave a mocking bow. Theia rolled her eyes and removed a vial from her jacket pocket, and downed it like a shot. It wasn't awful, as far as potions go, being mostly alphabet soup and aromatics. She felt it take effect after a few seconds and then turned to Matthew and, in perfect Japanese, asked him to lead the way.

• ● •

As they entered a hole in the wall karaoke bar, Theia was thankful she had brought her credit card. Taking the time to get paper Yen would have been more than she was willing to invest on this visit. The man at the front counter was truly impressed with her Japanese. She informed him she just had a really good tutor.

"So, who are we meeting?" Matthew asked in Russian, so as to not be overheard easily. It took a minute for Theia to shift the spell to Russian, but she managed to answer back.

"Paula. She's an avatar." Matthew's eyes bugged out a bit, Avatars were kind of a big deal. Even to organizations like PLEB, it still wasn't common or easy to detect or classify Avatars. All Avatars hold a small piece of a god or goddess' divinity within themselves. All of the ones Theia had ever met had been terribly unassuming and normal folks. Paula had helped her out a lot when she was first starting out, so it was hard for her to think of Paula as a celebrity.

"Well, I'm not gonna ask how you know her, but how can she help?" Matthew continued.

"She's an avatar of Apollo, and, if legends are true, he is kinda the whole reason I have the power I do." She said offhandedly, opening the soundproof door to a particularly rowdy booth.

"Wait... THE Apollo!?" Matthew managed, before the terrible singing inside the booth overwhelmed them. A Japanese businessman, of some stripe or another, was finishing a terrible rendition of 'Carry On My Wayward Son' by Kansas. As the music faded, a portly woman in a fuchsia evening gown began clapping enthusiastically. Her blonde tresses played across sun kissed skin, and she spoke in a commanding and powerful voice.

"Oh, Minato-San, that was splendid!" The woman looked to Theia and Matthew, as if just now seeing them, and politely bid them wait outside. Theia nodded and pushed Matthew back into the hallway. After a few minutes, a very grateful and weeping Minato exited the room. "Come in, Theia!" the woman's voice demanded.

"Prophetess, it's been too long." Theia said with a deep bow of respect. Matthew was a bit flabbergasted and quickly dipped into a bow himself.

"Oh stop, you willful child." Paula said with a healthy chortle. "You were good to come to me." She said plainly.

"You have no idea how happy I am to hear that." Theia breathed out in relief.

"Oh, you're not gonna be happy, but nothing is free. You know the drill." Paula said, gesturing to the karaoke machine. Theia had been dreading this part. Sure, she sometimes sang in her car, around Mason and Zoe, and enjoyed it. But, Matthew and Paula were not the ideal audience. Not to mention, the slow almost active burning along her throat, reminding her that she had met 4, maybe 5, divine beings in the last 24 hours.

"Do you know Medusa?" Theia asked, almost as an afterthought. Paula visibly stiffened.

"She has been dead for eons, Theia." Paula said, with polite finality. Theia couldn't help but wonder if she meant literal eons, or was just being colorful. All non-humans had a vague notion that human history wasn't very accurate, and that the age of myths might be much much older than anyone thought.

Theia shook it off. If it had been important, Paula would warn her. That's why she was here. She wrapped her hand around the slightly sticky microphone, and selected a song. She was feeling particularly melancholy, so she picked, 'Set Fire to the Rain'. The irony tickled her. As the music started, she stared straight at the screen, trying to forget she had an audience. As the small white words appeared, and she took a breath releasing just the beginnings of a note, the brand flared to painful life, and the room filled with blinding yellow light. Theia spun into a crouch, reaching for her gun on pure instinct, to have her eyes meet Paula's. She was radiating pure divinity and held a golden bow aimed at her, its silver arrow nocked and shining.

"The fuck, Paula!" Theia cried out. Theia could see Matthew pressed up against the wall, looking terrified, and she couldn't blame him. Even in the Orphic, Baku aren't dangerous or particularly powerful.

"I, Apollota, Prophetess of the house of Delphi, and Avatar of Apollo, demand you reveal your true form, deceiver!" The sound of her voice had that creepy double echo thing that gods liked to use. She was half manly Apollo, and half screaming Paula. Theia could feel the divine nature pulling at her, and she knew, even if she had wanted to, that lying would be very difficult. Apollo had dominion over guilt and law, and it would take a much heavier hitter than Theia to resist that.

"Paula... it's me, Theia, honest..." she managed to wheeze. If only she could get out of this oppressive energy

THE APOCALYPSE BEAD | 255

and get a second to breathe. Almost as if answering her, the brand cooled and a chill spread over her, and the relentless force pinning her to the spot, abated. Theia could now see the assault for what it was, almost psychic, more than anything actually controlling her actions or motivations. Even the light filling the room seemed illusory.

"You should kill her, and protect the bead." A barely perceivable shade of Ryan Randall stood just off to the side of Paula, and time seemed to crawl as she considered him. "She is tied to the Divine, she won't let you keep it. No power is stronger than the allure and temptation of the bead." Theia chose to ignore the obvious, and clearly arrogant, manifestation of the bead, and looked Paula in the eye. Time came back into focus, and the arrow was drawn back.

"Paula... Please help me." Theia said, letting go of all of the pretenses of power, letting the raw emotion of her situation play out with her words. Paula stopped and truly looked at Theia.

"You are not Theia any longer." Paula said, "However, I'm not sure that you are aware of that, yet." The light subsided and the bow broke into tiny motes of light and disappeared. Paula smoothed her now golden dress, and flopped back into her chair. She gestured to the couch next to her, as the instrumental track of the Adele song that Theia had picked, played on as if nothing had happened.

"Thank you, for trusting me." Theia said, sitting stiffly and trying to get the brand to stop glowing like a road flare. Matthew was still pressed against the wall, the whites of his eyes very visible.

"It's alright, Mr. Davis, there will be no bloodshed." Paula said trying to calm the man. Matthew slumped onto the floor, his expensive suit wrinkling a bit.

"What did you see?" Theia asked calmly.

"It is more what I didn't see, child." Paula began with a sigh. "Theia exists and touches the lives of those around her. She has a future, a roughshod kind of destiny, and eventually, she learns to get over the bullshit a bit."

"Paula..." Theia said trying to keep her on topic.

"Right. While all of that still exists, where you are is blank. Just a jagged hole in the fabric of reality itself." Paula took a sip of her beer. "However, my gift is a god's gift. We can only perceive the realms we live in, unlike mortals that might run off to an alternate dimension or have a misadventure in a doomed timeline, we as beings of the firmament, cannot."

"So, whatever has happened to me, really isn't of this world." Theia scrunched her face up. "The Norns had said similar, but it was in a dream."

"Perilously inaccurate." Paula agreed. "I see now why you came to me." Theia almost smiled. "Unfortunately, in the future, it might makes us enemies if you aren't careful. While I have no problem feigning ignorance of this encounter, if my pantheon comes down squarely against you, I will be hard-pressed not to get involved." Paula did seem truly upset at the prospect, which was touching.

"Well, how do I avoid that?" Theia pressed.

"As of now, you are an unknown. To gods and other divine beings, this makes you a potential problem they can't properly control, or an asset they haven't figured out how to exploit. What this shift has done to your capabilities can't be known. This magical scar across you neck could set fire to the universe, or make you really good at poker. There is no way of knowing for sure because we cannot see it! I can see your physical body, feel your soul, but I don't see the core of you as I normally can." Paula shook her empty beer bottle at Matthew. He took it and left the room. He seemed elated to exit and have a chance to collect himself.

"Okay, but what do I do with it? The Norns called me a Warden. This dead guy keeps showing up and talking about responsibility. I'm pretty sure it would be a terrible idea to give it to someone else, but I also really don't want it." Theia said, as the red light from the bead finally abated.

Paula put a stockinged foot on Theia's knee and nudged her. "You are an Oracle trained by the visage of Apollo himself, what an earth are you worried about?"

Theia did smile then; Paula was a literal god-send, and was always way more supportive than she needed to be, even if she was way too concerned with her social life. Theia took in a deep breath and balled her fists.

"Right, whatever this is," she gestured toward the large mark, "it will either benefit me or cause more problems, regardless of how unfair it feels, so I might as well buck up."

"I can tell you, the way you found it seems to indicate a bit of overlap between that world and this one. How much is impossible to know, but you should be cautious." Paula said. Matthew reentered the room with a fresh cold beer bottle and a cocktail napkin in hand. "Oh, darling, I mustn't." Paula playfully protested before accepting the beer.

"Great timing, I think it's time I found our killers, freed my name from PLEB suspicion, and maybe, save the world from a supernatural war." Theia said rising and looping her arm with Matthew's.

"I'm billing you for this." Matthew drawled between deep sighs.

"That would be quite unethical..." Theia teased.

"I'm a lawyer not a saint." Matthew stated.

CHAPTER

23

———— • ● • ————

Benjamin, while a bit bruised, was feeling okay despite the adventure. He was trying not to be amazed, as his side had taken several very strong blows. The damage should have been much worse than it was. This overlapping thing, for which he was sure there was a better term, was quite potent. He looked at Zoe. She was breathing heavily, and it was clear that she was pretty drained. After escaping the Avalon, Ben had suggested they find somewhere to sit and recover. They were close to the Union, a food court of sorts, on the UofA mall, and were trying to find a table.

"You recovered much faster than I did. I'd chalk it up to youth, but I'm not that much older than you." Zoe said sliding into a vinyl booth.

"Honestly, I'm a bit surprised myself. The Consumed is stronger than I thought." Ben could feel her in his shadow.

It didn't feel right to keep calling her it. Her name may have been lost, but she was clearly a person from some far-gone age. Maybe, they/them was more appropriate. He would have to remember to ask.

Ben took his phone out and texted Professor Wooly to see if he could meet them at the Union as opposed to his office. It seemed a bit risky to talk out in the open, but he didn't want to push Zoe or himself too hard after their ordeal. Ben caught himself scanning the crowd in the Union nervously. Any one of them could pose a threat.

"You look just like Mason when you do that." Zoe chuckled.

"Maybe I picked it up from him. I'll admit, I always thought it was silly when he did it in the past." Ben rubbed his forehead, the act of lifting his arm made his ribs hurt.

"Here." Zoe fished in her bag, and then slid what seemed to be a child's band aid across the Formica table between them. "It's a pain reliever. I keep them around for minor headaches and stuff. Assuming you aren't more seriously injured, it should keep your head clear." Ben smiled, took the little package, and applied it under his armpit. The relief from the little thing was almost immediate.

"Thank you." He sighed relieved.

"It's always good to have a witch along." Zoe said with a bright smile. She was being flippant, but it was true, her magic was far smoother and easier to maintain than runic magic. It was a hassle to use runic magic for healing, as the spell had to be crafted for the specific injury. It was nearly impossible to stock up items in advance, given the necessary forethought you would need.

"That is proving more and more true with every passing hour." Ben smiled. He remembered something from earlier, "So, now that we've survived a brush with mythological death, I have a question."

"Well, you saved my life as readily as I saved yours, so I'd say we are even, but I'll indulge you." Zoe said with a grin.

"Before the Minotaur attacked, you said you had a hunch about me." Ben stated it as nonchalantly as he could. He was dying to know what she had meant, but didn't want to seem over eager. Zoe sighed deeply and did some thinking for a moment.

"When you and Mason were telling me about your fight in the Lasso, against the flesh Golem, he had said that he first noticed you being different cause you were feeding the pumpkin vines magic." She said it quite suddenly, as if relieved to be talking about it.

"Yes, if he hadn't noticed, we probably would have died." Ben surmised.

"That's just it, they were conjured pumpkin vines." Zoe said as if it was obvious.

"I'm not following." Ben retorted.

"So, Mason, who is tied to the Second World, he could feed mana to a natural plant, maybe even convince it to keep moving, but, as proven by the Consumed, you aren't tied to the Second World." She took a breath, and in that shallow breath he saw her point. "Moreover, they were conjured, not natural in the slightest. Even a Shaman as prolific as Mason, would find it impossible to feed energy to a conjuration, hence, why he didn't even think to try."

"I mean it seems like something he would notice..." Ben said quietly.

"Not really, Mason has a very rudimentary understanding of actual magic. Everything he does is actually convincing natural things to move about or do him favors. Actual mana manipulation isn't something he is very good at, outside of elementals. From what he described, and you experienced, I'd classify you as a Witch, like me." She let the sentence hang for a bit.

"But, witches aren't two-natured, so if that was true, what about the Consumed?" Ben said gravely.

"That's just it, when you overlapped with it..."

"Her." Ben corrected as a reflex.

"With her," Zoe said cautiously, "It kind of proved that she was, in fact, your two-natured partner. No familiar or conjuration would have been able to mesh with you quite that seamlessly."

"So, by empowering the vines, and overlapping with the Consumed, I've done at least one thing that shouldn't be possible." Ben said putting his hand to his mouth nervously.

"Well, for as much as we know about magic, it is possible you are a hybrid or something. Both witches and the two-natured tend to be inherited abilities, at least the potential is genetic." Zoe said putting a hand over his. It was clear she didn't believe that per se, but was trying to comfort him. It was the kind of revelation that would have been pretty obvious to a practitioner like Zoe. She had studied both her natural magic, and had worked with two-natured people on an almost daily basis.

"Both of my parents are human..." Ben whispered to himself, as if it was rude to call them that.

"Which makes all of it even more mysterious. Don't worry, though, we will keep it to ourselves until we have figured something out. No need in getting you dissected by PLEB." She said with a jokey tone, that didn't quite land.

They sat in companionable silence for some time, until a 7-foot-tall humanoid sheep man approached the table. Benjamin recognized Professor Wooly immediately, as they had argued quite earnestly over the particular shade of hideous yellow coloring this disguise's waistcoat. The giant sheep man gave a deep bow before sliding into the booth next to Ben.

"Ah, Professor, thank you for making time to meet with us." Benjamin said, with a professionalism in his voice that his energy level couldn't match.

"Mr. Aguilar," Wooly said, with a head bob before turning to Zoe, "I don't think I've had the pleasure of meeting your companion." He said roundly.

"Ms. Halston." Zoe provided, reaching out a hand.

"Oh, no need for human pleasantries. My hands are quite illusionary." Wooly said with a chortle. Zoe lowered her hand, with grace, and placed it in her lap.

"Professor, I had a few questions." Benjamin started.

"I'm sure you do, my boy, but first, I have to know what transpired to have drained the two of you so thoroughly. And, perhaps to inquire how you hid your true nature from me all of this time." Wooly said with a twinkle in his eye. Benjamin had been afraid something like this might happen. He had never attempted to hide his magical nature before, mainly because, he didn't know he had one that could get him into trouble before.

"Well, that's tied to why I asked to see you." Benjamin skirted.

"He has only recently made the jump to post-human... late bloomer." Zoe assisted.

"Well, congratulations, my boy! Aside from the pervasive human opinion, you are better off." Wooly said, matter of factly.

"Yes, well, actually, aside from my change of status, I was hoping to ask you if you'd noticed anything else odd lately."

"Several things, I saw a cricket dragging a five-dollar bill into a sewage drain on the way over!" Wooly said jovially.

"He's going to be the talk of the drain!" Zoe chimed in, despite herself.

"Well, I meant odder than that." Benjamin tried to steer the conversation.

"Insects developing an economy is quite odd, Benjamin." Wooly said flatly.

"Professor," Benjamin tried again.

"It would almost indicate that there was some kind of insect market to which such a thing would be necessary. Which, of course, begs the question, why use human currency as opposed to something less cumbersome?." Wooly continued on, enraptured with his train of thought.

"Yes, but have you seen a Gorgon recently." Benjamin said in a whoosh of breath.

"Oh yes, she has been around campus a few times, with her friend the Minotaur." He said, appalled at Benjamin's rude interruption. "That's hardly odder than insectoid commerce."

"Wait, you have seen her, Professor?!" Zoe said suddenly.

"Yes, I thought it odd, but she was heavily glamoured, useless against Mara like myself. Intangible beings have a knack for seeing through illusions." he said, a bit of pride in his voice.

"You didn't think to report it to anyone?" Benjamin stated, a bit incredulous.

"My dear boy, if someone reported me to the authorities every time they saw me going about my business, I'd get nothing accomplished." He stated haughtily.

"Yes, but you haven't been extinct since the age of heroes." Benjamin put his hand to his face rubbing his eyes.

"Are they? I had no idea! You see them all the time in the Orphic realms. People are quite enamored with the Grecian monsters." Wooly began stirring a cup of tea that had definitely not been there earlier.

"Makes sense, but if they were here, they weren't in the Orphic realm." Zoe said, with a mother's patience.

"I can't keep track of what exists and what doesn't, young lady. I do have a social life." Wooly chided, adding the 'young lady' with emphasis.

"Okay, fair, but regardless of that, they aren't supposed to exist. How have they stayed hidden for most of human history?" Zoe said, expertly NOT rolling her eyes.

"They may have come through the hole." Wooly said, taking a sip from his illusionary tea cup.

"The hole?" Benjamin and Zoe managed at the same time.

"Well, it's more of a concept. It's always existed, but is also fairly recent." Wooly waved his hands in the air as if trying to wrestle the concept. "You see, for you mortals, it wouldn't seem that out of place. For you, nothing has really changed, but for the truly immortal, things have been odd for quite some time, and exceptionally odd very recently."

"So, there is a hole somewhere that ancient beings can crawl through?" Zoe removed a pad and pencil from her purse.

"More accurately, there was a space where nothing existed that has back filled into the human consciousness. These beings may have entered our reality last week, but humanity has felt them for much longer. Most of the pantheons are formed that way." Wooly continued.

"So, Zeus, who could have immigrated last month, has existed since ancient Greece?" Benjamin was managing calm, but losing the battle.

"No one as prolific as that, but anomalies or smaller beings might have. They get worked into the narrative by the human subconscious. Ripple backwards, your physicists are getting closer to actual time by the decade." Wooly sipped his tea.

"The Medusa isn't prolific?" Zoe faltered.

"Well, Greek myth is so pervasive in modern culture, basically anything that fell into the hole would probably get lumped into it. Anything unique anyway." Wooly took another fake sip of his illusory tea.

"Okay, so, Medusa, and the Minotaur could have arrived last week, but due to the nature of wobbly time dynamics, they could have been conceived of for eons." Benjamin surmised.

"You see it all the time. Bits and pieces of other realities seep in, humans can't reconcile the change, so they rationalize. That rationalization ripples forwards and backwards and permeates human myth. Dragons, vampires, demons, angels, cultures all over the planet began conceiving these concepts almost simultaneously. This is because they were once foreign." Wooly put his teacup in his jacket pocket, apparently done with the charade of it.

"How come no one is studying this?!" Zoe asked incredulous.

"You are! Amazing little creatures these humans! The Mandela effect, alternate realities, the Gap, all of these scholars are attempting to find the question to the answer that you already understand." Wooly gestured widely.

"So, mortals... us, are trying to reconcile these foreign reality bits with... science fiction?" Zoe slumped back in her chair.

"Honestly, I'm surprised none of your scientists have thought to ask one of the Immortals for an answer before now. Though, I guess without context, these concepts might drive someone mad. You don't feel mad, do you?"

"Mentally reeling, but sane." Zoe said wistfully.

"Okay, assuming all of that is above board and easy to understand, why now?" Benjamin focused on a part of the problem he could fix. "What do they want here, in Tucson, right now?"

"I mean, who knows what aliens are after, or if they even have a motivation. When vampires arrived, they just kind of started eating people." Wooly checked his pocket watch. "I do hope I've been helpful, I have a lecture soon."

"It's been enlightening," Zoe said with a heavy sigh.

"Don't want you to be late, Professor, but, if you happen to see any other Grecian myths running around, could you, please, text me?" Benjamin managed.

"Will do, my boy!" And with that, Professor Wooly stood and exited the Union, his sheep's tail wagging merrily.

"So, dimensional invaders, which have always existed in the collective subconscious, come to Tucson. Why?" Zoe underlined a large 'why' on her notepad.

"Honestly, I'm more worried about why they seem fixated on Theia." Benjamin removed his phone and began scrolling through his contacts. He texted Theia to see if she was awake yet, and placed the phone on the table.

"Assuming everything is connected, they were after Ryan Randall first, and have now moved on to Theia." Zoe corrected.

"According to Mason, Samael said that Randall had something that the Demons and Angels are both very interested in, and Theia did just develop pyrokinesis." Benjamin added.

"I mean, it could be a coincidence, but the other creatures that have gone missing have all been tied to the Fey." Zoe scribbled a thought web as she spoke.

"The Queen of the Deeps seems to be opposed to the situation, but the King of the Valley has been strangely quiet on this whole debacle, even so far as to let the wild fey roam as far as the border." Benjamin was leaning in to watch Zoe's scribbling. Benjamin's phone chirped, and as he turned it over, a golf cart smashed through the window across from them. The Union erupted in screaming.

CHAPTER

24

— • ● • —

Mason had only been out of the world for a few scant moments, before he came shooting out of the closing portal. As he spun into the air, with the momentum granted to him by the wind wisps he had cajoled, he counted five cultists, disguised as soccer moms, and the bowling shirt wearing Horace waiting for him, looking gratifyingly terrified.

"Get Jack." Even as Mason said it, he could feel Nosam tear away from him, and run towards the intersection. Mason ran his hands along his chest, with its numerous chains and bits of metal. His hand brushed the one he wanted, and he tore it free. Shamans, and other two-natured beings, typically worked with other creatures that hailed from the different realms they were associated with, convincing them to assist them. This could be a slow and expensive process, so, most chose to delay payment on a service rendered until a later date, and this process was represented by physical objects.

About a month ago, He and Theia had been trying to kill an ogre, and a small, but intense fire had broken out around them. The fire was completely unrelated to their actions, yet, he had convinced the fire to ride with him until he could find it a place where it could rage without being hunted by firefighters. The flames, still there, waiting, writhed in excitement as he connected to them at that moment, and with a whisper of exchanged energy, he chucked them towards a panel van that Horace's cultists had arrived in. It erupted into a hissing fireball that struck the van and became a raging inferno seconds later. The cultists ran towards, and shielded their eyes from the now intensely burning van.

As Mason was still airborne, he turned his attention to not breaking his neck, as he fell 10 feet towards the ground. In the much harsher gravity of the First World, the wind wisps weren't able to hold him aloft, nor do much to mitigate the speed at which he fell. Mason turned his shoulder and attempted to roll with the impact. He managed not to break anything, but he felt his shoulder painfully tear itself out of socket as he rolled. He laid his good hand on the hot pavement and immediately felt the presence of the Loci.

'Hello, welcome to Prol-Mart, how can I help you today?' came into his mind, in a clear friendly tone.

'Weapon!' He thought back pouring energy into this, mostly unfamiliar, elemental.

'I'm afraid weapons are not allowed on the premises, sir. Can I interest you in a shopping cart?' It thought back, as a shopping cart began to roll towards him. Mason took a second to panic. Maybe if he could punch through the pavement, he might be able to get to Sonora. She would be much more amenable to keeping him alive. His elevated pulse might even convince her to try. But, two of the soccer moms had recovered enough to turn their attention back to Mason, and summoned sickly green flames into their palms. Mason didn't have time to argue with the Loci, so he threw himself back, and instead sent a command to his boots.

'Get lost, guys!' he commanded, narrowly avoiding concussive bouts of flame. His boots tore at the seam allowing him to slip out of them. As soon as he got his feet under him, he took off at a run trying to circle around and get the burning van between him and the cultists. As he did so, the thin material of his socks let the energy of the Loci creep into his feet.

'Did you need anything else, sir?' the chipper voice returned.

"Manager! Get me a manager!" Mason cried out verbally. The cultists were becoming more bold and were improving their aim, as chunks of asphalt began shooting up from the craters their bolts were creating.

'I can do that sir, but I can assure you, I'm more than capable of rectifying this situation.' The Loci almost pleaded. Mason managed to get the van between him and the soccer moms just as a bolt of flame that felt like a baseball bat struck the side of his head. The attack only grazed him, and a chain hanging from his lapel disintegrated, as a spirit of luck fulfilled its obligation and absconded into the world.

"Get me a primal-damned manager, or I will write the longest email to corporate you have ever seen!" Mason yelled, as he made a 90 degree turn to keep the van between him and the cultists. He heard shouting as they rounded the van from either side. Where was Nosam?!

'Very well, sir, one moment.' the Loci said dejectedly. The Loci's presence withdrew, and Mason turned to face the cultists, who were forming a firing squad in front of him. Mason suddenly smiled, which caused the only brunette in the group to hesitate. Behind them, a 7-foot-tall, tawny hare-man hybrid flew over the van in a large leap, landing on one of the soccer moms. Her body crumpled grotesquely under the weight of the muscular rabbit. Jack then dropped to his hands and shot his powerful legs out behind him at the next woman, and she went flying like a bullet towards one of the other cultists. They both crumpled against the burning van, shrieking in agony.

Mason felt the tether between he and Nosam snap, and energy poured between them, Nosam fully manifesting. It meant that Mason was hemorrhaging energy, but, the results were hard to argue with, as the brunette was suddenly blindsided by a large white hound plowing into her, and tearing her back to shreds. Losing four of their number so quickly, Horace, and the remaining cultists panicked and took off running from the canine and hare.

'I'm with you, my chosen.' Sonora's voice touched his soul, the Prol-mart Loci having brought her directly to him. The asphalt under Mason exploded away from him, leaving untouched desert earth under his socked feet. Horace, sensing the shift in the battle, fell to his knees and covered his head. The remaining soccer mom was digging her fingers into the flesh of her forearm. Mason didn't know what her plan was, but he could feel large shifts of energy forming around her.

"No." Mason stated, and with an outstretched hand, the asphalt under the woman hissed and pooled into boiling tar. She tripped and screamed as her body was consumed by the black sludge.

Jack, his nostrils flaring, turned to Horace and flexed his legs. Mason held up a hand, and the Hare relaxed reluctantly. Nosam, his paws red and breath heavy, came to Mason's side. He faded slightly, and fed what energy he had left over to Mason, who stood and looked towards Horace. Ambient energy and sand swirled around Mason, as Sonora urged him to put an end to the interloper.

'We shall end him; he will feed the desert.' Sonora raged in his mind.

"I have need of him." Mason said calmly. Sonora was beside herself, but managed to attain a semblance of calm. Sonora was one of the more emotional Loci Mason had ever met; it; was one of the reasons he had chosen to dedicate himself to her. She was like an overprotective mother. The wind died down and Sonora retreated to the back of his awareness.

"Mason?" Jack said, in a guarded tone, his voice sounding foreign in this form.

"Now Horace... What in the hell was this?" Mason said in a condescending tone. His feet were definitely burning from the hot asphalt, but he couldn't focus on that now. Horace looked up cautiously from his cowering.

"I thought I could remove you," He hesitated, "go after Theia and the bead." Mason took a beat to consider the options. Horace and his cult were aware that Theia had the bead, but, not necessarily what it did or was.

"Your crew was pretty small. I assume this was a power grab?" Mason said, starting to grow a bit concerned by the scene around them. Jackson must have felt similarly, because he was shifting back to his human form and turned to the flaming van. Sonora was already swallowing the bodies; they were being slowly absorbed by the ground itself. It would have been more of a concern if they hadn't tried to murder him recently, and Sonora saw little difference between most humans and any other dead thing in the valley.

"Our lord, bade us steer clear of the situation," Horace swallowed, "I'm motivated to negotiate." Mason nodded his head. Jack had completed his glamour and the van seemed to sit in its place, the flames now gone. Mason hadn't been fully aware of just how fey Jack was.

"I don't really wanna tangle with anymore of your little cult and, I imagine, you don't want Samael finding out you've lost five cultists against his will?" Mason tried to surmise.

"You can't really have a mind to let me live. This is the third time I've tried to kill you." Horace instantly regretted his statement, but his incredulousness seemed genuine.

"Well, if I kill you here, Samael goes looking and maybe decides I had something to do with it." Mason held out a finger weighing the options.

"It would not take a huge leap of logic." Nosam added.

"Even worse," Mason extended a second finger, "Maybe he decides young Jack had something to do with it, and it goes Rabbit season." Jack gulped at that one. Mason was always flabbergasted at how he could be so timid and skittish after killing three literal demon worshipers wielding hellfire.

"Not a fan." Jackson chimed in.

"Or" Mason held up a third finger, "Mutually assured destruction. You limp back with a very good story about what happened, knowing full well neither of us wants any further trouble." Mason dropped his hand sliding it into his pants pocket.

"I know which one I'd pick." Nosam barked.

"I see your logic." Horace squinted his face. He moved to a sitting position on the hot pavement a bit bewildered. "Tenuous allies, though you hold most of the leverage."

"You did try to kill me Horace..." Mason sighed.

"Seems like an occupational hazard, but I can see the forest among the trees." Horace stood with a groan and held a hand out to Mason.

"So, you keep Samael off my back, and all of your cult buddies give us a wide berth. You get to keep serving demon dad without this black spot on your reputation." Mason held his hand out, but didn't grip Horace's quite yet.

"Deal." Horace said, a tad eager. Mason smiled a little too much as Horace's hand slapped into his.

"So observed." Jack stated, also sporting a toothy grin. Brambles burst from the handshake wrapping around the two men's wrist for a painful moment before fading into nothingness again.

"Betrayal!" Horace squealed, throwing himself back from Mason.

"Did I not mention Jack here is a bonafide Changeling?" Mason put his hand to his chin in an exaggerated oops expression.

"But he's a hare!" Horace was yelling.

"I mean, that's why we say demi-human not half-human; people can be more than one thing, Horace. Besides, if you have no intention of going back on our deal, there is no reason to be upset that it was geased." Mason explained. Nosam could be heard giving a hearty doggy laugh.

"You tricked me! I didn't know! It can't be valid if I didn't know!" Horace's voice was getting amusingly shrill.

"You are more than welcome to take that grievance up with the Damp Queen." Jack smiled. Horace was clearly upset, but he knew he couldn't weasel out of this now. Promises made to, or observed by, the Fey were very hard to wiggle out of. Sure, you could do it, but that marked you as an oath breaker to the Fey courts. Anyone tied to the fey, or with fey blood, would instantly know you were dishonest, and would attempt to bring you to court to answer for breaking a Geas.

"Well, then it's a pleasure to know we have an agreement." Mason tried not to be too giddy about Horace's facial expression, but he wasn't succeeding.

"I didn't know Shamans were so duplicitous." Horace grumbled.

"Technically, I did most of the shadier stuff." Jack said pointing at his chest.

"I mean, I'm definitely not NOT duplicitous." Mason said grinning, despite being in some pain. Nosam chuffed as he dropped Mason's ruined boots at his feet. Mason ruffled him, as he set about trying to convince them to change back into passable footwear.

"Am I meant to fly away on a broom?" Horace gestured towards the still smoldering but glamoured van.

"I mean, you can hardly be upset I blew up your van. You did try to kill me, Horace." Mason said, a smile in his voice. After getting rubber soles under his aching feet, Mason stood and handed Horace a card.

"A taxi..." Horace lamented.

"You can have them charge the Unseen Forces account, as a kindness." Mason offered the defeated Invoker his hand. Horace looked at it for a beat, and then took it, Mason helped him to his feet.

"What's next?" Jackson seemed antsy.

"Well, Judgment is working on getting us that info, Samael is out of the game, and I'm not sure if PLEB is still after me. I guess it's time to check in." Mason pulled his phone out of his back pocket, only to find it pretty thoroughly broken. "Okay, office for a new phone, then check in."

"Do you think there are any danishes left?" Jackson held his tummy as if he had never eaten before.

"We should get a pup-cup..." Nosam was a fiend for those tiny cups of whipped cream.

"Okay, food, then office, then check-in." Mason relented. How could he say no to such a good dog?

CHAPTER

25

• ● •

The trip back from Japan had been pretty easy. They had gotten pretty lucky and found a Japanese man having a particularly steamy dream, eerily similar to a man in Tucson napping at his desk. Sure, his coworkers would be really confused as to why Theia and Matthew were leaving his office, but that was hardly any of their concern. It was a quick jog back to the Unseen Forces office, and seeing that no one had sent her a multitude of texts asking where the hell she was, Theia felt like she had gotten away with this escapade.

However, seeing Mason, Jackson and Nosam eating tacos and drinking lattes in the reception area of the office, deflated those hopes.

"Why are you out of bed..." Mason asked calmly.

"I had a date?" Theia attempted weakly. Nosam did a doggy head tilt as if she'd said a word he'd never heard before.

"We didn't tell them about you trying to melt Waldorf." Statler added, not at all helpful.

"You tried to melt Waldorf?!" Jackson said in a playful tone. Mason held up a bag pleasantly shaped like a burrito, and hooked a chair with his foot. His bare feet were bandaged and smelled of ointment.

"If you knew him better, you would also try to melt him," Theia shot the gargoyles a withering glance, before plopping down in the offered chair. "What happened to your feet?"

"Horace and his soccer mom cultists tried to kill us. Had to lose my boots. It's over 90 out, so." Mason supplied. Theia nodded, understanding that asphalt in Arizona was not traversed without risk.

"I went to see Paula." Theia said, unwrapping heaven.

"I didn't know she was in town…" Mason said, leaving a purposeful pause for her to fill.

"Our lawyer gave me a ride to Tokyo." Theia said her mouth filling with burrito.

"I've never traveled by Baku, was it fun?" Mason said tossing a taco wrapper and missing the trashcan.

"Wait, your lawyer is fully supe?" Jackson asked a bit amazed, "An Orphic supe?"

"Maybe, keep that between us." Mason cautioned.

"We have to go to great lengths to get our leverets all the way through high school, and he can just stroll in and get a degree?" Jackson shook his head.

"It's easier for full supes to pass. They were born that way, no awkward puberty changes." Theia attempted to comfort the were-hare.

"We can worry about that after no one is trying to kill us." Jackson rushed to clarify.

"Speaking of which, have you heard from Zoe or Ben?" Mason asked.

"I was a bit outside my service area, so I was hoping you had..." Theia countered.

"I'm sure they are fine. The bead is with you, and PLEB doesn't even know Ben isn't human, so all the major players should be swinging at us, not them." Mason said, rubbing his sated belly.

"What's the worst that could be happening!" Jackson added jovially, around bites of vegan chorizo.

· ● ·

The Consumed had gotten Benjamin out of the way of the golf cart, but as he laid sprawled on the linoleum of the Union, he was concerned for Zoe. He looked about, but in the resulting chaos couldn't place her. He would be useless to her dead, so, Benjamin turned his attention to the busted window. A man wearing a Red sleeveless hoodie, and grey sweatpants stood in front of it, calmly chewing on a cigar. He was incredibly muscular and stood, easily, seven feet tall. His facial features had a hard blunt edge, like someone had sculpted it with a hammer. The man stepped over the small wall where he had casually tossed the golf cart, and cast his gaze around finally letting his eyes fall on Benjamin.

"Icarus, you busy?" He said as calmly as if he was requesting a lunch meeting.

"Are you with the Gorgon!?" Benjamin got to his feet, stumbling for a moment before he felt the cold clarity of the Consumed.

"Who?" The man seemed thoroughly confused, and then waved a hand dismissing it.

"Medusa? The Minotaur? A cabal of invasive mythical creatures come to collect a magical artifact?" Benjamin was finding it very hard to believe this man had nothing to do with any of it.

"No clue. I was sent to get you. Someone wiped the warding on you, means your vulnerable. Can't have a pretty thing like you falling into the wrong hands." The behemoth tossed aside his cigar butt and cracked his neck.

"I'm not available at the moment, kinda just started talking to my ex." Benjamin was desperate to sit down. The emotional exhaustion warring with his adrenaline.

"Shame." was all the man said. He started to breathe deeply and then, with zero irony, began expelling fire like vomit into the space between them. Benjamin was both motivated to get out of reach of it, and find Zoe before she was consumed by it. He needn't have worried, however, as the flames bent up and away from him before they could gain purchase. Both Benjamin and the walking meat slab looked about confused before Benjamin noticed Zoe standing a bit behind the newcomer, her hands in a casting pose and her forehead showing the difficulty of the maneuver.

"Get clear, this guy feels odd!" Ben called out. Zoe nodded and retreated behind the trashcan. From this angle it was unclear where she went, but Benjamin was relieved at least momentarily.

"Icarus, why are you being such a little bitch about..." The man began but was cut short as a blur of pink slammed into him knocking him to the ground. The six-foot-tall flamingo wasted no time digging taloned feet into the mystery man, as Levi, the Shaman for the University, came to Ben's side.

"You, ok?!" Levi held his hands out and water stretched between the two of them. Benjamin had seen Mason do something similar in the past when healing someone.

"Levi, what are you doing here?!" Benjamin was incredulous and then embarrassed. Levi was the shaman for the campus, it made perfect sense for him to be here. Benjamin had been protective of the young man in the past, knowing how much ridicule he'd suffered during his transition. Ben had been a much-needed support for him in that time.

"My job." Levi winked and slid a foot along the floor. The seven-foot mystery man had managed to get his limbs under him, but was suddenly jerked to the side and lost his balance again.

"I have no clue who this is, but he has little care of collateral damage. We need to incapacitate him quickly." Benjamin heard Mason's words leaving his mouth and wondered who he was becoming.

"No offense, teach, but this is a bit above your weight class." Levi knew him as a Runic, capable of magic, but not super competent in this kind of fight. Benjamin wasn't sure just how much he should reveal in this instance. Levi was a friend and a dedicated student, but they had never needed to test their level of trust before.

"If my gut is right, you might need our help. My friend is around here somewhere, and she is a reasonably skilled witch." Benjamin hedged. He felt bad, but Zoe had made him question what was going on with himself.

"He doesn't seem that tough." Levi said dismissively. As if on cue, Bertrand the Flamingo went flying from where he was standing to slam with a sickening crunch against a column. Levi was visibly shaken as the feedback reached him. The attacker was dusty, but not seemingly injured , and regained his feet with the ease of a man of his stature.

"If you don't cut it out, I'm gonna get..." He was cut off again as a torrent of water erupted from around the corner. As soon as it contacted the man, it flash froze, encasing most of his torso in frothy white ice. Benjamin could hear Zoe's whoop of victory from where she stood.

"Reasonably?" Levi whistled. It was a short lived victory, however, as the man in red simply flexed and chunks of ice scattered across the floor.

"ENOUGH!" The man bellowed. There was a short scream from the sidelines, and Benjamin's confidence dissipated. Levi shot into action, sliding across the floor toward the man. As he moved, he reached upward and yanked something toward himself. A 4-foot radius circle of the ceiling dislodged itself from above the attacker, and, all in a rush, a column comprised of the five floors above them came crashing down on him. Benjamin watched as Levi touched the resulting pile and it shot in on itself almost as if imploding, and then, blood and dust shot out from the attacker's resulting prison and everyone held their breath.

"What the hell WAS that guy?" Levi panted. Benjamin didn't have time to respond. A literal gorilla stepped around the corner with an unconscious Zoe draped over his shoulder.

"Here is your better, Terran." The Ape said, gripping Zoe's leg and squeezing menacingly. Zoe shot awake, screaming from the sudden torsion.

"Stop!" Levi and Benjamin managed to call out in unison.

"Release my master, and you may have the witch." The Ape said pulling harshly on the woman. Levi looked to Benjamin apologetically. There was no way this man could be alive in that pile of rubble, so what else could they try? Levi visibly relaxed his muscles, and the compacted rubble lost its rigidness and began to roll away. The large man stood in the center of it, wounded, but angry.

"Kong!" He yelled, boiling spittle splashing on the floor. The Ape seemed wracked with pain and much to Benjamin's surprise, it began rushing to the man and merged with him, in a similar manner to how Mason and Nosam had merged in the past.

"He's a shaman?!" Levi yelled back, confused. "What did you do, Benjamin?" Bertrand who had recovered somewhat, appeared at Levi's side. Benjamin caught Zoe moving herself into a seated position some ways away and hoped she would sideline herself. The man bulged his muscles and corse black gorilla fur spread along his shoulders. He swung down faster than a creature its size should have been capable of, and Levi just barely avoided the blow which left a crater in its wake.

Levi was able to pull a chunk of the floor free and it hovered between them, pulling on his connection to the campus, but it didn't last long under the devastating blows laid out by the enemy. As the barrier began to dwindle, Benjamin knew he had to do something, but he was new to combat, and even newer to being two-natured. It was in that moment that Zoe's theory came back to him. While he was new to combat, as a medium, he had years of practical and theoretical knowledge on more traditional magic, and if Zoe was right, he should be able to use that to his advantage.

Levi was putting distance between the ape-man and himself by turning the floor between them into a treadmill of sorts. Injured as he was, the brute didn't seem to notice right away what he was doing. Soon, though, he caught on and launched himself into the air. Benjamin sized the moment, and with little thought to energy conservation, thrust his arms forward yelling "Viento!". Wind ripped through the union slamming into the attacker like a freight train. His limbs were snapped back at disgusting angles, and he ricocheted off the ceiling almost comically. Levi ,sensing the opportunity, got his legs under him and stepped back into Bertrand. While he didn't pack on muscle his limbs lengthened and he now sported a cloak of bright plumage, in rich pinks and reds.

The attacker stood up from the cracked floor, his arms at unnatural and painful angles, and began laughing. Levi and Benjamin looked on in horror as his limbs snapped back into place, audible, even across the large building. He continued his maniacal laughter as he stood and took a step toward them. Levi, showing fear for the first time, looked back at Benjamin. Pain and regret played across his face, and Benjamin wasn't sure if he could go on. While not nearly as experienced as Mason, Levi was no slouch when it came to conflict, if he saw no hope, then what could Benjamin do.

The maniac took a deep breath, air visibly heating as it entered his lungs. Benjamin closed his eyes, resigned and hopeless. The flames, however, never came. Benjamin shot open his eyes to see Zoe panting over the man, a long sword clutched in her white knuckled hands. The Man's head rolled a few feet away coming to rest, its lifeless eyes looking at Benjamin. The Consumed, keening like a banshee, descended on the head bludgeoning and tearing at it until mush and a stain were all that was left. Benjamin and Zoe stumbled to each other and embraced.

"Bastard was too cocky." Zoe panted.

"To be fair, I didn't see you coming either." Benjamin almost sobbed. Levi crashed into them wrapping his arms around the two of them.

"One of you owes me a long explanation," was all he said, as his feathery cloak tickled them. Benjamin began laughing in a probably unhealthy manner, the tension and adrenaline leaking from him.

"Where the hell did you find a sword?" Benjamin managed to get out, between bouts of mad laughter.

"It's a dangerous world, you shouldn't go at it alone." Zoe said smiling up at him. "Its a one off, though, snicker snack, and then its just plastic again."

"You keep an enchanted long sword in your purse?" Benjamin asked incredulously.

"It's always good to have a witch along, remember" Zoe started laughing as well. Levi cut the celebration short and kind of shook the two of them.

"I don't know what's going on, but I know something big is moving around out of sight. Neither of you have the time to deal with bureaucracies, time to skedaddle." Levi said gently pushing them.

"What are you gonna say about all this?" Benjamin said gesturing at the very destroyed union.

"The truth mostly, a crazy, fire-breathing shaman attacked the campus. I stepped in and took care of it." he took a beat, "With no help from anyone else I might add." He winked at Zoe. Benjamin's phone chirped and he fished it out of the rubble to see a brief text message from Mason asking where he was. It made his chest tighten a bit. How was he going to explain this to him? Why did he feel flustered by a concerned text? He surmised he was in a hyper emotional state, and he should try to keep his mind thoroughly off of Mason for the time being, though there was something to be said about almost dying that makes one reconsider their life.

'We made it through. See you soon.' Benjamin texted back, adding just enough emojis to annoy the grumpy shaman.

"I'm assuming that's Mason, checking in," Zoe guessed, "based on your smile." Benjamin blushed profusely and shoved his phone in his pocket. Levi pretended not to notice, like a gentleman.

"I think it's better we go see him in person." Benjamin coughed. They hustled out of the Union and in time made their way back downtown before anyone thought to question them.

CHAPTER

26

• ● •

"**Y**ou were attacked TWICE?!" Mason was incredulous. Benjamin winced at the force of Mason's anger. Jackson on the other hand was ecstatic.

"The Minotaur, and a Dragon dude!" he beamed. "It sounds terrifying, but also very very cool."

"It was neither a big deal nor very cool." Zoe said flatly, leaned exhausted over her desk. "But it was also not our fault, Mason." Mason could tell what she was trying to get at and sat back in his chair, crossing his arms.

"The red hoodie, fire breath guy sounds coincidental, but the Minotaur and Medusa can't be happenstance." Theia mused from her favorite chair, that she had dragged into the common office space.

"According to the theories Professor Wooly put forth, I'm pretty confident they are after the bead." Benjamin found his voice now that Mason was calmer.

"While its fire powers are cool," Theia paused, "I can't imagine that it has anything stronger than your average witch would use it for." Theia absentmindedly rubbed at her neck where the bead had merged with her brand.

"Well, if the Norn's are to be believed, and Professor Wooly is 100% above board, then Medusa and her monster squad might want the bead because it comes from their universe." Benjamin said, gesturing as if arranging his thoughts in the air in front of him.

"Okay, assuming that is true, wouldn't that mean the end of their branch of the multiverse?" Benjamin seemed skeptical.

"Do you have any details on what's inside the bead?" Zoe asked. Theia paused. She had seen that vision of a strangely empty campus and dead college boy, but wasn't sure what that had meant.

"Nothing conclusive..." was all she would commit to.

"Can we find out? Go somewhere?" Jackson asked, not sounding very confident. Most of the room turned to Zoe and Ben. They were the two most versed in traditional magic, and had the market cornered as far as what was possible.

"Theoretically." Benjamin provided.

"It would be a terrible idea." Zoe added quickly. "Crossing into a known realm, such as faery, or the shadow, without knowing where you want to go, or what you are looking for, is ill advisable. Even if it was possible, we would have no way of knowing if we could get back ."

"I'll go!" Waldorf sounded off upon hearing he might not survive it.

"Shush." Zoe continued. She turned to Theia. "If your powers had more of a grasp on it, you or another powerful oracle would be the safest choice."

"I know I'm new to solving supernatural problems, but couldn't we just give them the bead?" Matthew spoke up. Most of the group had forgotten he was there, "I mean, best case scenario, they take it somewhere far away from here." The bead flared, causing Theia to break out in a pained sweat.

"I don't think it considers that an option, as appealing as it might be." Theia said her voice slightly breaking under the strain.

"Even if that was possible, these interlopers have caused significant problems in our world. I'm not sure if I'm comfortable with letting them get away with it, and letting bygones be bygones." Mason said a touch of anger returning to his voice.

"Okay, so we fight," Theia was relieved when the bead seemed to go back to sleep. Perhaps, deciding to protect it had placated the damn thing. "Now, what do we know?"

"Medusa, a witch, and possibly more, are willing to do just about anything to get the bead." Mason provided.

"A powerful witch..." Zoe commented.

"Let's not forget the spider..." Jackson added.

"Right, with everything else going on, I'd almost forgotten." Mason capitulated, "The spider, if related, is responsible for at least the Vampire deaths, if not all of the other ones we've been going after."

"Why would Medusa hire us to find Randall's killer if she was working with the one who killed him?" Theia asked.

"I think she never really cared about that. We know Randall had the bead, and she was much more concerned about finding that. Maybe the thought was that we would stumble onto it in some way." Zoe surmised.

"I mean, if that was the plan all along, it did work. I did find the bead." Theia rubbed at her neck, which was quickly becoming a nervous tic.

"If that's true, then it's easy to connect the spider thing to the invaders." Mason concluded. "What else?"

"The King in the Valley." Jackson stated.

"Right... wild fey at the borders, he should be doing something about that." Mason replied. Nosam rolled over and chuffed in frustration. "And all of the victims had connections to the fey..."

"If you wanted to move about the city without drawing to much attention to yourself..." Theia had the beginnings of a thought.

"With a minimum usage of magic..." Zoe said picking up the thread of thought.

"You'd use one of the Mirror realms!" Jackson exclaimed.

"So," Theia said, holding a calming hand up. "Chances are, our interlopers are huddled up somewhere in faery.

"So, if we want to find them we'll have to go find them in the near infinite madness realm of the fey..." Mason let out a puff of breath and looked at Jackson, who was the most versed with the fey.

"Impossible," Jackson replied. "If you don't know a road that leads to them you could end up literally anywhere. There are no rules of geography there. On any given Tuesday, the road leading to a particular place can change. Unless you knew where the road went... It is admittedly confusing." He slumped into one of the plush couches, frustrated.

"Couldn't you use your gift, like we did in the Dream realm?" Matthew said, sipping at an overly sugary coffee.

"I've tried before, but unfortunately the situation is different." Theia said, seeing confused faces. "When we went to Japan, the chances of success of getting to Japan were high. So, there were a lot of threads that reached that conclusion. It was just a matter of sorting through that clump to find the most advantageous one. Even then, there may have been an even better outcome that I missed. Faery has an ever-shifting tapestry with a very small clump, that could end up anywhere we would want to go. So, finding those threads is possible, but, it would take a lot of time and energy." She sighed. "But it is possible."

"Well, something I can speak on with a bit of expertise, is on the situation with PLEB." Matthew said shifting to a positive tone. "The case against Theia is laughable, even by PLEB standards. It looks more like you guys just pissed off the lead agent, rather than their being any actual interest in some sort of wrongdoing." Mason and Theia's eyes met.

"Fuck." they said in unison.

"Something I said?" Matthew said looking between them. At that moment, Mason's phone dinged. He fished it out of his jacket pocket only to have their fears confirmed.

The mysterious person they had been trying to find, the powerful witch meddling in their affairs and covering for the interlopers was...

"Meredith Carsen..." Mason said out loud.

"It makes sense..." Theia said, in that infuriating way that she and Mason talked.

"She made sure we were motivated and on edge." Mason added.

"Kept me distracted and tried to neuter me." Theia continued.

"Oh..." Zoe said morphing it into a sigh.

"And for the cheap seats?" Jackson said, with only the slightest annoyed tone.

"Meredith Carsen. She's the witch. The one hiding the monsters and making all of their disguises." Theia said rubbing at her forehead. Mason looked down at his phone, then held up a photo that Judgment had just texted him. It was very clearly Meredith Carson speaking with the disguised Medusa.

"WHAT!?" Jackson exclaimed.

"What I don't get is, why not just kill us... Why put us on the path to finding the Bead, and then try to stop us from finding it?" Mason said grumpily.

"Does it matter? A shockingly powerful witch, who may or may not have usurped a kingdom in faery, has been casually serving you paperwork!?" Jackson's arms were getting hairy due to the stress of it all. Suddenly, a sweet smell, almost like incense, filled the room. It took the edge off the tension, and helped him regain his composure. Theia looked at Matt, who winked over his coffee cup.

"Okay, so our fey problem, PLEB problem, and Medusa problem, are all the same problem. That's handy." Mason said breathing deeply from the Baku's calming aura.

"And, assuming the guy who attacked me and Zoe was unrelated, we still have a definite way forward..." Benjamin smiled at an unseen thing at his shoulder, probably the Consumed. Mason frowned at that.

"What do you think, Ms. The Consumed." Mason said authoritatively. Mason had no direct power in the shadow lands, but a Shaman of his clout had a modicum of authority across all the realms. The Consumed was dragged into the material world clinging to Benjamin like debris in a shipwreck.

"What my angel wants, is what I want." She appeared and whispered into the room, her ravaged face unmoving and horrifying.

"Well, that's a refreshing change of pace." Mason shot a sly look at Nosam who growled.

"Don't blame me for your contrary nature." Nosam said stretching. Theia couldn't help herself and burst out laughing as the release of it combined with the mildly euphoric fog, and led to a round of boisterous laughter and wiping of eyes.

"If nothing else, we need to remember we haven't survived all this by chance. We've gotten this far by knowing our shit and sticking together." Theia straightened her smile out and refocused the room. "That's how we end it too, knowing our strengths sticking to a plan. Which reminds me does anyone have a plan?" Theia said looking out at the faces in the room.

"I don't wanna be that guy, but I'd be a liability in the fey." Matthew said, placing his coffee cup down decisively. "Not that I'm much of a heavy hitter, even in my own circles."

"Unless we can open a true gate to faery, I'm pretty nerfed too." Mason said crossing his ankles. "Nosam can't cross the natural crossings."

"Me and Benjamin should be able to work that out, with some time..." Zoe said smiling knowingly at Ben. Benjamin flushed a bit but also smiled.

"Now we just need a way to find them, and not get lost in Fae,ry." Jackson added. Dramatically, as always, a hideous popping sound came from the small bathroom off of the lobby. They all jumped to attention, spells crackling at fingertips and guns clearing their holsters, as a small black blob rolled through the open door.

"My queen may be able to help..." Coincleach hissed.

CHAPTER

27

• ● •

Theia looked at the large shower drain with apprehension. She remembered what Coincleach's brand of transportation had felt like, and wasn't super ecstatic to do it again. She, Jackson, and Benjamin stood staring at the black blob as it inched a slow circle around the drain. Theia fiddled with her Dora the Explorer watch, hoping the magic was still strong enough for this hopefully quick visit to the Fey. Mason and Zoe were working on the gate ritual. Mason had wanted to come along, but without Nosam, he would be better utilized here in the material. Zoe had insisted they take Benjamin, stating clearly that his magic paired with Theia's new abilities, would be enough if trouble kicked off. Jackson was their liaison, so he was forced to go by default, whether he wanted to or not.

"You know, most changelings never ever get a chance to meet one of the monarchs... much less twice in a week." Jackson said gulping.

"Prepare your flesh." Coincleach gurgled as he started to spread out. The bead seemed almost nervous as Coincleach's 'body' touched Theia's feet. She thought about trying to comfort it, but decided against it. There was a line of familiarity she wasn't willing to cross yet.

"That... is a sensation." Benjamin choked out as the putrid smell intensified. He clutched his hands nervously at his sides.

"Just focus on staying awake, that's the trick." Jackson added, maybe just for his own benefit. As the cold slimy mass reached her thighs Theia took an ill-advised deep breath, her head swooning from the fumes. In a rush, she was completely consumed and with a wrenching of her guts she was on her knees in a perfect black void, the smell of mildew and damp air filling her lungs.

She looked about but couldn't see anything, the blackness being as absolute as it was. However, bobbing orbs began igniting around them. Not enough to really see any details of the cavern being revealed around them, but from them, she could make out the kneeling but awake form of Benjamin and Jackson.

"Everybody okay?" Theia asked, unsure of just how many creatures were in the darkness with them.

"Conjuration is a hobby. While that experience was unique, I'm used to these type of sensations." Benjamin provided. It was hard to tell if the light or his skin was particularly pale at the moment. Jackson just held up his thumb in an all-good gesture.

"Hello, Child of Apollo." the strange multifaceted voice of the Deep Queen reached her from what she thought was straight ahead, but couldn't be sure.

"It is an honor to speak with you again." Theia forced herself to her feet. In her peripheral, she saw Benjamin do the same. Jackson managed to make his kneeling position look respectful, but didn't trust standing just yet.

"I apologize for the sudden call to court, but things have changed." The voice seemed almost nervous.

"It was convenient, as we have grown close to completing the task you set for us. We believe we have identified who has harmed your changelings." Theia added, hopefully reminding the Queen that they weren't slacking off.

"It is good that you bring pleasant tidings, for ours are ill." The Queen's voice seemed to be circling them. Theia forced a mental picture of some large snake or other predator out of her mind. Jackson managed to get his feet under him and seemed tense, like a coiled spring.

"I assume you are aware of our situation, but I wasn't aware things had gotten worse on this end." Theia continued to face forward, something in her lizard brain told her it would be dangerous to follow the circling voice.

"Indeed, my spies have determined that the Valley Kingdom is without a Monarch." The Queen said it casually, like she had misplaced a sock.

"Impossible..." Jackson said with horror in his voice.

"The Valley King is arrogant," the voice continued, "It would not be difficult to flatter him into a situation that would endanger him. He relies too much on his power, does not think of the..." Theia felt breath on her ear. "angles." Theia knew flinching would be ill advised, but everything in her was screaming.

"Be that as it may, we also require a service from your Majesty in order to complete our quest." Theia said, really wishing that someone else was having this conversation.

"You require a guide to the farther. One who knows the old paths." The Queen sounded far away again.

"If such a thing is within your power to grant." Theia stated, knowing that, while her words could be seen as a challenge, lesser language might be just as offensive.

"This has already been provided, but may require instruction and introduction. But first, payment must be discussed." The Queen said close to Theia's face. The breath smelled sweet and cool.

"What would you have us do, my queen?" Jackson said confidence and strength returning to his voice.

"I mean to usurp the Kingdom." She said before laughing maniacally.

• ● •

Gates, portals and doorways into other spheres of reality, was something Mason had only briefly studied. He felt like a real idiot looking at the pages of strings of runic symbols and slowly growing pile of magical supplies. Zoe was in her element, with several, what could only be called, tomes spread out on music stands, so they weren't cluttering her workspace. Waldorf and Statler also made small suggestions and corrections as she moved through the process, earning their perch space.

"Don't worry Mason, they will be fine." Zoe said, incorrectly guessing what was eating at him.

"Theia is a badass, Benjamin is a Runic genius, and very recently, I got to see firsthand what Jackson is capable of." Mason said confidently. "I'm more anxious about sitting around being next to useless."

"Hardly useless, maybe not inherently at this juncture, but far from useless." She debated between two quartz stones that seemed almost identical to Mason.

"Right one has the proper sympathetic connection." Statler supplied.

"Thank you." Zoe said, returning the less desirable one to its resting spot on the shelf.

"What do you make of the man who attacked you?" Mason changed topics to something he could be helpful with.

"He was a strange one. Seemed to be some kind of Draconic Shaman. Had a Gorilla partner." She remarked while measuring herbs.

"Dragons are supes. They can't be Shamans." Was all Mason provided.

"I'm starting to think even our communities understanding of the hierarchy is flawed. Between Benjamin and this new guy, I'm not sure what is and isn't possible." Zoe realized her mistake almost immediately and froze while retrieving a tome she needed. Mason and Zoe had been friends for a long time, and he didn't miss the tension.

"What about Ben?" He asked calmly.

"I shouldn't have said anything. I,t's just a theory in any case." Zoe said plopping the tome on the corner of her desk. Mason considered just dropping it, but if Benjamin was hiding something it could be pertinent to the task at hand.

"Zoe." She had heard that tone a million times. It wasn't a demand, but a reminder that she could trust him. If she had heeded that voice it in the past, maybe her life would be different now.

"I don't think Benjamin is a medium." She said in a rush of breath and a strained tone.

"Okay." Trust again.

"He shows a capability for magic, that just shouldn't be possible for a two-natured. And, also, when he fought the Minotaur, he definitely fused with his partner." Zoe sat down, her to-do list forgotten for the moment.

"If that's true, there is no telling what he is. I've never heard of anything like it." Mason sat across from her a tad deflated himself. The two-natured, while paired with a supernatural being, are thoroughly human otherwise. Magic, the true stuff Zoe did, was not possible.

"There is no precedent as far as I know, but this dude in the hoodie seemed similar." Zoe gestured and her thermos of tea sailed across the room to her hand. It was rare for her to use magic for things she could do herself, but she clearly couldn't be bothered at the moment..

"Thoughts?" Mason said to his partner. Nosam seemed to look at the middle distance between them for a long while.

"I feel like I should know, did know, could know, but don't..." He said in a strangely cryptic way.

"Well, that's concerning..." Mason put his head on the desk with a thud. "He kissed me..." It was Zoe's turn to sound incredulous.

"When?!" she slammed her hands on the table, her ritual prep be damned.

"Right before we all split up. He said he wouldn't reject me." Mason crossed his arms over his head so his blush wouldn't show.

"I mean, you've always liked him; I can tell." Zoe said in a conspiratorial tone.

"Of course, I do. The only reason it didn't work out before is because we wanted different things, but now..." Mason thumped his head again in frustration.

"Whatever is going on with Ben has nothing to do with how he feels about you, Mason." Zoe scolded.

"Sure, but if things get complicated, there is no way he's gonna want to casually date." Mason let out a groan.

"Let's walk before we run. Save the world, then worry about boys." Zoe chided.

"You're right." Mason sat back up, his face still pink but fading.

"Right, now run down to the Ave and get me everything on this list." She handed him a slip of paper with tiny writing on it. Mason looked down at it and sighed. He HAD wanted to feel useful. So, he grabbed his keys and sighed even deeper.

• ● •

Theia wasn't sure how to feel about this course of action. Regardless, she stood stock still as a fish-like fey strapped her into a breastplate and greaves.

"Weapon?" the attendant gurgled.

"Uh... I have my gun. I don't think I want to be closer to anyone than that." She had been training in swordplay with Mason, but wasn't confident.

"Iron?" The attendant seemed almost appalled.

"Oh, I guess that's a good point." Theia remembered that wielding iron in a sanctioned war between fey could reflect badly on the Queen. "It's steel, but maybe a crossbow?" The attendant nodded at the wisdom of that, and shuffled to a rack of crossbows and began pointing out how to use them. Theia listened politely, but internally, she wanted to call Mason and have him storm the castle in her place.

The Queen had asked them to prepare for battle, and had then ushered them into these well-lit armories filled with everything a young party of conquerors could ever need. Theia had spent most of her dressing time reading the tapestry as best she could. Reading the threads in Fey, however, was frustrating and random, and she was already annoyed by the effort.

After being dressed and armed, she was escorted into a waiting room where Ben and Jackson were uncomfortably waiting. Benjamin was dressed like a mage out of Lord of the Rings, complete with conical hat and staff. His robes were scaly but moved like cloth, and his staff was slightly taller than he was, and held the largest chunk of tiger's eye she had ever seen. Jackson was in his hybrid form wearing layers of thin green metal with a leaf motif, not what she would have expected from the Damp Court.

"Hail, and well met, compatriots!" Theia attempted with a humorous tone.

"I look ridiculous." Was all Ben managed, fiddling with his hat.

"To be honest, I feel pretty cool." Jackson said, moving about and twisting. "It even shifts to match whatever form I take!" he exclaimed, as he transitioned into the form of a large Hare resplendent in armor.

"They don't really expect us to fight, do they?" Benjamin already seemed fatigued holding the large staff.

"They do, but I doubt we will see much resistance. If the king truly is missing, his subjects will be listless and chaotic. The weapons and armor are more to protect us than anything else." Jackson explained.

"They wouldn't protect the throne?" Benjamin asked, finally giving up and leaning the staff against a wardrobe.

"The monarchs serve an important purpose amongst the fey. Without one, they return to their basic natures, chaos and selfishness. If the Infernal and Celestial realms are places of Order and structure, the fey realms are their opposite." Jackson explained with deference.

"But, you hear all the time about all the rules and laws of the fey realms. They literally serve as oath keepers for most supernatural treaties." Theia commented.

"That's the monarchs. They, by there mere existence, enforce all of that. If one were to leave its demesne, the fey who existed in that kingdom grow wild again." Jackson sipped at a comically small teacup. Theia was jealous that Jackson, being fey by nature, could eat the food here without much consequence. Benjamin and Theia couldn't, without risking complications, and she was starving.

There was a small cough at the entrance of the waiting room. The three 'mortals' turned to see a small man standing in a violet spider silk suit. He had sandy blonde hair and a mottled skin tone, mixing pale white skin with a cool brown tone. He leaned against the door frame and looked quite annoyed.

"Does the Queen need us?" Theia asked. This didn't look like anyone she had seen so far, and didn't look like a damp fey in the slightest.

"I'm here to see him." The fey said, pointing at Benjamin. He didn't seem pleased, and said 'him' with a vehemence you reserve for unliked family members. "Unfortunately." he added. Confusion gave way quickly to recognition, as Ben looked at the fey man.

"Lathair." Benjamin whispered in awe. "She.. the queen, meant.."

"Oh cripes," Lathair, pushed off of the door jam and stood about an arm's length from Ben, looking him up and down. "I'd hoped to never see you again."

"I don't understand, why do I know you?" Benjamin seemed transfixed by the fey.

"Oh, they scrambled you right good." Lathair whistled. "It doesn't really matter. I'm surprised you don't have the chew toy with you."

"This feels very awkward." Jackson whispered to Theia. Theia shushed him, enraptured by the exchange. Lathair held out a hand to Benjamin and sighed deeply.

"Let's get it over with. The Queen made a promise, and a solitary fey like myself won't get far without the backing of a monarch." Lathair whined. Benjamin raised his arm in a similar stance and laced fingers with the fey.

Wind erupted into the room, making Theia cover her eyes. Energy poured from the pair, and bright circles of finite symbols manifested at their feet. While Theia had never seen a life pact before, she was aware of what they were was supposed to look like. She was also painfully aware that this shouldn't be possible. Benjamin was a Medium, tied to the shadow realm. Lathair screamed fey, vibrant and alive.

"It is done." Lathair spoke with finality. At their feet, seven slightly glowing circles were quickly fading, having made a ruin of the mossy carpet they stood on.

"It's wonderful to see you again, or meet you." Benjamin said, confused.

"Don't even get started. I'm only doing this so I can retain my independence, not get all weepy and subservient." Lathair spit on the ground between them. "Though, while you are in the fey, I will do my best to guide you." Lathair said quietly..

"I understand this isn't what you want, and I will try not to lean on you." Benjamin said, as if talking with an old friend.

"Then, we have an understanding." Lathair looked at Theia and Jackson. Jackson gave a small wave. Theia hadn't noticed that Jackson had shifted back into his human form; the armor now making him look thin, like a child wearing his dad's armor.

"Mason know about this?" Theia asked. She could feel the warmth of reconciliation through their bond. It was making her giddy and forlorn and was thoroughly confusing.

"I don't think I can pretend it's not a thing now." Benjamin said, by way of explanation.

"Well, welcome to the team, Lathair." Theia said, adjusting the strap on her crossbow.

CHAPTER

28

— • ● • —

Mason liked Fourth Avenue. He would never admit the small thrill he got, driving under the train tracks. The eclectic mixture of people there milled about, mindless of the world outside this little pocket of bohemian heaven. It also served as the de facto hub for supes and non-humans of all types. They had long been drawn to it, but only recently realized its scope, as people started coming out of the broom closet.

At a stop light, Mason looked at the list again confirming that most everything could be purchased at one specific store. And, while he felt the pressure of the time crunch they were under, he couldn't help but park a tad farther away than was strictly necessary. Nosam agreed emphatically, enjoying a good walk as much as the next dog.

As they rounded the corner onto the avenue proper, Nosam spotted her. Meredith turned into a local coffee shop.

Mason froze, thinking that the only thing that this could be was a trap. She might as well have placed a plate of cookies under a propped-up milk crate, and hid in the bushes. He didn't have much choice though. If he did nothing and she decided to take hostages, he'd never forgive himself.

'Hey Fourths?' Mason only had to open himself for the elemental of Fourth Ave to fill his senses.

'Why, hello, Mason. Is that a bad guy?' The spirit of Fourth Ave was an odd one, somewhere between wise sage and new age nut job, inconsistent and a tad moody, but also indifferent.

'It is, Fourths, any chance you can get Sonora to focus?' Mason had doubts he could get to her twice in the same day, but Fourths was a friend, and much more helpful than the parking lot from earlier.

'She's real deep, brother, but I can try... You sure you don't want me to stay and help out?' The tone was almost condescending but not defiant. Fourths was hurt.

'Try her, just really quick, and then rush back. I don't think anything is gonna happen, but if it does, I'll be glad of the help.' With that compromise, the spirit faded from his senses, presumably to try and rouse Sonora. They waited a few minutes in tense silence before the presence returned. Mason wondered if he looked like a crazy person, squatted like he was and touching the sidewalk.

'The saguaros are blooming.' Fourths thought at him.

"Shit." Mason cursed. There was no way she would miss something that important to her.

'Okay Fourths, here is the plan.' Mason thought back.

Mason, against his better judgment, stepped into the cafe. There was an iced coffee sitting on the counter. It had his name displayed prominently on it, in sharpie. There was even a small cup of organic whipped cream sitting next to it.

"You don't think she would poison a pup-cup, do you?" Nosam said his wagging tail betraying his excitement. Mason smiled at the dog and waved at the barista. She strolled over wiping her hands on her apron.

"Did you make these?" Mason tried not to sound paranoid.

"Sure did, a real hot business mommy ordered them and then described you perfectly. She's out back on the patio." The woman turned back to the espresso machine, indicating she was a little too busy for Mason's nonsense. Mason took the drinks and headed towards the patio. Meredith sat there, puffing on a vape pen and stirring a very foamy cup with magic. Her finger outstretched and twirling.

"Afternoon, Mr. Wallace." She said calmly without looking at him.

"Ms. Carsen." Mason said before sitting across from her. Mason placed Nosam's pup cup next to him and gently asked the bench seat to widen to accommodate his companion. The bench gladly capitulated and groaned a bit under the strain of them both. Once they both sat facing the witch, Mason took a sip of his bribe. It was heaven, perfect in every way. It took all of his willpower not to smile down at the cup.

Nosam gently lapped at his own, never taking his canine eyes off of Meredith.

"You've impressed me," Meredith said, "the practitioners of this world are all rather self-absorbed, but your little band is quite capable." She turned to Mason and dipped a finger in her drink before raising it to her lips.

"You're not half bad yourself." Mason loathed complimenting her, but he had to admit she was good at what she did. She laughed a little too loud at that and removed the spoon from her cup.

"The Magic of this sphere is thin, easy to push around. It's much thicker where I come from." She assessed Mason. He wasn't sure if she wanted to kill him, marry him, or possess him. "I'm not sure how you escaped my lasso or my Golem, but after that fiasco, I've refrained from trying to kill you in a hope we could speak frankly."

"All the Franks I know are very eloquent. I will try to live up to their legacy." Mason said with a smile. Meredith didn't find this nearly as amusing, but pushed past it.

"I do not wish a war with this sphere. I and mine only wish to move on to the next. With the bead." She was all business now, pretense gone.

"If things had gone differently, that might be an option. We can't trust your intentions now, seeing as how you killed so many locals." Mason said, making a point to sip his coffee absentmindedly.

"I'm aware of your intentions, as well as your group's little foray into Faery." Meredith traced a symbol onto the table. It sparked but didn't erupt into anything dangerous.

"Won't be long til we find your clubhouse, and put a stop to your scheme." Mason was trying very hard not to enjoy his coffee.

"What scheme? I came here for a purpose. I was stopped in my tracks by a plucky group of friends, and now I have to defend myself against them. Who, pray tell, is the unreasonable one in this situation?" Meredith slammed a well-manicured hand against the rough wooden table.

"I don't want to talk in circles about murder and general distrust, but I am able to." Mason remarked.

"Do you think your inherent resistance to magic will protect you? Is that where this cockiness stems from?" Meredith's hair began to rustle slightly in an unfelt wind. That did give Mason pause. It was true, magic had a hard time with him, but a fireball was a fireball.

"If it makes you feel any better, most people I meet find me infuriating." Mason said sipping loudly.

"Let it be known, I attempted to reason with you." Meredith said standing.

"Nosam, update the minutes." Mason said with undue confidence.

"Duly noted, sir." Nosam replied.

"Enough insults." Meredith threw her hands into the air. Clouds flooded the sky, and the smell of ozone filled the air, so intensely, that it burned Mason's nose. Meredith's hair tossed about as if in a hurricane, and she brought her hands down and a deafening crack of lightning struck Mason and Nosam. She cackled gleefully, until she saw, not charred and smoldering corpses, but slightly singed statues.

From across the street, Mason clutched his head, the sudden returning of his consciousness to his real body making his ears ring. Nosam looked up at him with serious eyes.

"Don't worry, bud. Agatha is already delivering what Zoe needs, so we can skedaddle." Mason took a moment to send an energy laden high five to Fourths. 'Good job on the simulacra.' he thought to the elemental.

'I'm gonna take a nap. That lightning strike was legitness.' Fourths said, his consciousness fading. Before the wicked witch had even decided what to be angry about, Mason and his dog were unlocking the jeep.

• ● •

Soon, Theia was on horseback flanked by Jackson, Benjamin, and an annoyed Lathair. Jackson had forgone a horse, as his hybrid form was a bit large to ride comfortably. Theia looked out at the desert landscape and sighed deeply. There were plenty of fey creatures standing between them and the castle in the distance. There were also quite a few fey in their ranks, but she was dubious of ancient style warfare.

"Pardon if I sound ungrateful, but what are our odds here?" Theia said, bemused by the spectacle of it all.

"I don't go to war very often either, Theia." Jackson said his tall frame putting his head at her waist, despite the height of her horse.

"Why are we doing this, again?" Benjamin said, trying to hold on to his large staff and the reins of his horse at the same time.

"Presumably to gain favor with the Damp Queen, and put an end to the wild fey at the border." Theia answered unsure.

"If you want to go after your other interlopers, having this region of Faery stabilized, is your best bet." Lathair explained. "Otherwise, we are likely to meet a lot more opposition the whole way."

"Right. Now, I get that. But, how will The Damp Queen take control if she hasn't left her own domain?" Theia was painfully aware of her absence in the field.

"The Damp Court is democratic." Lathair explained, with a sigh reserved for small children. "Any one of her subjects on the King's throne will mean that she controls this region." Lathair pointed down the line to some snazzily dressed, pale, elf looking characters. "Those are the heads of the noble houses of the Damp Court."

"How can you have a democratic monarch?" Benjamin asked so Theia didn't have to.

"Upon joining the Damp Court, all new members give some piece of themselves, a bit of flesh, an eye, some hair. This ensures that any decision made in Court, is instantly made by the entirety of the Court." Lathair fidgeted in his saddle and Theia felt for the faery man. He was only here because of his connection to Benjamin.

"Fascinating. So, when the Queen speaks, she does so with the authority of everyone. Instant democracy." Benjamin said with undue wonder in his voice.

"Exactly. It's one of the draws of the Damp Court within Faery. It only causes problems when there isn't a majority opinion, which has caused schisms in the monarchy." Lathair stated.

"Schisms..." Jackson said with a shiver.

"Only thing worse than one queen, is two opposing ones... Its why most kingdoms rely on just one monarch," Lathair concluded. One of the previously pointed out pale elves approached them.

"Oracle, we are ready to hear the plan." He said handling his horse and spear expertly.

"Well, I've gone over the threads, and the most success is gained by plowing down the middle while the flanks repel the defenders. My group, and a few of you princely types, push through to the throne room, and then it gets confusing." Theia said, her confidence slipping into a more skeptical tone.

"Confusing?" The elf asked.

"Well, at that point, the magical topography vastly changes. The threads sever. Whoever takes the throne changes the outcomes, but I can't see them that well. It's as if they don't truly exist. It's like a bunch of different maps stacked on top of each other. As a whole, they indicate information, but it's impossible to tell which item is on which map." Theia was a tad relieved to be talking to people who took her gift for what it was. The elf just nodded and returned to his little group to relay the information, no questions, no doubt, no probing comments trying to prove her a fraud, just acceptance and action.

Before she had much time to revel in the acceptance of her gifts, drums began booming from further back in the ranks. A horn blew and her horse surged forward. The horses seemed to understand what they were doing better than either Theia or Benjamin, and they just did their best to hold on. Theia had chosen this course of action, because it led to a minimal loss of life, and kept her little group mostly isolated from the fighting, which was ideal for her.

Most of the battle wasn't visible from their place within it. Theia spent most of it just trying to stay on her horse. She didn't dare swing her crossbow forward, as it meant she would have to let go of the reins. She knew from her visions, however, that the large trolls near the edges of the throng were battling the near crazed fey, with little regard for their own wellbeing. She also knew from her studies, that unless the fey were killed with iron, any deaths would not be permanent. In this way, the fey could freely engage in the sport of war, without having to really mesh themselves with the consequences.

Soon the gates of the castle loomed ahead, foreboding and very closed. The broody elf from before looked to Theia for guidance, and she nudged her horse forward. She looked at the elf almost apologetically for what she was about to do.

"We seek an audience with the King and bear a delivery most cumbersome!" She yelled up at the gates, which, after an agonizing moment, swung in on themselves allowing them deeper inside.

"Deceit?" the elf seemed incredulous, which, given the fey's reputation, rang hollow to Theia's ear.

"You asked for easy, not honorable." Theia stated plainly. She knew none of the assembled fey, which now included

Benjamin, could tell a strict falsehood within Faery, but Theia, being human, had no such issues.

The guards within the gate looked up at the opening doors with horror, and were quickly routed by the Elven knights. Theia tried to remind herself that the violence and gore weren't real, like they would be in the First World. This warfare was the fey realms favorite pastime, but it didn't console her much. Soon, Theia was being helped down from her horse, and she pulled the crossbow forward with just enough precision to loosen a bolt into a mad looking fey about to stab Benjamin from a hidden nook. That one action solidified which of the scenarios the tapestry was revealing. That didn't occur in each iteration.

"You two, guard this door." Theia said, pointing at two of the larger elves. "There is only one guard between us and the throne room, but most of you fall to him before Benjamin clinches the deal." Theia could have elaborated, but if they hesitated, it would lead to injury on Ben's part. The princes had to take on the guardian. Fighting had erupted in earnest in the courtyard, and Theia was glad to be entering into the cooler interior of the castle.

Inside was chaos. Desert fey of all stripes, were losing their minds. Between defecation, screaming, and the occasional fornication, none of them seemed to have a scrap of sense. It appeared that, whatever their most basic urge was, that was how they were composing themselves. If Meredith had caused all of this madness, she had a lot to answer for.

The group moved through the halls of the castle, all but ignored by the assembled courtiers. As they passed a lavish dining hall, Theia scooped up a particularly shiny goblet and tucked it into her belt. No one so much as looked their way as their small group quickly covered ground to a grand staircase. At the top of the plush stairs was a large set of gilded doors. Theia gestured to the princes, and they pushed at the doors to open them. She put a hand on the elf who had approached her earlier.

"What's your name?" Theia asked. It was a rude question in Faery. One should either already know someone's name or use their title, but she had to know if she had everything right.

"Fane." The knight said a tad bewildered.

"Okay, Fane, I need you to stay near me to keep me safe." Theia said with a smile. Fane seemed to like the whole chivalry thing, and raised his shield in a respectful salute to her. Theia turned to Benjamin.

"What am I supposed to do?" Benjamin asked.

"You'll know." Theia said with a wink. The future was a delicate balance, and telling someone their own was not always a good idea. Give them exact instructions, and many will panic trying to remember what they were supposed to do. Those seconds of hesitation led to things going sideways 80% of the time. It was better to tell someone that they would succeed and let them react naturally to a situation.

As the large doors fully swept open, the assembled princes looked at each other bewildered. Sitting in the grand hall before the throne, was a small pinkish red dragon about the size of a house cat. It looked up at them startled as the doors locked into place. It sat on a small mound of cups and tilted its head in their direction. Theia looked away, not wanting to see what happens again.

The small dragon shifted colors, its shimmering scales turning black with green accents. It raised its little snout and a cloud of black smog billowed out from it. The princes were immediately consumed by the cloud. The sound of shouting and laughter quickly followed. Benjamin, seeing the danger, raised his staff and a strong wind whipped up around them, dispersing the cloud before it could reach them. As soon the smog faded, Ben could see what was happening within it. The princes were giggling or screaming as they stabbed at each other mercilessly, driven to madness by the dragon's smog cloud. Theia nodded to Benjamin after the smoke had mostly cleared, and she stepped forward with the fancy goblet in hand.

"I brought this for you." She said in a sweet voice. The small dragon cooed and stood on its haunches reaching for the shiny cup. She dropped it into his little claws and his scales returned to their pink, red brightness. While the little dragon arranged his new prize on his pile, Theia gestured for the rest of them to move around the little guy and up to the throne proper.

"Truly, without your insight, the day would have been lost, milady." Fane said looking at the small dragon and his dead companions.

"It would have taken longer, but you would have managed it eventually." Theia tried to keep her tone light as she gestured to the throne. Fane looked at it with awe and removed his helmet. His first few steps up to the throne were taken slowly, until excitement overtook him and he ran up and sat upon it with a flourish. He truly did look regal sitting upon it, but nothing else truly shocking happened. Jackson and Lathair shuddered, and a sense of calm emanated from the throne.

Outside it began to rain.

CHAPTER

29

——— • ● • ———

Theia looked out at the expanse of Faery. The desert was dotted with green vegetation giving the landscape an almost spotted visage. The fey from the area were all gathering to reaffirm their loyalty to the new liege lord, and their shifting bodies made the whole vision surreal.

She and Jackson had decided to remain in Faery, while Ben was escorted back to the First World to assist with the Gate spell. Units of the damp army were cleaning up those fey still in the throes of rebellion or madness. Theia looked out over the mountains to the horizon, curious but also anxious at what awaited there. She couldn't quite see what was coming, and that was always thrilling to her. Ever since she had manifested her gift, her life had followed a set course, measuring the ripples and split threads. She had learned to avoid heartache, misfortune, and missteps, but it all seemed so exhausting now. What if she hadn't wasted hours deciphering every small detail, and just turned it all off and walked forward?

Her mind wandered to visions of the past. She had been giddy after her first date with Gideon, yet, she began pulling out her cards and seeing what the future held. She had seen the grief, the pain, but also the potential joy and contentment. It had scared her. She'd been young, and Gideon wasn't going to grow old with her. No matter how much joy sat on one pan of the scale, the other held loss for one of them. She brought a pipe to her lips and let the soothing smoke of whatever was packed inside it, dull the feelings, allowing her to pack them back into the file cabinet of her mind.

"Copper piece for your thoughts." Gideon's voice lilted from behind her. She cursed herself. Thinking about Celestials was never a good idea if you were trying to avoid them.

"I didn't think that hard, so I'm assuming this isn't nostalgia." Theia said, not giving him the satisfaction of turning to speak with him.

"Honestly, Theia, you might have seen a terrible life for us, but I remember one really good night out of the deal." Gideon said with too many teeth.

"Nope, no thank you." Theia said, "What do you want?"

"I'm attempting to be kind, Theia." Gideon's tone lost its frivolity.

"How did you even find me?" Theia said, turning and resting her elbows on the small wall of the tower.

"The Celestials notice when the monarchy shifts. The rest was luck and intuition." He removed a cigarette from somewhere and lit it, as he brought it to his lips. The smell of it made Theia sigh a bit with the recollection.

"Okay, but you still haven't told me why." Theia pushed, puffing on the pipe again.

"I've been feigning incompetence, but it's time to give up the bead. The brass doesn't like it being in the hands of some human girl." Gideon was clearly quoting someone else.

"Several points," Theia said, angrily, "Not human, not a girl, and, it's stuck in my neck! Did you bring a machete? I could hack it off right quick!" Theia's anger was more of a defense than a true emotion.

"I told them you wouldn't appreciate the description." Gideon pinched off the cherry of his cigarette, and with the sound of metal against cloth, a sword slid out of his other sleeve.

"Is that it, Gideon? You're gonna kill me?" Theia stared deep into his blank white eyes.

"I don't want to, Theia." Gideon had shaky emotion in his voice.

"What would prove it to them? That I can keep it... at least until they find a way to transfer it." Theia pushed off from the wall, the beginning of a scheme forming in her mind.

"I'm listening." Gideon said calmly.

"I don't know if your boss is aware, but some inter-dimensional party crashers are in Faery. They are up to something; they too want the bead. Tried to kill me for it." Theia was pretty sure she was stretching one of those facts, but she liked her neck where it was.

"If you were able to protect the bead from the outside forces seeking it, they might be convinced to reassess." Gideon relaxed the grip on his sword.

"I'm sure if one of their trusted agents put the proposition forward, they would at least consider it." Theia put as much sincerity into the statement that she could. The sword glowed for a moment and was gone.

"How can I help." he said a sigh in his voice.

• ● •

"Zoe, I understand your point, but if this symbol falters, we could all end up as goo upon arrival." Benjamin said emphatically, pointing at the symbol nearest him.

"You worry too much." Zoe said waving off his protestation.

"I'd survive it." Lathair said with a snotty tone from Zoe's office chair. Mason was watching the fey like a wolf stalking a rabbit.

"Lathair, if you aren't going to help, you are more than welcome to await us in Faery." Benjamin said with practiced ease.

"And miss out on your adorable thinking face?" Lathair said, making eye contact with Mason. Mason's nostrils flared and Nosam growled softly.

"You should really use stone for the medium," Statler said with a whistle. "That plywood does not look up to the task." Zoe threw her arms in the air.

"Do the men around here want me to go make sandwiches while they critique my work, or should I finish this!?" Zoe slammed her sharpie on to the half-completed circle.

"I don't mean any disrespect, Zoe." Benjamin apologized.

"I was kinda hoping you'd smite me, honestly." Statler added. Zoe huffed and stomped into Theia's office.

"Who are you again?" Mason said grumpily for the third time, staring daggers at the lounging fey.

"I'm one of Benjamin's other selves." Lathair said making the words sound silky and filled with innuendo.

"And to clarify again, you have no urge to explain how that is possible..." Mason said clenching and unclenching his fist. Nosam circled the office, the excess emotion pouring off of Mason and into him.

"A pooka is under no compulsion to answer any mortal man." He made mortal seem like a slur as he spoke.

"It's just odd that all this madness befalls Benjamin the same week that some similar madness attacks him with a golf cart." Mason cracked his knuckles.

"Trust, no one will miss Fafnir." Lathair said with an eyeroll.

"Ben, will you please compel this mouthy asshole to answer me straight!" Mason bellowed.

"I already told you, regardless of the temptation, I promised I wouldn't assert dominance over Lathair." Benjamin said without looking up from his reading. Lathair stuck his tongue out at Mason with an elfish giggle. Mason chucked a stapler at the Pooka. It struck the back of an empty chair as Lathair transformed into field mouse and slid under the desk. Mason moved to the desk only to find the sharp point of a long knife pressed to his neck.

"I might remind you; you need me a lot more than I need you." Lathair said with a cold seriousness.

"Not forever, pooka." Mason said pushing his neck against the point drawing a bit of blood.

"Mason, enough!" Benjamin scolded. "Honestly, you seem more concerned with Lathair than whatever Meredith has planned.

"Pooka can't be trusted, Ben." Mason said, the small wound on his neck dripping blood below his shirt collar.

"Well then, get your head out of your ass and help me hold this steady, or do you need a time out as well?" Benjamin said struggling with the large sheet of plywood.

"Ben..." Mason started, but was cut short by a flash of white light. After they had blinked the spots from their eyes, Theia and Gideon stood in the reception area. Gideon looking horrified at the various art supplies threatening his white suit.

"I thought Gideon was a bad guy?" Waldorf called out disappointed.

"If you're going to do a dramatic reveal, can I run to the little gargoyles room first?" Statler added. Mason chucked a stack of post-its halfheartedly at Statler.

"I got bored, so I asked my ex for a ride." Theia said with a smug smile.

"I don't know if one date really makes us exes..." Gideon said exasperated.

"What we shared meant nothing to you?" Theia said mock anger in her voice.

"Oh, burn him up!" Statler exclaimed. Zoe threw the door open and smiled at Theia and Gideon.

"Not that I don't have faith in you all, but Gideon here can open a gate to Faery." Theia said, pointing at him with her thumb. Gideon shifted awkwardly but didn't say anything.

"I mean, I feel like we almost cracked it." Benjamin said holding up the plywood.

"I mean, Gideon tried to kill us pretty recently, Theia." Mason tapped his foot for emphasis.

"I mean, not very hard…" Gideon said with a shrug.

"Don't be a sore loser, Gids." Theia said patting him on the shoulder.

"Lathair, are you prepared?" Benjamin said, stretching and only wincing a little at the movement.

"Meredith must know we're coming." Mason reminded them. "She tried to kill me while we were shopping."

"Honestly, if we wait, it will be just more opportunities for people to kill us. So, we might as well go to the source." Theia said with a huff. "Jackson is getting some mounts together from the Valley King. So, all that's left is for pretty boy to show us the way."

"Pretty?" Mason said incredulous.

"Flirt." Lathair returned.

"With Gideon on the team, I think we stand a chance of pulling this off." Theia said, leaning against the wall. There was a gentle knock at the door before it swung in of its own accord. Matthew stood a bit bewildered on the other side.

"I smelled Theia," he said a bit suddenly. Theia pushed off of the wall and stood before him.

"How can I help you?" Theia said nonchalantly. Gideon looked at the Baku and his wings unfurled. Mason looked at the two men. Matthew, in gym clothes, cut an impressive figure, and Gideon seemed perturbed to see him.

"I just wanted to bring you something." He locked eyes with Gideon and handed Theia a small pouch. "I might not be much help in Faery, but these are poppy seeds from the dream-realm. They protect dreamers far from home." He met Theia's gaze and smiled.

"It's a love triangle!" Statler yelled in a whisper.

"It's happening!" Waldorf answered in kind.

"Enough." Zoe scolded, but winked at the gargoyles.

"I appreciate it." Theia said a trace of blush rushing to her cheeks. Without being able to peek, Theia wasn't sure what else to say.

"Gideon." Matthew said in a slightly defensive tone.

"Mr. Davis." Gideon was also a bit guarded.

"Do you guys know each other?" Mason couldn't hold back as he blurted out the question.

"We dated when I was in law school, I wasn't aware you knew each other." Matthew explained.

"Shit." Theia said, as she put her face in her hand. Statler and Waldorf audibly gasped. Mason burst out laughing and Nosam bit into his calf trying to get him to stop.

"Wait." Matthew started, as Theia swung the door closed, shutting him out.

"Can we please go get killed by the bad guy now?!" She shrieked, red filling her cheeks fully.

"That's your cue, angel boy." Lathair said, barely concealing a shit eating grin.

• ● •

Sometime later, they stood in the courtyard of the Valley King's castle. Fane waved down to them from the balcony of his throne room. He had physically changed, taking on more aspects of the old king, filling out his frame and sporting the beginnings of a beard. But, Theia didn't have time to worry about the political climate of the near fey as she took stock of her group.

She, Benjamin and Jackson were still in their fey gifted armor and weapons, astride solid, but oddly colored horses. Mason was on foot and wearing his very modern looking armor. Neck to feet layered plates of metal, and Kevlar, making him look like Batman. He adjusted the large backpack he wore, the weight of the dirt inside it constantly shifting. Nosam was by his side standing shoulder to shoulder with the horses, smiling in a very non-threatening way at the nervous equines. Zoe wore more traditional modern body armor and military style fatigues. It clashed with her floral bag filled with potions and other magic supplies, which she busied herself double-checking from her highlighter yellow mare. Gideon stood off to the side in his traditional white suit and flexed his wings. They all were sporting their colorful cartoon watches. Lathair, currently a raccoon, peeked his face out from underneath Benjamin's giant wizard hat, and chittered pointing west.

"We have our heading, Captain!' Mason said with a smile. Nosam crouched down on the ground, and Mason climbed on to his back, apologizing for the inconvenience.

Theia gave a respectful bow to the King, before urging her lime green stallion west. They moved past assembled desert fey, all waving and cheering the departing heroes. Theia made a mental note to tell the Admin about all of this. It was straight out of one of his campaigns. Jackson was exuberantly waving at the gathered crowd, drinking in the adulation. Benjamin looked a bit uncomfortable with the attention, and Lathair hid under his hat quite annoyed by the whole thing.

As they rode, guided by the chittering pooka, the landscape changed from the recognizable desert, giving away to scrubland and then eventually rolling green fields. It was nearly impossible to tell how long they had been riding, but eventually hills began to swell on the horizon and the sun began to dip closer to the earth.

"Ow." Benjamin exclaimed, as the raccoon yanked on his hair beneath his wizard cap. Theia pulled on the reins and circled to look back at him. Benjamin removed the hat, and Lathair stood next to him in his elven form.

"We are getting close, but the air is wrong." He sniffed at the air around them. "I don't think this could rightly be considered fully Faery anymore."

"More information, less fey nonsense, please." Mason grumbled, Nosam panting happily beneath him.

"I'm being as succinct as I can be, hound face." Lathair said looking about. "This part of Faery should be flooded with fey magic, and it is, but it smells wrong."

"Well, regardless, we should push forward." Theia said, looking up at Gideon flapping in a holding pattern overhead. They continued onward, and the hills gave way to valleys of towering gray stone. Gideon began to fly lower and closer to the group, as the whooping of some other flying monstrosity could be heard from within the stone crevices. No one spoke much, as the air grew tense with anticipation and thick, syrupy magic. Before long, they rounded one last corner, and the space opened up onto a cliff overlooking a raging sea.

Sitting near the edge of the cliff, was a large, classical ancient Greek temple, reminiscent of the Parthenon. Its gleaming marble looked bright and freshly carved. Theia was taken aback by the mere spectacle of it, but the feeling quickly soured as she saw the large, too large, webs covering the base of the structure.

"We've arrived." Lathair said, the usual contempt missing from his voice.

CHAPTER

30

• ● •

The structure's columns formed a wall of webs. The thick strands weaving between them meant the building could only be safely approached from the front. Theia wasn't sure if the webs would be sticky, as large as they were, but was very keen not to find out. As they moved towards the entrance, Benjamin examined the strange substance.

"It's ever so slightly pink, and the smell is familiar." He said, getting his face uncomfortably close to the stuff.

"It's blood." Mason said, Gideon nodding his agreement.

"Why would it smell like that?" Zoe said, the slightest bit of panic in her voice.

"I, for one, don't want to find out." Jackson said swallowing hard.

The group continued on in quiet contemplation as to the implications of a large spider that could spin blood webs. At the front of the structure, the open doorway was a dark rectangle. No light seemed to penetrate that darkness. They all stood looking into it, a foreboding feeling reaching each of them.

"Why is everything in Faery awful?" Gideon said, relieving a bit of the tension.

"Buildings in Faery are always reflections of the things that live in them." Lathair commented solemnly. The comment was undercut slightly by his raccoon image on Benjamin's shoulder, but they all nodded.

"Okay, Jackson, Gideon, and I, in the front where stabbing is most likely. Zoe, you and Ben stay in the middle as you have the most ranged potential, and Theia, we aren't sure what you can do, so you bring up the rear and try to catch an ambush." Mason said, his serious face on.

"I told you my sight isn't good short term anymore, and in Faery, even long-term sight is difficult." Theia said, annoyed with her current handicaps.

"Sure, but you still have a lot more experience than Zoe and Ben. You're sure to catch something they might miss." Mason said, with a reassuring smile. Theia had needed to hear it, as her confidence had been shot since they had gotten to Faery. They entered the black, gaping hole in the otherwise bright countryside. The darkness was palpable, and none of them could see absolutely anything. However, light began to spill from Gideon, displaying a large room carved from marble.

Zoe gasped in horror. They saw the King. He was held aloft, his wrists being attached to the far walls on either side of the room by vine like webs. His lower half was just...missing, and gore still dripped from the vivisection. He looked very dead, and the pool of blood beneath him had grown quite large.

"Impossible..." Jackson said clutching at his head. Lathair also recoiled and chittered in horror.

"What's impossible?." Mason said stern but calm.

"Monarchs are immortals..." Lathair managed to croak out, visibly struggling with something. Even Ben seemed to be straining in pain.

"Okay, but pull yourself together." Gideon scolded.

"It's the corpse. The presence of a Monarch carries a calming sensation. The presence of a Monarch's corpse is wrong. I'm not sure how much longer I can be around it." Lathair whispered, clearly trying to hold it together. Jackson was squat down covering his head with his hands. Mason, quite suddenly, reached for the backpack, and a thin but sturdy spear of sandstone formed into his hand.

"If this is here, it would be the perfect place..." He couldn't finish the sentence before the floor gave way and dropped them to their butts. As they began sliding into an even darker abyss, Gideon was able to grab Theia and fly up and away from the pit trap. Theia regaining her senses, looking in horror as the others tumbled into that darkness. Benjamin, being born by the largest hummingbird she had ever seen, rose out of the pit. Lathair turned to them and gave a brief shake of the head in his new bird form.

"Put me down! We need to go after them!" Theia yelled. She was smart enough not to struggle and fall out of Gideon's hands, but it was a close thing.

"Theia." Gideon put on a voice that seemed to speak volumes, but she wasn't hearing it.

"Now, Gideon!" she shrieked. Gideon began lowering towards the sloped floor, and they watched in horror as it pushed itself back into place sealing itself with an audible rush of air. Theia resisted the urge to cry out in agony. She had seen a future with Mason. He was assuredly fine, but it also came with the knowledge that she had been wrong before.

Gideon flew to the far side of the room and hovered, letting Theia get her feet under her again and run to him. They were at a doorway leading deeper into the temple. Benjamin and Lathair joined them.

"What the hell was that?" Benjamin said, panic evident in his voice. Lathair changed into his raccoon form and kind of curled up, one eye always on the King's corpse.

"It looked like an enormous trap door." Gideon stated.

"We knew there was a spider here, but that was insane." Theia was attempting to sound comforting to herself, if noone else.

"We have to find a way down there! I could try a conjuration." Benjamin was already making hand gestures. Lathair put a paw on his leg.

"Faery doesn't have a normal relationship with the space-time continuum. If you conjured them, or attempted a teleportation or gate, you'd be just as likely to toss them into the ocean as help them out." The raccoon said, a bit dazed.

"Well, we can't just do nothing!" Benjamin cried out, his emotion raw and near the surface.

"Perhaps, there are stairs that lead down. For all we know, there could be an elevator." Gideon said calmly.

"Gideon is right. Mason would push forward and find another route." Theia reached out with their connection, but it was hard to make out Mason with so much of Benjamin's emotion flooding the metaphysical space.

"We'd know if he was hurt, right?" Ben said sensing her.

"In theory yes, and I know this doesn't help, but it would be easier if you got a hold of your emotions a bit." Theia said trying to be understanding.

"Ever since I bonded with Lathair, all of my emotions have been in hyper drive. I'm struggling to get a baseline." Ben said, taking some deep breaths.

"You are connected to Faery; emotion is an issue for us all." Lathair said plainly.

"Shall we see what's gonna try and kill us going forward?" Gideon said.

"We still haven't seen Medusa or Meredith, or anyone really." Theia responded with a harrumph of frustration. Gideon nodded and walked down the hallway.

The next room was much like the last, with high ceilings, and seemingly carved out of the same solid piece of marble. It was clear that the inside of the building was much larger than the outside, as each of these rooms seemed larger than the building itself. To make matters worse, this room was filled with grotesque statuary. Ben audibly swallowed and Lathair climbed back onto his shoulder, finally free of the dead king's influence.

"I must ask the Nephilim to remain here. My master wishes the others to continue." Medusa's voice suddenly echoed off of the high ceilings, making it impossible to determine where it was coming from.

"Not gonna happen." Theia called back, drawing her gun. Gideon put a hand on Theia's shoulder.

"Medusa is more than a passing threat. She is probably the most hazardous to you and young Benjamin. I'm partly divine. She will be hard pressed to turn me to stone." Gideon sounded confident, but Theia knew it was possible, if not improbable.

"Yes, but it would be nice to have a mini-nuke when facing Meredith." Theia whisper-yelled at him.

"If we cannot reach a consensus, we can attempt to extract the bead from your statue." Medusa's voice filled the space accompanied by maniacal laughter.

"Whatever is happening, it's happening soon, Theia. I don't know if we have the luxury of choice here." Benjamin said his eyes heavy lidded.

"What do you mean?" Theia asked abandoning the whisper.

"Something is stirring deeper inside, something big. If you would take a moment, I'm sure even you would be able to feel it." he added. Theia closed her eyes, annoyed, and reached out. The threads while not being clear to her sigh,t were almost blinding and hummed with potential. Ben wasn't wrong. Whatever was happening was beyond the scope she had words to describe.

"I'm not happy about this." Theia said loudly to the room. "It feels like some sort of cartoon, and I did not sign up to be the protagonist." she said to her companions.

"It might be Ben... so self-centered." Gideon said in a dismissive tone. Theia slapped him on his glowing arm, but took a deep breath and put one foot in front of the other towards the door at the far wall.

"Be careful, Gideon..." Benjamin said meekly.

"Wait... Theia." Gideon caught her arm and she instinctively turned to the angel. He leaned forward and laid a gentle kiss on her forehead. Warmth spread through her, and light began to shine from her. "For luck," was all he said as he pulled back and faced the room around them.

"For luck..." Theia repeated as she turned back towards the third super scary doorway, and the thrum of magic.

• ● •

"For a trap..." Mason said as the rumbling ceased. He was sprawled out, his limbs entangled by what was most likely a giant web. He sighed and looked about, but it was just as dark in here as every other room had been.

"Mason, I think we found the spider." Jackson said from somewhere off to his right and a bit below him.

"Zoe, you good?" Mason called out.

"Yeah! Uncomfortable, but I'm okay." She sounded much closer to the ground.

"Anyone got a light?" Mason regretted not bringing a fire spirit, but it would have been an ordeal to keep it lit all this way.

"One second. I think I can reach my bag." Soon, light filled the room from below. Zoe was holding a very bright glowstick. Mason could finally get a feel for the room.

It was a cavern of some sort, the ceiling made of flat sculpted marble, but the walls seemed more like natural stone that was more reminiscent of a burrow. Webs, thick as power lines, filled the room in a crisscrossing chaotic way that had little rhyme or reason. Jackson was within eyesight, but he couldn't see Zoe.

"I think I can get free. I'm only, like, six feet from the floor." Zoe called out. Mason heard glass clinking and soon after, feet hitting stone.

"Any chance of a rescue?" Mason called out, unable to turn his head.

"You're pretty high up, and I didn't think to pack two solvent potions." Zoe said, disappointed in herself.

"What about you, Jackson?" Mason said, turning his eyes to the shifter. While Mason watched, Jackson wriggled a bit and then shrunk into his armor. Soon, the head of a tawny hare stuck out of the neck of the armor. It assessed the situation, wriggled some more, and then leaped, clearing most of the web's strands. Jackson shifted as he flew through the room, landing in his hybrid form like someone out of a superhero movie.

"Okay. Now, how do we get you down?" Zoe called up, trying hard not to look at the very naked Jackson. Mason put his mind to it and also felt for Nosam.

'I'm here.' Nosam thought to him. 'I was caught in the crushing of the floor. I'm attempting to reform.' His physical form must have been mangled enough to where he had to return to his spiritual form. He'd be okay, but it would take him a few minutes to manifest fully.

It was then that Mason saw the spider. It was the size of a large truck and a deep black color. It looked like a black widow, slick and hairless. It moved along the web with a grace Mason would have thought impossible for such a large creature. It was heading determinedly toward Mason. Mason was very glad that he had made sure to evacuate his bowels before coming on this adventure, because he would have shit himself.

'Nosam...' Mason thought, adding as much panic to the thought as he could.

'I need more time. But, despite its size, it IS a natural spider.' Nosam thought back. Mason felt like an idiot. If it was in fact a natural spider, not some supe or other planar being, that meant the webs were, in the most technical sense, of the First World.

Mason reached out with his magic, suffusing the strands entangling him. They stirred and a consciousness reached back to him.

'You are food.' the web thought back to his call.

'What? There must be some mistake, I am a spider.' Mason had one shot at this.

'You are?' the web sounded confused, which was good.

'Clearly, look at my hard outer shell.' The web seemed to think on that for a moment.

'You seem like a human to us. Two arms, two legs. Humans are food.' It was sounding surer of itself as they spoke.

Speaking in this way was faster than talking, and while the conversation was pretty fast, the spider was still approaching.

'You have my extra limbs pinned together. Quite uncomfortable I might add. If you loosen, I can stretch them out for you.' Mason split his attention between the web and his backpack, giving it instructions.

'Very well.' the web loosened around his limbs but still held fast to the rest of him. As it happened, sand leaked from the backpack attached to his back, and four long spindly spider legs wriggled.

'See?' Mason said as if the Web was an idiot.

'If you are a spider, how have you gotten caught in me?' The web was truly confused now.

'That's why I'm talking to you. What kind of web grabs on to a spider?' Mason could feel Nosam manifesting, rushing the process in case Mason needed him.

'That is most embarrassing! My apologies!' The web immediately started to recede, no longer sticky to Mason. The Spider must have sensed some change as it was rushing to him now. Mason had his head free and turned to the floor, hanging on to the web, to keep from falling. The floor was maybe 15 feet below him, but he didn't have time to climb down fast enough to avoid the spider.

Mason let his body go limp and used his six new limbs to catch the thick strands as he did his best to control a free fall from the web. He'd managed a few feet without gaining too much momentum. Pain shot through him, and he snapped his head up to see the spider digging its fangs deep into his arm. He felt the numbing poison rushing into his body and looked to Nosam, tears blurring his vision.

'It's the only way,' Nosam thought back knowing his mind instantly. 'I will take the pain, you will need a clear head.' A connection between the two of them slammed home and the pain vanished. Only the swift numbing sensation was left. Mason sent power into the sandstone legs, and they began to harden and sharpen. He breathed deeply one last time and urged the sand to strike.

If Mason had been able to feel pain in that moment, he was sure he would have passed out from the pain of the spider's leg, sharp as any axe. It cleaved his arm from his body and he dropped uncontrolled towards the floor.

CHAPTER

31

——— • ● • ———

Gideon stood still in a way that was only truly possible with an inhuman body. Gideon wasn't very old by his people's standards, but he had learned fast, and had quickly gathered a flock of his own. He held his breath and let his awareness spread to the room around him.

His aura of light actually made the room a confusing mass of shadows that distorted into monstrous shapes. He ended this effect so his eyes could adjust to the darkness. While he waited, he listened. The room was tomb silent, save for the far-off sound of running water, probably a fountain or leaky faucet. He tried not to linger on the growing scents. People tend not to think about the smell of reptiles, but it began filling the space. The smell of Rot was also prevailing. Gideon knew it was only a matter of time before the Gorgon struck, but he was also curious about how she would. If it had been him, he would have made his move as soon as the light went out. Maybe she was too far away to strike him without alerting him. More likely, she was still unsure of what he was capable of.

Nephilim, like most mixed breeds, run the gamut of abilities. Some are super strong or fast, others possess a preternatural magical gift or other weird powers. If she truly was Medusa, and had died in the way the stories had told, then Perseus had definitely been a Nephilim. Though, historically, they were called demi-gods back then.

Gideon spread out his pinion feathers and felt the air currents around him. What was she waiting for? She couldn't possibly hope to get him with her petrification gaze. Both of them were the products of divine meddling, so they each had a certain level of defense against the other. In the mortal realm, Gideon would have the distinct advantage of being able to call on his father's power. But this deep into Faery, he would be hard pressed to bring any of his Invoker abilities to bear. Unless she had done extensive research, however, she wouldn't be aware of this, nor anything besides his underlying nature, which he did little to hide.

The strike came from behind and with little warning. If it hadn't been for his sensitive wings, he probably would have lost the fight right there and then. She wielded a long knife that was truly terrifying to his magical senses. The blow was a sweeping one. It would slash against his legs, probably an effort to hobble him. But, unfortunately for the Gorgon, he could fly. He avoided the blow, and was able to become airborne. He turned towards where she had attacked from, only to find her gone. She was fast for something as large as she was. The temptation to stay in the air was strong, but without his own magic, the fight would become a stalemate that would put Theia and Benjamin at risk.

Gideon lowered himself enough that his toes brushed the marble floor, but kept his wings engaged. If need be, he could use them to escape into a vertical position. Being a serpent, Medusa would always be slightly less capable in the air. There was a shriek from above, and she was on him. She must have climbed one of the columns and dropped on him from above. Her powerful tail slithered over him, her weight and muscles crushing the breath out of him.

"It will be over soon, Nephilim." She whispered near his ear. The snakes in her hair tickling the side of his face. Gideon slowed his breathing and flexed his muscles. Eventually, even his bones would break, but he was holding on for now.

"And, what would killing me accomplish?" Gideon asked as calmly as he could manage. Surprisingly, the tension around him eased slightly.

"Nothing," The Medusa cooed. "But it would please me." She gripped his chin in her too strong hand and forcefully pulled it towards her.

"Surely, if this is going to be my end, I demand that you have a better reason than mere pleasure." Gideon said, holding his chin aloft in defiance of her.

"If I had known the girl had such a pretty bird in her retinue, I would not have waited so long." She dug her nails into his cheek, and blood poured from the sudden wounds.

THE APOCALYPSE BEAD | 353

"Ah, this is a racism thing." Gideon said, a mocking smile in his voice despite the situation.

"What?" The Medusa seemed taken aback. She seemed young in the moment, like a girl presented with her own flaws for the first time.

"I get it. Cursed by the Gods, life's so unfair." Gideon was able to wiggle his fingers a bit. "Anyone divine is suddenly the bad guy. No ambiguity, no nuance, just hatred and blind fanaticism."

"You know nothing about what the Gods took from me!" She hissed, her anger distracting her.

"The Olympians sure. I have nothing to do with them." Gideon said, sending energy to his cheek. He could feel the bleeding slow. It would stop soon, but he needed her distracted.

"Yes, the Jealous God rules this land. He forces the denouncement of all who come before Him. Blessed are the meek... what nonsense." Gideon was almost disappointed he couldn't watch Medusa roll her eyes.

"Ah, common misconception. I am not associated with the Christian god." Gideon said, "Though I admit the white clothes, the wings, it's all very on brand. However, I, myself, am just tied to the divine concept of light, I was born of light, and I will fade with the coming of the void." Gideon tried his hardest to give a pretentious facade most people were so fond of.

"No matter, if she wishes you dead I will not deny her such a petty thing." Medusa said the tension in her wrist returning.

"You know light..." Gideon strained and his hand came free. He was able to gather the pools of light he had hidden in the grooves and cracks around him. All the little motes of light rushing to him, going completely unnoticed by the Gorgon, who only had eyes for him.

"Enough!" Medusa shrieked, her hand jerking his chin hard enough that, if he had not relented, his spine would have snapped. As his eyes met hers, he crushed the motes of light, causing the reflection at the back of his eyes to rebound stronger. Medusa stared deep into Gideon's eyes a wicked smile on her face, but all she saw in them, were her own.

The effect was immediate, and her face twisted in horror, hardening and turned a chalky white. The effects spread quickly, as if rushing to complete some purpose they had dreamed of their whole life. This curse given to her by the petty gods ended its cruel game. Soon, Gideon was dangling from a nine-foot Gorgon statue made of rough unpolished marble. Luckily, he had distracted her enough that the grip she had had on him was uncomfortable but not life threatening.

Gideon took a shallow breath and looked at the Medusa. She was beautiful, monstrous for sure, but with power and grace and a delicate bone structure. She had worn false eyelashes, an odd bit of vanity, he thought. He pitied her and instantly felt guilty. She had been a strong warrior, but he had been her end. He let his body go limp, but when the marble caught on his suit and did not release him, he looked to the ceiling and sighed deeply.

"Fuck."

• ● •

Theia's heart beat in time with the thrum of magic that suffused the temple. The stark white hallway seemed to stretch on for miles in front of her. The Bead was growing hot again, as if it was just now realizing the danger she was in. She looked at Ben and the scraggly raccoon walking beside them. She couldn't help but worry that Ben might have had a happy life, if she and Mason had just kept their distance from him. The Consumed, who hovered a few feet behind, met Theia's eyes with her own. Theia felt almost comforted, and she knew, whatever would have been Ben's fate, he was clearly better off having other people around him to face it with.

Then, without warning, she was alone. The walls of the hallway giving way to an empty void. Theia sighed and knew that she was about to see the disheveled form of Ryan Randall looking back at her with concern on his face.

"What are you planning?" he asked, pretense forgotten.

"Wish I could tell you. A freeloader has made it very hard for me to plan my future." Theia shot back.

"Do you think you will obtain mercy by giving the interloper the bead?" Ryan said in a monotone.

"First of all, let's drop the dramatics. I know you aren't Randall, you are the Bead. You just think that taking his form will make me more comfortable talking to you. Second, I'm pretty sure we are in mortal danger, and, consequently, I'm not in a huge rush to let her take you." She said, trying not to be disrespectful, but missing the mark on purpose.

"You are not strong enough to face her. Turn back." The Bead pretending to be Randall continued, unmoved by her sass.

"Ok, buddy, you need to start working with me. I don't know how you've done things up until now, but we need to work together. I get that you're a dangerous, apocalyptical, both figuratively and literally, but if you keep messing with how I get things done, neither of us is going to survive long enough to collect Social Security." She said continuing to walk forward, despite not getting any closer to where she might be going.

"I..." The Bead hesitated, "I have always had a guardian. Someone who fears me, and keeps me contained."

"I'll be honest, I've been battling creatures stronger, faster and deadlier than I am, most of my adult life. Having you around makes me feel like I can stand up to the things that make me and mine feel small. I'm swiftly gaining an addiction to that feeling. You have to trust me. Know that I'm not looking to get rid of you for the first good payday that comes along. I didn't pick this responsibility, but I've never shied away from a challenge." Theia felt silly trying to rationalize with a piece of jewelry, but she needed the thing on board with her plan.

"I'm not sure I know how to help..." It was clear the thing meant it literally. It didn't know how to work with her as opposed to through her.

"Well, maybe, try listening." Theia said annoyed.

"Perhaps."

Theia was back in the hallway. Benjamin, Lathair, and the Consumed were all looking back at her as if she'd gone insane.

"You, good?" Lathair asked.

"Yes, sorry, the Bead needed a pep talk." Theia said before drawing her gun and continuing on.

"As someone who has also just started having magic friends who talk in their head, I can say with confidence, it does get easier." Benjamin said waiting for her to catch up.

"I can't imagine having more than one." Theia let out a sigh.

"Well, Connie doesn't talk much." Ben said, looking up at the wraith.

"Connie?" Theia asked looking from him toward the chewed-up woman.

"I'm trying it out, 'The Consumed' is pretty dramatic." Ben admitted.

"Well, let's get our game faces on and get this over with." Theia said, not willing to touch on issues like 'The Consumed being called Connie'. They managed to smile at each other before pushing forward into another room. This one was aglow with red light.

Every inch of every wall was madness. Glowing, blood red madness. Thick threads of red string had been woven and shaped into patterns and shapes that her brain knew better than to dwell on. She looked more closely at a three-dimensional floating shape near her, and was a bit horrified to find it was fleshy. It was smooth and wet like a tendon or blood vessel. They all dripped incessantly, so that the room seemed to have a warm rain throughout.

Theia strolled into the room casually, and then swore under her breath as the light Gideon had gifted her winked out. She looked down at her feet. She had crossed a ring of runes about 10 lines thick. She cursed herself for her idiocy. Mason would have never just strolled into a magical trap like this. It was going to be impossible to escape it with magic or otherwise. She turned to warn Ben just as he crossed the threshold of runes as well. She watched as the realization dawned on him, and they both began looking for Meredith.

The light from the fleshly shapes was bright enough to see by, but stained everything blood red. Details were hard to discern. As if on cue, Theia saw her, Meredith, standing on a small dais near the middle of the room. She was naked except for a bit of gossamer cloth she draped over her shoulders, the pulsing red light of the room making her look like some kind of goddess.

"Isn't it glorious?" She said, raising her arms to the fleshly 'art'.

"It's a bit much, honestly." Theia responded.

"You, of all people, should be able to appreciate it. To see beyond the surface of it." Meredith scolded. "You have come much farther than other guardians, you should stand in awe of your achievement, and Arachne's artisanship."

Theia was confused at first, but then looked more broadly about the room. She focused her eyes on the whole of what was around her, instead of the individual pieces, and gasped. It was the Tapestry. It was warped and much more three dimensional, but she couldn't deny it, she was looking at a physical representation of the Tapestry.

"What the fuck are you." Theia said in a whisper she knew Meredith would hear.

"If I'm honest, I don't rightly know anymore. I've been recast by a hundred realities, reshaped by the unconscious minds of its people. Cast in role after role, so often that I can barely remember what I was originally ." She seemed to grow sad for a moment touching her chin. "I do know that I am always cast as a woman, cursed and vilified for knowing something or wielding power some man could not. Hecate, Circe, Hel, Eve, an evil queen, and countless other names."

"And your Grecian monster squad?" Theia said hooking a thumb back towards the way they had come. She hazarded a look at Ben. He stood alone, stoic but determined. She couldn't spot Lathair or Connie anywhere, however. She hoped this meant they had something up their sleeves. It was a comforting thought, because hers were very empty.

"Kindred souls. Cursed, punished, imprisoned on the whim of cruel gods and even crueler fate." It was clear Meredith had been waiting for this opportunity. She gestured and swayed about as if in the ecstasy of creation.

"Okay, so you made a really gross blanket of the tapestry. Why?" Theia had to goad her into wasting time, so as to give Benjamin his moment.

"I'm looking for paradise." She said intently, as if that were some great revelation.

"This seems like a lot to go through in order to fund a reasonably priced lake house." Theia said. But, Meredith could not be shaken from her revelry even by sass. Which was sad; Theia was good at sass.

"Do you know what makes the fey unique?" Meredith asked, ignoring Theia's comment.

"Is that rhetorical, or..."

"They have no gods. Not truly. The greater powers of the universe place figureheads and monuments to control them, but they are by their nature free of the meddling of divinity." She gestured to the macabre tableau surrounding them. "Somewhere in their fate, in the essence of their being, is a map. A map that leads to a universe where the gods are dead. I seek to find this dead world, and bring its fate to the oppressed and maligned masses of the greater universe."

"So, you killed a bunch of changelings to make a road map?!" Theia called back in horror.

"You seek to muddy my work with your thin view of morality." Meredith scolded. "However, I feel, of all the ants that I've crushed, you, at least, are capable of understanding the deeper truth of it. You've joined with one of the beads, and have seen the callousness of the gods and how they hide and manipulate even their own mistakes, so mortals cannot stand against them."

Theia had never been a huge fan of bullies, and, admittedly, gods were some of the worst bullies around, but all this seemed like madness to her. The bead, which had been quiet as if in contemplation, began to stir, almost as if roused by the woman's passions.

"I've learned I can use the beads to slip into the crawlspace between realities, and find the missing pieces of my great work." Benjamin had been strangely quiet up until this point.

"What happens when you leave a world? What does the bead leave behind?" He said pointedly.

"Sacrifices must be made, winged-one." She looked at him as if she had just realized he was there.

"Wait. Do you know what I am?" Benjamin asked a bit too desperately.

"Of little consequence." She said dismissively. "If it's any condolence, you will most likely survive my departure."

"Joy." was his only response. Meredith began dramatically walking down from her dais.

"Your kind have always given me a wide berth, but, I suspect, not for much longer." She reached the base of the dais and sauntered toward them.

"How likely is it she's going to give me a clear explanation?" Ben asked Theia.

"She's in full Disney villain mode, very unlikely." Theia responded.

"In that case, you can finish Lathair." Theia and Meredith both looked confused for a moment before Magic came rushing into the room in a deluge. Lathair tossed away the rock he had been using to scratch a line through the runes of the circle they had crossed. It seems he had hung back as a cockroach and had been slowly working on it this whole time, using his fey gifts to hide the sound.

As soon as the ward fell, the bead erupted in flame at her neck filling her with burning energy. Meredith threw up a hand and a flash of bright red energy scoured the floor toward her. She dodged out of the way and rolled into a shooting stance. Lathair leaped into the air and then seemed to burrow into Ben's back. This overlap was much more subtle than the one with Connie. Ben's hair grew into long pale blonde locks. His frame narrowed into a lither constitution, and his ears took on an elven bent. As Meredith lunged at him, black energy pouring from her hands, Ben dodged and was suddenly a pigeon flying out of reach. As he did so, his shadow leaped forward and the Consumed lunged from it sinking her fangs into Meredith's neck.

CHAPTER

32

— • ● • —

Mason's vision was blurring. Even though he couldn't feel the pain of his injury, his body was still registering the trauma. Nosam was howling and wincing in pain, which just added to the emotional agony of it all.

"Mason!" Zoe rushed to him and was reaching through her bag desperately for anything that could help. The giant spider dropped a few feet away and lunged for her. The tawny blur of Jackson slammed into the spider's side, throwing it off its feet. He rode it to the ground, pummeling it with his powerful legs before leaping off some distance away. The spider gave chase.

"It's okay, Zoe, I just need to focus for a second." Mason got back into contact with the pile of dirt and sand he'd brought with him in his pack.

'We have killed you...' Was all the collection of elementals could think of.

'Not if you listen closely. I can't focus with the blood loss. I need you to stem the tide.' Mason thought as clearly as he could about how to stop his body from hemorrhaging blood. The elementals listened and rushed into action. Little clumps of dirt and sand began coalescing at the amputation site, staining red quickly. Soon larger particles joined the first group, followed by stones fusing and forming a kind of cap on his arm. Soon his body started to normalize, but he was far from peak condition. Mason opened his eyes to see Zoe staring at his arm in awe.

"Blood loss!" she exclaimed and fished a thick red potion from her bag. Mason was not excited about what it was going to taste like, but took the bottle and downed it as fast as possible. He wasn't sure what to expect, but, as the syrupy liquid suffused into his system, he felt stronger and more capable.

"Help, please!" Jackson called out, barely avoiding being speared by a spider leg the size of a 2x4 and as sharp as a razor blade. Zoe looked at Mason before removing a squirt-gun from her bag and joining the fray.

'I need you, old friend. Share the pain with me.' Mason laid a hand on Nosam's heaving flank, and the pain came rushing back. He found it hard to imagine that this agony was only half of what Nosam had had to endure. Nosam's eyes cleared, and he met Mason's gaze. Soon, he began changing into long tendrils of smoke, his essence sublimating with Mason's. Together the pain was immense, but they were also strongest when sublimated. A strong spectral canine claw manifested where Mason's lost hand would have been. It was an odd thing, just floating there not connected to his body, but he was able to flex it and was grateful to Nosam for it.

'Let's focus on keeping all of our pieces for the rest of the week.' Nosam thought back weakly.

'Deal.' Mason rose to his feet, the white fur and heightened senses of Nosam filling him with confidence. Whatever was in the squirt gun seemed to terrify the spider, as it recoiled from anywhere the liquid pooled. The smell of mint and soap filled the space.

"Hit the deck!" Jackson yelled, as he slid beneath the giant spider's head, and from flat on his back kicked up into the creature. There was audible crack of chiton and the thing screamed in protest. Blue spider blood splashed across him before he again rolled away from the creatures stabbing feet.

'Okay, guys, I need you on full defense. We will focus on attacking.' Mason thought to the backpack, whose volume was concernedly lower than when they had started.

'Right!' the tiny combined voices called back. Mason surged forward, letting gravity and momentum propel him forward. The spider had managed to knock Zoe to the ground, sending her gun careening across the floor. Mason felt the backpack shudder as a sheet of sand and dirt shot from it and lodge itself in the spiders dripping maw. Zoe scrambled to her feet and was fumbling with her bag.

Mason used the distraction to get under the creatures flailing legs and slash at the wound Jackson had made earlier. The claw gained purchase, and it ripped into the spider's body, widening the hole. Liquid streamed out. Jackson tackled one of the creatures back legs trying to throw it backward, but the thing was just two big for such a tactic. The spider flung out with its leg sending Jackson sprawling.

Mason smelled ozone, just as the sand and rocks formed a rough shield on his back. A peal of thunder rang out, deafening him, and lightning struck the spider from overhead. Mason looked over his shoulder to see Zoe holding a taser aloft, panting but smiling. Mason took the opportunity, as the spider twitched and shrieked, to lunge at its wound, digging his claws and teeth into its flesh. Mason had a strange moment of clarity, and thought that it tasted a bit like crab, and worried about his shellfish allergy.

He couldn't hear the blows coming, but as the spider stabbed at his body, sand raised up to meet every blow. Sand and rocks showered down on Mason, and they lost their group cohesion. There was another flash of light, hot and flickering, probably fire, and Mason and the spider tumbled as a large column of marble slammed into the creature's thorax.

Mason felt numb and cold, his body nearing the end of its energy. Yet, he continued to dig into the spider like a dog at the beach. Chunks of flesh and blood sprayed and covered him. With a final thrust of his arm and a cry of triumph, Mason ripped a vital organ of some kind from the creature's body, then collapsed.

• ● •

Zoe rushed to the dead spider and hauled Mason out of the hole he had dug into the thing. She fished a universalantivenom from her purse and depressed the plunger of the syringe. When the liquid squirted free, she jabbed it into Mason. It was not done elegantly or with any kind of precision, but she was a witch not a doctor.

Jackson was nearby trying to say something to her, but her ears were still useless after that lightning bolt. She felt stupid for not working the sound dampening effect into the taser. That was magic 101: if you use lightning, remember its loud. She fished a pair of earbuds out her pocket and pushed them into her ears.

"ARE…YOU…OKAY?" Jackson was yelling slowly and loudly. Zoe gestured for him to come closer, and gave him one of the earbuds. "Oh, that's much better." he said at a normal volume.

"Sound clarifying headphones." she said applying first aid to Mason's wound. The little dirt clods were trying their best, but with Mason passed out they were struggling to defy physics.

"Okay. Is Mason going to be, okay?" Jackson said looking down at Mason's pale form.

"It looks like Nosam is keeping the furnace going, but he's gonna need time and a bit of luck. He was digging into the damn thing's venom sacks. It's not nearly as deadly absorbed through the skin, but he definitely should have known better." Zoe tutted as she got the stump tied off and cauterized. He was lucky she'd brought so much fire magic.

"You don't think that thing had babies, do you?" Jackson said, taking a low, but panicked stance. It was a tad humorous to watch a 7-foot-tall shifter panic.

"If you can find a Male spider her equal maybe, but I doubt it." Zoe slapped a couple pain relieving Band-Aids with little puppies on them around Mason's arm. "If the Grecian theme holds, this was probably Arachne. So, she wasn't born a spider."

"Oh..." was all Jackson could muster.

Zoe, calm now, could begin to feel the tug. Some great thrum of magic was sucking at the world like a vacuum. The pull of it almost had a heartbeat, some dark and primal rhythm that made you want to run, and hide, to protect your young from some great threat on the horizon. Something anathema to the concept of reality, had just poked its head into the world.

"Jackson, we need to find a way out of here." Zoe said ice pooling in the pit of her stomach.

"I'll look around." He darted off in that way that only rabbits can, searching the perimeter of the large room. Zoe sat back on her butt having done as much for Mason as she could. She laid a hand on his cheek watching him dream. She thought of her daughters. They were always so angelic when they were asleep.

CHAPTER

33

• ● •

Meredith cackled as the gruesome form of Connie tore at her throat. Theia watched as she reached up and just tore the wraith from her neck, chunks of her flesh coming off with it. The ragged hole of her neck knitted and healed as swiftly as the damage had been done.

"Nice trick," Meredith said dismissively, spitting a bit of blood on the floor. "But I am beyond you." A streak of black energy shot out from her arm, barely missing Ben as he rolled in the air. Theia squeezed off a few rounds at Meredith's torso, the bullets ripping into the woman. She just laughed again, and with a wave of her hand, sent Theia tumbling to the ground, the wind knocked out of her.

"Many, many heroes have tried to stop me. You are no different." She dug one of the bullets out of her flesh and looked at it. "You are not even the mightiest of your little rag-tag band. By now, Arachne has slain your shaman and witch and the Nephilim has surely perished to Medusa."

Ben landed on a broken pillar and shot off a peal of magic of his own. Meredith sidestepped the bolt, but, it became clear to Theia, that he wasn't trying to hit her. The runes he had already damaged took the full brunt of the attack, and the room became a figurative geyser as magic rushed through that small hole.

It was like the room was depressurizing magically, like in a sci-fi movie. Theia could feel whatever small magic she naturally possessed struggling to manifest, like a match in a hurricane. Meredith shrieked in anger and lobbed a screaming purple orb of magic at Ben. He had already shifted into a hummingbird and was rounding a pillar before it left her hand.

"Destroying the tapestry's restraints will only quicken the destruction of your world, you fool!" Meredith gestured and a pair of bloody wings erupted from her back. She took to the air after Benjamin. Theia squeezed off some more shots, but couldn't get a good lead on her in the air. Theia squatted behind a pillar and fished a new magazine from her pocket. The Bead was still strangely quiet despite the circumstances.

"Theia." Connie was at her shoulder. Her cold fleshless hands touching her gently. "We have need of you."

"Who? You and Ben?" Theia said in a whisper.

"Yes." She said in that infuriating slow tone of the long dead.

"Okay, I'm not exactly built for this kind of conflict, Connie." Theia said, trying to keep a watch on the magic flinging around the room. The fact that Ben and Connie could form effects in this torrent was scary impressive.

"Benjamin wishes to find an empty world. The tapestry is a map, he wonders if you can use it." The Consumed hissed.

"Maybe. The bead is more handicap then help at the moment." Theia said struggling to hear herself over the magical 'noise'.

"Meredith is too strong for us to overcome. We must change the stakes." Connie whispered in her ear. "The pooka keeps us from death, but even a trickster is eventually silenced by the cat."

"I'll try..." was all she could manage. Then the Consumed was gone, back in the fight and nipping at Meredith's heels while Benjamin took cheap shots at her.

Theia quieted her mind and spread the tapestry out in her mind's eye. It was almost instantly sucked away by the deluge in the room, like it was made of smoke. She threw her arms up in frustration. This was too much. She thought about her companions, the strength they had, the capitol they could leverage against fate. She felt the hole where Mason should be and convinced herself he was fine. She felt the small flickering flame of her power and cupped her metaphysical hands around it and let the hopeless emotion wash over her.

Then she squared her shoulders and got over it. Yes, she was just one person, yes, she had only the one gift, but if Benjamin needed that gift, by god, was she going to use it. She reached for the burning hole inside of her that the bead had made its home in, and yanked as hard as she could.

'Get out here and help!' she commanded it. The world around her faded and she was standing in that dark void. Ryan Randall did not appear, but a version of herself sat before her, wrapped in red flames and sitting with her knees pushed into her chest, hair falling over her face.

"I have been listening." The bead answered back in her voice. It raised its head and looked at her through its hair.

"Okay, ready to help then?" Theia said, painfully aware that a magical war was playing out over her very vulnerable form.

"I'm ready to try." Was all it could manage. Theia tried to spread the tapestry out in this space, and it appeared between them warped, but solid.

"Okay, we need to find the perfect moment in this mess." Theia said reassuringly. She took the threads closest to her and began tracing them, but without fail they tangled into a knot near the edge of the bead's distortion.

"I must listen. You must change your perspective." The bead stood and walked to the tapestry that hung in the air. It placed its hands on it and kind of slid to the side. The tapestry rotated on its x axis, and was now standing vertical in front of her. Some of the knots clarified but now other parts were unreadable.

"Okay, but it's still not readable." She said coming to a new knot.

"I am not of your world, and I am outside my own. Your near perspective is more complex than you are used to." The Bead summoned a sphere of flame into its hands. "In this form, the sphere is unaltered." The bead flattened the sphere into a disc. "But in order to put it on paper, you must distort it, and make it unrecognizable. The tapestry as we see it together cannot be represented as you currently read it."

Theia felt like an idiot child. She clasped her hands together and slowly brought them apart forcing the mental image of the Tapestry to stretch into a 3-dimensional model like the room they were in. The knots became just threads that passed over each other. Fate wasn't distorted, it was just much more complex than she had previously thought. She had become stronger, not weaker.

"Okay, great. Now, help me pick through it." Theia said as she walked down the threads.

• ● •

Benjamin had never considered himself a distraction before. Lathair assured him mentally that it was a noble profession. Connie was latched on to Meredith and their wings had tangled together. Ben had a moment to check on Theia, who was hidden behind a pillar her eyes squeezed closed. The respite was momentary though, as Meredith threw Connie, one handed, into a pillar.

Benjamin reached down into his combined form, and took on the form of a house fly, taking a moment to observe Meredith. She cast her rage out into the room looking for him, and like every other time he had attempted to hide, she zeroed in on him immediately. How was she doing that? He was truly changed, even his magical signature shouldn't be distinguishable from all this rushing magic around them.

Something had to give soon. His new, larger, magical reservoir had a bottom, and the rushing mana around them meant he had to spend much more energy to do just about anything.

'Lathair, about this plan of yours..' Benjamin thought, as they dodged yet another nasty looking red lash of magic.

'It will work.' Lathair thought back, already picking a new animal to try next.

'I trust your thoughts on the matter, but I'm not sure."' Benjamin said. Lathair ballooned out into a grizzly bear and landed a solid blow at Meredith's flank, sending her sprawling to the floor below. Then, just as quickly, he shifted into an elephant and landed on her, his bones rattling but not breaking, held up by Ben's magic. Ben could feel the woman's body crumple underneath the weight of the 6-ton body. She was mending, but even she would need a timeout after that. Ben assumed the hummingbird form and huddled with Connie in a dark corner.

'Theia just needs to get us the right spot.' Lathair thought back. Connie reached out a tendril of magic and Ben connected with her as well. Magic flowed into her. She was perilously low, not having any way to restore herself in Faery.

'I have never done what you are saying should be very simple...' Benjamin argued, while Connie watched Meredith slowly collect herself.

'You have, you just don't remember. Not knowing, and not remembering are vastly different states of being, Benjamin."' Lathair thought back, frustrated.

Using Lathair, Benjamin took a large breath of fey energy from the room, and sent a wall of concussive wind down into Meredith, breaking her freshly healed spine. It made his vision blur, and he almost lost his precarious footing. Connie steadied him with her grave cool hands.

'Okay, so Theia gets us the specific point. Then what?' Benjamin asked gathering energy for yet another strike at the witch.

• ● •

Theia and the Bead had already found several near perfect realities: one, where there were no humans, and plants had claimed the earth, another, where humans had never evolved, and yet another, where using magic turned you slowly to stone. No world was truly void of all life. Then she saw it, a tiny cluster of threads. She looked into them and saw an endless empty plain. It almost pulled at her, and it was hard to tear herself away.

"This is it!" She said pointing. The Bead took note of it and looked out to the horizon.

"I have found it on Meredith's model." It added helpfully. Theia clapped her hands and did a little dance of excitement before returning her body to the situation at hand. Meredith was screaming and rapid-fire attacking Ben with what looked like barbs of marble pulled from the floor.

The Bead pulled her attention to the spot they had found. It was near the dais where Meredith had been standing on, surrounded by a little spiral of unsettling red threads.

Theia reached out her hand and wreathed it in red flame, making it glow. She reached into that part of herself that was connected to Ben and Mason and, again borrowing the power of the Bead, called out with all her might.

'I FOUND IT!' she screamed, over and over.

'Okay! We hear you! Please stop yelling.' came Benjamin's calm voice.

'It's near the dais! Bea highlighted it.' She thought at him.

'Bea?' He thought back.

'I'm trying it out.'

• ● •

Benjamin smiled as he launched himself toward the area that the Bead had highlighted. He needed to get Meredith close, so, as he neared the dais, he purposefully landed wrong, and pulling on Lathair's impressive rolodex of long-cons, grasped at his leg in feigned agony. He sent a sputtering bolt of magic, that fizzled long before reaching its target, and put on an air of exhaustion. Lathair swore up and down that this would work, but Ben was dubious.

Meredith let the marble chunks fall to the floor as she moved toward Ben. She was filthy, and despite her amazing healing capabilities, also looked exhausted, though, Ben could sense her well was far from in danger of drying up.

"I had always wondered if I could defeat one of your kind." she said, reaching down and entwining her fingers in his hair, and pulling his neck into a weird angle as she looked into his eyes.

"I can help you." Ben begged, fake tears welling in his eyes. The Consumed cupped her hands around the small glowing spiral of threads filling her mind, and with it she deepened their connection.

"Oh, a coward as well? Willing to throw this world that incubated you away, as if it meant nothing." Meredith slammed his face into the marble dais without releasing his hair. Benjamin gave a quite real groan at the sudden pain.

"Stop, I beg of you." Ben didn't need any help on that one.

"I shall grant you no such weakness or shame as my mercy." She whispered to him.

"Very well..." Benjamin said making the decision. He reached out with his magic, and took the mental picture Connie held, and threw every scrap of magic he had towards it. He felt the lasso of magic snap closed and he spun and gripped Meredith in a bear hug and pulled them into the trap.

The sensation was a lot like falling. They had momentum but there was no wind or friction. Ben felt his stomach lurch at the sensation, but his mind did not register any movement. Soon, heat, air, light and gravity all reappeared. They were falling in earnest now, tumbling through the new world's atmosphere. Ben saw the ground coming towards them, and pulled Connie to him. Their forms overlapped and he spread their wings to slow his descent. Violent urges, and cold, undead logic appeared, but were counteracted by the jovial nature of Lathair who held them aloft mentally.

Benjamin released Meredith, and watched her fall to the barren land below. She impacted with an impressive dust cloud and didn't get back up right away. Benjamin touched down on the ground and looked about. The sky was blue like back home, but there were no clouds in this sky. Nothing dotted the landscape, and it was a purely flat, endless, expanse of gray dirt as far as the eye could see.

"What have you done!" Meredith screamed as she rose to her feet. She lashed out with her magic, but Ben pushed it off course. Connie clearly had some experience in countering magic, he had to remember that.

"I wouldn't waste what energy you have." Ben said calmly. "You won't be able to find any magic here." He said gesturing out at the lifeless world. He watched as Meredith reached out and felt nothing, confirming what he said.

"Then it is to be your prison as well…" Meredith said with a laugh in her voice, not a victorious laugh, but the laugh of a defeated woman.

"I'm sure one day I'll figure out how to escape." Benjamin looked at her with pity in his eyes, "I'm hoping you do as well, and in that time, you abandon this crusade of yours." "Even if I do, it will just be a temporary reprieve until I can kill you." She said narrowing her eyes in rage at Ben.

Ben could feel energy trickling in from beyond the barren world. Unlike Meredith, he was a child of that in-between place, and he could feel that now. As slow as the flow was, though, he lamented that it would take so long that he may never see Mason again. It was also highly possible Meredith would manage to kill him here, so far from home.

• ● •

Theia sat defeated, looking at where Ben and Meredith had been struggling. Ben was gone, completely gone. Not even a trace of him remained in that special place the three of them now shared. She could even feel Mason again, but she was still missing a piece. It happened quite suddenly. Ben had used her, to sacrifice himself. She had felt his thoughts in those last moments. His plan was to slingshot them both into the world devoid of people, devoid of magic. There had been a small hope that he might someday be able to find his way home, but he hadn't had a lot of confidence.

"Fuck that." Theia threw a hand back and a wall of flame coalesced over the broken circle of runes. The magic of the room stopped rushing and snapped back into equilibrium. She stepped up to the dais and saw the well-worn spots where Meredith had used the macabre map to move the temple from world to world. If Meredith could move the whole temple, Theia could snatch up one post graduate student.

'Okay Bea, it's time to do the heavy lifting.' Theia thought at the Bead.

'I am with you.' It said, as Theia's pattern filled to the brim with hot energy. It coursed through her, and then she sent all of it she could to that little speck in the center of that spiral.

The speck yanked on it voraciously, pulling more and more energy from her without any sign of slowing. Theia had no way of knowing when she would reach that particular world, and how much energy Bea could give, or even if this would work at all, but she was sick and tired of sitting around and moping. There was no way she was going to let this upstart of a brand-new baby supe throw his life away.

Her energy was flagging but she kept pushing it forward. Bea couldn't send her energy fast enough to keep up with the demands of the tapestry. Theia wasn't going to make it. Suddenly, she felt a warm but cold, compared to Bea, energy join her own. It was Mason...

It wasn't much, but the energy from Mason and Nosam was soon bolstered and flowed in smelling of daisies. Zoe... Theia turned her attention back to the task at hand and just when she felt she had nothing left, it stopped. She had him she could feel him, faintly, but he was there.

She smiled, and pulled. Pulled him home, and as she did so she began to plan on just how she was going to burn this place to the ground.

CHAPTER

34

· ● ·

The inside of the damp temple sprawled out before the mighty heroes. Large stone steps led to a bloody alter, barely perceptible in the inky darkness. The group's humble wizard held his staff aloft and whispered words of power to it. Gentle amber light bloomed from the staff, illuminating the oppressively dark cave.

"Thank you, Benitus." A gruff dwarf wearing leathers said, giving him a playful swat on the arm.

"Oh, stop, Finley. Not all of us can see in the dark." A powerful redheaded woman with a strong build said, thumping her large hammer on the ground.

"I have a bad feeling about all of this." an elven man said, his armor clanging as he looked about slightly panicked.

"Well, nothing good has ever happened after someone said that, Jangles." Finley said to the quaking elf. "See anything, Berda?" the dwarf said bringing his attention to the large woman with the larger hammer.

"The place does have a feeling of foreboding." She placed a foot on the first stair to the alter, when, suddenly, a deafening roar shook the space. Manifesting near the alter, an inky black dragon comprised of shadow appeared, staring down at the mortals foolish enough to invade its lair.

"And, that's where we will end our session." Cole said, his face illuminated by his professional studio lighting. Theia and Mason let out and audible groan of frustration, and Jack sighed with angst. Benjamin just kind of looked at all of them, confused.

"Don't you dare.." Mason threatened.

"That's all for us today, join us next time!" Cole said pleasantly, before pressing a few keys. The lights on the cameras winked out. Cole had a shit eating grin on his face.

"I agreed to one session, Cole!" Mason bellowed.

"You are more than welcome to let the mystery of the Lost Temple remain a mystery, Mason." Cole said, tapping his fingers together.

"I cannot believe you named your Cleric... Jangles." Theia said to Jack, scorn in her voice.

"Forgive me for wanting something original," he retorted. Mason was trying to collect all his dice and gear with his one good arm, all the while grumbling to himself.

"Let me help." Benjamin moved to help Mason as tenderly as he could, making sure to leave room for Mason to do some of it.

"I saved the world, you know!" Mason said to Cole.

"And, I am very grateful," he said, a devious smile in his voice.

"Nosam!" Mason bellowed again. The hound stuck his head into the room.

"Are the cameras off?" The dog totem inquired.

"Yes." Theia called to him. Nosam came trotting into the room, a suspicious dollop of whipped cream on his snout. Benjamin hefted the large bag Mason had brought, before leaning over and planting a kiss on the grumbling Shaman's head.

"We will come back next week. You're not doing any world saving for at least another week. You promised." Benjamin reminded Mason, and rolled his eyes at Theia.

"I could, you know!" Mason said, mostly to Cole.

"So, how are you guys holding up after your little foray into heroism?" Cole said, producing a perfect cocktail from seemingly nowhere.

"Well, Zoe is up in Washington for a visit, and the rest of us are just taking some much needed R&R." Theia supplied.

"Me and Arty just closed on our house!" Jackson supplied enthusiastically.

"Congratulations!" The gathered friends said in unison.

"Yep, the domestic life for the Thumpers." Jackson said puffing out his chest.

"Ugh, that reminds me. I need to start rat proofing mine." Theia whined. The assembled faces all scrunched up at that prospect.

"I'm gonna have some work done on the boat in lieu of payment from the Deep Queen." Mason said joining the conversation, despite his grumpiness.

"I'm putting mine directly into an emergency fund. Next time the world needs saving, I'm running away to Bermuda." Theia said pointedly.

"You really must tell me again everything that happened. Its gonna make for a killer campaign: 'Mad Witch Sets out to Find a Plane with no Divinity'." Cole said, a bit of grandstanding in his voice.

"Well, she got one," Benjamin said flatly, "and, hopefully, she never escapes."

"Benjamin, the man asked for a story." Theia said.

"It all started with a body…" Jackson said, forebodingly, as he began telling the story. Theia checked her phone. She had two texts: one from Matthew and one from Gideon. She ignored both of them and turned her phone screen off. The temptation to immediately check the tapestry was strong, but she resisted for now, happy with letting fate decide for a bit.

• ● •

Theia dropped a box on the deck of Mason's House Boat/ House. It had been three months since they defeated Meredith, and she was helping Benjamin move in. Zoe was arranging boxes on the lip of the moving truck they had rented.

"Why do all of my friends have a million books!" she cried out in frustration. Theia smiled to herself and hauled her way up onto the boat. As she collected her box and moved down the stairs, she was still taken aback when she entered the house. While not any larger on the outside, the space was at least four times the size it had been on the inside, before Mason's fey contractors had gotten to it. It was still essentially one big room with a bedroom and bathroom off the main space, but it was exceedingly larger.

"You can put that down anywhere." Benjamin said, sporting an uncharacteristic tank-top and board shorts. Theia placed the box on the kitchen counter and leaned on it a bit. Mason exited the bathroom spraying a deodorizer behind him. Theia smiled at her old friend and sighed.

"Calling it quits already? Ben has so much stuff, and I lost so much." Mason said with a smile, indicating his stump arm.

"You know, between the two of you, you have three arms and a magic ghost dog. Why do I even have to help?" Theia responded with a smile.

"Well, seeing as you were the one that convinced Ben to register as a supe, and that led to his landlord charging him a 'Magical Insurance Fee,' this is kind of your fault." Mason retorted.

"Oh, stop," Ben protested.

"How was I supposed to know he had a posty hating landlord!" Theia shot back.

"Most of them are pretty supeist." Zoe said, as she descended the stairs.

"It's a small price to pay. There was no way my involvement in the Union attack wouldn't come out eventually, and I'm working for Professor Wooly now. So, that was a pay cut regardless." Ben said trying to keep the peace.

"I'm just worried. You guys haven't been dating that long..." Theia cautioned.

"I mean, if you count from the first time they dated, its been a year." Nosam said from his fluffy doggy bed.

"You would support this." Theia said to the hound.

"We love Ben and Connie very much. Having them here will be great." Nosam said his tail thumping. Connie came floating through the ceiling, her usual stark nakedness now covered by a flowing white dress. Some of her hair and face had returned as well. Compared to when they had met her, she was practically a cover girl now.

"The resonance is bad. Much work must I do." Connie said to no one in particular.

"This is the danger of two-natured cohabitation. The vibe is gonna get wonky." Mason plopped down on his work stool looking over the large chunks of metal splayed out before him. Theia walked over and peeked over his shoulder.

"This the new arm?" she asked.

"It's gonna be, once I can convince the pieces to get along." He said, poking one of the odder shaped chunks. "Tungsten is very stubborn."

"I can't believe you and Lathair stopped bickering long enough to find all of this." Theia said with a whistle.

"He has good connections... for a pooka." Mason said begrudgingly.

Theia lowered her voice conspiratorially, "Everything been normal?"

"He's showing potential with both the Orphic and the Celestial. That is unprecedented, but I'm trying not to panic." Mason answered in kind.

"Well, I got a hold of Nessa. She should be arriving any day now." Theia said in a more normal tone.

"Why she insists on using that damn posty travel site I will never know." Mason said rolling his eyes. "It takes forever to get tickets."

"Well, as you will soon be very familiar with, things get weird when Mediums sleep. She likes the peace of mind." Theia responded, while Mason grumbled.

"Regardless, do you think we should ask her?" Mason said, suddenly changing the subject, and looking at Zoe.

"Now? She's already helping you move. I don't wanna bum rush her." Theia said suddenly nervous.

"Gideon and Matthew will be by later. So, if she storms out, there will still be plenty of people to help." Mason said with an eye-roll.

"You know what I mean!" Theia balked at him bringing up the two men. She still hadn't made any decisions about either of them.

"Hey, Zoe?" Mason said, ignoring her. Theia straightened up, and Nosam stretched and trotted over to stand next to Mason. Benjamin, seeing their body language, also shuffled over, Connie floating lazily by his shoulder.

"Yes..?" Zoe said looking a tad puzzled.

"Me and Theia have been talking, and now that everything has died down..." Mason began.

"And **PLEB** has finally finished the Meredith investigation..." Theia added.

"We wanted to ask you a couple of things." Mason said, squaring his shoulders.

"Ok." Zoe said, a bit defensive.

"Well, for starters, we would like you to be a full partner in Unseen Forces." Mason said without ceremony. "We'd still need you to do the same stuff, but you'd just be doing it cause you're the best at it, not because you have to." Zoe put her hands to her mouth and immediately got emotional.

"What he is trying to say is, we'd be lost without you, and its high time we acknowledge that." Theia said, worried that she might say no.

"I'm sorry," Zoe said, tears coming quickly. "Of course! It would be an honor." She hugged the two of them, almost knocking Mason out of his stool.

"Whoa, there." Mason said trying to keep his balance.

"The second thing is a little more awkward." Theia squeezed out around the hug.

"Oh?" Zoe said, wiping her eyes of her happy tears.

"Well, we had never asked before because you're a witch." Mason began.

"And, we just kinda always figured you'd join a coven someday." Theia quickly added.

"Right. We just didn't want you to say yes just because we asked. We know how important covens can be." Mason continued.

"Wait." Zoe said her breath catching.

"That is to say, and only if you're interested, we wanted to know if you'd be interested in joining our Circle, letting us be your coven." Theia said, all in one breath. Zoe started bawling, unable to hold back her emotion, and she hugged them again. She suddenly reeled back, somehow making eye contact with both of them, her eyes wide with excitement.

"Should we have a ceremony?!" she said her voice filled with frantic energy.

"I think that's a yes!" Nosam said with a doggy grin.

www.ingramcontent.com/pod-product-compliance
Lightning Source LLC
LaVergne TN
LVHW041245170125
801534LV00005B/1077